DEVILS
&
WIZARDS

PAUL WOLFF

DEVILS

&

WIZARDS

PAUL WOLFF

Copyright © 2024 by Paul Wolff
Cover Design by Sienna Arts
Developmental Edit by S.G. George
https://www.ladybirdediting.com/

For more information, email: lordwolff1@charter.net

ISBN 979-8-9936613-3-9 (hardback)
ISBN 979-8-9936613-4-6 (paperback)
ISBN 979-8-9936613-2-2 (ebook - Kindle)
ISBN 979-8-9936613-5-3 (ebook)

For Harlow, Ross, Emmy, Beau, and Jayme

Thank you to my wife Samantha. Her support and honest feedback helped keep me on task and bring this project to completion.

Content Warning

"Devils & Wizards" is a work of fiction recommended for mature readers 18 and up. There is content included that could trigger individuals that have experienced trauma or have specific sensitivities to certain topics. The following is a list of content that can be expected in this novel. Reader discretion is advised.

- Violence
- Gore
- Decapitation
- Sex
- Rape
- Nudity
- Occult
- Magic
- Animal death
- Confinement
- Child abuse
- Suicide
- Dead bodies
- Fire
- Poisoning
- Cannibalism
- Devils and demons
- Hostages
- Profanity

PART I

1
The Escape

The sounds of heavy breathing and groans of a young man in the throes of passion filled the finely appointed bedchamber. The room had all the dressings befitting the young daughter of a wealthy family. The colorful oil paintings adorning the walls depicted whimsical forest scenes filled with fairies and unicorns. A finely crafted doll that once held a position of honor on the large feather bed was cast on the floor. The young man that had forced it to abdicate its position took its place, albeit naked on the sweat, soaked sheets. The young woman who once held a childish doll in high regard, was riding the young man hard.

"Randall, keep it down! Someone might hear you!" Madeline's eyes closed tight as her hips moved even faster and rhythmically.

"I can't h-help it." Randall groaned eyes also tightly shut while his hands clutched the sheets.

Madeline pressed a pink silk pillow over Randall's face to muffle his noise as they climaxed. She removed it from his face after he began thrashing, struggling to breath. Not that quickly though. She enjoyed inflicting a little torment.

Randall relaxed with his arms outstretched as if crucified. His eyes were partially covered by his disheveled brown locks. Madeline still sat atop him teasing him tugging at the few hairs that sprouted out of his chest. A smile spread across his face until Madeline plucked out one of the hairs.

Young Randall had the physique of a bookkeeper rather than a valiant knight serving a king. A bookkeeper in service of Lord Mayor Geoffrey Walters, Madeline's father. He was engaged in a dangerous game in the mayor's own house. The Lord Mayor and his cronies, whose books he was cooking, were embezzling city tax funds. Randall was decently compensated as he was quite the clever bookkeeper. However, it was not enough to keep him loyal to his employer. The weekly meetings going over the accounting at Geoffrey's mansion now included the secret rendezvous with Madeline afterwards. He would double back through the garden and climb the trellis into her open bedroom window where she waited. He fancied cute, plump, and curvy Madeline. He felt this affair was fair compensation for helping cover the Lord Mayor's and the other's extravagant lifestyles on the dukedom's shilling.

"I'm not done yet. Do you have any more life in you?" Madeline purred tracing her finger across Randall's nipple before giving it a pinch.

"I don't think so. I need what little life is left in me to get home. I must be at the Custom's House early tomorrow. You know, keeping Port Gwynn's accounts straight for the dukedom. Important stuff." Randall said self-importantly.

Madeline rolled off the bed and pulled her white nightgown over her head, wriggling into it until the hem touched the floor. She smiled at Randall, her face framed by long red locks and sun kissed with freckles. The picture of innocence once again.

Randall smiled back pulling one foot through his braise before losing his balance and toppling backwards over the chair his clothes rested on. The loud crash caused by the breaking of the chair as well as Madeline's scream was soon answered by a loud knocking on the door.

"Madeline, are you alright? Open the door!" A matronly voice called through the heavy wood door.

"I'm ok, Mother. I accidentally knocked the chair over." Madeline was in a panic waving her hands frantically at Randall, who was struggling to tie the drawstring on his braise.

"Why is this door bolted? Is there someone in there with you?" The Lady Mayoress now pounded on the door.

"No, mother. Just me." Madeline threw Randall's breeches into his face while kicking the rest of his clothes under the bed.

Another voice was now at the door. The familiar gruff voice of Lord Mayor Geoffrey talking to his wife, but the conversation was not discernable. Randall held his breeches in his hands and shrugged his shoulders in confusion. Madaline pointed at the shuttered window to make his exit. Randall finally understood as she pushed him toward it.

"I'll toss the rest of your clothes out when they're gone. Just hide in the bushes." She whispered.

Randall gave her a quick kiss on the lips and pushed the shutters open to look below at the gardens. He looked back at Madeline and shook his head.

A city guard wearing the tabard of Port Gwynn over his mail hauberk was making his rounds on the pathways through the garden while humming to himself. The guard was taking extra care to shine his lantern into the shrubberies looking for any trespassers skulking within.

Madeline pushed Randall into the huge cedar lined wardrobe that occupied one side of her room as the pounding on her door rattled the paintings.

"Open the door this instant, Madeline!" The voice of her father rumbled as the wardrobe doors shut with a click.

"Yes, father!" Madeline stepped back after turning the bolt and clasped her hands behind her back.

The Lord and Lady Mayoress entered the chamber and surveyed the room noting the smashed chair, bed in disarray, and open window. Geoffrey was a rotund middle-aged man with a thick black beard and short cropped hair graying at the temples. He wore layers of fine clothing atop which was a dark, thick fur cloak clasped to his left with a silver brooch. The metal hilt of a dagger peeked out from under this garb. His wife, Cecilia was wrapped in a robe over her silk nightgown, and her bosom was spilling out. Her greying brown locks fell well past her shoulders

Geoffrey's concern quickly turned to suspicion noting one of his tankards from the cellar tasting room on the writing desk. He lifted it to his nose then took a taste. "You have never liked Grummandy beer. What's going on in here?"

"I know you enjoy it so much that I wished to expand my taste palate and give it another try. It's a little stronger than the drink I usually take with dinner. I stumbled and broke my chair. I'm sorry." Madeline rubbed her leg to feign a minor injury.

"Oh, dear, are you hurt? Ladies should never partake of that. Leave that horrid drink to a big brute like your father." Cecila crossed the floor quickly to Madeline's aid.

Geoffrey stood in the room with arms crossed eyeing the bed again. Madeline leaned against the desk for support as her mother inspected her 'injured' leg.

"You poor dear, it doesn't look bruised at all, nor did you break the skin. Nevertheless, you best sit down and take your weight off it." Cecilia walked her to the bed.

Madeline did her best to shift the covers before she sat down to cover the wet spot Geoffrey's eyes locked on. The attention turned to the cedar lined wardrobe when Randall had a sneezing fit and the cabinet shook. Lady Cecilia gasped, springing to her feet, and backing away. Madeline held her breath.

Randall threw the doors open, stumbling out disoriented, and sneezing violently. Cedar allergies blew his cover.

"You!" Geoffrey exploded going red in the face and drew his dagger from his belt.

"Run Randall!" Madeline cried.

Randall struggled to see through his red watery eyes and his mess of hair in his face. He made a dash through the door but missed, running into its frame. He knocked himself out cold and was sprawled on the floor wearing only his braies, with one foot stuffed into a leg of his breeches.

***

Randall awoke on the ground of a stone floor. His head was pounding, and he was in darkness. He tried to remain calm to keep his wits and discern his current situation. He was gagged and a burlap bag was over his head. His hands were locked in irons behind his back. How long he had been here, he wasn't sure. Where he was, also a mystery.

There was the sound of a key turning followed by a metal door opening and multiple footsteps around him. Then the gruff voice of his employer spoke.

"Get him up." Geoffrey barked orders at the two Port Gwynn guards that were with him.

The men pulled Randall up and removed the bag. Randall's eyes adjusted to the light of the lantern that Geoffrey had aimed into the small cell he was being housed in. He was being held in Geoffrey's secret dungeon in the mansion's undercroft. He was still wearing only the undergarment from that night in Madeline's room, along with dried blood smearing his face from the split on his forehead.

Geoffrey eyed Randall up and down as the guards each held him under each arm. He then delivered a speech aimed at Randall, but really for the benefit of the guards. "So, it has come to this now. I was too generous granting such a position to a young learned lad when you first came to Port Gwynn. You didn't waste time misappropriating coin from the city's coffers to support a lavish lifestyle not afforded to the common citizen. Levying an additional tax on the already burdened people will now be necessary as the Duke will be collecting the quarterly tax and we will now be very short."

This news didn't resonate well with the two men that were holding Randall.

The older guard tightened his grip on Randall's arm. "We'll make sure this package is delivered promptly Milord."

Geoffrey passed a small bag of coins to the older guard for the men to split. "Good, they're expecting you this morning. As always, keep this to yourselves. I prefer to deal with enemies of the people in this manner rather than waste the time of the courts with one as guilty as he."

Randall could not say anything on his behalf with the gag still in place. This also made it impossible to use his powers of the arcane arts. He mostly kept this secret to himself in the kingdom where its practitioners are branded heretics and dealt with in nasty ways. Randall had a good idea where he was going as there were special entries logged in the ledgers for 'waste disposal.'

"The little bugger just pissed himself." The younger guard grinned a yellow smile.

The guards led the prisoner into the undercroft. The vaulted ceilings were twelve feet above, the walls had niches lined with large casks of wine, and individual bottles stored upon dusty wooden racks. The large chamber was dimly lit from a single torch in a sconce on a supporting pillar. Geoffrey and his lantern waited next to a large empty oak wine barrel, the lid laying on the flagstone beside it.

Rats scampered along the wine racks away from their approach, save for an unnaturally large one lurking in the shadow. The creature sat on its hind legs watching everything from the floor. It sniffed the air, then ducked behind a large cask. Randall made brief eye contact with the large rodent before the men's rough handling reminded him of the situation at hand.

"Let's get on with this." Geoffrey stepped back, turning the lantern to the barrel.

Randall's guards dragged him forward, as the odor of soured wine assaulted his nose. Light from the torch flicked wickedly above the barrel, and in the dim illumination he saw that nails had been driven all through the side walls. An extra little torment Geoffrey added for the betrayal. Randall put all his strength into one last effort to pull away, but it was for naught. The guardsmen dropped him headfirst into the barrel.

The tips of the nails were not enough to be fatal to Randall, but caused great discomfort. His head was turned and the weight of his body rested mostly on his left shoulder. Nail tips pierced the skin on his backside and he felt a trickle of blood running to his shoulder blades. His feet were still poking out of the barrel until the younger guard pushed them in to put the lid in place.

Randall could only let out a muffled groan. The pain continued to burn through him all over as they nailed the lid on. The old barrel was not perfectly sealed; the few holes and cracks allowed the him to see out.

"Okay, the wagon is backed to the gate. Load it up." Geoffrey turned and aimed the lantern at the stonework ramp to a landing ending with a pair of metal doors. Wooden crates of various sizes were stacked and organized along the pathway from the wine cellar. Some crates had tags of parchment tacked onto them with handwritten lists of the contents. Others were just branded with the name of a merchant company and port of origin. Many of the crates of goods, like the wine barrels, were not exactly legally obtained.

"May as well do this the easier way." The older guard said. A hard kick teetered the barrel over. Randall's position shifted from his head and shoulders onto his side to be pierced by the nail tips.

"Whoopsie." The younger guard snorted at Randall's muffled groans escaping the barrel.

The mayor was pushing the doors open as the guards rolled the barrel up to meet him. Reaching the top the guards set the barrel on the flat side, and mercifully for Randall, he was upright. He was, however, covered in small punctures from head to toe. Drifting out of consciousness, his head fell against the side of the barrel with a nail tip poking into his cheek bringing him to. Pulling away he found the gag was snagged on a nail. He shifted freeing himself from the gag, and spat out the cloth filling his mouth.

The wagon was backed up, and the driver was finishing hitching a pair of oxen to the neck yoke to pull it. Randall's barrel was loaded into the wagon with the young guard taking a spot beside him, the older guard sitting on the bench with the driver.

Outside the stone wall surrounding the mayoral mansion, the streets were awakening with foot traffic. It wasn't uncommon for Geoffrey to send out his driver with his trusted guards to pick up supplies and make deliveries, so this morning's activities would not draw suspicion.

Randle kept an eye on the outside world through the crack during the ride. The cobblestone streets were not very smooth, and the bumpy ride added to his discomfort with the occasional poke from a nail tip. He stayed quiet, not wanting to reveal he was free of the gag.

Wagons and carts with wares were pushed by merchants themselves or drawn by horses to the market square. Wattle and daub buildings were cramped close together in various stages of upkeep and repair, depending on how successful the local business owner was. Doors were opening, windows unshuttering, and front stoops swept. Colorfully painted and carved wooden signs hung from chains off eaves at some store fronts. From Randall's vantage, he knew they were going in the opposite direction of the other traffic. He would need to attempt something before they reached their destination.

The young guard pulled a large red apple out of his pouch and sank his yellow teeth in it. The driver kept focused, navigating the street and shouting out at passersby to clear the path. The older guard beside him kept a watchful eye on each alleyway they passed and every person that was ahead of them. Travel on the road went on for a long while with no stops. The wagon continued to a busy crossroad, and within a few turns down the street the smell of the air changed as they approached the docks at the High Port. The cobblestone gave way to hard packed earth with ruts. Wooden boardwalks were used for foot traffic with wall-to-wall stone and wood warehouses, saloons, and brothels. A seawall, designed and constructed by the city's engineers hundreds of years ago, protected Port Gwynn from countless storms and other threats. Wooden docks ran along it and out into the bay, which was very busy this morning. Small fishing boats set out, and large carracks docked and unloaded their underdeck cargo with block and tackle systems.

Randall recognized the area immediately. There were whispered rumors of individuals that crossed the mayor and became part of the "night soil," which was the waste that was removed from the city's sewers, cesspits and privies and loaded onto barges for dumping out in the bay. Whether an offender was dumped alive or postmortem in multiple pieces, he was not sure.

Randall looked through the crack again and saw an open wagon passing them on the opposite side of the road. The bed was filled with baskets and cloth bags with a father and son driving it.

His mouth freed of the gag, he recalled a simple spell that required only a spoken incantation.

"Ut hic de mecum in infernum!" Randall whispered.

There was a brilliant flash of light within the barrel and then another flash as he was instantaneously transported into the bed of the other wagon. He now lay across baskets filled with raw fish. His hands still in irons behind him, he looked up and saw that the wagon continued going forward, but the young guard's attention was on the barrel with an expression of bewilderment.

"What in the nine hells?" The startled man shouted turning to see Randall atop the baskets.

"Please get me out of here! I can pay you!" Randall was eager to cut a deal to escape the mayor's men.

"Get off me cart! I don't want trouble." The driver dressed in drab work clothes smacked Randall with the horse crop.

"Ow! Stop you bastard!" Randall tried to dodge, but each time the leather tongue connected on his bare skin with a snap, his cries came out in high pitched squeals. Rolling off the cart, he landed on top of baskets of fish that spilled out onto the ground. Still covered in his own blood from the barrel he now had fish guts to add to the mess.

"Oy, over there!" The older guard called from the wagon some sixty feet further down the road. He slapped his gloved fist on top of the younger guard's helm and pointed in Randall's direction. The younger guard retrieved a stashed crossbow.

"Recludo velox!" Randall's magic words made the shackles behind his back open and clatter to the ground. Randall rose to his feet, fighting for balance.

The fishmonger's wagon made a speedy escape in a cloud of dust as Randall pivoted to watch its departure.

"You! Don't move!" ordered the older guard as he climbed out of the wagon. Randall pivoted again to face the guards. The younger guard was cranking the wench on the crossbow, drawing back the bow readying a bolt. Shirtless dockworkers turned with cargo they were unloading. Wagons and foot traffic moved off the road and came to a stop. Spectators from the warehouses and the other business stood in the open doorways and windows. A group of dirty street urchins in the alleyway next to a brothel watched with anticipation.

Randall was not going willingly and found himself running without thinking in the direction of the kids in the narrow alley. The children ducked into hiding places.

A crossbow bolt lodged into the edge of the wall of the brothel missing Randall's head. The narrow alleyway continued forward another hundred feet and opening onto a busy cobblestone thoroughfare.

"Pssst! Come quick!" A rail thin girl no more than eight, with matted brown hair and wearing a sack dress, called from a dark hole in the stone wall at ground level.

The girl crawled down into the darkness. The opening was barely over a foot wide, but it looked like his only option as the sounds of the shouting guards quickly approached. Randall dove in headfirst and fell into darkness onto a muddy floor. He turned his head and saw the outside light extinguished as the secret door slid back into place with a click.

Randall sat up listening to the muffled voices and footsteps of the guards as they rounded the corner into the alleyway. He couldn't make out the words said, but he knew they were moving away, taking their search further down the alleyway.

In the dark stillness it turned to absolute silence, and he could hear his own heart pounding in his chest. He turned his head from side to side, listening for the little girl that led him here. Nothing. Though only a few minutes passed, it felt an hour.

Finally, his ears caught a sound. Squeaking and chittering creatures were entering the small chamber, and half a dozen glowing red eyes surrounded him. He sat trembling, and then all was quiet again. The glowing red eyes were focused on him. One of the creatures brushed against the back of his neck. He could smell its foul breath and heard it sniffing him over. The others slowly closed in, and Randall closed his eyes tight. He felt their noses touch him, whiskers brushing against him, and the sound of their chittering. He pulled his knees up close, ducked his head into them, and wrapped his arms tight readying for the moment they would begin to rend his flesh and devour him alive.

"I can smell the fear in his blood!" A voice of a young boy chuckled.

Then nothing. The creatures backed away from him.

"Pssst." The little girl called out to him once again.

He raised his head up, opening his eyes. The little girl was crouched in a narrow passageway that was no taller than four feet high, a small oil lamp dimly illuminating her and the surroundings.

Randall looked wildly around the room. Six dirty street urchins leaned against the rough masonry walls supported with timbers. Randall looked over his shoulder toward where he entered. A young, barefoot lad sat on the stone ledge below the concealed portal smiling and kicking his feet. He picked at his fingernails with a knife as he stared at Randall.

"Hey! His Lordship will see you now. Come on." The little girl motioned for him to follow and hurried down the passageway with the lamp.

"Go on!" The boy on the ledge laughed.

Randall pulled himself up and hurried into the small passage as the light in the chamber dimmed to blackness. He walked stooped over following the lamplight.

Looking over his shoulder he saw many pairs of red glowing eyes staring back from the darkness. Randall picked up his pace until he was only a few steps behind his rescuer.

2
Izzy

R andall knew the passageway was descending deeper below the city. The ceiling was now arched with worked stone, allowing him to straighten and stumble upright. The passage remained just wide enough that he didn't bump into the sides. No longer was the stone path covered in mud; however, it was slick with moisture.

The girl held the lamp ahead of her as she navigated through the tunnel effortlessly. Randall was exhausted. Weakened by hunger, thirst, and his wounds; he stopped and slumped against the wall.

"Please. Stop. I've had a hell of a morning." He sat on the cold floor looking more even more pitiful. "Who are you? Where are you taking me?"

"I'm Izzy, Mr. Randall. There is no time for rest here. His Lordship will not like this." The girl put one hand on her hip while she shined the light on Randall.

"What? How do you know my—"

Izzy cut him off, throwing him a cross look, and furrowed her brow. "Mr. Randall, His Lordship knows of everyone and all the goings on in Port Gwynn." She paused for a moment and looked at Randall with a bit of pity as he caught his breath. She sat the lamp on the ground and pulled a blood-soaked parcel out of the leather pouch she wore on her side. Izzy revealed a piece of raw meat and held it out for Randall. "Here, I was going to save this for my breakfast. I just nicked it from the butcher's shop."

Randall cautiously reached out with his free hand and took the meat. He slowly brought it up to his nose to sniff it. It was fresh enough, although hunger wouldn't let him judge it too closely. Normal situations would have called for it to be roasted until it was only slightly pink inside, served smothered in onions, seasoned with fresh ground peppercorns and a pinch of salt. He was not discriminating now. He devoured it and hoped she had a bottle of wine hidden somewhere else on her person. No luck.

"Thank you. You are very kind." Randall honestly meant it as he wiped his lips with his hand.

"Mr. Randall let's go now. Not too much further." Izzy picked the lamp up and urged Randall to follow.

The passage didn't follow a straight path and had turns and twists, as well as variations in the angle of the grade of the floor. One consistent thing was that the rough brick walls glistened with moisture and the arched ceiling had straw-like stalactites adhered to it. The journey ended at an alcove.

"Please watch your step here, Mr. Randall." Izzy shined her lamp to the floor and pointed to a thin wire placed across the passageway.

Randall followed Izzy's steps, carefully bypassing the tripwire. He surveyed the wire and found it ran to a mechanism attached to a loaded crossbow aimed chest high in a niche. Poisoned undoubtedly. More bolts were in a small crate nearby, and the wall above had several notches scratched into it. The tracking of uninvited visitors, obviously.

Izzy set the lamp on a stone ledge in the alcove and lifted a mock brick hiding a catch in the wall. Pushing the switch caused it to click and pivot open. A portal was revealed that was just large enough to crawl into. Izzy put the lamp into the crawlspace and looked at Randall.

"Mr. Randall, you go first, and I'll close the door behind us." Izzy pointed to the small tunnel.

"Where does that go?" Randall was frightened and suspicious of what lurked beyond.

"To His Lordship of course. It won't be much further." She wrinkled her nose and made a frown showing her impatience with this line of questioning.

There didn't seem to be any other options at this point. Face knife wielding urchins and the mysterious glowing red eyed creatures, or present himself on bended knee to His Lordship. He poked his head in the small tunnel and looked ahead as far as the lamplight would illuminate. The crawlspace was tight, and was dug into earth shorn up with rough timbers. The air was heavy and stale, and as he made his way in, it felt as the weight of the earth was crushing in on him. Crawling forward on his hands in knees with the lamp proved a test of his endurance. He really wished he was dressed for the occasion, or dressed at all.

"Mr. Randall, not too much farther and we will be in the undercity." Izzy stated.

"The catacombs?" Randall responded nervously, eyeing Izzy with a raised eyebrow.

"Yeah, it's called that too." Izzy said, nodding her head. "Will you hurry up please?"

Randall turned his gaze forward then, taking a deep breath, reluctantly crawled onward. It wasn't much further along that the crawlspace came to an end at a wall that had a small mechanical catch and another door.

"Mr. Randall, when you pull that latch, the door will open outward, above Old Jake. I'll be right behind you. "Izzy said.

"Old Jake?" Randall mumbled to himself and opened the door. Randall screamed out loud as his lamplight shined on the leathery face of a mummified corpse with mouth agape, seemingly in shock at the sight of Randall.

"Shhh, Mr. Randall, you'll wake the dead." Izzy said laughing.

"Damn you, and damn Old Jake." Randall shimmied past Jake and dropped onto the floor. Holding the lamp in front of him, to the left, and then right, he saw that he was in the catacombs below Port Gwynn. The walls were lined with niches filled with generations of family remains of the long departed. Most were just stuffed full with jumbled bones of entire families. Family names either carved directly into the stone, or on rotting wooden plaques with the faded names painted on them. The passageway was a mere five feet wide and carved directly out of limestone. The temperature was much cooler here, causing Randall to shiver.

"I'll take that Mr. Randall. Let's go." Izzy took the lamp from his hand and pressed onward, merrily whistling a tune.

"I think I recognize that. It is a song I've heard the dock workers sing when they are loading cargo." Randall stumbled along, listening to the tune. "Definitely have heard it before."

Randall began singing along with Izzy's whistling in a cracking voice.

The morning, I rose
The cock was up first
I reached for the eggs
It crowed out a curse

You choked the chickens
You punched all the clowns
Beaten the bishops
You...

"Mr. Randall, it's just around this turn." Izzy resumed whistling and made the corner.

Randall made the turn and stopped, face to face with people dressed in gray cloaks with hoods pulled over hiding their faces. They wore simple leather armor, and one held a wooden club, the other a thin rapier. Izzy stood behind them, the lamp silhouetting their forms in the darkness.

"Make it easy on yourself. Don't move." With blinding speed, he raised his rapier and pointed the tip within an inch from Randall's throat.

Randall froze in place with his knees locking and his eyes fixed on the blade. He followed the length of it to the gloved hand that was holding it and up to the large gray cowl covering his captor's head and stared into darkness that hid his face. Except for the eyes. They glowed red. Randall stared into the eyes and features of its face became clearer. It was the face of a rat.

Randall gasped as the other came behind him and grabbed his arms, restraining him. The same glowing red eyes and rat face was under the hood too. Lowering his blade, the rat man returned it to its sheath and pulled out a sap.

"Sorry Mr. Randall. His Lordship prefers to keep the way to The Nest a secret." Izzy said

"What? Wait. No!" Randall looked over to Izzy and watched her transform into a childlike rat wearing the sack cloth dress holding the lamp. Izzy looked up at him with glowing red eyes.

The rat man cracked the sap across Randall's head, knocking him unconscious. Izzy extinguished the lamp, and the three continued their trek to His Lordship's Nest with their prisoner.

3
Catching Up with Friends

Geoffrey sat at his desk in his study with the handful of prominent co-conspirators for an emergency meeting that evening. The doors were locked, heavy curtains drawn. The room was lit by candlelight, and a low fire burned in the hearth. The well-appointed room was paneled with fine hardwoods, furnished with overstuffed sofas, chairs, and a large collection of books on the shelves, none of which Geoffrey had read. Hunting trophies were mounted on the walls that Geoffrey often boasted about. Tonight, the bodyguards and drivers for his prominent visitors waited outside in the courtyard with their horses and carriages.

Thom Clarke, the director of the board of customs, paced the floor in front of the stone hearth, nursing a glass of wine. He poured another glass from one of the open bottles Geoffrey had brought up from the cellar. He stopped in front of a brass framed mirror on the wall to inspect the appearance of his well-groomed pointed beard before downing the glass.

"Slow your consumption Clarke." Bishop Bennett rolled his eyes. "I'm sure Geoffrey has a good reason to include us in this matter after keeping us in the dark about his former bookkeeper." The Bishop was not in his formal vestments, preferring simpler robes and a brimless gray head covering all but his face. He leaned back and heaved a sigh. "To think that he was also a practitioner of the 'dark arts.' You knowingly allowed him to work for you rather than having him arrested and face judgment in the divine eyes of The Mother. The elimination of these practices has been forbidden for centuries. Word of this reaches the capital and they will send an inquisitor to Port Gwynn for an investigation. I can assure you that bribery will not make an inquisitor look the other way." He leaned forward wringing his wrinkled hands.

Captain Madok of the Port Gwynn Guard nodded his head in agreement. Sitting in another overstuffed chair next to Bennett, he set his empty glass down on Geoffrey's desk. "I wouldn't have known a thing about this if that boy didn't spread gossip of the bookkeeper's escape at the barracks. Involving my men to make Randall disappear with the help of the 'colorful' individuals you employ is bad for our business agreement. I've had to put the guards on high alert at the city gates, docks, and shipyards. You are a reckless fool!"

Thom's hands shook as he poured his third glass and drank without adding a word to the conversation. He was only a nervous spectator in this meeting.

"Now listen-" Geoffrey began to rise, but Captain Madok cut him off.

"I respectfully ask you to shut up, Lord Mayor!" Madok pointed his finger in his face. Geoffrey returned to his seat. "I have a few of the men posted at his house now. I just don't want you to involve any thugs for hire. Obviously, there was something personal involved for you to go out of the way to foul things up fabricate this story. Now I'm left to tie up your loose ends."

Thom dropped the glass, scattering shards of glass and wine across the floor. Bennett rolled his eyes, shaking his head. Geoffrey turned red.

"So, what is it, Lord Mayor? Did he even move money out of the city treasury? Maybe dipped his hands into our cuts? What else? Say it!" Madok stared into his eyes.

"My daughter, Madeline." Geoffrey turned his head shamed.

"What? So, he broke her, did he?" Madok chuckled.

"Enough, Captain Madok! I understand now. This sorcerer obviously put an enchantment on young Madeline to corrupt her purity. This act of devilry, however, is secondary to the fact that stealing money from me is a stealing from The Mother herself! Those funds were being used for the ongoing construction of the private sanctuary for Port Gwynn's elite, as well as a place for receiving visiting high ranking church officials. The ceilings are being painted by-" Bennett was cut short.

"Whatever. I know you are worried that your lack of these extra finances may also prevent you from affording secret sessions provided by Sister Lucia. Sending girls to your 'private sanctuary.' It is only girls you pleasure yourself to, or do you also request boys?" Madok sat back into his chair, smirking.

Thom's knees grew weak, and he slumped against the wall with his hand against his forehead.

"Captain Madok!" Bennett struggled to stand up, but the overstuffed chair proved to be the best restraint for an old man.

"Don't get up on my account Bishop." Madok stood and pushed Bennett back in his seat by his shoulder. "Geoffrey, give me some names and I'll visit his acquaintances and regular haunts. Assuming he hasn't left the city already."

"Very well. I will be addressing the citizens tomorrow morning, declaring Randall an outlaw. I'll have posters posted about town as well. The printer is making the woodcut with his likeness at this moment." Geoffrey looked over to The Bishop.

"I shall have word spread to the faithful, of this heretic in our midst, and the church will supply its guard as well to track down this outlaw. Captain Madok, we shall speak of your falsehoods directed at me at another time." Bennet managed to push himself out of the chair with some difficulty.

"Am I to ask for forgiveness with an additional tithing?" Madok snapped back.

"Of course." Bennet waited at the door, and Captain Madok obliged, opening it for him to pass first.

Geoffrey sat at his desk staring into space, and Thom stood over his broken wine glass. Geoffrey looked over at Thom without speaking a word.

"What would you have me do?" Thom said with knees knocking.

"Clean up the damned mess you made on my floor. See yourself out when you're done." Geoffrey exited leaving the door open.

Outside in the courtyard Bennett's carriage waited by the fountain. The carriage was an elaborately decorated vessel with highly polished brass accents. Four horses drew The Bishop's carriage, as the increased weight from metal armor plating, was hidden in the woodwork. Even though The Mother protects her servants, Bennett liked to take extra precaution in case of would-be assassins. Two church guards kept watch with crossbows at the ready as his driver opened the carriage door for him.

Madok's mount was held by city guardsmen dressed in the standard chain armor with Port Gwynn tabards over them. The captain walked over to The Bishop's carriage as Bennett was settling in and his guards were getting into their stations on the front and back. Two pairs of glass sconces illuminated the comfortably outfitted red velvet interior. Bennett tried to pull the door closed, but Madok blocked it with his boot.

"Geoffrey's handling of his bookkeeper will come back on all of us, if word gets out of Gwynn and catches Duke Payne's ear." Madok said in a subdued voice.

"Without a doubt I'm sure that conniving man is already plotting a way to make one of us look like an incompetent, treacherous fool as a cover. The Duke is a reasonable man, and The Duchess is one of The Mother's faithful. I have influence with them and can assure you that I will not hold any blame for any corruption that Geoffrey, or you or anyone else, may direct at me." Again, Bennett tried to pull the door closed, but found it impossible with Madok's boot in the way.

"Fine Bishop. The Mother would seem to favor some of her children more than the others." Madok said, pulling his boot from the door.

"Very wise Captain." Bennett slammed the carriage door shut, and locked it. Bennett's driver drove the team of horses forward as guards kept watchful eyes along the path exiting The Lord Mayor's estate.

Madok climbed into the saddle of his chestnut riding horse and a pair of his guards followed suit. Thom exited the mansion, descending the stone stairs leading to the courtyard. Thom's luxurious carriage rivaled Bennett's in fine craftsmanship and comfort. However, he didn't have it outfitted with armored protection, nor had bodyguards along for the ride. Thom climbed into his coach and leaned out the window.

"Captain. A word please?" Thom called out. Madok rode alongside the carriage as they followed the path out of the courtyard.

"What is it, Mr. Clarke?" Madok feigned concern.

"I'm not some common criminal. Word of this reaching Duke Archibald will most certainly result in a full audit of Geoffrey's record keeping and an investigation into each of our involvement. I cannot-"

"No, Thom, you are not a common criminal, you are rather uncommon. There aren't many common criminals that can afford to have two sailing vessels under construction in the shipyards, and a third docked in the harbor, on your salary. I imagine The Duke will spare no expense on the finest spikes to mount our heads on his castle wall." Madok smiled describing their possible future.

Thom gasped and fell back into his seat and closed the window.

Madok laughed as he caught up with the guards at the gates. "Gents, we are going to be busy for a bit. The Lord Mayor will be issuing the list of names of the outlaw Randall's contacts in Port Gwynn."

"To the garrison then, Captain?" Asked the guard on his left.

"No, first a round of ale at Smitty's. Things are about to become interesting around here again." Madok replied, as the three riders exited Geoffrey's estate.

Geoffrey watched through the window of his bedchamber as each party left the grounds. The Lady Mayoress, Cecilia, sat at her vanity brushing her hair in the mirror. Legs crossed in her silk nightgown; she spoke without turning. "Geoffrey, what is next?"

"We find Randall before Duke Archibald gets word." Geoffrey sat at a writing table, dipped a quill in the ink, and began compiling the list for the captain

.

4
The Nest

Randall awoke with his head aching from the blow. Eyes still closed he reached with his hand to touch it and felt a lump, which was also warm to the touch. He slowly opened his eyes and found himself lying on a wood frame bed, covered in a wool blanket, on a straw filled mattress. Much better accommodations than he had previously found himself in with The Mayor. Hardly luxury. He was in a small room with rough masonry work that served as a supply room. Sitting on the small wooden table by his bed was a wooden plate of food and tankard of warm beer. There was a wedge of hard cheese, boiled potatoes, and a piece of bread. One candle lit the room, and it was almost burned to its end.

He sat up and threw off the blanket. Someone had washed him, tended his wounds, and put a night shirt over him. Next to the bed on the floor lay a pair of simple slippers. He slipped them onto his feet and leaned over the table to devour the feast before him.

While chewing on a piece of bread, his attention was turned over to wooden boxes and cloth bags in stacks around the room. In the center of the floor was a wooden platter with food scraps piled onto it, that was teaming with rats. They showed no fear of Randall, nor paid any heed to his presence. Randall kept his distance from the rodents, as he finished the beer with a burp.

Randall took the candle, and slinked across the floor avoiding rat tails and other obstacles on the floor. He stepped into a narrow hallway loaded with small crates, casks, and bags. Rats scurried across the floor and the stacked supplies. At the end of the passage, he heard voices and laughter.

He edged his down the passage with curiosity. Looking into the chamber, he guessed he was still in the undercity. It was a large common area filled with people engaged in all manner of activities. There were men smoking pipes and drinking at benches, barefoot street children chasing after a chicken, couples romantically engaged in the many alcoves along the wall. There was a cacophony of sounds: shouting, laughing, singing, cursing. A central fire pit, that lit and warmed most of the room, had a thin shaft in the ceiling for ventilation. Skewers of meat were held over the coals by a few hungry men, and a large cauldron hung over the flames cooking a stew tended to by a hefty cook in a tattered dress. One musician played a reel on a fiddle as Izzy danced.

Randall scanned the room and no one paid him any attention. There were several other passages in the large room allowing egress from the common room. He deduced there was a large network of tunnels with secret doors connecting the city with the catacombs and the sewer system. Certainly, there were several secret entrances to the surface, like the one he was duped into following Izzy into. Just how long these people have been living unbeknownst to anyone above, was one of the questions running through his mind. The other, who was his host referred to as 'His Lordship?'

As he stood at the end of the passage, he was surprised as a large, wet, brown rat the size of a small dog ran by. It was the rat he caught a glimpse of in the undercroft of the Mayor's mansion. The creature ran to the fire pit and stopped to shake water off on the cook.

"Damn you Flynn! Not funny at all!" The woman pulled the ladle out of the cauldron and tossed it at the creature who dodged it effortlessly. Hot stew splashed onto the ground and the ladle bounced with a clang until it came to a rest at a man's feet.

"Careful there Agnes. That's a dangerous weapon you're wielding there! Flynn could've been killed!" He laughed, revealing a grin of only two yellow buck teeth. He turned to the rest of his drinking buddies, and continued their conversation.

The giant rat stood on its hind legs and outstretched its paws toward the warm coals. Agnes shook her head and went back to her stew. A man holding a skewer of meat presented it to the giant rat, which sniffed it, then bit off a piece.

"Pretty good eh, Flynn?" The man then took a bite for himself.

Randall watched the scene disgusted, and fascinated at the same time. The giant rat grew larger by the flickering light of the fire pit. The fat body thinned out as it grew in length. The naked pink tail shrank until it disappeared inside it. The paws transformed into hands, and claws shortened into fingernails. The creature took on a hybrid bestial human form and continued transforming. The snout shrank, and rat features began taking on those of a man. The brown fur covering the body began to become sparser, burrowing under, leaving only brown skin. Within seconds, the transformation was complete. What was once the giant rat Flynn, was now the nude man Flynn, warming at the fire.

"Give this fool a blanket and a pair of trousers!" Agnes laughed.

Someone quickly complied, tossing a dirty wool blanket at Flynn. Flynn caught it in his arms, and wrapped it around himself like a cloak. He looked at Randall with piercing dark brown eyes and a wry smile. "Our guest has awoken. Did they feed you?" Flynn spoke in a thick islander accent with genuine concern. "You were quite a mess when you were brought in two days ago. I think Gerard may have put a little too much force behind that whack to your head."

"He was asking for it!" Gerard looked up from the bosom of the woman his face was buried in to answer. He laughed, then continued his business with his lady friend.

"Hello, Mr. Randall. I'm glad you are feeling better. You smell better too. Agnes cleaned you up, and tended all those wounds." Izzy smiled as she walked over to him.

She took Randall by the hand and walked him to the center of the room by Flynn and the firepit. His eyes darted back and forth at all the people sitting, lounging, sprawling, and walking about the large room. It was crowded with at least twenty other occupants and the different smells of body odor, food, and the feces of normal rats that ran freely throughout began to overwhelm him. Randall heaved, and his lunch exited as he doubled over.

"Mr. Randall, are you ok?" Izzy voiced her concern.

"I'm sorry." Randall wiped his mouth on his sleeve and straightened back up.

Flynn offered him a tankard of water, which he gulped down. Smiling he pats him on the back. "I think we had better visit His Lordship before you fall over dead."

Flynn put an arm around Randall for support as he and Izzy walked him out of the common hall. They took one of the winding passages out of the hall lit by small oil lamps distantly spaced out on stone ledges. Other passages branched off in directions from their main path as well, and there were alcoves for the denizens in this strange warren to sleep, some vacant and some occupied. Personal belongings and crude pieces of furniture were hoarded the alcoves. Randall could not fathom how these people could live in such conditions. It seemed far worse than anything he had seen any poor family struggling to survive even in the worst slums of Port Gwynn.

They stopped in front of an alcove with a wood partition in front of it for privacy. "Wait here a moment. Let me get myself together." Flynn dropped the blanket as he stepped into his room. Behind the partition he got dressed in black breeches, blue tunic, then strapped a black leather belt with a rapier and dagger to his waist. He called the others into the small room, feeling suitably dressed, while lacing up his boots.

Flynn's alcove seemed much larger than the other's they had passed by only because it was neat, organized, and not packed full of junk. A simple bed, footlocker, small writing desk with a chair were the only furnishings in the tiny room. The floor was covered with a mish mash of woven rugs, and old tapestries covered the walls to make it a tad cozier. On the bed he laid out patched brown breeches, a stained yellowed pullover shirt, and a threadbare, blue felt cap with a mangled black feather.

"These should work for you. Better than running around in that nightshirt." Flynn pointed toward the clothes, encouraging Randall to get dressed.

Randall inspected each article before getting dressed. Finally, he put his nose in the cap and sniffed. Whoever the previous owner was must have worked in a tannery, judging by the pungent smell of urine. His facial expression let Flynn know that he was less than grateful for his charity. However reluctant he was, he set the cap on top of his head and brushed his hair behind his ears.

Izzy inspected Randall's ensemble and nodded approvingly. "You look very handsome Mr. Randall." She smiled up at him.

"You are too kind." Randall took this as a genuine compliment.

"Very good. Let's go meet His Lordship." Flynn led the way through the labyrinth of tunnels passing other large common rooms with people participating in various activities. Things as mundane as candle making to group love making. Privacy and personal space didn't matter to them. Nor did living amongst all the rats in the city, who they shared their communal home with.

Their destination found them in a large rectangular chamber lined with tables, and lit by torches in sconces with a central firepit. The ceiling was barrel vaulted with a mural painted to appear as a moonlit sky. Young children filled clay jugs of water from a well to distribute throughout the nest.

Two women outfitted in hardened leather breastplates, and bracers sat on top of a table in conversation. The lady that was of islander descent wore her hair in short, corn row braids. She was eating an apple impaled on her dirk. The other woman had short, choppy red hair and her fair skin had scarring from burns on half of her face. Her blind eye on the scarred side was clouded over making her appearance even more intimidating. She cut slices of raw potato with her dagger, and ate them as she talked.

"Sauda, Red! Where's His Lordship?" Flynn called out to the bodyguards.

"He's lightening his load in the privy." Sauda laughed and bit into the apple.

"Don't you need to be in there to wipe his arse?" Flynn said with a broad smile.

21

"You are being quite the twat today, Flynn. His Lordship overdid it again with the drink, and had a bit of a meat pie that was off. I guess it sat in the sun to long when it was snatched off the cart. The flies didn't seem to mind it much." Red laughed and continued eating the slice of potato.

Flynn walked to the far corner of the hall where a curtain was drawn in front of a niche. A walking stick with a silver cast metal handle resembling a rat, leaned against the wall. "Ermm. Your Lordship are you-"

"Piss off Flynn. Let me die in peace." A voice coughed behind the curtain.

"Peter, I'm coming in." Flynn drew back the curtain revealing His Lordship, Peter, sitting on the floor. He was leaning against the privy box cradling a jug lovingly in his arms. "Let's get you out of there." Flynn snatched the jug from Peter and passed it to Izzy. He assisted Peter into standing with his walking stick. He walked him to his designated thronelike chair at a table on a dais.

Randall was underwhelmed by 'His Lordship.' He was an overweight man in his early fifties, with gray in his hair, and a week's worth of white whiskers on his chin. He dressed in layers of old clothing a wealthy merchant once owned, but was tossed out with the rubbish. All were patched, motheaten and in need of a good washing. On his feet he only wore a pair of mismatched stockings with his toes peeking out of holes.

Izzy placed the jug on the table in front of Peter. "Thank you, child." Peter leaned into the table and emptied the jug in a dirty cup. "Hair of the dog." He made his toast, then took a drink. He eyed some of the scraps of food left on the table that might help with his hangover. A slice of bread that had only a few bites taken out of it looked like it would do the trick.

Flynn got down to business. "This is Geoffrey's bookkeeper, Randall, we've been keeping tabs on. We fed him and got him patched up a bit. Seems he is under the weather. Threw up his dinner all over the floor in Agnes's mess hall."

"Sorry sir, I'm much better. It was just..." Randall stopped as he spied a few rats on the table sharing leftovers with Peter. "Yes, much better. Thank you."

"Have a seat boy." Peter motioned to a chair opposite of him. Randall watched as a fat black rat sat on its hind end on a platter of chicken bones finishing off the last piece of meat. It watched him as it ate without any worries.

"What is it you intend to do with me?" Randall got straight to the point. Flynn took Izzy by the hand and joined Sauda and Red across the room.

Peter sat up straight in his chair and instantly became sober and serious. "Okay then. I have known of you, and the work you do for the Lord Mayor since you first came into his service. I had my spies reporting to me all that transpired over the past year of his shady dealings, and your involvement. You won't plead ignorance, will you?"

"No sir, I wouldn't deny—"

"Good, I'll continue. Three days ago, the Lord Mayor had his coureur deliver a message to a couple of my boys that work in the 'disposal service' to get rid of some *rubbish.* That's *you,* if you aren't keeping up. I learned you were being held in Geoffrey's private little dungeon under his estate, after you disappeared from the public eye around that same time. Something about Geoffrey's daughter and you? Regardless, my boys were going to deliver you to me, and not the bottom of the bay in a barrel. Your escape has just created a new wrinkle in my plans, since Geoffrey knows you are not fish food and are somewhere, hiding out in the city."

Randall raised an eyebrow. "Your plans?"

"Why yes. As the bookkeeper, You know the exact amount of coin hidden away in their vault. I also assume you know the location of said secret vault. That is the one thing they have managed to keep hidden from my spies. One thing that has kept our secret is those that live above do not know of our society existing here for the past century. However, the existence of a secret vault filled with ill-gotten coinage was revealed to a pretty courtesan by a drunken bookkeeper, leading us to this moment." Peter smiled ear to ear.

"Umm." Randall stammered. "Did I say that?"

"Oh yes. Tessa reported that tidbit, after which you were given special interest by my top man Flynn. He discovered your imprisonment, and had been skulking about the Mayor's manor with the house rats, gleaning what information he could. The thing that stood out was learning you have working knowledge of magic. Confirmed by Izzy, witnessing your escape from the transport, firsthand. That is such a rarity, since practitioners of it are typically dealt with by the religious police. The likes of Bishop Bennett especially. Do you have any more tricks up your sleeves?" Peter asked with curiosity.

"Well, first I must study the magic formulas from my spell book. I tend to forget them often when I use them. All I have committed to memory now are a few simple cantrips that I used for practical jokes. You know, once I changed the taste of this annoying sailor's beer at the pub to hot piss." Randall stopped, noting Peter wasn't interested.

"Since you made your escape from the Lord Mayor and have been our guest, things in Port Gwynn had become quite busy. My first thoughts were to have you turned you in for a small reward. There are posters posted across the city at every establishment with a reward for £50 for you dead, or mostly alive. A more profitable plan is robbing Geoffrey and those other sneaky bastards blind and scurrying off with their secret slush fund." His Lordship smiled broadly, ear to ear, with a twinkle in his eyes.

"I don't understand why you would want to risk doing this, as you have managed to live in secret for so long? I think Geoffrey would have the city torn apart to find his money and who was responsible." Randall was very concerned with that prospect, and the room seemed to spin a bit.

"Bring the boy some water!" Peter called out over to a young girl filling a jug of water at the well. "That's exactly what I hope he will do. The kind of chaos that will get that fool removed from his office, once it comes to the attention of that old fossil, Duke Archibald Payne. It's harder for us to earn coin provided by our 'protection' services when he's sneaking his extra tax burden on everyone. Especially when he's hitting some of the legitimate businesses I own." Peter dipped the bread in a bit of cold gravy from another plate before stuffing the remainder in his mouth.

Water was poured into a dirty cup that was sitting on the table already. Holding it in both hands, Randall gulped it down. He scanned the table for any scrap of leftover food not picked over by rats. Nothing.

"Sir, after I tell you where they have the coin hidden, would it be possible to smuggle me out of the city?" Randall said with hope.

Peter looked Randall in the eye and let out a laugh from his belly with projectile bread crumbs flying onto the table. "My boy, you are not only going to tell me where the stash is, you are going to help us retrieve it."

Randall gasped with wide eyes. "I don't have my book to study to relearn spells. I would be a liability. I'm a lover not a fighter."

His Lordship rolled his eyes and then gave him a stern warning. "Boy, you are indebted to me for saving your life. You will face the same risks as the other members of the team. When the coin has been successfully removed and brought here, then I may decide whether to let you go. I assume your book was not on your person at the time of your capture?" Peter picked up a half-eaten olive off a tray, tossed it in the air, and caught it in his mouth.

"No, it's hidden at my house, which I'm sure is being watched." Randall voiced his concern.

Peter searched the tray for another olive, but came up empty. "Not to worry boy. Once you retrieve your book, we'll be in business."

"Sir, I did say that my house is going to be watched, just waiting for me to return." Randall had a bad feeling about this.

"What's the worry boy? I'll be sending an expert sneak thief along with you." Peter pointed a fat finger across the room. Randall looked over his shoulder locking his eyes with Izzy's.

"Yay!" Izzy clapped her hands, beaming with delight.

"A bodyguard as well." Peter waved over to Flynn.

"Fulathela Chilongola at your service, Randall. Friends call me Flynn." Flynn made an exaggerated sweeping bow, with a wide smile.

"You, see? You're in capable hands. Now, you will get your damned book, after we get that baby face disguised." Peter said waving Randall away.

5
Ada

The Cathedral of the Merciful Mother stood as the largest, and one of the oldest buildings in Port Gwynn. Construction began half a millennium before the present day, and took almost one-hundred years to complete. The engineers made this marvel of stone construction as beautiful as it was defendable. Guards could be sent along the crenellated parapet that ran along the perimeter of the entire building, providing defense with heavy crossbows. Large cauldrons for boiling oil, set in strategic positions, in case of siege upon the city, which happened more than one time in Gwynn's long history. In the present day those defenses were abandoned and only a handful of church guard were kept, more as a ceremonial force with a few exceptions.

Stained glass windows, depicting the most important events of The Mother, and those that had risen to sainthood. The massive wooden doors, giving entry to the nave, had bronze relief sculpture, telling the story of The Mother and the birth of the world. The interior nave was finely finished out with white blue veined marble flooring, statues carved into the likeness of The Mother and The Saints, pews crafted from rare hardwoods, and a pulpit and altar adorned in gold fixtures.

Bishop Bennett had received an updated report from the captain of the church guard. Some of the church guards were imbedded with members of the city guard led by Captain Madok over the past few days since Randall's escape. Embezzlement of the church's revenue, that was also taxed in the kingdom, was an offense that would have him removed from his position.

It happened to a few other high-ranking clergy in the recent past. It most often led to imprisonment after an investigation by the Chief Inquisitor. Once, a priest was given the option of leading missionaries into the Goblyn Badlands to spread the word of The Mother to the savages. That was an unsuccessful mission trip. One missionary escaped, and witnessed his comrades turned into the main course of a banquet honoring the goblyn chief. Self-preservation was Bennett's top priority.

"This is troubling news Captain. This heretic may have escaped the city." The Bishop slumped in the frontmost pew in the empty cathedral, addressing Captain Ashdown, who stood before him in highly polished plate armor.

"Your Grace, since his disappearance, additional city guards were posted in the harbor in the event he tries to sneak on board a ship. All the buildings, businesses, and homes in that area have been searched. The Lord Mayor also has this Randall's residence under constant surveillance, with a few guards inside. One of our guards stationed with them, on the slim chance he would return. My assumption is, someone is hiding him in the city. However, Captain Madok investigated Randall's few acquaintances and places he frequents, turning up nothing. It seems the lad is not too well loved by anyone enough to do him any favors at this point." Captain Ashdown paused the conversation as a teenage girl entered the nave.

"Your Grace. I have finished cleaning the sacristy. Is there anything else you would have of me?" The girl was dressed in a simple gray dress that touched the floor, with a white apron and matching bonnet exposing only her face. She held a straw broom in one hand and a feather duster in the other. She made a point of not making eye contact with Bennett.

"Yes child. The north aisle needs to be attended to before your duties are complete tonight. Isn't Sister Lucia here? She oversees you. Now leave us be." Bennett waved the young girl away.

"Sorry your Grace." The girl turned with eyes focused on the floor, and retreated to the north aisle, to begin her new task.

The captain crouched down onto one knee and spoke in a whisper to Bennett. "Your Grace, there is one more thing. There is a newcomer I have in the ranks. This young woman appears to have powers she was blessed with, and performs in the name of The Mother. I have never seen anything of this nature before."

Bennett felt a chill over him, and nervously looked in Ashdown's eyes. "You suspect heresy? Someone to usurp, and create an insurrection? Someone to destroy the faith, deceiving the faithful with witchery?" Bennett was more concerned a true believer was granted powers by The Mother, and acted as a direct conduit to her. This could mean even bigger trouble than Randall, the bookkeeper, on the loose.

"Your Grace, I did not know, which is why I wanted to bring it to your attention. She came from a parish church in a hamlet some fifteen leagues to the north, with a letter of recommendation from their priest. She had training in armed combat, but nothing out of the ordinary. The thing I saw her do, was call upon The Mother and heal a wounded man. I saw the knife wound close before my eyes where she laid her hands upon him. She called upon the same power and brought sight back to a blind child. Word of these 'miracles' have just begun spreading through the city. She is the one currently stationed with the city guard, watching Randall's house." Ashdown said, concealing his excitement.

"I am both intrigued and troubled by this, Captain. I need a meeting with her as soon as possible. Please arrange for tomorrow, after the evening's service. I will want to know why this member of the guard wasn't brought to my attention beforehand. When has there ever been a letter of recommendation sent on behalf of a recruit?" Bennett was cross at this point in the conversation with Ashdown and ready to end.

"As you wish, your Grace." Ashdown rose and exited the nave as Bennett watched the doors closed behind him.

Bennett rose from the pew and scanned the empty cathedral hall. The light from the setting sun through the large stained glass rose window above the large entry portal faded as brass candelabras provided the sole illumination. The loud metallic crash from the north aisle caught the bishop by surprise.

"Oh no, no, no!" The voice of the girl came from the direction of the source of the noise.

Bennett swiftly made his way to the north aisle and found Ada, setting up the brass candelabra she had accidentally knocked over during her cleaning routine. Melted wax and candles, and one broken arm lay across the marble floor.

"Your G-grace, I'm s-sorry." The girl, with head bowed, struggled to get the words out. Bennett struck her across her face with an open hand, knocking her to the ground.

"You fool, girl! The Mother's house is to be respected, as is her property!" Bennett shouted enraged.

The girl wept and tears ran down her cheeks onto the floor. Her head covering lay on the ground beside her, and long curly dark locks were hanging loose.

"Look at me when I address you!" Bennett commanded.

The girl slowly raised her head, and then opened her eyes to look into the Bishop's eyes, as she sniffed. She was of fair complexion in skin, contrasting her dark hair. Her pretty face and large sad brown eyes eased Bennett's fury.

"I apologize for that child. I let my anger take control for your mistake. I was too harsh with my reaction." Bennett's tone softened, and he extended his hand to her. "What is your name young lady?"

"Ada, your Grace." She reached out her small hand toward the Bishop's.

Bennett grasped Ada's hand with his wrinkled hand, and pulled her to her feet. The girl was a several inches shorter and he looked down on her face, studying her features, holding her hand. Ada was fearful, not daring pull away or make any sound. He tightened his grip on her hand and turned her around to face away. Ada skin crawled as his fingers ran through her hair, and felt his hot breath on her neck as he leaned in to sniff. Almost immediately, Bennett released her and took a few steps back.

"Do you currently reside with the sisters in the convent?" Bennett inquired, raising an unruly white eyebrow.

"No, your Grace. I live at home with my mother and younger brothers. I just started working here this week. I also work..." Ada stopped when she saw Bennett crack a small smile.

"I see, I see. I assume you are being paid the standard two pence per week?" Bennett asked.

"Yes, your Grace. It is most generous and helps to—" Ada was interrupted again by Bennett.

"Yes. Child, there is a better paying job opportunity needing to be filled. It provides room and board and pays two shillings a week. One shilling would be sent to your family and the other paid directly to you. The steward of my manor needs additional staff, and he was requesting an additional chambermaid." Bennett relaxed, and the tone of his voice became caring and grandfatherly.

"It is very generous your Grace. I don't think I should do it, as I wouldn't want to accidentally break anything at your home. I t-think I s-should..." Ada stammered, and Bennett waved his hand to shut her down.

"You will take this job now as you will be working to replace the candelabra you so carelessly damaged. One shilling will still go to your family, and the other toward the replacement cost. I will discuss this further with Sister Lucia, and I'll send my steward for you soon. This is non-negotiable. Do you understand?" The Bishop's eyes narrowed and Ada felt the burn of his gaze on her as she looked at the floor.

"Yes, your Grace. I understand." Ada said defeated.

"Good. Now finish here and then you can leave." Bennett turned, walked down the nave, and turned to the south transept exiting to the cloister.

Ada walked and sat in the nearest pew, sobbing with her face in her hands.

6
Gong Farmer Blues

The phony beard and nose, that Peter's 'Master of Disguise' attached to Randall's face, made him unrecognizable. Combined with the fecal matter smeared on his ragged clothes, no guard would stop him for questioning. He pushed the wooden wheelbarrow, half filled with human waste, through the dark cobbled streets of Gwynn. Tonight, the Lord Mayor's former bookkeeper was one of the 'Nightmen.' The scooping bucket hung over his shoulder from a chord and swung with each step he took. Very few lampposts were about town. Port Gwynn was mostly lit by the waxing moon and starlight.

"I think I'm going to lose it." Randall only had dry heaves since the contents of his stomach were emptied a few blocks back.

"Keep it together man! There are people up ahead. Keep moving and act like you are supposed to be here." Flynn's voice came from the shadows in a whisper, as he followed Randall.

A large rat ran ahead of Randall and ducked into an alleyway. It stood on its hind legs to sniff the air. It dropped back down and scurried ahead to the next alleyway, through the neighborhood, and waited. Sounds of revelry were up ahead, as a group of drunken men had exited the tavern and were staggering and singing in Randall's direction.

"Move it, Randall." Flynn's voice came from the shadows behind him again.

Randall lifted the arms of the wheelbarrow and rolled it forward toward the group of young men. It was obvious these four were the grown sons of the wealthy business owners in Port Gwynn. Randall sang an ode about a harlot he had learned recently. He made his voice sound like the 'gong farmer' he was pretending to be.

"Miss Mary is the girl for me
She never let me down

Paul Wolff

Invited me up for a cup of tea
Then she threw me on the ground
Mary shagged me once
She charged for twice
Took me for a dunce
And gave me the lice"

The revelers were walking arm and arm and caught the stench upwind from them before they saw Randall. They moved to the other side of the road covering their noses with handkerchiefs and picked up their pace.

"It's late, the damn nightmen are out now. We should have left hours ago." A young man in a fancy brown leather doublet, and green felt hat with a large feather, announced.

"Yeah, then maybe you wouldn't have lost your week's allowance your daddy gave you to that card sharp!" A young man, with skinny moustache and pointed goatee, laughed.

The group continued forward paying Randall no further attention. Another young man wearing pantaloons, in a shiny gold fabric, stepped up to the flower box under a shuttered window where Flynn ducked under for cover. Flynn pressed against the wall as the golden pantaloons dropped to the man's ankles. His aim was not the best, as half of the yellow stream missed the box entirely soaking Flynn's blue tunic. He pulled up his golden trousers, and hurried on his way to join his group.

"I'll remember that little bastard for next time." Flynn said as he continued following Randall from the shadows.

Randall stopped short of the wall of wattle and daub homes. One city guard was drinking from the metal cup chained to the pump in the center of the courtyard. A tall light post lit the area, while Randall stayed just outside it.

"Which one is yours?" Flynn whispered.

"The second one from the left. Looks like there is a light inside it. Probably a welcoming party inside, waiting for me." Randall spoke softly.

"Ok, Izzy. Check it out." Flynn whispered to Izzy in her giant rat form.

Izzy scurried along the row of houses after darting across the courtyard, as the guard took another drink from the pump. She arrived at Randall's house and sniffed the air. Inside there was at least two people, judging by the conversation through the shutters.

"Oy! What are you doing skulking over there?" The guard took notice of Randall, who was lingering too long on the edge of the courtyard.

"Sorry sir, just taking a breather. I've got to clean out the privies on this block." Randall said, doing his best gong farmer impersonation.

"Well, go to the alley. You're stinking up the place, you gob!" The guard shouted, waving him away.

"Right away sir! G'night to you!" Randall lifted the wheelbarrow up and hurried to the alley way.

Izzy crawled up the wall and into the planter box, under the front window. Randall neglected taking care of the flowers, so it was overgrown with weeds, providing cover. She listened through the shuttered window and heard two guards, one of which was a woman. She stood in the box and eased up to peak in the crack between the shutters. The best she could see was that both guards were set up in the front room at a small table, helping themselves to whatever food and drink was left in Randall's pantry. One guard was dressed in the city tabard, and the woman was part of the church's guard.

Finished with his drink, the guard headed back to the apartment. Izzy ducked into the box under the tangle of weeds, unnoticed. When the door closed, she scurried into the alley joining Randall. Flynn caught up to them shortly thereafter, and tossed her clothes and equipment to her.

In seconds, the giant rat transformed into her human form. Izzy pulled her dress over her head, then stashed her other items in her pockets. She appeared again as when Randall had met her only a few days before.

"Okay, if everything goes to the plan, we shouldn't need these. However, its best you have this." Flynn withdrew a dagger from the bag and passed it to Randall. "Ever had to use one before?" Flynn asked with a grin.

"Only to carve a ham at dinner." Randall took the small blade and placed it in his rope belt.

"Not to worry, it's the last defense. You just plunge it directly into your heart before they can arrest you." Flynn said in a stern voice.

"What?" Randall was taken aback.

"Just kidding, Randall. Just stay calm when you get the book, and walk the cart back to the safehouse. We will all meet there. No guard in town will search you with your stench. Just make sure that compartment on the cart's underside is closed tight before you move."

"Yes, yes, yes. If you can keep them occupied once you lure them out, I can be in and out quick." Randall said with the utmost confidence.

"Good. Get in there as soon as we draw them out. Now Izzy." Flynn drew his rapier from its sheath, and Izzy ran across the courtyard to the edge of the lamp light above the water pump.

Izzy let out a blood curdling scream in the direction of the guarded house that gave Randall a fright. Flynn stomped across the courtyard in Izzy's direction pointing his blade shouting. "Come back here you filthy urchin! I'm going to skewer you!"

Izzy ran screaming as the door swung open and the first guard stepped out.

"Oy! What's all this?" He shouted at Flynn.

"Mind your own business!" Flynn yelled as he darted after Izzy, screaming for blood.

"Looks like we've finally got something interesting on this watch tonight! A bloody child killer! Everyone on your feet!" Three guards rushed out with weapons drawn and took up pursuit. The city guard with swords, and the woman of the church guard wielding a mace.

Randall slinked toward his front door, which was left wide open. Scanning the courtyard and other houses, only a few residents seemed to be awakened, peering out of their second story windows. Their attention was focused on the street where the guards had just run out of view. Randall took a deep breath, and entered his former residence.

A single oil lamp sat on the table in the front room, where he used to take his evening meals. Spread about it were dirty dishes, a deck of cards, and a dagger stuck into it next to some crudely carved initials.

"Bastards! No respect." Randall cursed under his breath. Randall lit a candle from a sconce, and took it with him.

The first floor was ransacked, and gone through thoroughly, by the city guard. Geoffrey probably personally made sure that everything was suitably broken, searching for any secret ledgers hidden away. Hopefully, the secret compartment in his upstairs bedroom where his spellbook was hidden away wasn't discovered. Randall took the narrow stairway leading to his bedroom.

Looking through the door, he saw that his furniture, including a small writing desk and wardrobe, were overturned, and linens were bunched up in a pile atop the bed. Randall kneeled on the floor and studied the wall, which was fitted with decorative wainscoting. He gave a disguised button a push, and a section swung open, revealing the secret compartment's contents.

The leather-bound spell book was stored within, along with a stash of coins, and small bags of various reagents for magic. Scanning the floor of the room, he found his finely tooled leather belt with pouch. Randall put on the belt, then gathered all the small bags and book.

"Hey, shut your noise. Wait your turn. I'm still trying to catch some winks." A cranky voice came from under the linens.

Randall was startled to find one more guard still in the house. A chain shirt, helmet, and sword belt complete with sword were laying at the foot of the bed, on top of other clothing and equipment he overlooked.

"S-s-sorry." Randall mistakenly answered.

The guard tossed the quilt off his head and looked directly at Randall. Squinting his eyes, he immediately recognized him. "Well, you've got bigger balls then I thought!"

The guard jumped out of the bed wearing only his braies. Randall tripped backwards over the desk and hit the wall.

"Don't move, little bugger!" The guard ordered as he crouched down, moving toward his sword on the floor.

Randall drew Flynn's dagger from his side, attempted a menacing stance. "D-d-don't bother. I'm just leaving."

The guard kept eye contact with Randall, and continued to reach for the sword, unconvinced. He found the hilt, and wrapped his fingers around it.

Randall was shaking and began pleading. "P-p-please don't."

"Hey! He's upstairs! Get up here!" The guard shouted to alert his comrades, who were away on the chase.

Randall pushed himself from the wall, with his shaky hand still pointing the blade. He tripped over the desk falling into the guard who was drawing his sword.

The dagger plunged deep into the guard's shoulder spraying Randall's hand with blood. The guard fell backwards yelping in pain. Randall grabbed his book to make a quick exit.

"He's stabbed me! He tried to kill me!" The guard cried, following Randall down the stairs.

Randall ran to his front door, and saw his neighbors in the courtyard looking in his direction.

"Look! It's Randall! The damned criminal!" A man in his nightclothes pointed directly at him. The others in the group, dressed in various sleepwear directed their attention to him.

"He's come back! Where are the guards? Guards!" A woman sharing a blanket with her husband screamed.

"Don't you move!" The wounded guard was at the foot of the stairs, with sword in hand, and the dagger protruding from his shoulder.

Randall darted across the courtyard, not impeded by his neighbors. The guard stepped to the doorway, leaning on the frame for support. "Help me, please." He cried sliding to the ground, losing consciousness. The couple ran to the guard's aid as others followed Randall, shouting an alarm.

***

Flynn and Izzy were a block ahead of the guards easily out pacing them. Izzy darted into a black narrow alleyway, between a closed eating establishment and a clothier's shop. Flynn continued forward, ensuring the guards were still following. Izzy crouched down in the darkness, and her eyes glowed red, as she transformed into her hybrid rat/girl form. The guards trod past the alley, not taking notice. Seconds after their passing, she crept out and ran for the safehouse.

Izzy hid in a dark doorway hearing more footsteps. It was Randall, running in her direction, gasping for breath. He already tossed the hat, and was peeling off the phony beard and nose. Behind him the sounds of the guards closing in. Luckily, he still had his book under his arm.

The shrill sound of a whistle blow, pierced the night. "Guards! The outlaw Randall is on Mourning Road!" The distant voice of a pursuing guard shouted. Again, the whistle blew.

"You're going the wrong way!" Rat Izzy shouted to Randall as her nose and whiskers twitched.

"Where do we go? They are around the corner!" Randall squealed.

"We can hide out in the mausoleum. You know the one in Lamentation Park? Let's go!" Izzy ran without waiting for Randall. He took the hint and followed through the alleyway.

Flynn kept a steady pace on the parallel, street thinking that the others would take an alternate route to the safe house. Izzy and Randall burst through the alleyway onto the street, nearly colliding with Flynn. Flynn joined them as they crossed the street to a corresponding alley. A guard spotted Flynn and blew the shrill whistle once again to redirect their pursuit.

A few more turns, through dark city streets and back alleys, found the three at the stucco covered, stone walls surrounding Lamentation Park. The iron gates were bound with a heavy chain and padlock. Beyond the gates were the granite grave markers, marble monuments, and mausoleums under a canopy of huge live oak trees. The entrance to the old catacombs was no longer in use by the city. However, in a moment's notice, persons from The Nest could gain entrance and hide out from guard patrols until the coast was clear. This was only to be used as a last resort, but never at night.

Izzy scurried up the sheer wall nimbly, using cracks and small imperfections as finger and footholds. She crouched on the top. "Hurry Mr. Randall!"

"How am I supposed to do that?" Randall was dumbfounded.

"The wall isn't that high. I'll give you a boost. Now quick." Flynn tossed his book to Izzy, who caught it effortlessly in her paws. He cupped his hands for Randall to step into and lifted him to reach the top of the wall.

"I haven't the strength." Randall exclaimed, trying to pull up.

The shrill sound of the whistle blew again, and the sergeant of the guard yelled. "Surrender now, and you won't get hurt!" The two teams of guards combined for a total of six well-armed persons, running in their direction.

"Shite!" Randall suddenly found the motivation to pull up and over, into the waiting bushes.

Flynn scaled the wall with little effort as the guards closed in. They rushed to the gate in time to see the three disappear, deep into the darkness of the graveyard.

"Dammit, which key is it?" The sergeant fumbled with a large ring of keys. The third key worked. "Get the lanterns lit up and we'll split into two groups. You, stay outside the gate and lock it behind us." The sergeant took one other with him. Juliana of the church guard led the other two into the gloomy shadow of Lamentation Park.

7
Into the Dark

Izzy held the lock picking tools in her nimble, rodentlike fingers and worked on the lock to the iron gate to the mausoleum. "You will need to lock this behind us to gain us some time." Flynn said with his blade drawn, keeping watch out into the darkness. Some moonlight and starlight filtered through the branches of the trees, causing shadows to play all around the stone markers.

"Got it, Flynn." Izzy opened the squeaky gate. Flynn pushed Randall through the door and backed into the hall scattered with leaves and twigs. Izzy closed the door and began locking it behind them.

"I need some light. I can barely see anything. Et erit lux!" Speaking an incantation, he touched a rock that was on the floor, causing it to glow, bathing the passage in a bright blue light.

"Randall, what the hell?" Flynn turned and glared at him.

"I can't see in the dark. I'm not like you two." Randall picked the stone up and held it before him.

"Uh, oh. They see us." Izzy finished locking the gate as the light from the pursuing guard's lantern shined on them.

"Randall, this is twice now things are running afoul because of your ineptness. At the end of the hall is the catacombs door Izzy still needs to open!" Flynn ran ahead followed by Izzy.

Randall saw the guards closing in, then heard the whistle blow. He tightened the grip on his book, held the 'light stone' before him, and ran after the others.

He caught up with them at a solid iron door, upon which was painted, *DANGER! No Admittance*. A granite plaque was affixed overhead, with the inscription, *Northern Catacombs,* chiseled into it. Izzy was frantically working on the lock. The marble walls around them had burial vaults, from floor to ceiling, with family names on bronze plaques. Members of the elite of Port Gwynn were interred within these walls.

At the opposite end of the hall, the shouts of guards echoed off the walls. Izzy had made quick work of the lock and Flynn grabbed the pull ring.

"I don't think this has been opened since the incident." Flynn said in a pained voice, as rusted hinges slowly gave and allowed him to forcefully pull it open.

"The incident?" Randall held the light rock up, illuminating a stone stair beyond the door. Stale air exhaled forth from the depths through the portal.

Randall and Izzy hurried in and Flynn looked back to see the city guards entering the mausoleum. He pulled the iron door shut behind him.

"We're out of time! Down the stairs now!" Flynn pushed past them leading the way down.

The walls were smooth masonry of perfectly fitted stone work. Metal sconces were set in the wall at ten-foot intervals for torches, but all were empty. The dust on the floor they kicked up with each step showed this area had been abandoned for some time.

The three entered a small chapel used for services when the dead were interred into the catacombs. A stone altar and platform for the body to be laid upon, were in the front of the room. The room was divided by two rows of stone benches. There were several arched niches in each side of the chapel that once housed statues, which now lay smashed to pieces on the floor. The fresco painted onto the plastered wall behind the altar had also been defaced. The heads of all the figures of the saints had been chipped off, and the large central figure representing The Mother was completely obliterated. Any other evidence of furnishings in this room had long been removed. There were two passageways on either side of the defaced fresco leading out.

"We better choose one and go. Our only chance is if they follow us down, we find a place to hide, and wait them out. These northern catacombs do not join the others that lead to The Nest. I'm not aware of any other exits to the surface either. Follow!" Flynn took the left passage without waiting for any response from the other two. Izzy quickly followed.

"The incident?" Randall muttered again and followed them.

✳✳✳

Juliana and her team were walking down the steps into the catacombs. Gregor held the lantern in one hand and his longsword in the other, leading the descent.

"Oh, no, no, no. I don't like this one bit. We should turn back and wait for the sergeant to come with us. This place has been kept locked up for a good reason, I'm sure. In fact, I would rather just say we lost them. Also, I don't want to be blamed for you smashing the gate open with that mace of yours." Gregor shook his head, stopping in the middle of the descent.

"I'm taking full responsibility for that, Gregor. It's more important that we take Randall and his accomplices in, and not worry about a little damage to the gate. You told me he had stabbed Edward, back at the house. We can't let that go. I'll lead the way, if you are unable." Juliana passed Gregor on the steps and continued into the darkness.

"Go on now. We bring them back, then no one's going to care about anything and we could collect that reward ourselves. The Captain said guards could claim it." Delvin gave Gregor a nudge.

"Can't spend it if your dead." Gregor grumbled as he caught up with Juliana, who waited just at the edge of the lantern light.

They entered the chapel and Gregor shined the lantern around the room. Juliana shuddered at the defaced room that was once hallowed ground. "Who would commit such sacrilege? Gregor shine the light onto the fresco." Juliana approached the wall inspecting the plaster chipped away on all the faces of the figures. "It looks like the plaster was clawed away. Look at the marks here. Claws for sure."

"Oh, no, no, no." Gregor was shaking his head again.

"Gregor, I think I hear something this way." Delvin pointed with his sword

into the dark void of the left passage.

✳✳✳

Randall and Izzy walked side by side as Flynn lead the way. The blue light illuminated the walls checkered with burial niches. The cloth that the dead were ceremoniously wrapped in were loose in many of the niches, and bones were strewn about the hallway. They passed through larger chambers and side passages finding the same thing wherever they went.

Flynn stopped in a large chamber, with a vaulted ceiling, with several stone sarcophagi and the stone effigy of its occupant lying atop it. Prominent citizens of Gwynn were interred in this room, from mayors to prominent knights, and clergy of centuries past. Burial niches lined the walls in the chamber as well, with most of their contents removed and scattered throughout the room.

"This must do. You two hide in that space there and I'll keep watch from behind the sarcophagus of... 'Sir Edgar.'" Flynn read the bronze plaque attached to it. "Extinguish that light, now!"

Flynn crouched behind the last resting place of Sir Edgar. Izzy crawled into a niche that had old wrappings and a few bones left inside it. Randall moved over to a niche near Izzy's and examined a femur that was lying on the ground. He picked it up to inspect it a little closer then dropped it. He squatted to inspect a humerus bone as well. He tossed it aside and looked across at more bones scattered across the chamber.

"Randall, get into that niche. Now!" Flynn struggled to keep his cool.

"Flynn, all these bones... they have been gnawed on. Toothmarks. Snapped in half and old marrow sucked out." Randall looked in his niche first, then crawled in.

"Yes, I know! Extinguish that light!" Flynn ordered.

Randall covered the rock within the folds of his clothing to hide its luminance and cradled his book.

The room was blanketed in absolute darkness, but Flynn was able to see everything in shades of gray. From within the burial niche, Randall attempted to control his breathing and calm himself. It was not going well for him, and he could hear the pounding of his own heart, and his temples began to throb with pain. Izzy scanned the room with red glowing eyes and listened with her keen ears.

The sound of approaching footsteps and lantern light was coming from the passage just outside the chamber.

"Oh, no, no, no. I'm not liking this at all. I've heard these catacombs go on for miles under the city. I've lived here my entire life and wouldn't go in when they were open. We should leave now and just have that door permanently sealed shut with them inside. Brick it up I say. Problem solved." Gregor gave unsolicited advice freely.

"Shine it in there Gregor." Juliana pointed her mace toward the chamber and tapped Gregor's helmet with a gloved fist.

"Easy." Gregor pointed the light into the room.

Gregor stepped to the edge of the chamber, shining the light along the back wall into the burial niches. "Looks clear. I reckon they found themselves another way out."

Flynn crouched low behind the sarcophagus, prepared to fight.

"No, Gregor shine it into all the niches on the walls." Juliana and Delvin stepped in behind Gregor.

"There! Somebody is hiding in that one!" Delvin pointed toward the movement he spotted.

Randall closed his eyes tight awaiting a sword through his skull. Flynn readied his blade, preparing to strike from behind at the right moment. Izzy held her little knife, ready to give them a fight.

Delvin reached into the shadows of the niche and yanked a handful of hair. "Come out ya bastard! Else I'll skewer you and take you back in pieces!"

A pale hand, with purplish bruised flesh, took hold of Delvin's wrist and dug long yellowed, razor-sharp fingernails into him. Delvin screamed, losing all strength and muscle control, and dropped his sword. Pupil-less eyes, white as eggshells, on the cadaverous face locked eyes with Delvin. The creature's smile revealed razor-sharp, yellowed teeth.

"Brethren, young lambs for the slaughter! Feast with me!" Its voice hissed, and its breath smelled of rot. It released Delvin's hand, allowing him to collapse. The creature pulled itself out of the black niche, and its snakelike tongue licked blood off its long fingers. Standing over Delvin's prone body, it turned its lifeless eyes on Gregor.

Insane laughter came from various niches around the room as more of the creatures pulled themselves out of their holes. Flynn jumped up from his hiding spot, crossing both sword and dagger across his chest. Juliana did the same and spun on her heels. A dozen of the creatures slunk forward from all around them.

"Mr. Randall, we need to help Flynn! Come on!" Izzy darted across the floor and stood with her back to Flynn.

"A damned wererat too!" Gregor's light caught Izzy as she ran. "What other cursed creatures live under here? Oh, no, no, no! We've got to go, now!"

"Hold your ground Gregor! Delvin needs our—" The creature lifted Delvin in its arms, and pulled his chain mail coif off his head. It sank its yellow razor-sharp teeth deep into his neck, ripping the flesh with a spray of blood, then threw Delvin back to the ground.

"We starve. We have not tasted flesh for far too long." The creature tore onto Delvin's body, consuming him alive.

"No!" Gregor turned, another creature dropped from the ceiling, knocking him on his back. Gregor's kettle helmet was sent rolling, and his smashed lantern set his own arm alight. He waved the flaming appendage as his flesh melted and his fingers fused together in the flames.

The creature crouched in front of him, its laughter a rattling chuckle. This creature had patches of long, stringy, white hair on its head. The breasts on its naked body sagged like empty sacks, and folds of skin at the belly hung loose.

Randall escaped the confines of his niche, providing light with the stone as he moved in next to Flynn and Izzy. Flynn swung at four of the creatures, driving them back on his own. Six more spread out to block the passage.

"No please!" Gregor pleaded, as his tormentor crawled over on top of him.

Juliana's heavy mace connected with the beast's head, crushing the skull and rolling the naked body off Gregor. It lay flat on the ground oozing a black ichor.

"On your feet, grab your sword! We will survive this!" Juliana called out.

Gregor scrambled to his feet. A dead man's foot stepped on the blade of his longsword before he could arm himself. He looked up into the milky white eyes of death, as the odor of carrion overwhelmed his senses. It grabbed his head with both hands, sinking claws into his skull like a hunter's trap. It lifted Gregor, shaking him violently, then tossing him to the floor. Gregor's lifeless body lay at Juliana's feet, his head twisted around backwards.

"Let us share the fight against these hell spawn creatures." Juliana called to Flynn as she defensively retreated toward him past four dead men ravenously consuming Delvin's body, now stripped of armor.

"Aye!" Flynn lunged and drove the point of his rapier into the belly of one that stepped in. He twisted the blade and pulled it out. The creatures' organs spilled out, as it fell to the floor in a heap.

The four temporary allies were now in the center of the room standing back-to-back. Gregor's killer stepped cautiously over his body. The three blocking the exit dived onto Gregor and immediately stripped him out of his armor and consumed his warm flesh.

Two of the dead men lunged at Flynn, but the swing of his blade held them back. A dead woman ducked under his backswing, snatching Izzy's arms.

"No! No! Please no!" Izzy screamed into its lifeless white eyes framed by long greasy black hair.

The creature sunk its teeth into her neck and shoulder, ripping her flesh from her. The creature's chin was dripping in Izzy's blood, and she went limp in its arms.

"Izzy!" Randall and Flynn screamed in unison. Flynn turned, but a slashing claw drove him back.

"Flynn, I've got one last spell that may help." Randall dug into his reagent pouch and pulled forth a rotting banana peel.

"Do something then!" Flynn shouted, kicking one of the creatures back into a pile of bones.

"Lubrica cum humida!" Randall spoke the words waving the peel at the floor under the three undead creatures.

The peel was consumed by the magics used in the conjuration, and the floor beneath the dead ones became slick. Almost comically they lost their footing, one by one as they slipped and fell, fighting to stand again.

Izzy lay prone on the ground, but was no longer in rat hybrid form. She now appeared as the little girl in the sack dress, as Randall had first met her. Blood flowed from the wounds on her little body.

Juliana swung her mace smashing the clawed hand of the dead one that reached for her. The creature's hand was hanging broken at the wrist, with sharp bone shards poking through its skin.

It howled and backed away. "A curse be upon you! Your soul will never find rest when we devour your sweet flesh!"

The other dead, swarming the bodies of Juliana's fallen comrades, looked up from their gruesome feeding. They were covered in warm blood and held entrails in their fingers. They slowly rose with anger and hunger in their soulless white eyes.

Juliana pulled free the silver pendant that was hanging from a leather cord around her neck. It was a stylized depiction of The Mother standing with arms outstretched to receive. She forcefully held it before her, attracting the lifeless eyes of the undead that were approaching her.

"I command you in the name of The Mother to retreat! Flee from here!" Juliana's voice boomed in the chamber. She turned to face each of the dead with the symbol in hand repeating the chant over again.

The creatures held their arms out defensively trying to block the silver symbol from their lifeless eyes to no avail. The hideous sound of them gurgling, hissing, and howling blasphemous curses toward her could not drown out Juliana's chanting. They began backing as far away as they could from her. Some crawled back into the niches from whence they came. The ones on the slick floor crab crawled away until they were free from Randall's conjuration. She looked over to the eviscerated bodies of Gregor and Delvin laying on the floor as unidentifiable piles of gore.

"How long can you hold them back?" Randall cried.

"I'm not sure. This is a first for me!" Juliana shouted back.

Flynn sheathed his sword, and scooped up Izzy. She lost a lot of blood and her face was dead white. He draped her limp body over his shoulder and backed away as the female creature cursed him, retreating into a niche.

"We should leave now!" Randall yelled to the others as he entered the passageway under the blue light of his stone.

"Agreed." Juliana said ending her chanting. She backed out into the passageway holding the symbol in front of her.

"Quickly, back to the stair. I'd rather deal with the guards than them!" Flynn shouted to Randall.

"You knew about these things living below and you just referred to it as 'the incident?'" Randall snapped at Flynn.

"Poor choice of words, yes." Flynn admitted.

They stopped in the desecrated chapel to catch their breath. Flynn laid Izzy across the stone platform and put his ear to her chest. "She still has some life in her, but she's almost gone." Flynn said.

Randall listened down the hallway, clutching his book. "I don't hear them. I think you changed their minds about eating us."

Juliana stepped over toward Izzy. "Please, allow me to help her."

Flynn drew his rapier, and put himself between Izzy and Juliana. "Stand down! The truce is over."

"Please, When I sleep, I have visions of events that may come to pass granted by The Mother. I don't know why, but I have seen this child in them." Juliana looked and pointed at each of them, "You, and you, as well. There was nothing in my vision about turning you over to The Mayor." Juliana pleaded with Flynn.

Flynn was compelled to lower his rapier and step back. Juliana removed her gauntlets and closed her eyes. She gently placed one hand directly onto Izzy's wounded neck and stroked her hair with the other, then closed her eyes. "Mother, I call upon your divine mercy to heal this child."

Randall and Flynn watched as Juliana's hand glowed with a soft white light. Just as quickly, the light faded. She lifted her hand and the bite marks closed, leaving only small scars as a reminder. Izzy forced her eyes open rubbing tears away with her hands.

"Momma, I'm hurting." Izzy's wounds were healed and the danger of dying gone, but she still felt the pain. Izzy was orphaned and lived on the streets since she was four, but on rare occurrences still cried for the mother she barely knew.

"Izzy, you're okay! I thought I was going to lose you." Flynn pulled her up and gave her a big hug. "I am indebted to you, my lady."

"Flynn, we need to get the hell out of here. I can hear guards coming from the other hall this way." Randall urged him along.

"I need to rejoin the others, and let them know we were ambushed by the ghoulish dead. I will pray that you may turn to follow The Mother's divine wisdom. The Mother has a higher purpose for you. Leave here at once." Juliana pulled a stone from her belt pouch and saying a small prayer, it glowed with a soft white light. She held it aloft, and entered the dark passage.

"You heard the lady, let's go!" Randall said and held his blue light stone up into the stairway.

"No argument from me." Flynn concurred.

"Me either Mr. Randall." Izzy agreed.

Flynn set Izzy on the ground, then took her by the hand. Within another hour, they found their way to the safehouse.

8
Madok's Warrant

The sergeant's report to Captain Madok was not well received, especially learning of the death of two guards, and the stabbing of another by Randall. Juliana was brought in for an intense interrogation by Madok. The escape of Randall, with the help of two accomplices, raised more questions than answers given.

Geoffrey's reception of the news from Madok was taken even worse. In a rage, things in his office, were thrown and smashed and the foulest of curses shouted, while the Captain stood stoically in silence. The undead creatures, that killed city guards, needed to be dealt with after being ignored for years. Randall risked returning to his home to recover something of great importance. Randall also had allies that were lycanthropes, and *that* woman allowed them to escape.

"The sergeant reported Randall was in disguise and pushing around a cart for emptying privies. His cart was discovered abandoned behind his house and had a secret compartment for smuggling. My gut tells me the lowlifes, you were originally shipping him off to for disposal, have some involvement in this. I don't trust that woman from the church guard, nor her story. Because of her, two of my men were killed and that little prick escaped. I don't want any of that fool, Bennett's guard involved in this. They can all guard the poor box at the cathedral." Madok's pressure valve released.

"I'll send word to Bennett that his involvement is not needed in this matter further. Take some men and arrest those gong farming brothers and tear the place apart. If they have him or been aiding him, I want them all dumped into the bottom of the bay with the rest of the shite tonight." The mayor angrily responded.

Geoffrey sat behind his desk then penned the warrant for the Madok. After sprinkling the pounce to dry the wet ink, he rolled it and slid it into a bone tube.

Madok took a few steps to the door, stopped and turned back to Geoffrey. "Lord Mayor, I don't know why you even bothered with that. None of those fools can read." Madok shook the tube.

"It's for appearances. Giving the illusion of our great legal system at work." Geoffrey laid a fresh sheet on his desk, dipped the pen nib into the inkwell, and started writing, without looking up at the captain.

Madok exited mayor's mansion and joined his two men, in the courtyard holding their mounts. It was only a few hours after sunrise and the rest of the city was just awakening for business.

"We'll need the wagon and plenty of manacles. Meet me at the dockside and bring five more men with you, sergeant." Madok ordered.

"Sir, I thought I might be allowed to return to the barracks, as my duty ended with the morning sun." The sergeant was not very enthusiastic as exhaustion set in.

"Noted. Now get the damn men and wagon as you were told. I want everyone there within the hour." Madok shouted.

"Yes sir." The sergeant said, mustering enthusiasm.

Madok and the guard arrived at the docks after a ride through the city streets, which were already bustling. Fresh breakfast breads on carts, and baskets of fruit lined the road for sale to hungry dock workers. Madok purchased a pair of sweet pastries for them, which they ate as they made their way.

The gong farmers of Port Gwynn were all employed by the brothers Mark and Bert, whose family operation had been in service for three generations. Their work was a necessity in a city the size of Gwynn, but their work was only carried out after dark and completed before the morning sun awoke. Services were paid through tax revenue; however, Mark and Bert expanded their business model. This included clients needing other things to be disposed of with the 'night dirt' at the bottom of the bay. They were good at their work and 'special' rubbish was weighted down to prevent it returning with the tide.

The brothers home base was a two-story structure, first floor of stone and the upper made of wood. The smell coming from it attracted all manner of vermin and flies swarmed around it. Mark and Bert's personal living quarters were on the second story, shared with their families. The lower story housed the tools of their trade. The upstairs apartment had an exterior stairway separate from the downstairs, to avoid need to walk through the mess below. Even so, it did not prevent the smells below from fouling the living quarters. The brothers and their families referred to it as 'the smell of money.'

Madok spied on the building from a distance, noting all windows were shuttered and the gate closed. While waiting for the other guards to arrive, they saw a large mastiff chained at the foot of the stair to the apartments. It rose and watched him suspiciously. The many wrinkly jowls on its black face made it more intimidating, but it hadn't taken an aggressive stance.

"That beast needs to be taken out before it alerts those shite peddlers." Madok pointed.

"Aye sir. I can get him in one clean shot." The guard loaded the bolt on the crossbow and took aim.

The bolt lodged deep into the large dog's neck, dropping it dead on the ground without a noise. Madok nodded his head approvingly. Within minutes the sergeant arrived with more men and the wagon used for prisoner transport.

"Perfectly timed." Madok said. The men took positions around the building as he and two guards ascended the wooden stairs.

One brute of a guard wielding a maul waited for the command from Madok to smash the wooden door in. The wooden balcony was littered with garbage and ragged clothes were hanging to dry across it as well. A few children's toys, in various stages of repair, were also strewn across the way.

"On the count of three..." Madok said in a low voice while drawing his sword.

The maul smashed at the door, splintering it and throwing half to the floor and the other hanging from one hinge. The three ran into the large open living area the brothers' families shared. The giant open room covered the entire floor, with makeshift partitions separating sleeping areas and the kitchen. Privacy was a luxury this family did not seem to care about. It was a dark, filthy, hoard house having walking paths through junk collected over the years, and the smells that went with it. The place was unoccupied at this moment.

"Dammit! They were tipped off." Madok cursed.

"Sir! There's a trap door here in the floor." The brutish guard pulled on a ring opening the door, which had a wooden ladder going to the lower floor. From below, the sound of hasty movement could be heard.

The three descended the ladder and did a quick cursory scan of the large stone room. A single lit lantern hung low from the center rafter overhead. Tools of the trade were stored about: dried feces encrusted wheelbarrows, buckets, shovels, carts. Tack and harness for the mules were stored within as well. Dirty straw covered the floor.

"Foul odors may curse us with the fever. I have no idea how these people don't carry the sickness." The young guard said covering his nose.

"They haven't gone far. They must have a hiding place in here, sir. I know I heard them." The brutish guard said, walking cautiously with the maul.

There was the sound of a click, from the opposite side of the room. Madok pointed in the direction, and the others complied silently. The three walked across the straw beneath which large smooth flagstones fitted perfectly together as the floor. A large flagstone in the corner of the room not covered in straw immediately caught Madok's attention.

"No chance to cover their tracks. See if you can pull it up." Madok said to the young guard.

The young guard kneeled over the large flagstone and ran his fingers along the edges, seeking a handhold. Finding success, he pulled it up and slid the stone out of the way. Descending into darkness, a tube was carved into the rock. Metal rungs, for hand and footholds, were mounted into the wall and the air had a stale smell to it.

"Grab that line and the lantern. Lower it down and let's see where this goes." Madok said to the brutish guard. "You tell the sergeant I need him and the others to get in here now."

9
Separation of Church and State

B ishop Bennet closed the evening service, leading the congregation in a prayer to the Merciful Mother. His heartfelt performance, with head bowed, eyes tightly shut, and hands gripping the ornately carved pulpit, moved all those in attendance. He asked for The Mother to guide Randall, to realize the error of his wicked ways, and come forward to turn himself in. The Mother would act with mercy to those that repent their sins.

Geoffrey sat with his family in the frontmost pew. The Lady Mayoress and daughter Madeline sat, in their finest gowns reserved for church, with eyes closed, hands tightly clasped and heads bowed. Madeline dried her eyes and blew her nose into her handkerchief throughout the service. Geoffrey frowned with his arms crossed staring directly at Bennett unblinking, except to roll his eyes during exceptionally over the top moments. Bennett avoided eye contact with Geoffrey during services.

The midweek evening service was not typical for Geoffrey's attendance, but he wanted to sit in on The Bishop's meeting with Juliana, after receiving a report of the previous evening's events. The nave was clearing and the faithful exited their class appropriate portals. Bennett took his place at the designated portal for Port Gwynn's more elite citizens. Many of the church's most generous donors passed through, and Bennett always made the time to have a small conversation with each. Always thanking them for their past donations, and letting them know about the most urgent needs of the faith.

Geoffrey stayed behind while Cecilia and Madeline exited to board their coach. Captain Ashdown and Juliana walked up through the nave to meet Geoffrey and Bennett. Bennett held firmly onto the hand of wealthy parishioner, patting it with the other, as his family stood alongside. They smiled and gave an approving nod at Bennett's every word. Another generous donation for the orphanage's restoration was procured, and made official with a handshake. Half of which, would be funneled to the construction costs of the new wing to Bennet's manor house.

Bennett smiled as that last family made their way to their waiting coach. His expression took a dour turn as he turned to the next group he was about to receive. Geoffrey, Ashdown, and Juliana stood patiently, waiting for the schmoozing to end.

"Let us walk the cloister while we talk." Bennett led the others, as the acolytes closed the doors and removed liturgical items from the altar for storage. He waved to one of the young robed acolytes to accompany them with a lamp.

The cloister walkway was dark, and shadows danced in the light. The boy carried the lamp on a long pole, struggling to keep it aloft over their heads. The sound of their steps emanated throughout the open gallery, echoing between walls and pillars. Juliana was out of her guard attire, and walked in a simple gray gown and common slippers. Her dirty blonde hair was cut short off the shoulders and neatly brushed straight. Captain Ashdown walked alongside her, clad in his polished breastplate carrying his helm under his arm.

"I was hoping for a chance to meet with you before there was the controversial events of the previous evening." The Bishop said, as they stopped before a large pair of doors that were reinforced with iron bands and set with large pull rings.

"Your Grace, it was originally my intention to bring in the accused, but the events in the catacombs changed following the deaths of my men. I told the captain that The Mother had shown them to me in a vision. She hasn't revealed their purpose to me yet, but I know it's not to rot in the dungeons." Juliana spoke in her defense again.

"Those were not your men. Those were guards of Port Gwynn, whose lives were lost due to the actions of the outlaw and his accomplices. You aided them, and allowed them to escape!" Geoffrey's voice boomed, and he aggressively pushed his finger in Juliana's face.

"Lord Mayor, I agree that the lives of those men were lost due to his criminal actions. Obviously, this young and naïve child was bewitched by Randall—" Bennett tried to respond.

"I am no child, nor am I naïve. I did—" Juliana was in turn cut short.

"Shush!" Bennett's face reddened in the lantern light, and his wrinkles and creases became more pronounced. "Your service of The Mother in her guard has been revoked. You are to join the Sisters for the time until we determine the next course of action to take. Sister Lucia will provide you with a cell for your housing, so you can pray and ponder your actions. This begins tonight."

One door opened outward, and a tall, thin, elderly woman dressed from head to toe in a form hiding habit. She had a thin cane in one hand to provide her support, as she walked as well as to provide a quick retribution to one that strays from the Mother's teachings.

"Come child, I've been expecting you. I'm looking forward to the chance to speak. You will be provided for with more appropriate clothing first." Sister Lucia looked Juliana up and down with watery, red-rimmed blue eyes.

Juliana stepped through the door without dissent, and Sister Lucia pulled it shut. Captain Ashdown and Geoffrey looked at each other, slightly puzzled. The Bishop clasped his hands together and smiled.

"She'll be serving as a missionary and travelling to the badlands within a week." Bennett said with relief.

"I object to this, Your Grace. Perhaps her judgement was clouded by the events of the evening, but I believe I should have some say in her punishment. I believe she does have promise and a higher purpose." Ashdown said.

"You said you had your own reservations about her when we last spoke. Sister Lucia will observe and report before we move forward. That is how it will be." Bennett walked back to the cathedral as he spoke.

"There are other problems aside from that girl. Madok found an escape tunnel those gong farmer brothers had at their place. The passage was trapped, and one of the men was killed by a poisoned dart. Currently the area is locked down, and they're sending in a specialist to help find and remove more traps. Madok believes that there is something larger than just Randall and those 'Shite Brothers' here in Gwynn. There's a network of criminals and cursed rat lycanthropes, from what we got out of that girl's interrogation. Silvered weapons will be needed to kill the things according to Madok." Geoffrey spoke, as he followed.

"So, they can transform into a rat-like person? There are other such cursed people that transform into other bestial abominations. They will all need to be eradicated." Great concern was reflected in Bennett's voice.

"Easier said than done. Madok is under the impression that there is more than one point of entry to whatever lies below the city. These people have been walking the streets in plain sight all along. Just what Randall's involvement with them is and what they are using him for, I'm not sure, but I have my suspicions." Geoffrey stopped before the doors to enter the cathedral, as the young acolyte lowered the lamp and ran to open the door for them.

"My guard is willing to support the city guard again now, since she has been discharged and confined, Lord Mayor." Ashdown offered.

"No thanks." Geoffrey grunted. "Things are going to get ugly, and I expect the job will be carried through all the way. Bishop, we can discuss more in private, if you will share your carriage and take me home."

"Of course." Bennett dismissed Captain Ashdown and prepared for an unenjoyable shared ride with the Lord Mayor.

10
The Not-So-Great Plan

R andall sat on the floor in the corner of the small room, pouring over his book by the light of a single candle. The straw filled pallet he sat on didn't offer much comfort. The worn gray blanket he was using was warm enough, but it had a personality of its own as far as odors go. He wasn't sure how many others had holed up here in the past. He did know that someone had fleas. He picked one off himself and dropped it in the candleflame as he studied. It was well into the second day, sharing cramped quarters in the secret room.

Izzy was curled onto her own pallet under a similar gray blanket. Her bloodied and torn sack dress was discarded in a corner, though her other belongings lay on the floor beside her. Her eyes were closed tight, brow furrowed, while making rat-like squeaks, as she dreamed of the catacombs.

Randall looked over to Izzy with some concern, then returned to his studies in his spellbook. There were several spells in his book he had read over, but never actually used or committed to memory. The spells he used in the past were for getting around Geoffrey's mansion to sneak into Madeline's bedchamber. His current situation called for something more.

The door to the room was barely three feet tall, and the ceiling was only five feet high. Getting around in here meant stooping over to walk. There wasn't enough room for Randall to pace in.

The knock at the door was a sign that Flynn had returned, from a little foray into the tailor shop above. Randall leaned over to pull the bolts at the top and bottom of the door. The other side of the door was camouflaged to appear as the cellar wall. Flynn crouched down with a basket holding fresh baked wheaten bread and kippers.

"Our host is very generous." Randall said, taking the basket from Flynn and setting it in the center of the floor.

Flynn pulled the door shut and bolted it, as Izzy sat up sniffing the air.

"Is that breakfast Flynn?" Izzy sat up wrapped in the blanket, leaning over the basket of food.

"More like lunch. It's well past the noon hour according our host. He said there is a lot of activity on the street, and the city guard has been going door to door, searching businesses and residences for us. They did a quick look around Rowan's shop earlier, but didn't search the cellar." Flynn sat cross legged on the floor.

Izzy and Randall reached over to the basket. Randall tore a piece off the loaf and Izzy began nibbling on a kipper. Flynn grabbed a kipper for himself.

"The Brothers' place was raided, and its occupied now. Word is that woman who saved our necks down below was taken into the cathedral, apparently discharged from service in the church guard for letting us go." Flynn washed the fish down with a drink from a water jug.

"I like her. She was nice." Izzy said thoughtfully.

"What do we do next? Rowan wants us out tonight. I don't fully trust him. The little fat man gives me the creeps. However, this doublet he gave me is rather nice." Randall adjusted the overly large collar covering his neck on the finely embroidered garment.

"Show some respect Randall. Rowan has been an ally to us for years." Flynn closed off that part of the conversation.

"Sorry." Randall sighed.

"I don't like these things." Izzy tossed the pair of small brown shoes away. She had on velvet green knee breeches, a white shirt, and red vest. "I look silly. Danny and the others will make sport of me. I'll punch him in the eye if he does." Izzy made a threatening gesture with her fist.

"I'm sure you will." Flynn smiled at Izzy. "However, we need to figure out a new game plan. If they found the passage leading to The Nest from Mark and Bert's place, they will eventually overrun it with a large force. There are plenty of traps set and secret doors to foil them for a short time, but I believe The Mayor's men will find it. Peter has collapsed tunnels, in the past, during raids on different 'business partners' establishments. The 'Shite Brothers' didn't have the forethought, or time to do it, as they made a run for it." Flynn said shaking his head.

"I need to get out of this town. There is nothing for me here except certain death, and it sounds to me, you're about to become homeless. I've been studying a spell in the book I haven't used before, but might be just the one to get me safe passage out of here. Its illusionary magic, that will allow me to take on the appearance of another person. This can get me past the guards at the gates, if they don't look too closely." Randall hoped the others would be impressed.

Flynn's eyes narrowed, and Randall felt them burning through him.

"Er, um yeah. It could, uh work." Randall stammered.

"Maybe it will. However, I believe the whole reason you are still breathing is because you have a job to do. If The Nest is being invaded by the city guard, we will need a bit of coin for relocation costs, so to speak. My friends will be able to put up a good fight against those poorly trained soldiers down there, while making their escape." Flynn began cleaning under his nails with a dagger he pulled from his boot.

"You're not suggesting we do a heist, while the city is on high alert?" Randall's heart sunk deep into his stomach and began burning in the acids.

"Ooh! This sounds fun! Better than playing with those mean dead people. They were biters and didn't fight fair." Izzy called out, making stabbing motions her knife.

"Geoffrey's vault is guarded, and I'm sure filled with lethal traps to deter thieves. I never visited the inside of it. I only recorded what was being brought in for his ledger in the offices. I never went below. Even if we were to get in and out of there, how would we make it anywhere carrying a bunch of loot?" Randall knew this was going to be a worse idea than fleeing into catacombs.

"This is the best time. Hit it when they are occupied elsewhere in the city. I can get messages sent through Rowan, to other safehouses where others will hole up, if they evacuate The Nest." Flynn smirked.

"This is not a well thought out plan." Randall shook his head, hoping Flynn's mind would change.

"Mr. Randall, I think you're nice, but I will stick you in the bum with my knife if you don't do as Mr. Flynn says." Izzy suddenly appeared quite menacing in the dim candlelight as its light glinted on her eyes. In the short time Randall has known the little girl, he had never seen this more sinister side of her.

"I'm sure it's not going to come to that Izzy. However, Randall, your life is only as worth as much to us, as the service you are to provide. Understand?" Flynn looked unblinking into his eyes.

"Yes." Randall was quickly concluding, Flynn and Izzy were not quite trusted friends yet.

"If you get us in safe and undetected, with the aid of your magic, Izzy and myself will take care of the vault." Flynn said with confidence. "There is not time to wait and see what is going to happen. After we hit it and take what we can carry out, there is another safe place nearby to make a stash and hide out."

"Very well. The Customs House in the High Port is far from the action in Low Port. Maybe, there would be less risk." Randall accepted that the ever-evolving plan Flynn was cooking up, would be suicide.

"So, about this new spell that you learned. How long can you keep up the deception?" Flynn enquired.

"I'm not sure. I'm not even sure how convincing it would be. It would be best to take on the appearance of someone I know. Someone with access to the Customs House and won't raise suspicions being there." Randall said thoughtfully.

"Anyone I would know?" Flynn looked at Randall sideways.

"Probably not. The Director of the Board of Customs, Thom Clarke." Randall nodded his head and bit his lip, thinking of the timid yet corrupt man, was up to neck in the conspiracy.

"I don't know that name. Would he be someone that would draw attention and be recognizable, if seen out on the street in the night?" Flynn asked.

"He sometimes visits a brothel in the area. I saw him there when I was... Randall felt slightly ashamed at the admission.

"Hold on a minute, you're talking about 'The Siren's Cove' run by old Madam Stella? That is the one that is a short distance from The Customs House." Flynn mused. "Been there myself, when I had extra coin in my pocket. Stella has a safe house nearby that we could slip in, after the job." Flynn stroked the hair on his chin. "It's in the basement of a warehouse she has ownership of. Seems she was going to branch out and do something 'semi-legit' businesswise. Her silent business partner is Peter of course."

"That's all fine, but what is the plan after we pay a visit to the Customs House? Somehow make it out of there, with the most powerful men in Port Gwynn's secret stash of money, then hide out in another cramped basement?" Randall ran out of breath recapping Flynn's plan.

"Still working on that. Several things to factor in." Flynn nodded his head.

"What?" Randall's eyes narrowed.

"Whether or not we all make it there alive." Flynn smiled.

11

Assault in the Dark

"Behind you!" The sergeant shouted a warning to the soldier fighting a sword wielding rat man.

The man-at-arms swung around lifting his shield arm as a child rat, dressed only in brown breeches, leapt at him with a dagger. He fended off that attack as the rat man, now to his flank, lunged forward with its rapier. The tip of the blade drove under the mail coif deep into his neck. Blood flowed out over his tabard as he dropped to the floor gurgling.

The invasion of The Nest had turned into a life and death struggle. Captain Madok led a force of twenty men into its depths, with the intent of bringing in Mark and Bert, but were met with resistance from its entire population. Several of Madok's guard were slain.

The large common room was the rallying point of the remaining twelve men under Captain Madok's command. Tables and benches were overturned and the remaining rat men that fought were springing in with rapiers or daggers, and dodging the swing of their swords. The glow from the firepit's coals cast nightmarish shadows from the action on the walls.

The rat boy leapt at the sergeant who was rendering aid to a fallen comrade. The sergeant made a quick slash with his longsword across its belly. It rolled away, holding in its guts with its hands, as the blood stained its white underbelly.

The creature winced with the pain from his attack, as its belly wound closed. It rose to its feet, looked at its bloodstained belly, then to the sergeant.

"Sergeant! Finish it with the silvered dagger!" Captain Madok called out as he finished another wererat with a silver headed mace.

The rat woman tried to defend herself as she lay prone. When she couldn't hold back Madok's relentless attack, the silver head of the mace caved in her face, as he wildly bludgeoned her repeatedly. When the last breath left her, Agnes reverted into her human form. Her face unrecognizable.

The sergeant plunged his silvered dagger deep into the chest of the rat boy. It staggered back a few steps and collapsed. As the life left its body, he transformed into a skinny boy of twelve, with brown hair and freckled face. Izzy would not have a chance to punch Danny in the eye for teasing her as she promised. The sergeant ran forward and pulled his dagger from the boy's chest and prepared for his next foe.

The remaining wererats scattered, taking different tunnels, leaving Captain Madok and his remaining men alone with dead wererats and city guardsmen all around.

"This is unbelievable." The sergeant exclaimed, looking around wildly. "These vermin living beneath us."

"Captain, what are your orders sir? Do we pursue?" A guardsman frantically asked, catching his breath.

"No, this is beyond anything I imagined. We must retreat to the surface. Leave our dead!" Madok shouted.

"Captain, what about him?" The sergeant pointed his weapon at Mark, who was slumped against the wall holding his belly from a sword wound. Bert lay dead on the floor with his neck slashed wide open.

Mark looked up at Madok. He made a pained cough as blood trickled down his patchy beard.

"They brought this on themselves, and he won't make it if we carry him out. Someone else will need to take over their family business. Leave him." The captain ordered.

The captain scanned the room, tallying the bodies of his fallen men and the dozen denizens of The Nest. "Return the way we came. You, take the rear and watch our backs."

They made their move into the dark narrow hall leading out of the larger common chamber. The man in the lead held a bullseye lantern before them as they moved out single file. The Sergeant backed out, keeping an eye on the rear. He saw the glow of red eyes spying their retreat into darkness.

"They're returning!" The sergeant shouted, as he paused.

Three arrows found their mark, piercing his mail coat, driving deep into his chest and belly and another lodged into his wooden shield. He attempted to turn to run, but after taking two steps he collapsed.

"Sarge has been hit!" cried out one of the men, who turned to go to his aid.

Two more arrows were shot out from the chamber, and one caught his shoulder, the other a direct hit in his face. He fell across the sergeant.

"Run!" Cried out the next in line from the back.

"You two! Shields up. Back out." Madok barked as his numbers were decimated.

The rear guard took positions with their heater shields together. Another volley of arrows was launched into the passageway, lodging into their shields. The wererats followed from a distance.

"Ade, move it in front!" Madok shouted to the lead man, who was hesitant to move forward into the inky blackness.

The lantern illuminated the roughhewn corridor some sixty feet ahead, causing a small cluster of normal sewer rats to scatter in the light.

"Captain, I don't think this is the way we came!" Ade called back.

Another volley of arrows launched from the rear, was deflected by the guard's shields except for one. The arrow met its mark, lodged deep into the soldier's inner thigh, passing through to the other side. He bellowed and fought to stay upright, as blood flowed from the wound. He staggered backwards against the wall, forcing his shield arm up. His femoral artery severed, he slid down the wall, crying.

Another arrow struck the side of his head, not even slowed by his mail coif. He crumpled to the ground.

Madok furiously stuffed an oil-soaked cloth into a ceramic flask he held in his hand. Another guard took the rear position, and they continued to retreat as they were fired upon by the archers.

"This will gain us a little time." Madok lit the cloth with the flame from a firestick. As flame consumed the oil-soaked rag, he lobbed the flask at the wererat archers.

The flask landed at the rat men's feet, shattering and covering the floor, and them with flaming oil. The rat men cursed rolling on the ground, and patting the flames down.

The lantern bearer, Ade, led Madok's shrinking force further down the narrowing passageway. They took more turns, and side passages, until all direction was lost.

"Definitely didn't come this way!" Ade called out as the passage dead ended in a closet sized room.

"Let me through." Madok squeezed through, as the rear guard kept his eyes to the back. "Shine that light in here. Quiet everyone!"

He held the lantern into the room, flooding the small space with light. One wall was of stonework, unlike the other. He tapped the wall, listening for changes in the sound. Identifying what appeared a hollow area beyond, Madok felt around the wall and, found a loose piece of masonry. He ran his fingers around the edge of it, then tried pulling on its edge to no effect. He then gave it a push, and the stone gave with a *click,* and a small square section of the wall pivoted open, swinging inward. A foul odor, and the sound of dripping water attacked his senses in the blackness.

"Captain, they're coming this way." The man at the back of the line called out.

Ade shined the lantern into the secret doorway which dropped to the passage below. Before him was a cylindrical masonry tunnel lined with ancient, perfectly fitted bricks. Black water, that appeared less than knee deep, stood at the bottom. Rubbish and more unpleasant things floated atop it, washed from the city streets above.

The rear guard cried out, as glowing red eyes approached. Two well placed arrows to the neck ended his life.

"Into the sewer, now!" Madok grabbed the lantern from Ade, and shoved him through the door.

Each man splashed down into the dark tunnel, until it was just Madok and the last man holding the shield. Another guard ignited a torch in the larger tunnel. Madok passed the lantern off and then went through it boots first splashing down on his feet.

"They're on top of me!" Cried out the last guard, as he abandoned his shield and grabbed the edges of the portal to pull himself through.

Madok reached out his hand and took the man's arm to pull him though. The other men backed away in the tunnel, watching the sight, as two pairs of rat hands dug their claws into his shoulders, playing a tug-o-war with his life.

"Don't let them take me!" He cried, as his helmet fell from his head into the water below.

Madok held the man's arm with both hands, desperately pulling. He saw the gray rodent face of a red eyed wererat just behind the man, staring back into his eyes. While the other wererats held the guard back from Madok, it opened his throat with a curved dagger blade. It shoved its fingers into the gaping wound spreading it wide open, spilling his blood down the side of the tunnel.

Madok released his arm and drew his sword, backing into the opposite wall. The body was pushed into the tunnel, splashing into the foul water. Laughter erupted from the darkened portal, and the door closed shut with a click. No trace of a door could be seen.

He turned as the light in the tunnel began to dim and the sounds of footsteps splashed off in the distance. His six remaining men were fleeing deeper into the sewer. Madok chased after their distant silhouettes in the torchlight, splashing through the muck.

12
A Tale of Two Thoms

'Thom Clark' sat next to the wagon driver, stroking a finely groomed graying beard. The streets in this area had a good amount of foot traffic late into the night in High Port. The sounds of lively music, from the open doors and windows of a popular alehouse, could be heard as patrons sang along swinging flagons of drink.

"I feel a tad parched. Perhaps we should stop for a drink. The proprietor of that fine establishment carries Grummandy beer." *Thom* said.

"No stopping driver. Keep it rolling." The voice of Flynn came from under the tarp in a whisper.

"Yeah, Mr. Randall. We're working." The voice of Izzy, scolded him from a wooden crate.

"Father said no stops until the drop-off." The teenaged driver kept his eyes forward, hands tight on the reigns.

Randall was disappointed, giving a sigh of disapproval. He adjusted the satchel holding his spell book over his arm, then folded his hands in his lap. The *clip-clop* of the horse's hooves on the cobblestones and the wooden wheels of the wagon became the only sound on the street as they drove onward, and the way was soon only lit by moonlight.

Randall touched his chin again, rubbing the illusionary beard.

"I hope this is going to work. You say you can see this pointy beard, because I can't feel anything there except a little stubble since my last shave." Randall said nervously.

Flynn pulled back the tarp, scanned the streets, then looked at Randall.

"I see it just fine. Don't try to convince any guards that you are, who you are. Don't try to imitate the man's voice or mannerisms. I'm sure the night watch doesn't have enough interaction with him, other than to recognize him by appearance. Trying to pretend would raise suspicions. When you get in, we will wait for you to open Thom's office window." Flynn looked to Randall for a response.

"Yes, as I said his office is upstairs. I also said the vault is in the basement." Randall looked ahead at the dark road and businesses that were closed for the night.

"Since the ground floor windows have bars in them, we're not getting in that way. However, once we are in, we deal with any problems on the inside as they arise." Flynn said anticipating Randall's objections to this mission.

"It's just up ahead, Flynn," the driver said looking forward to the Customs House. A large building with a lower floor of masonry and overhanging upper story of wattle and daub. Light could be seen through the barred windows on the ground floor, that had thick panes of dirty glass with an opaque glaze of grime.

"Great, Victor. This is where Izzy and I will get off. Luckily, no guard posted outside." Flynn slid off the wagon, and helped Izzy to the ground. "Victor, after you drop old *Thom* here off, wait ahead in that alley, and I'll make it worth your while with a little extra cut from your father's payment."

Victor smiled and drove the wagon up to the front of the door. Izzy and Flynn disappeared into the darkness, slinking along to the rear of the building. Randall mentally prepared himself for anything. He had acquired another dirk provided by Rowan 'just in case' and adjusted his belt and frilly collar around his neck.

"Well, I've lived a long enough life I suppose. In case I don't make it out of there, it's been a pleasure making your acquaintance." Randall offered his hand to the driver to shake.

"Shut up and get off my wagon. I'm expecting my cut tonight, and if you cross me, I'll cut your throat myself." Young Victor put his hand on the hilt of a dagger on his side.

Randall quickly climbed off the wagon and stood between it and the steps up to the building. He looked at the large brass inlaid double doors, above which a large brass sign engraved in bold letters "Customs House" was mounted overhead. He turned back looking at Victor, who was sitting staring him down.

"Well, what are you waiting for?" Victor said a tad annoyed. "I'm your driver dropping you off. You can't just show up like you walked here."

"Yeah." Randall climbed the few steps and rapped on the door with his fist. He waited, looking down at his boots and then back at Victor.

A small viewing portal slid open and a pair of eyes appeared squinting at Randall looking him up and down. The little portal slid closed. Randall turned and looked at Victor shrugging his shoulders. There was the sound of a bolt sliding and a bar lifting from the other side of the double doors. Randall stood up straight clearing his throat and faced forward.

One door slowly opened and a hulking middle-aged man with a shaved head, wearing leather brigandine armor, holding a spear stepped out. He didn't speak, but just stared at Randall, making him very uncomfortable.

"Will that be all Mr. Clarke?" Victor called out.

"Um, yes. Thank you." Randall paused before turning his head in Victor's direction.

Victor drove the wagon down the dark street and Randall watched it disappear into the darkness. He turned his attention back to the man at the door, who still stood in place eyeing Randall. The man moved to the side and encouraged him to enter, without saying a word. Randall walked inside, and the guard immediately bolted and barred the door.

Randall was familiar with the layout of the Customs House, having reported often to Thom Clark's office working on the ledgers for the conspirators. He was not sure how Flynn and Izzy were going to sneak past the guards to the basement. He walked across the polished hard wood floor of the large open room, lined with rows of tables for inspections, and desks for the clerks. He set one foot at the base of the carpeted stairs, when a voice called out.

"Mr. Clarke. I don't know how we missed you leaving your office." Another man, also dressed in brigandine armor, was sitting in a chair leaning against a supporting pillar. He stood up and walked toward Randall. He was shorter and a bit more vocal than his companion, with a full head of unkept hair. "Somehow you barred that door behind yourself, and changed your clothes too." He stopped a few paces from Randall and looked at him sideways, squinting with one eye.

Randall took one step up the stairs.

"I, uh, clumsy me spilled ink on myself and had to change. I, uh, left out the back door." Randall took another step up the stairs, hoping these two would not question him about the building's lack of a back door.

"Back door? Are you saying you went out through the dock entrance down below, without us seeing you?" The man took another step toward Randall. His bald companion grunted in support, as he too stepped forward readying the spear in two hands.

"You know, that's what I refer to as my office window. I can climb down from there easy enough, just not back in." Randall was grasping now. He backed up the stairs several more steps.

The two guards looked at each other and smiled, each stepping up onto the stairway.

"You need to stop right there and walk yourself back down these stairs. You may look like Mr. Clarke, but you sure as hell ain't him." The man drew a skinny dagger from the leather scabbard at his waist. "I promise not to hurt ya. I can't make the same promise for him though."

His companion gripped the spear tighter in both hands and grunted approvingly with a yellow smile.

Randall stepped back onto a landing before a turn in the stairway and stopped. The two men were continuing to slowly approach with their weapons at the ready.

"Okay, we'll come to you then. Just stay put. Maybe Mr. Clarke would like to help sort this out." The two continued slowly walking up the stairs, then suddenly sprinted at Randall.

Wild-eyed with fear, Randall instinctively held his hands before him with his palms facing the men, as to block their approach.

"Flamma Illum!" Randall shouted out magic words. From the palms of his hands orange and yellow flames fanned out, hitting the two charging men in the face, then stopping almost as soon as they were conjured.

The heat from the magical fire set hair alight as well as the leather brigandine they wore. They screamed as their exposed flesh burned, blistered, and melted. The bald brute shielded his face with his hands, then toppled down the stairs snapping his neck. The other fell forward, sprawling dead across the stairs, as his armor continued to smolder.

Randall stood on the landing bewildered at what he had just done, nervously blowing on his hands. Randall had never taken a life before, and now he was responsible for the deaths of two people.

"Well, that's more powerful than when I used it to light the fire in the hearth." Randall was in awe of himself, inspecting his hands for any signs of scorching.

A man's voice from atop the stairs made a cry of terror, and Randall ducked down, raising his hands over his head defensively. Thom Clarke covered his mouth with one hand to hold back his screams and the other on the rail for support. His eyes were on the smoldering corpses of the guards. He then looked over at Randall in his illusionary disguise appearing as him.

"D-d-d-don't hurt me! Is that you, Randall? You stay away from me!" Thom backed away from the rail with his hands up.

"Sorry about that, Thom. I didn't want to hurt anyone. We didn't think you would be here this late." Randall tried to look as unthreatening as possible.

"W-w-what do you mean we? How many of you are there?" Thom moved toward the open door to his office.

"Just some friends. We'll be out of here in no time. If you would just..." Randall climbed the stairs, hands up, trying to be unthreatening, but it didn't work. Thom jumped into his office slamming the door.

Randall ran to the door, heard it lock from the inside, and then a bar dropped for added reinforcement.

"Thom, I promise I'm not going to hurt you." Randall pounded on Thom's office door with his fist.

"Go away you evil magician! You won't turn me into a toad!" Thom shouted through the door.

"Don't be silly Thom. I don't have the powers of transmutation ...yet." Randall said, the last bit under his breath. His confidence was growing, bullying Thom Clarke through a locked door.

Randall listened with his ear to the door. Thom squealed, and there was the sound of something breaking.

"Uh, Thom. What are you doing?" Randall stepped back addressing the door.

A minute of silence passed. There was the sound of the bar lifting, and then the bolt sliding from inside the office. The door slowly opened, and on the floor in front of his desk, Thom lay unconscious. A broken flower vase with fresh cut flowers was laying by his head, upon which a lump was growing.

Izzy, in her rat girl form, poked her head around the door and looked up at Randall. The window to the outside was open, and Flynn was just pulling himself in through it.

"I thought you were going to wait for me to open the window for you?" Randall said to Izzy. He crouched beside Thom, examining his head."

"Flynn though it best for us to sneak in since this window was already open and we heard quite the ruckus you were making." Izzy stepped away from Thom. "I imagine he may wake up with a nasty headache. I don't think I hurt him that bad." Izzy held a single white daisy to her nose to sniff it.

Flynn pulled the windows closed and latched them shut. The finely appointed office had polished hardwood paneling, bookcases and cabinets overstuffed with ledgers and documents. Izzy jumped onto an overstuffed green tufted chair in the corner of the room. Her little rat feet dangled, not touching the ground. Randall stepped over Thom and examined the papers spread about the desk.

"Looks like Thom was trying to prepare for the quarterly taxes that Duke Archibald will soon collect to fill the King's coffers. He thinks he's clever enough to fool the Duke's accountants and collectors." Randall looked from the abacus and to the papers. "Maybe the Duke will only put his head on a spike at his castle."

"Randall, you are you again." Flynn pointed to his face, as the illusion of Thom's likeness faded away and Randall's youthful features were restored.

"Aww, you're handsome again Mr. Randall." Izzy transformed back into her human form. She tucked the daisy into her hair by her ear.

"What do we do with him?" Randall asked, pointing at Thom.

"Izzy will bind him and then we'll hit the vault. Victor is waiting close by with the wagon, like we discussed." Flynn tossed a length of hemp cord to Izzy, that he pulled from his pouch. He stepped out of the office and looked over the railing at bodies of the guards. Flynn's nose curled at the smell wafting upwards of seared flesh. He looked at Randall, who was now standing in the doorway.

"What?" Randall looked at Flynn who was staring him down.

"Very impressive. You can do more than conjure up candlelight and make floors slick." Flynn surmised.

"I'm working on it." Randall said, as he watched Izzy.

Izzy had one foot placed in the small of Thom's back, and pulled tight the cords bound around his wrists and ankles, hogtying him.

"I'm getting better at this too Mr. Randall!" She stepped back, smiling proudly.

A low moan came from Thom's lips.

"Thom, where are the keys to the vault?" Randall asked politely

More moaning from Thom and his head raised up and immediately dropped flat on the floor. Randall checked Thom's pockets finding a ring of iron keys that jingled as he held them up.

"One of these it, Thom?" Randall shook them in front of his face. Thom opened one eye looking at the keys and moaning one last time, fell unconscious again. "This is going to be easy!" Randall smiled broadly with confidence and stood spinning the ring of keys on his index finger.

Izzy clapped her hands together and smiled.

Flynn rolled his eyes.

13
Scrambled Eggs and Potatoes

The remainder of the raiders on The Nest splashed through the sewer tunnels beneath the city. The last of the lantern oil was used by Captain Madok, to slow the wererats from overtaking them. Now only flickering orange light of a single torch lit the way through the cylindrical tunnels.

"Sorry boys, I don't know the way out of this damned labyrinth. It doesn't look like they are giving us chase anymore, at least." Madok stayed positive.

The water level was lower at least. Only up to their ankles now in drainage and raw waste. Madok was sure everyone on this little expedition, including himself, would fall ill in the upcoming days, from trudging through the filth. No time to dwell on it now, though. Reporting the findings of a whole underground secret society in Port Gwynn, and the brothers' exit from the world of the living to Lord Mayor Geoffrey, was what was pressing on him.

"Captain! You ain't gonna believe this." Rik called out.

Madok pushed his way through the tunnel to the front and took the torch. The tunnel ended on a narrow ledge to a large natural cavern, that spanned out of the range of the torch light. Water cascaded down the rough slick walls, splashing down twenty feet below, onto jagged rocks into an underground stream.

"What is this, Captain? Did we find the gates to The Hells?" Rik looked across the span.

"No, this cave was incorporated into the city's sewers when Gwynn was built buy our father's, father's, fathers and several more fathers before. We follow that stream and it should lead out." Madok pointed down to the water below.

"Captain says this is the way out, guys!" Rik called back to the others.

Captain Madok looked at the layout of the cavern, with torchlight reflecting on the moist cavern walls and live cave formations. He noted holes cut into the rock, along with a few iron spikes driven in for foot and hand holds.

On a narrow ledge about twenty feet below, a thick knotted rope was secured to allow for further descent to the cave stream below.

"It looks like this way has been used by those bastards for getting around as well. Light up another torch and toss it over to that dry area. Rik, you go first to make sure the way is good for us to follow." Captain Madok gave his orders which went unquestioned.

A second torch was ignited and lobbed onto the area pointed out landing just shy of rolling off to be lost in the stream. Rik secured his equipment, then cautiously made his descent. Carefully gripping the spikes with his hands and finding the foot holes with his boots, he climbed down as the sewer water splashed over him from the tunnel overhead. His feet touched the narrow ledge after navigating the twenty-foot climb. He looked up to see Captain Madok watching him from the mouth of the tunnel, along with Ade who held the torch.

Taking the torch off the dry ledge, he looked down below at the cavern stream, which was only another ten feet below, easily accessible with the knotted rope. What may have once been a clean freshwater stream, was polluted. The generations of the poor Port Gwynn citizens not having privies serviced by the gong farmers, dumped their chamber pots in the sewer drains.

"Captain, looks like we can all make the climb. The smell down here is not nearly as foul as where you lot are." Rik called up to the others.

"All right, you two follow when he's halfway down." Madok tapped the next in line on the back, giving them the go ahead. "Rik, climb the rest of the way down and light another torch at the bottom."

"Yes Captain!" Rik called back to Madok, then furthered his descent by rope to a dark ledge along the stream.

Rik pulled a torch from his pack, igniting it with a single firestick. He held it forward and above his head to illuminate the natural passage, that was slowly carved from the flow of fresh water over the course of a millennia. The ledge running alongside it was damp, but not as slick, as he slowly advanced beyond the sewer runoff. The other men were climbing down in pairs until Madok and Ade were last to make the descent.

Rik continued forward, watching his footing on the narrowing ledge, which soon came to an end. The stream continued onward to the end of the cavern, exiting through tunnel fifteen feet wide.

"Captain, there's no dry ground this way. We'll be swimming the rest of the way." Rik called back.

"The water doesn't appear to be fast moving. It's only a stream, not a damn river, so we can walk it like in those tunnels." The Captain called back.

The others began to catch up to Rik, who was hesitant to step into the stream. Rik looked to the impatient man behind him.

"What are you waiting for?" Ade huffed.

"Would you mind taking the lead?" Rik passed the torch to Ade, who hastily stepped down into the stream. Rik cautiously stepped down afterwards, followed by the other men and Madok.

The group plodded through the muck of the stream, which started less than knee deep. It became almost waist deep at an area along the way. The water was nearly to their chests, when it opened into a chamber that smelled far worse than anywhere else, they have been in the city sewer system. Refuse, piled at the far end, was creating a blockage. The perimeter of the natural chamber was dry, being slightly elevated.

Ade climbed the debris that was choking the exit with garbage, human waste, and drift wood. Looking over into the tunnel beyond, he felt a little blast of fresh air and heard the wind whistling through. Faint daylight was ahead.

"Captain! I think we are almost out of here like you said it would be! I think I hear the sea hitting against the South Cliffs! It must be dawn!" Ade called out joyfully.

The other men cheered as Madok pushed forward through the murky water. Stoic as ever.

"Let's not go tugging each other's privates just yet. Once we reach South Cliffs we will have to climb up and march it back to Port Gwynn." Madok always knew what to say to kill a little joy.

"Eh, what's this?" Ade picked up a human skull partially buried in the hill of refuse he was perched atop. He held it up presenting it to the other guards. "I think I have an idea where bodies of some of missing townsfolk may be turning up. Well, hello..." He dropped the skull then drew a human femur out of the mess. Then he found another human skull.

"Well, what is it?" Madok asked as, he stopped his approach.

The other men nervously stretched to see each new body part that was being recovered.

"Captain, we need to hurry out of here." The guard dropped the skull and removed his helmet, then began rubbing his head feeling a bit unsteady.

"What's the matter Ade?" Rik said with concern.

"I felt a ravenous hunger all the sudden. I could see us all, including myself in here. It was like I was looking through something else's eyes." Ade looked up bewildered, with a touch of fear in his voice.

The other guards and Madok immediately drew weapons.

"Quickly! Everyone out of here!" Madok called out.

Another guard shook his head, trying to get the image out, and had a desperate look in his eyes. "I see the same thing, Ade!"

The others felt the overwhelming hunger and images flashing in their thoughts and overtaking their own sight and feelings. Panic ensued as the men begin moving in every direction, except for where Madok called from. Ade thrust the tip of the torch into the refuse pile freeing up his sword hand, and balanced himself atop it. Another torch bearer ran to a ledge on the edge of the small chamber and scanned the room. Madok backed his way out the way they came as the others tried to make their way out of the water.

"Look! By your leg Ade!" Rik called out from his perch on a dry ledge to his comrade.

Ade looked to his feet and saw a slimy stalk ending in a large, bulbous amphibian eye staring at him. It had pushed its way out of the refuse and was swaying almost snake like scanning everything in the room.

"This can't be happening!" Ade leapt off the pile and was caught in mid-air as a sticky spiked tongue broke out of the garbage pile. It coiled around him like a giant python, then pulled him into the refuse pile

The mound of refuse broke open, and a giant toad-like creature pushed its way out on its powerful legs. Each foot ended with long thick talons, and its brown hide was warty. Bits of debris from its nest stuck to sharp barbs that grew across its skin. Its two eye stalks scanned the room like a pair of cobras preparing to strike. A gaping mouth large enough to swallow a man whole, opened wide revealing rows of sharp teeth, and foaming with saliva. The long spikey tongue was ready to strike again, as the beast let out a loud roar shaking the insides of the cavern.

"Back this way fools!" Madok ordered again as he retreated to the tunnel.

The creature's tongue struck like a serpent at Rik, knocking him prone, and dropping his sword. A second strike from the tongue caught him. Rik was drawn into the beast's open mouth that smelled of carrion and feces. Powerful jaws cut through his mail, biting him in half. The remainder of Rik dropped into the muck.

The remaining men attempted to climb out of the water to the ledges, when the beast splashed into the center of the room. The creature dispatched two more, leaping and crushing them against the cavern with its giant body.

"Nigel, I'll flank it!" Madok quickly made his way up a slick ledge, covering the short distance to the rear of the beast, that was busy eyeing the last remaining man in the team.

The beast struck out at Nigel, but he was quicker with his blade and slashed its tongue in half. The beast emitted a howl of pain as it withdrew from him.

The beast was poised to leap upon the guard, who prepared a defensive position. Without giving a second thought, Madok leapt atop the beast's back, straddling it with his legs. Immediately, the creature was distracted from its former prey.

The beast's eye stalks caught Madok in its sight as it thrashed furiously. Madok stared back directly into the froglike eyes and hesitated.

Madok was overcome with emotions of fear and anger, and in his mind saw himself atop the creature from its perspective, through its own eyes. The beast had a telepathic link between it, and his men. It's would be prey.

Clenching his teeth and closing his eyes he attempted to shake the image from his mind. He tightened his legs around the monster's back to steady himself. Taking his longsword in both hands, he cried out and swung it at the eyestalks.

A few swings of the blade severed the stalks, dropping them into the muck. Madok regained his own vision. The blinded creature leaped around the cavern in a rage, attempting to throw Madok from its back

Madok drove the end of his sword between the shoulder blades of the beast, as it thrashed about splashing the walls of the cave. Nigel rejoined the fray, as it turned its back to him. Madok sunk the blade further into its back, before it rolled over on its side, to throw him off.

The pale underbelly of the creature was exposed just above the water, as it thrashed about. Madok clambered onto the remains of the refuse pile, looking to the exit tunnel. He looked back as Nigel drove his blade into the belly of the creature. He pushed it in with the weight of his body, while screaming triumphantly. He pulled is sword free after the body went limp.

"Well done, Nigel." Madok called out, offering his hand to his lone companion.

"Thank you, sir." Nigel called back breathing heavily, as Madok pulled him out of the water.

Madok pulled the torch from the refuse pile, and climbed down to the exit tunnel.

"Ade was right. I can feel the breeze. It's a shame we all made it here and then this." Nigel lamented over his dead friends, looking across the chamber and the carnage that played out.

Madok pushed the torch into Nigel's hand, then recovered one of his fallen men's longswords. He slid it into the sheath on his belt with a sigh. Not saying another word, he stepped into the narrow water filled tunnel.

The men exited the tunnel to the cliffside, where the foul waters drained over the jagged rocks into the treacherous bay far below. The morning sun was blinding, as their eyes adjusted to its warm light. Madok looked at the sheer cliff face above them.

"I need some scrambled eggs and potatoes before I deal with this shite." Madok grumbled.

"What?" Nigel looked at the Captain.

"Never mind. Catch your breath, we've got some climbing ahead of us." Madok slumped down on the ledge against the cliffside. He removed his boots to dry his waterlogged feet. In under a minute, he was snoring.

The sergeant quickly followed Madok's lead, and he too slept under the morning sun.

14
The Vault

Randall took the lead, descending the staircase to the basement with his light stone. Its soft blue light bathed everything with its cool glow, making everything appear from deep indigo in the shadows to pure white at its lightest.

He held it ahead of himself, turning a full circle at the bottom of the steps, acting as a human lighthouse. Flynn and Izzy were still on the stairs a few steps above, looking across the vast basement. In the center of the southern wall was a set of large doors leading to the docks. Large ornately carved wooden pillars were spaced at regular intervals, providing support to the ground floor some twelve feet above. Two rows of tables lined the floor, each twenty feet in length, across the span of the basement. Atop these were crates, leather bags, cloth sacks, and barrels of various imported goods. These were being held for the inspectors, and the contents inventoried in log books at a large central desk. Various quills, inkwells, a set of weights and measures, and an abacus were scattered on the work station.

"Any ideas where to look?" Flynn stepped onto the floor. He looked in a crate holding rolls of silk.

"I assume there will be a hidden entrance. Something that appears mundane enough to go without notice. Maybe we should go up and splash some water in Thom's face, and slap him around a bit for the information." Randall was becoming more open to extortion, and the other criminal activities of his companions.

"I already got his purse. It had ten pieces of silver in it too!" Izzy proudly tossed Thom's leather purse up in the air, and caught it repeatedly.

Randall looked at the bag, which was obviously filled with more than the few silvers.

"I will need to teach you how to count higher than the fingers on your hands." Randall said with a chuckle.

"Mr. Randall, that's not nice. I counted ten pieces of silver I was going to split with you. The other twenty-four gold coins I'm keeping for myself." Izzy turned her nose up at him.

Flynn departed the debate and inspected the layout of the room. Tight fitting flagstones made up the floor, and the basement walls were set with uniform masonry. Along the walls were heavy wooden cabinets filled with containers of merchandise. Each was tagged with the emblem of the shipping company, and a list of the contents.

He ran his hands along the ornamentation on the cabinets, pressing and pulling them in hopes to trigger a catch that might release hidden compartments. So far, no luck.

Izzy crawled around the counting desk in the center of the floor. She knocked on its panels, in search of a secret compartment.

Randall walked the floor, looking side to side at the wood columns. They were cylindrical in design, about 5 feet in diameter and rose 12 feet to the ceiling. Each had different themes carved into them in relief and were highly polished and varnished over. One had sea serpents wrapped around one pillar with ships being crushed in its coils. Another depicted several musicians performing on lutes, recorders, harps, and a variety of percussion instruments to merry dancers. Another depicted several carpenters using tools of their trade, constructing a house.

Shining the soft blue light on each pillar, he checked them for anything noteworthy, other than exorbitant cost that must have been paid to commission the artists to create these works. Randall inspected several more before stopping at one that differed from the scenes of the others. The relief carvings on this one were life size depictions of soldiers armed with a pike and holding a tower shield before them. He walked around the pillar, looking it up and down.

"Come have a look at this over here." Randall called out to Flynn and Izzy. The others joined him around the column. "This one seems to stand out to me. Just a gut feeling."

Flynn and Izzy began looking at the column closely. Flynn checking around the upper portion and Izzy closer to the floor. Izzy ran her hands along the relief of the rectangular shields, which were five feet in height, touching the floor and the shoulder of each soldier depicted.

"I think this does something Mr. Randall." Izzy said proudly, as she pressed her ear to the shield, then knocked on it with her fist. "Sounds like there may be a space behind it. I see a thin seam around this big shield."

Izzy looked at the circular boss on the shield. Squinting her eyes and manipulating it with her nimble little fingers, she pressed the rivets that were carved on it. One pushed in with a *click*, and the boss rotated downward revealing a metal keyhole. Izzy squeaked like a mouse, and looked at the others with a big smile.

"Excellent Izzy!" Flynn was proud of his little protégé's expertise in this skill set.

"Mr. Randall, do you want to try those keys?" Izzy beamed.

Randall held out the iron key ring and tested the different keys in the hole, fumbling with each. Once he was almost out of keys, he found the fit. It slid in and turned easily. The sound of the locking mechanism made clicks and then the entire shield moved slightly, revealing a space beyond.

He withdrew the key, and pulled the shield open like a door. Beyond, was a four-foot-high rectangular portal that entered the column. Shining his light in the hollow space beyond, revealed a narrow square shaft with an open elevator car suspended by chains from a system of pullies and cogs. There was a hand crank on the car to manually raise or lower it and a lever that worked the braking mechanisms.

"I wonder how they kept it a secret after building it?" Randall speculated the engineers and artisans employed for this may have been dumped in the bay with the night soil.

"It looks like that is meant for one person at a time to use." Flynn said with caution.

"Uh, yeah." Randall agreed. He looked at Izzy, who just transformed into large rat and was shaking off her clothes. Izzy sat up on her hind legs, looking up at Randall and twitching nose. "I suppose one person and one... rodent."

Izzy squeaked angrily at being called a rodent.

"Sorry, Izzy. Rat." Randall corrected himself.

Randall gathered Izzy's equipment, and put it in his satchel. Izzy crawled through the doorway sniffing around the interior of the column. Testing the floor with one paw, she stepped into it. She scurried around sniffing, then stood up on her hind legs to inspect the chains and pullies overhead. She looked at Randall, encouraging him to enter.

"I'll stand watch out here. If there's any problems in there, I'll climb down to help. If this is the vault where they're hidden all the coin, it may take a while to bring up." Flynn patted Randall's back as he entered the lift.

Randall studied the controls for a moment, then released the braking mechanism. The hand crank turned easily, with a system of pullies, and the lift began to steadily descend. The mechanical parts were well-oiled, and silent.

Flynn looked down the shaft, watching the glow of Randall's light stone dim the further down it went. Flynn stepped away from the column and hid behind a table with neatly stacked crates. One had its lid removed and was filled with apples. He grabbed one and ate it as he kept watch.

Randall and Izzy reached the bottom of the shaft, which went fifteen feet below, to land in a closet sized room with smooth walls and low ceiling. Opposite the lift was an iron door set in the wall.

Izzy hopped off the lift into the room, and transformed into her hybrid rat/girl form. Stepping up to the door with her nose twitching, inspecting the lock, the tri-spoked handle, then the edges around the door itself.

"What is it Izzy?" Randall said, as he stepped into the room.

"I want to make sure there are no nasty surprises." Izzy continued her inspection.

"Good thinking. I wouldn't expect anything less from the Lord Mayor." Randall kept his distance as Izzy peaked through the keyhole.

"Mr. Randall, I can't find anything on this door that looks like it would be a danger." Izzy stepped back, giving Randall some space.

Randall again pulled the keyring out and tested keys one by one in the key hole. None fit it. "Well shite! I imagine Geoffrey doesn't trust old Thom to hold onto the key."

"Let me give it a try Mr. Randall. Can I have my tools please?" Izzy held out her paw.

Izzy unrolled the bundle with her tools onto the floor. Running a finger across them, she withdrew a few special lock picks with hooks, and jagged rakes. She went through each meticulously, trying to use her specialist skills to unlock it. Several minutes went by and only failure.

"All right, I prepared a spell for this eventuality." Randall stepped up to the door, concentrating on the handle and the keyhole. He closed his eyes and spoke the incantation. "Recludo velox."

There was the sound of clicking of the tumblers as the key hole rotated. Izzy looked up at Randall and smiled, showing her four large orange incisors. This always disturbed Randall, but he returned the smile anyway. With both hands, he turned the handle and pulled open the vault door.

Stepping over the threshold into the vault, Randall held the light stone in front, illuminating the room. It was slightly larger than the room they had left. A blank, non-descript small, square wooden table sat in the middle of the room. Atop it, a metal coffer, and along the walls, rows of empty shelves. Two iron bound wooden chests were on the floor against the far wall.

Izzy maneuvered herself over to the chests. She inspected each closely, sniffing them and running her paws across them, searching for hidden catches to disarm any traps. Satisfied that the chests were clear, she lifted the lid to the first to peek inside.

"Mr. Randall, its empty!" She said with dismay. Randall's smile quickly changed to a frown. Izzy moved to the next chest following the same routine and turning up the same results.

"That bastard!" Randall shouted.

"What's the problem?" Flynn suddenly appeared, standing just outside to vault door.

Randall was startled by his companion's stealthy appearance. He composed himself and pointed to the chests.

"It's empty. Nothing. Geoffrey must have relocated everything in the days since everything went down." Randall waved his arms angrily as he spoke.

"All right, let's get out here. Peter is not going to take this well, and the city is going to be on high alert with this botched burglary. Especially when Clarke, and the two dead guards are discovered." Flynn had more concern in his voice.

"I imagine they took whatever was in this as well." Randall picked up the steel coffer on the table.

"Mr. Randall, I didn't check the coffer yet." Izzy warned as Randall lifted the lid.

Lifting the lid of the coffer, it revealed three thin glass vials, filled with a clear liquid, and protected in a cushioned red velvet lining. As the lid opened, stoppers were pulled from the vials, causing the liquid to immediately turn to gas, and fill the entire room.

Randall wavered, his eyes rolled up, and he collapsed on the floor. Izzy attempted to flee, but she succumbed to the gas. She transformed into her child form on the ground. Flynn was also caught by the gas, and hit the floor.

All three lay on the floor of the vault, unconscious, as the gas slowly dissipated over the course of a few minutes. Quiet stillness was only broken by the sound of Randall snoring. Within the hour the light from his spell expired and the entire place was black.

15
Juliana's Deliverance

Sister Lucia stood beside the doorway into the small room that was to be Juliana's new home. A few candles provided illumination, as well as a tiny square window near the ceiling that allowed the light of a waxing moon in. Inside was a simple bed with a straw filled mattress, a square wood table, chair beneath the window, and pegs for hanging her clothing. The cold, bare, slate floor looked very unwelcoming. A small wooden carving of The Mother and a worn prayer book sat in a niche beneath the window.

In her arms Juliana carried the clothing more appropriate of the sisters that served The Mother. She stepped in the middle of the room, taking in the disappointing accommodations.

A young teenage girl, in a simple dress with head covering, stepped into the room carrying a wash basin. She set it on the table with a washcloth and a chunk of lye soap, but too close to edge causing it to crash onto the floor. The shattered basin and water covered the floor beneath the window.

"Fool girl!" Sister Lucia stepped in to the room, swatting Ada across her backside with her thin walking stick. Ada let out a pained cry, standing in place, staring at the floor.

Juliana stepped back, fighting to hold her tongue.

"Gather all those broken pieces and then fetch the mop to clean up the water." Sister Lucia pointed everything out to Ada with her walking stick.

Ada got on her knees, picking up pieces of the basin, placing them into her apron. Juliana knelt to help the girl.

"No, the girl must take responsibility for her mistakes." Lucia quickly stopped Juliana, blocking her with her walking stick.

"Sister, The Mother tells us we must be merciful and forgive those that err." Juliana calmly stated, and gently pushed away the sister's stick. She helped pick up the last pieces, placing them into Ada's apron.

"At least the girl won't be my problem anymore come tomorrow." Sister Lucia disregarded Juliana's words and watched as Ada carried out the broken basin, head bowed, avoiding all eye contact.

Juliana watched with pity as Ada exited her cell, then turned to Sister Lucia.

Sister Lucia stood at attention, holding her walking stick much like a military officer's baton. She looked Juliana up and down very disapprovingly.

"All personal property is now unknown to you in the service of The Mother. She will provide for you all basic needs. Shelter, food, and clothing. We have a very structured schedule that we will discuss further, after morning prayers in my office. Unfortunately, your opportunity to bathe this week was impeded by the girl's incompetence. Get some sleep. Call to prayer is just before sunrise." Sister Lucia exited the room, closing shut the door behind her.

Juliana hung the habit she was provided on the peg. The other article of clothing given was a simple gown for sleep, with a scarf to cover her head. She dreaded the thought of her hair being cut short with shears, as was common for those in the sisterhood. She believed in her heart that this couldn't be the plan that The Mother had for her to serve her.

There was a knock on her door, and Ada slowly opened the door. "Sister, I am here to finish cleaning the floor." Ada entered the cell carrying a bucket and mop in her hands with head down.

She sat the bucket on the floor by the large puddle of water that had spread across the room. "I'm very sorry for being trouble sister. I'll be out of your way as fast as I can."

Juliana watched as Ada began mopping the floor and wring the head of the mop out by hand, into the bucket.

"Let me help you, please." Juliana put her hand gently on Ada's shoulder and took the mop from her. She motioned for her to sit and finished the mopping.

"You shouldn't be doing that, sister. That was my mistake." Ada pulled the wobbly wooden chair out and sat down.

"My name is Juliana." She said as she wringed water into the bucket.

"I am Ada, sister. Pleasure to make your acquaintance." She said, with hands folded in her lap; eyes cast downward.

"Sister Lucia said you 'won't be her problem after tomorrow.' What did she mean by that?" Julian asked, as she leaned the mop against the wall and sat on the bed.

"I will be working and residing in Bishop Bennett's manor house. I am to pay off damages to church property. Pay will still be sent to my mum to help take care of the family. I'm sad that I won't be able to go home to see them for a long time. His Grace said that I will have to be in service for a year before the debt is paid." Ada seemed to feel her fate could not be altered at this point in her short life.

"Like me, you were not given a choice it seems." Juliana sighed. "I don't believe that in The Mother's teachings, we are to be forced into servitude under those, who are also servants unto her. My years of tutelage, under my parish priest Sabina, is quite a departure from what I have seen in this city. It seems that The Mother's words have been twisted and corrupted. They are being used in ways that go against Her words."

"Thank you for being so kind, sister. I'm finished for the evening, so I need to hurry home." Ada rose to her feet, gathering the bucket and mop.

"Perhaps I'll be able to visit with you in the future. I will say a prayer to The Mother for you, to provide you guidance and to Saint Vittoria to provide you strength." Juliana smiled.

"I would like that. Who is Saint Vittoria?" Ada smiled.

"Saint Vittoria served The Mother many years before ago before her martyrdom, defending against the heathen barbarian invaders from the north. Other's serving in my Order, followed her service to The Mother as guardians of the faithful and as Her voice to spread Her word." Juliana replied.

"Thank you, sister." Ada curtsied, then stepped out the door.

Juliana watched from her doorway as Ada walked the long hall, carrying the mop and sloshing bucket. All the other doors to the sister's rooms were closed, and only a few candles in wall sconces lit the way.

She watched as the girl turned the corner and left out of her view. She could still hear her footsteps in the distance, and then nothing as the silence of the place was stifling. She strained to listen and heard voices. One was Ada and the other was Sister Lucia, but she couldn't make out what was being said.

Juliana slipped off her shoes, carrying them in her hands and stepped out of her quarters into the hall's cold stone floor. She quickly made her way to the end of the hall, stopping at the turn. Peeking around the corner, she saw at the far end of another hall Sister Lucia, watching Ada as she returned the mop and bucket to a closet.

Lucia stood with her hand on her stick, growing impatient with what she perceived as Ada's ineptness at the tasks she performed. She continued to scold her, as the two walked out of view down a turn in the hall.

Juliana advanced to the end of the hall, stopping for a quick listen again before looking. She saw the two at the front door. Sister Lucia pulled a ring of keys from her belt and unlocked the door. Pushing one of the doors open, a church guard clad in plate armor stepped through.

"See the girl out, then return immediately. There are important matters to discuss in my office." Sister Lucia ordered the guard. "Child, I know the girl they send to replace you, will not perform the simplest of tasks with your level of incompetence. I imagine His Grace will turn you out onto the streets when he becomes frustrated with your stupidity." Lucia gave Ada a quick swat with her stick across her legs.

Ada yelped, though most of the sting was taken out by her dress. The real pain was caused by the sister's words she endured during her service under her.

The guard walked Ada out of the convent, into the cloister, pulling the door shut behind him. Sister Lucia paced the floor before the door.

Juliana, seeing the scene unfold before her, raised her suspicions and concern for their real plans for her. Within a few minutes the guard returned, and Sister Lucia locked the doors. Lucia walked in front and the church guard followed, with the noise from his bootsteps and metal armor disturbing the peace of the quiet halls. They disappeared around the corner.

Juliana waited a moment and then made her way to the door to check it. She would need to acquire the key from Sister Lucia.

 She advanced through the silent halls stopping at the closet door saw Ada use earlier. The hinges could use a light oiling, but there wasn't enough noise to rouse the other sisters. Wide open, there was no light to see inside. She guided herself with her hands, feeling for the shelves running her fingers across them, identifying objects as she touched them. She stubbed her toe on the mop bucket, but held in the pained cry she wanted to release. A supply of wide pillar candles, used for the sconces, were on the shelf and a box with long fire sticks beside them.

She struck a fire stick and lit the candle, illuminating her surroundings. The closet had an unpleasant musty and mildew smell. Mops, cleaning brushes, rags, and a barrel with chunks of lye soap were in here. There was also a supply of tools for small repairs. Mallets, saws, hatchet, nails and even scrap pieces of iron and wood, on a work table.

She looked over the items, and decided a mallet could act as a weapon in case of an emergency.

She continued through the dark halls with the items, past more closed doors of sister's cells. The far end of the convent was a dining hall, kitchen, larders, and a small chapel. No other sisters were quartered here, other than Sister Lucia's private quarters and office. Ahead there was light showing from under a door. Juliana set the candle on the floor, and crept to the door with the mallet at the ready, in case the guard was still in the meeting.

She pressed her ear to the thick polished wooden door, that had a brass plaque centered on it engraved '*Abbess.*' She heard their voices, but the conversation was too muffled from her side of the door. The Mother prepared her with the means to deal with anyone impeding her escape from the convent, she just needed to face the challenge.

Juliana slowly pushed the door open a crack. These hinges were well oiled, and the door opened easily without a sound. She looked through the crack and could see only a small section of Lucia's office. Rows of bookcases on a wall filled with large leather-bound books and scrolls, with loose papers overflowing out of the shelves. She could also see a corner of the desk.

"No, you fool! Repeat it again and without any mistakes!" Sister Lucia's voice was quite irate, and was followed by the crack of her walking stick.

Juliana pushed the door open further, expecting to hear the plot for her death and disappearance gone over again in detail. A far more disturbing scene was playing out.

Sister Lucia was leaning against the desk without her head covering, exposing her short cropped white hair. The guard, naked on all fours, with his head buried deep beneath the Sister's robes. His naked well-toned buttocks had welts from Lucia's walking stick, which she held in hand. Neither noticed Juliana in the doorway, as she pushed it open all the way.

"I thank you Mother for what I am about to receive. I am only here to service you." He said with gusto.

"Yes!" Lucia struck the man on his backside with her walking stick anyway.

Juliana stepped into the room and looked from side to side, seeing that every piece of armor and equipment was stripped off the guard and scattered through the room, with his sword belt hanging on a cloak peg.

Lucia raised her head up, locking eyes with Juliana.

"You!" Her words came out in a squeal. She threw her robe off the guard's head and slid off the desk.

The man turned his head with a mane of brown curls to Juliana, then smiled.

"Oh, you invited another to join us tonight! She is a pretty lass." He said, still on all fours.

"You didn't bolt the door, you idiot!" Sister Lucia backed around the desk. "She's the one that His Grace removed from the guard, fool!"

"Juliana? I didn't recognize you. I uh..." He rose to his feet with hands held palms out, trying not to show any aggressive movement. "You should lower that mallet, and step back." He slowly reached for his sword belt."

Juliana didn't back down and called upon the divine powers bestowed on her by The Mother. She locked eyes with the guard and delivered the divine magic with her words. "By Her power you are rigid! Hold fast!"

The man fought as his joints began to feel as if they were fusing in place, becoming inflexible. His movement became jerky, and as he reached for his sword belt, he ceased moving. He was immobile, save the darting of his fearful eyes and the expansion of his chest with every breath he drew.

"What have you done? You are a heretic in league with fiends from the Nine Hells!" Lucia moved behind her desk to shield herself from the young woman.

Juliana dropped the mallet and took the hanging sword belt off the peg then strapped it around her waist. The naked man's eyes followed her, unapproving this turn of events.

"Give me the key and I'll be gone from this den of hypocrisy." Juliana approached Sister Lucia with her waiting hand.

"This will not go unpunished. What harm you deal to a servant of The Mother; you do unto her!" Sister Lucia admonished Juliana, as she approached her from around the desk unfaltering.

"The key, Sister." Juliana's hand waited open.

Lucia slowly opened the top desk drawer and withdrew a ring of keys of a variety of shapes and sizes. She pulled a large black iron key, with the head shaped like folded angel wings, and placed it in Juliana's hand.

A small stack of gold coins set on a corner of the desk caught Juliana's eye.

"I assume that was meant to pay for his services?" Juliana pointed at the coins.

"You insolent girl!" Lucia didn't like being called out.

"I'll split it with him for his trouble." Juliana scooped up half the coins, placing them in the small pouch that was on the sword belt, after dumping out his few personal items onto the floor.

Sister Lucia reached into the desk drawer again and unsheathed a hidden dagger.

Juliana sprung back and shouted. "In the name of The Mother, provide Sister Lucia the rest she will need to find the strength for her penitence."

Lucia stopped before she could approach, and her mouth opened impossibly wide and eyes tightly closed as she yawned loudly. She took one step toward the desk, sprawling across it and immediately, snored loudly in deep slumber.

Juliana ran through the halls to unlock the front door and escape the cloister. She ran across the grounds in the starlit night of a waxing moon. No other church guards were on duty at this time. Lifting the bar and pulling the bolt back on the doors, she exited the courtyard of The Cathedral of the Merciful Mother. Pushing the door closed behind her, she calmly walked out onto the dark streets of Port Gwynn. Thoughts were to what she was being called upon to do in Her service.

She would need to remove herself from as far from the cathedral as possible before the divine intervention she had called upon ended, and the real trouble began.

16
A Kind of Hangover

Randalls eye's opened to total darkness. His head was throbbing, and his neck and back sore and stiff. He only knew he was laying on a floor. Slowly, it was all coming back to him. He was in the vault in the Customs House. The light stone was no longer illuminated, so he knew he was out for longer than an hour. The others must also still be down here with him.

He did his best to roll over and, on all fours, felt around on the floor for his elusive light stone. He ran his hands on the broken glass that caused the problem in the first place. Little shards of glass pierced the palm of his hand, causing him to draw it back quickly with a curse.

He heard Flynn moan from the outer room.

With his other hand, he tried again to find the stone. Success this time.

"Wait before you do anything Randall." Flynn said in a whisper.

"What is it?" Randall felt a droplet of blood fall from his wounded hand.

"We've been out for some time. There may be others above now." Flynn warned, as he rubbed his head in the dark.

"My head hurts, Flynn." The soft voice of Izzy came across in the darkness, quite pained.

"Mine too, Izzy. That knock out gas does that. The pain will leave soon. Sooner, if we had water to drink." Flynn rose slowly, still feeling woozy.

"I can't see anything. I need some light." Randall stated once again.

"Quiet, you two. I'm going to take a quick look." Flynn stuck his head in the shaft and looked upwards.

The vertical shaft had no sign of light from the open door up top. Flynn strained to listen, and heard a commotion from the ground floor.

"Izzy, help him into the lift. You two will need to ride up together. I think it may be morning, and we might be in some trouble." Flynn climbed onto the lift and pulled himself up, hand over hand using the chains. Once he reached the top, he pulled himself through the once secret door in the pillar.

The large room was as they had left it the night before, with no other persons poking around just yet. From the stairs to the ground floor, light was visible and he heard voices and movement.

Izzy pulled her clothes and other belongings out of Randall's bag and quickly dressed herself. She guided him into the lift, which was tight for two, but not uncomfortable. Randall felt around blindly for the crank with his good hand. The other hand was still stinging from the glass cuts in the palm. Izzy stopped tying the string on her shirt to place Randall's hand directly on the lever to speed things up.

"Thank you, Izzy." Randall said as he turned the crank, causing the elevator to lurch upwards, then steadily rise at a slow pace.

"My arm is going to twist off turning this damned thing. There's still glass in my hand too." Randall issued his complaints to the little girl.

"Mr. Randall, we are almost to the top." Izzy pulled the lever to lock the lift, then pushed past Randall to exit through the column door. She grabbed Randall by his sleeve, and helped guide him into the room.

"Psst, Izzy, over here." Flynn stood by the locked doors to the dock tunnel, motioning them over.

Randall's eyes were adjusting to the little amount of light that was coming down the stairwell. Sounds of excited voices and many feet walked the floor above. Randall guessed whoever was up there, broke through the barred front door to get in. They would have found the night watch dead, and Thom tied up in his own office.

Flynn already lifted the bar off the doors, and Izzy had her tools laid out working, on the lock. Randall squinted, straining his eyes along the tables and saw some food stuffs. He grabbed a burlap sack and dropped of apples and potatoes into it. He tossed it over his shoulder and joined Izzy and Flynn.

"Did you get anything good for breakfast?" Flynn whispered, as Randall stumbled through the dark.

"Nothing too exciting, but it should help stop our stomachs from complaining for a moment. Randall laid the sack on the floor, then turned his full attention to the stairs.

"Got it." Izzy said proudly, as the heavy padlock opened.

"This can't be good." Randall pointed to the stairs, hearing them creak.

The light from a lantern was now shining down the steps, illuminating the area at the foot of the stairs.

Flynn pulled open one door enough for them to pass through. Izzy grabbed Randall by his sleeve and pulled him into the passageway. Flynn stepped through the door, watching as three men descended the stairs. He gently pulled it shut and turned to join Randall and Izzy.

Two guards and one of the customs controllers stood at the base of the stair surveying the room. The controller was dressed in a green doublet, under which the puffy sleeves of his white silk shirt were exposed. The black slouch hat atop his head, covered neatly trimmed white hair. He was extremely nervous and beads of sweat ran down his forehead, which he wiped with a handkerchief. The two city guards with him looked like they were ready for anything.

"Thom said that there were others helping him. A little wererat and a foreign islander man, that climbed up in through his office window. He said Randall must have been let in by the watchmen, before murdering them with dark magic. I have no idea what they could have been after, as they had not touched the safes upstairs. As I said before, the only other way they could have left, aside from Thom's office window, would have been the dock tunnel." The controller wiped his brow.

The guard holding the lantern shined it across the room illuminating the rows of tables with goods, the counting desk and then to the tunnel doors.

"Looks like the bar is up and the lock is on the floor. They must have left through there." The guard focused the light on it.

"I need that boy to get the lamps lit down here, so that we can take a quick inventory and see if anything is missing. Send Phillip down here now!" The controller shouted up the stairs for the young boy employed as the Customs House lamplighter.

The guards walked further into the room and aimed the lantern along the walls and to the carved wood columns.

"Oy, what do you make of this?" The man holding the lantern shined it on the column leading to the secret vault. The shield door was wide open and the lift was in view.

"I don't know. I have never seen that before." The controller joined the guards.

The guard held the lantern in and inspected the lift. The controller poked his head in, giving it a quick look.

"I've never seen anything like this in all my born days. What is it?" The guard was intrigued by the simple machine.

"It appears to be a mechanical lift. Here's their target. This had to have been built a few years back, before operations were moved into this building." The controller wiped his brow.

"I remember the construction went on for months." The guard recalled, while tugging on his chin hairs.

"Clarke was overseeing the construction..." The controller stopped in mid-sentence, but kept the thought to himself. "Please, let's check the dock tunnel now."

The lamplighter was down the stairs with the jug of lamp oil, filling and lighting the lamps needed to illuminate the room. The controller and the guards made their way over to the tunnel doors.

***

Randall and his companions made a hurried escape through the passage way, which was only fifty feet to the High Port docks. The second set of doors, opened on to the boardwalk on the cliff face. These were also barred and locked from the inside, and an outer iron gate chained and padlocked.

Izzy was an expert at picking locks, and these were proving to be no problem for her. The morning sun had been lighting the sky for a few hours now, and there were several cargo ships docked. The large padlock clicked open, and she removed the chain. Flynn pushed the door open and all three exited.

"Hold it a moment." Flynn secured the chain back and locked the padlock again to slow down the guards.

"Hey, I wonder if any of these would have worked on these doors?" Randall remembered the key he had taken from Thom the night before, pulling them from a pocket out and rattling them.

"Now you remember." Izzy said looking rather cross up at him.

"Hey, any idea what's going on in there? They should have had an inspector here a few hours ago." Said a large man with a shaved head. His skin was leathery brown from the sun, and his thick graying beard looked like it meant business.

"Uh, no sir. I think they are closed for the holiday." Randall said trying to not make eye contact with the old salt. Izzy and Flynn started walking down the docks.

"I'll be damned. What holiday is this? We haven't been in port for over a month." The old salt scratched his head.

"It's a new one the Mayor declared in a proclamation last week. A duty-free day on goods brought into Port Gwynn." Randall walked faster, to catch up to Izzy and Flynn.

"I'll be damned. That's highly irregular." The old salt stood confused, with his arms crossed in front of the gate.

Other sailors and their captains waited along the long boardwalk, in front of their docked ships, watching them as they passed. A few vendors with carts of were selling smoked fish, breads, and fresh fruits to those who were waiting. Another, selling warm Grummandy beer from his wagon, was doing well this morning, with men lined up with waiting tankards to fill. Sea gulls made themselves a general nuisance to the vendors and pedestrians. A few strategically launched droppings onto unwary passerby's head.

"We need to get off the streets to the safehouse quickly. I have a feeling the area is about to crawling with the city guards." Flynn said, as he led them to a set of wood stairs alongside the white rock cliff face. It would be a short climb to the bustling street level.

Paul Wolff

There was some foot traffic from sailors making their way up or down, depending if they just arrived or were departing from Port Gwynn. A low stone wall at the top along the cliffside was host to a sleeping pelican, while several squawking seagulls flew overhead.

A man sat on the wall, a little way from the snoozing seabird, tossing scraps of bread in the air for the gulls. He was dressed in loose and airy breeches and wearing an open vest, showing a variety of scarification and tattoo designs on his chest and arms. A sword belt held his rapier and dagger, a deterrent to anyone who would dare touch his coin purse. His kinky black hair was cut short, and his earlobes were stretched and filled with plugs made of carved ivory. As intimidating as the man appeared, the birds didn't seem bothered too much by him.

He smiled as Flynn and the others topped the stairs. He nodded his head and began to laugh, then waved his finger at them. After the three were caught by his attention, he immediately went back to his task. He tore another crust off the bread tossing it into the air for the hungry gulls to fight for.

"Uh, do you know him?" Randall asked concerned, looking over his should at the man who paid them no attention now.

"Yes, that's Musa. Obviously, he's watching for us. There're probably others from The Nest posted around High Port. Probably to report to Peter that we're out. We better get to that safe house quick and wait. I'm sure they'll send someone wanting a full report and the location of all the loot we took." Flynn said, as he urged them to follow along into a side alley.

"Musa smells bad, and he's not very nice." Izzy commented.

"Aside from smelling bad, is there anything else I should know about Musa?" Randall asked.

"Yes, he's Peter's top assassin and spy. We both came from the same island nation years ago. The city I was from was a center of art and culture and commerce. Musa's people were raiders and pirates. We both happened to come to here years ago as much younger men, under much different circumstances. That is a story for another time though." Flynn waited for the passing traffic, then crossed over to the other side to the next alleyway. Randall and Izzy followed.

"Flynn, he going to be a problem?" Randall said, with some concern as they continued their pace keeping watch over his shoulder.

"It won't be good when we report back empty-handed days later, after The Nest was raided." Flynn pointed over to a large windowless wooden building across the way. "There's the warehouse. We may be able to eat, and get a little rest before someone comes to talk."

"Good. I'm hungry." Izzy said, as she darted across the road. Flynn and Randall followed, entering through a large open doorway, past the wagons and carts parked in front.

17
Monkey Business

Juliana made her way through the streets of Port Gwynn in the pre-dawn hours, avoiding guards walking their beat. Along the way, she concealed the sword, wrapping it in some bed linen she snatched from an alleyway hanging to dry. A gold coin was tucked in a pocket of a shirt on the line as compensation for the donation. A generous offering.

She was overcome with exhaustion of a sleepless night playing this game of evasion. There was no plan, but she had enough coin on her person to get provisions, and possibly transport out of the city with 'no questions asked.' The events from the convent with Sister Lucia and the guard, would make it impossible for her to remain in Port Gwynn.

The morning glow of the sun rising on the bay caught her attention. Juliana basked in the warmth of the yellow orb as an orange sky was revealed through purple clouds of the sunrise. High Port was coming alive, as trade ships were docking and offloading. People pushed carts with ready to eat foods for the sailors, dockworkers and warehouse workers that were starting the day hungry.

She slid off the low wall and made her way to a cart, filled with freshly baked loaves of bread and kippered herrings. The purchase made with a gold coin raised the vendor's eyebrow, as he had to make change with most of his shillings. Breakfast was served at least. She took a drink from the water pump in the center of the courtyard, which was surrounded by the offices of different trading companies. The prominent merchant's guildhall was opening its doors this time of the morning, with a few foreign traders arriving wearing robes and turbans, being greeted at its doors.

Thinking it better to rid herself of the weapon, she bartered with a smithy who didn't have any problems purchasing a weapon obviously forged for the city guard. He had a few simple martial weapons in his 'secret stock' for sale. An exchange for simple flange headed mace seemed to be a better fit, and what she was comfortable fighting with. No doubt the smith would make a tidy profit from resale on the sword.

She went down the cliffside stairs to the boardwalk leading to the piers for incoming ships. Securing passage on board one of the ships, to go anywhere else, felt like the first step to find what The Mother wanted of her. Perhaps in the future, to return.

Juliana was rejected by several ship captains waiting along the boardwalk, as their business would be keeping them in Port Gwynn for a time. However, one old salt seemed open to the idea. The stop in port was only for a day, then they would set sail westward to the next port, Sommer Harbour, a week away. Currently he, like the other captains, were waiting for the inspectors to check their cargo hold and manifest. The Customs House seemed to be off to a late start today.

Pushing several gold coins into the captain's large calloused hands, he smiled and promised her a nice little clean cabin. She returned to the streets of the Hight Port to gather supplies for her journey with the remaining coin she had.

Spending more coin in the market area, she replaced the dress in favor of clothes more suitable for travelling. Men's breeches, tunic, boots, along with a backpack. She purchased some travelling food: dried salted meats, hardtack, and a skin filled with warm ale. She finished it out with a bedroll, and blanket should she find herself needing to hole up in a farmer's barn for a night. She still carried her prayer book and wore the symbol of The Mother around her neck.

Exiting the trader's place of business, a small detail of Port Gwynn guards hurriedly pushed their way through the street. Their sergeant had a determined look in his eyes. Two carried a small battering ram with hand grips between them.

Juliana stepped back into the crowd out of their view, watching as they passed by. Their destination was just a little further down a block away at the Customs House. Her curiosity peaked, she walked in the direction of the customs house, noticing a crowd of people on the steps of a building that was usually opening at daybreak rather than this late in the morning.

The collectors and inspectors were angrily shouting and waving their arms, pointing to the locked doors and the open window to the offices above. The sergeant was explaining that this morning they were stretched, as there was ongoing trouble in the Low Port, that was at the top of the City Guard's priorities since the previous day.

Juliana watched as two men used the small battering ram began bashing at the double doors. After a few minutes, they finally broke through the bar holding them closed. The sergeant led the guards through, followed by the men of the Customs House. One of the inspectors ran out of the building and vomited on the steps.

"Murdered! Must have burned them alive! It's horrible!" The inspector wiped his beard on the sleeve of his robe.

The crowd of men and women gathered around the steps, gasped at the report, and attempted to approach for a better look. A pair of guards stepped out the door for crowd control, as others searched the building.

Juliana stepped back as more curious gawkers gathered. One other person walked away from the crowds that caught her attention. Chuckling as he walked on the opposite side of the road past storefronts and other foot traffic, he didn't pay any attention to Juliana. However, his exotic appearance with scarification and tattoos, walking barefoot through the street, made her take notice. Tunefully humming, he walked past a distracted street vendor, and with a little sleight of hand, pilfered a small loaf of bread from his cart. Without a pause, he continued tearing off a piece and laughing, while stuffing it in his mouth.

The rapier, hanging from his belt, served as a warning that this was a dangerous man whose attention she shouldn't attract. Stopping and stepping into a covered open-air food market she had previously visited; she watched the man at a safer distance. He turned to the short stone wall along the cliffside, where the steps led down to the boardwalk and docks.

He peered over the wall for a brief time, then turned and sat on it. He tore pieces of bread feeding himself and alternately tossing it into the air, for the waiting seagulls that gathered.

"Miss, either you need to buy something, or kindly step away. You are blocking these nice folks." A merchant shooed Juliana away from his booth, so that a group of women could look over the vegetables laid out across the table in baskets before him.

"Sorry sir." Juliana was briefly distracted by the merchant. She stepped to the side and looked across the way again to the man on the wall.

She saw three heads appear climbing up the stair way and briefly pausing before the man. She recognized them as the three that she pursued into the catacombs and briefly fought alongside, only a few sleepless nights before.

"Randall." Juliana whispered.

She watched the three dart across to her side of the road, before disappearing through the alley next to the market. Looking back to the man on the wall, she saw him stand up and stretch his arms out, as if waking from a nap. He continued walking down the road, whistling.

Juliana ran through the market stalls and booths, dodging purveyors and their clientele alike. The center of the market had brick ovens, and stacks of wood for fuel baking breads and meat pies. Slaughtered animals hung from hooks, and butchers cut choice meats, for their customers, with cleavers on large block tables. Juliana ducked under counters, bound over food tables, and squeezed between angry vendors, as she followed Randall, Flynn, and Izzy as they passed alongside the market.

The market building was also open to the street, that had warehouses lining the way. She stayed at the edge of the market building and watched as the three, led by Flynn, ran into one of the larger buildings that was bustling with activity.

Juliana stepped onto the street and crossed over, darting in front of a wagon driven by a team of horses, narrowly missing being run down. The driver shouted several choice obscenities at her, but never slowed.

She stepped through the large doorway, into a huge open building with rafters overhead. These supported the roof and the block and tack systems to load goods to the loft in the back half. Crates and barrels were being offloaded from a few wagons, that had been brought inside.

"Excuse me, young lady!" An old gentleman wearing a slouch hat with an enormous peacock feather protruding from it, called over to Juliana.

"Um, yes." Juliana looked him over as he approached with ledger under his arm.

"They're almost done unloading so you're next up. Do hurry with paperwork." The old gentleman pulled a pair of magnifying spectacles from his pocket and placed them on his nose, causing his eyes to appear three times as large through the lenses.

Juliana was caught a little by surprise by the giant eyes, but kept her composure.

"Sir, I don't have it." Juliana replied attempting to look past him searching for the three amongst the crowded floor of the warehouse.

"Tisk-tisk. We all have a job to do, and you obviously are inept at yours." He pulled an ink vial from his pocket and pulled the stopper out. "Hold this young lady."

Juliana did as he asked, holding the ink vial in her hand. The old gentleman opened the ledger in his arm and pulled the feather from his hat. Dipping the tip in the ink vial, he wrote notes in his ledger with flowing handwriting.

"I really don't have time for this, sir." Juliana was growing cross with the old gentleman.

"Now who are you driving for?" The old gentleman looked across to the other page of the ledger, looking at the trading companies that were expected for the day.

Juliana took a quick glance at the names in the ledger, while he dipped the quill tip in the ink vial in her hand.

"Merchant Adventurers of the Red Isles." Juliana said, forcing a smile.

The old gentleman looked over his glasses at her shaking his head. Then made a note in his ledger. He let out a sigh, as he blew on the ink.

"I'll call for you when we are ready. Now go out and wait with your wagon. I don't have time for young girls to be getting in the way and distracting the men. Whyever, would they hire a girl to do a man's job?" The old gentleman slammed his book and stuffed the peacock feather back into his cap. He swiped the ink vial out of Juliana's hand, and walked over to the warehouse workers, who were pulling up an enormous crate with the block and tackle.

The men struggled with the oversized piece of freight that swayed back and forth as they pulled it upwards.

"What's the problem lads?" The old gentleman stopped at a safe distance, eyeing the crate overhead.

"Sir, I don't think this is one is full of bolts of cloth." The young man said with clenched teeth, as he pulled the rope.

"They are always getting these things mixed up. I can't trust them to give me the proper shipping paperwork. Let's see..." The old gentleman opened his ledger, then looked up at the swaying crate.

"Sir, I can't hold it!" The young man cried out, as the swaying crate fell to the floor as he fought to keep rope in his hands.

The crate hit the ground, narrowly missing the old gentleman, who dove for cover behind a barrel. Moving in for a closer look, saw airholes drilled into the crate, and could hear heavy breathing.

A hairy gray fist burst through the crate. Another gray hand broke apart another piece of wood creating an opening for the huge silverback gorilla to push his way through.

The warehouse men turned and ran past Juliana, and the old gentleman ran, holding his hat on with one hand, and carrying the ledger under his arm. The gorilla was heavily sedated during its transport from the ship, but the dosage wore off too early. The animal was an illegal import for a wealthy collector's zoo. Very confused, angry, and hungry, the large primate bounded out the open door on all fours to the street where further mayhem ensued.

The old gentleman hid under a now overturned wagon, as the beast disappeared into the open market causing even more chaos. Throngs of people vacated the open market into the streets, screaming and shouting. The old gentleman consulted his ledger again and read through it with his spectacles.

"Shambaa Islands Trading Company. They'll get bad marks for this!" The old gentleman buried his face in his ledger, weeping.

Paul Wolff

Juliana turned her attention away from the scene on the street, that was now becoming a larger spectacle than the Custom's House break in. She walked past the destroyed crate on the ground, that was full of produce and animal feces. She looked along rows of crates and stacks of other items, searching for Randall and the others.

"Pssst, hi lady." Juliana spun around hearing Izzy's voice.

Atop a wooden crate next to the wall, the little girl stepped out curiously looking Juliana up and down.

"Why are you in here?" Juliana asked, as she looked around for the others.

"Oh, we're going to wait here until later, when its safe outside again. We heard the noise, and I was sent out to look. That was a big monkey." Izzy said, smiling.

"Where are your friends?" Juliana asked.

"They just went down into the secret room. No sooner did we go in, then we heard the loud crash. The funny looking old man is rude, but he is nice enough to let us stay. Would you like to have breakfast with me?" Izzy was excited to see Juliana, grabbing her hand, and leading her through the crowded warehouse floor.

Juliana was unsure whether to trust the little girl, but she followed anyway, as she led her to the back farthest end beneath the loft. Offices in the back, were overflowing with shelves of ledgers, pigeonholes full of rolled up documents. In the center of the main office was a large wooden slant top desk, that had a tall worn stool set up to it. It was covered in stamps, pads of inks, papers, pens, and the inkwell to dip them in.

Izzy kicked a small panel at the bottom of the desk with her toe, causing it to fall open. She stepped on a pressure sensitive plate inside the compartment, which triggered four audible 'clicks.' Smiling at her success, she pushed the desk, which easily slid with a small section of the wood floor. A narrow wooden staircase descended underground, illuminated by a hanging oil lamp.

"Lady, you go first please." Izzy stood by the desk smiling, as Juliana looked around the room nervously and then down into the stairwell.

"You will follow?" Juliana asked.

"Oh yes!" Izzy smiled, nodding her head.

Juliana stepped onto the first step, which creaked as she put her weight on it. Then she slowly took the next step and ducked her head, under the low ceiling. Halfway down, she looked back over her shoulder hearing the steps creaking, as Izzy stepped in. Izzy pulled two handles on the underside of the flooring, and the desk glided back into place on a pair of well-oiled tracks and with four clicks, it was locked back into place.

"Some very clever people built these things." Juliana mused.

"His Lordship is smart. He has a lot of smart people that do this work." Izzy said, as she motioned for Juliana to continue.

"His Lordship?" Juliana said to herself.

At the bottom of the stairs was a small room with a low ceiling that had bedrolls and dried foodstuffs in small crates, along with two small kegs with water and wine. Izzy walked over to a small door and knocked on it, with her little fist.

"I'm back! There was a big monkey scaring everyone. Please let us in." Izzy beamed.

A bolt slid on the other side of the portal and slowly began to open.

"Wait, what do you mean 'us'?" Randall peeked through the door and spotting Juliana let out a little *yelp*.

Randall attempted to pull the door closed, but Juliana swiftly moved up and kicked it full force, hitting him in the head knocking him to the floor.

"Lady, that wasn't nice." Izzy scolded her, with her hands on her hips.

Juliana stepped through the door into the small chamber. Randall laid sprawled out on the floor with his hand cradling his head, which now had a small gash. Flynn drew his blade and leapt to his feet, ready to strike.

"What did you do that for?" Randall attempted to sit up and fell back moaning.

"Because of you three, I was dismissed from the church guard, forced into a convent, and spent the entire night walking the streets of this city alone. Now I've lost everything for allowing you to escape. Just by chance, I find you again, on the run, after committing more malicious acts." Juliana stood boldly before Randall and Flynn without showing any signs of fear.

Izzy pushed in and stood over Randall, blocking Juliana from approaching any further and drew her knife.

"Well, what do you think you're going to do? Arrest all of us? Turn us over to the guards?" Flynn made a defiant laugh.

Randall attempted to sit up again, pushing up with one elbow. He pulled his hand from his head that was covered in his own blood. "Why, I'm going to..."

Izzy planted her foot in Randall's chest without looking back pushing him back to the ground with a '*thunk*' to his head. Izzy twirled the knife in her delicate small fingers and then flipping it into the air she caught it by the tip, ready to plunge it into Juliana's heart with a quick throw.

"You hurt Mr. Randall, Lady. You said we were *mal-ish-us*. I don't think that is a nice word." Izzy pinned Randall on the ground, under one foot.

Juliana lowered her head. Izzy and Flynn looked at her confused. Randall groaned, applying pressure to his head.

"I believe The Mother has a plan for all those that are truly her faithful. I am only a vessel, to deliver Her Word or to act on Her behalf, as a channel for Her divine power. I don't know yet what it is she is calling me to do, but now I think she has brought us together once again, for reasons unknown to me yet." Juliana looked at the three and gave an uneasy smile.

"What do you mean? I brought you here, meanie!" Izzy said, sheathing her knife.

"You are talking religious nonsense. I've prayed to many gods and not one has called on me to do anything, nor have they done anything for me." Flynn said, lowering his blade.

"Believe what you wish, but I know it to be true. The Mother has chosen me, and each of you have a part to contribute to whatever it is I must do." Juliana looked around the room and then to the floor, behind here where a bedroll was spread out. She sat down on it and leaned against the wall, removing her boots.

Izzy and Flynn looked at each other, very confused.

"Izzy, if it wouldn't be too much trouble, could you please get off of me." Randall managed to speak.

"Oh! Sorry, Mr. Randall." Izzy stepped aside then dropped to the floor to look at his head. It had a small split that had a steady stream of blood oozing out of it when he removed pressure.

"That will probably leave a big blue bruise there, too." Flynn said, inspecting the wound.

Juliana set her boots down and crawled over to Randall. She looked over Randall and the wound she inflicted on his head. She leaned in close to look at the gash and her hair brushed against his face.

Randall's eyes darted downward, and he saw the top of the cleavage of her very perfect breasts down her shirt. He quickly averted his eyes upward, and all he saw was her lips above, pressed tightly together inches away. He closed his eyes tight, as he felt her soft hand gently cup his head. Randall was getting woozy with all kinds of funny feelings.

"Mother, I call on your divine mercy to heal this man." Juliana spoke, and her hand glowed with a white light, that grew in intensity and brightness.

Randall felt the throbbing pain from the wound ease and then disappear. The gash fused together, leaving no trace or scar. Izzy and Flynn watched in amazement, as it unfolded.

"I'll clean him up, if you can fetch a cloth and water." Juliana said to Izzy, as she inspected Randall's head.

Flynn sat back on his bedroll, leaning against the wall, and Izzy returned with the requested items. Juliana helped Randall sit up and cleaned his face and hair. He tried to not be so obvious about catching glances of Juliana's bosom, thin waist, and hips trying to imagine them free from the constraints of her clothing.

"I have booked passage on a ship out of Port Gwynn, and I want all of you to join me." Juliana said, dipping the cloth back into the bowl to moisten it again.

"I'm in." Randall immediately volunteered.

"No, we are not in." Flynn overruled Randall's quick lovestruck response. "We are waiting here, until we can return to The Nest. That Clarke fellow is going to have all the city looking for us again. I'm sure that Musa was not just out there birdwatching either. Rowan and his son are expecting payment for their trouble, and Peter is going to want a report of the last few days activities. I would say, I need to send a message to him, but Musa is probably already delivering a different message."

Juliana dropped the rag into the bowl with a disappointed look toward Flynn. "I understand you feel you have these obligations to these people you must uphold. I will not attempt to sway your mind to do something you do not wish to freely do. However, I know there is a higher purpose, and She will guide us to fulfill what She calls on us to do."

"Is that right, Flynn?" Izzy asked.

"No, Izzy. She is just talking nonsense." Flynn said, as he took a potato from Randall's bag and sliced off a piece to eat.

"Allow me to at least get some rest here with you. I have not been able to sleep for days now it seems. I just need to be on board the ship by this evening." Juliana said, making her way over to the bedroll, stretching out on top of it and covering herself with a blanket.

"That is actually my bedroll." Randall said, with hope and lovestruck eyes.

Juliana curled up under the blanket without responding. Izzy crawled over then laid down next to her, sharing the bedroll and pulling the blanket on herself as well.

"Maybe you are still nice. I'm Izzy." The little girl snuggled against her back.

"Pleasure to meet you Izzy. I'm Juliana." She rolled over and shook Izzy's hand. Izzy had a smile from ear to ear.

"Flynn here." He said, popping another chunk of potato in his mouth.

Randall sat cross legged on the floor and withdrew his tome from his bag. He opened it up under the light of the oil lamp and began thumbing through the pages, mumbling.

"I'm Randall by the way." He said, without looking up, as he studied the incantations in the book. His ran his finger along the words and flipped through the pages, until he stopped on the one. He tapped on the title of the highly illuminated text for just the spell he was looking for. He looked up and smiled. This one proved useful for him to seduce Madeline in the past.

18
Unsafe House

Hours passed slowly in the small room, as time was killed by mostly sleeping on the floor on the thin bedrolls. Randall slept propped up against the wall, with the leather-bound tome resting open in his lap. A small bit of drool, from the corner of his mouth, dripped onto his shirt while he dozed. Flynn performed stretching exercises, free of his shirt and boots. Juliana sat reading aloud from her small book of prayers and songs, as Izzy stood behind her putting her hair in a braid.

"You have pretty, soft hair, Juliana." Izzy said, as she used pieces of twine to tie off the one simple long braid, effectively pulling all the hair out of her face.

"Thank you, Isabel. I can do yours now if you would like." Juliana closed her book and took the carved bone comb they had found amongst the supplies.

"Isabel?" Randall lifted his head up, wiping his chin on his sleeve.

"Yes, Mr. Randall. That's my proper name my mamma called me." Izzy said, as she sat in front of Juliana, cross-legged.

"Your mamma?" Randall asked.

"Of course. Everyone has a mamma." Izzy shook her head at such a ridiculous question.

Flynn leaned over and whispered in Randall's ear. "She's an orphan now. I had found her begging on the streets when she was barely four. She was badly bitten in a fight with one of the other children from The Nest, and then she gained our gift."

"It was mean for Danny to bite me. He's my friend now though. I would still stab him if I had to." Izzy responded, without looking up.

"Good ears." Randall said to Flynn. Flynn agreed nodding his head.

Juliana combed through the tangles in Izzy's hair, and used Izzy's knife to cut out mats.

"This is quite extraordinary. Izzy never lets anyone touch her hair, though she is quite the expert at braiding other's hair." Flynn mused at the sight.

"A wash tub would have been nice. We could have bathed and washed the grime out of our hair. However, having this comb has been nice." Juliana said, as she ran it through Izzy's hair.

Randall's eyes and ears perked up at the sound of that. He would enjoy a bath as well. However, his thoughts were of Juliana. Sitting in a bathing pool, filled with rose petals, while another lovely young woman used a sea sponge to gently bathe Juliana's voluptuous body.

"Mr. Randall, are you ok?" Izzy was concerned at the blank, faraway stare he was shooting in Juliana's direction.

"Uh, yes. A visit to a bath house would be nice. I haven't been in ages." He shook his head and closed his tome, keeping it strategically placed, covering his lap.

There was a soft knock on the door, causing everyone to look up at each other. Flynn crouched beside the door, slid the bolt aside, then pulled it open. The others leaned over to see who came to pay them a visit.

"Well, hello, Sauda. You are a fine sight to behold!" Flynn smiled offering his hand as the young woman ducked in through the door.

Randall remembered his brief encounter with her in The Nest, when he was first introduced to Peter. He recalled her as one of his personal bodyguards. She happily took Flynn's hand, entering the room amongst the other occupants.

"Who is she?" Sauda was taken aback when she caught sight of the new companion.

"That is Juliana. She was part of the reason we encountered trouble the night we went after Randall's book, but she is also the reason we were able to escape with our lives." Flynn offered up.

Juliana began to rise to her feet, but Sauda put her hand on the hilt of her sword, and, with the wave of the other, motioned for her to sit back down. Izzy frowned at the obvious threat made toward her new friend. Flynn was understanding of Sauda's wariness and wanted to defuse the initial mistrust.

"We are supposed to return to The Nest at once. Everything has finally calmed in High Port since the morning activities. There are arrangements made to sneak you out. Luckily, that big ape didn't cause too much trouble. A little bribery encouraged the guards to skip snooping around here. However, others will be back to investigate, and who knows if they'll find this place." Sauda stated the situation, not looking for any questions.

"I'm not going with you. I'm leaving the city tonight." Juliana said, suspicious of Sauda's intent.

"Night has already fallen, lady. Time is something easy to lose track of below. Whether you leave tonight or not, will be for His Lordship to determine, once he hears you out. We leave now." Sauda waited for everyone to exit the room before following.

At the top of the stair, the second bodyguard from The Nest waited to receive them in the office above. Red held out her hand to receive each, and help them into the room. Her scarring from the burns that covered part of her face, left Randall with many questions he decided not to ask as she pulled him out.

"Who is this little tart?" Red asked, as she pulled Juliana out last with a sneer. "She a new plaything of yours, Flynn?"

"She's my friend!" Izzy stomped, angrily.

"She saved us in a fight below in the catacombs. She's going to be leaving Gwynn. She's not any problem for The Nest." Flynn said in her defense.

"Let's move it along. A lot has happened at The Nest since you've been gone." Sauda said, exiting the secret passage, then pushing the desk back into place.

Outside the office, the warehouse was dark. Randall cast his light spell on the stone, which bathed the area with the soft blue light. Many shadows were cast from the stacks of inventory under the loft area, up to the ceiling rafters. He was nervous that all may not be well, and his companions shared the same sentiments. Red led the four of them single file and Sauda took the rear.

The group stepped out from under the loft, to a wagon with horses hitched to it, ready to go.

"Who is this woman?" A voice with a familiar thick islander accent, called out from above in the darkness.

The four quickly looked up to the loft, to see Musa looking down on them, with his arms crossed. Two other men stepped up on either side of Musa with crossbows loaded, ready for trouble.

"This is Juliana. She provided aid to us and was only sharing the space with us until she departs Gwynn tonight." Flynn called back up to Musa.

"I see. Here's where things stand now Flynn. The Nest was invaded for the first time since its existence, by the city guard. The accidental discovery was made when they raided Bert and Mark's place and found one of the hidden entrances. The guard was driven out after they took massive casualties, and that entrance into The Nest was collapsed. Some of our people were killed as well. They knew silvered weapons were needed to deliver death to us. By the time we got word of your unapproved and botched burglary of the Customs House, we already learned that any secret vault there was already emptied by the Lord Mayor and moved elsewhere. As things stand now, this apprentice magician boy is of no more use to His Lordship. His services are to be terminated tonight. As for this girl, I consider her another loose end to be eliminated."

"You can't. Juliana's my friend!" Izzy jumped in front of Juliana and pleaded.

"Stand aside, Izzy. You are too young to understand." Musa ordered.

Randall reached into his reagent pouch and quickly retrieved spider's silk from a web he collected in the safe room. Another spell he had studied earlier, was about to be tested. The crossbowmen were just taking their aim on Juliana and Randall, as Sauda and Red drew their swords.

"Aranea telam ingurgito!" Randall spoke the incantation as he held the web in his fingers, while gesturing with his hands the somatic component to the spell in the air.

A sticky mass of webs was conjured up, spreading across the floor of the loft and stretching to the rafters overhead. The thick mass engulfed Musa and the crossbow men, as well as the rows of warehouse inventory. They all appeared to be stuck fast!

Flynn and Juliana drew their weapons and faced off with Red and Sauda, both of whom transformed into their red eyed, rat hybrid forms. Red still appeared burned with scarring like her human form, with scar tissue where fur would be. Sauda appeared as a thin hybrid rat form, covered in thick black fur. Izzy drew her knife and prepared for a fight; however, Randall grabbed her and pulled her under the loft with him

"Red, Sauda! Don't do this!" Flynn went in a defensive stance, preparing to parry any attack from Sauda, who he faced off with.

"We are not after you or Izzy. Those two must be eliminated. For The Nest!" Sauda rushed Flynn, swinging her longsword at Flynn's rapier, knocking it aside and kicking him in the gut with one fluid motion.

Flynn doubled over and was knocked to the ground, but he didn't lose the grip on his blade.

Red held her sword in two hands, screaming. She leapt in the air with blade overhead and in a whirlwind spin, she brought it down on Juliana.

Juliana countered with her mace, deflecting the blow with a loud clash of steel and a flurry of sparks. She immediately swung her mace, but Red dodged and spun around, ready to strike again.

Overhead, on the loft, Musa was pulling with all his strength, to free himself of the sticky webs. His head was now free, and he strained to pull one arm loose as well. The two crossbow men were completely engulfed and struggling with their sticky bindings.

Flynn kicked up and jumped back to his feet from the floor.

"Stand down, Flynn!" Sauda ordered and swung her longsword, slicing its tip across his chest.

Flynn staggered back, grimacing from the cut that slashed his shirt and skin. He applied pressure to the wound with his hand as he staggered back, but it was already closing leaving no trace, other than the blood on his shirt.

Randall lost hold of Izzy, who had transformed into hybrid rat form. Izzy leapt out from their hiding place and landed on Red's back, preventing her attack on Juliana. She sank her orange incisors into Red's neck, twisting and ripping into her scarred rat flesh. She stabbed with her knife repeatedly into Red's leather breast plate while hanging on to her with her free arm, with little legs wrapped about her waist.

Red spun around trying to reach Izzy with her free hand, but Izzy was latched on to her. The wounds that Izzy inflicted upon Red did not cause lasting harm, as they almost instantly sealed closed with each stab of the knife. The pain, however, was felt each time the blade sank in, further enraging her.

Sauda turned her attention from Flynn, seeing Randall taking cover beside a stack of crates, as he watched the events unfolding. Stepping forward, she pointed her blade at Randall, letting him know his life belonged to her.

Randall's next move played quickly through his mind. He prepared the spell he had originally studied to have Juliana look at him more favorably. He put his hand to his lips and blew a kiss at Sauda, then spoke the arcane words, "Amicum gratissimum!"

Sauda stopped her advance, confused and uncertain, lowering her blade. Flynn was stepping forward ready to engage, but Randall motioned for him to stop. Flynn turned his attention away to Red and Izzy's fight, which was becoming increasingly heated.

Juliana was waiting for an opening to strike Red, but Izzy was latched on tightly and there was a chance of hitting her. Red suddenly ran back full force into a supporting post on the loft, crushing Izzy. There was the sound of Izzy's cracking ribs and cry of pain, as she released her grip on Red, and fell to the floor. Red spun around and plunged her sword into Izzy's chest, impaling her and pinning her against the column.

Izzy cried and screamed, thrashing, and then fell silent, losing consciousness. She transformed back into a little girl once again.

Juliana's mace connected with Red's back, and she knocked her flat to the floor. This only enraged the wererat, as broken bones fused back together, and split skin sealed closed. Red rolled across the floor away from Juliana's next attack, and the mace struck the floor, cracking the thick flagstone.

"Protect us from her!" Randall shouted to Sauda, as he pointed at Red.

Sauda under, Randall's enchantment, jumped into action, placing herself between Red and Juliana with her longsword at the ready. Flynn quickly moved to Izzy and pulled Red's abandoned sword from her chest. Izzy slumped over to the ground.

"What in the Hells are you doing?" Red yelled at Sauda, as she kept positioning herself between her and Juliana.

Red attempted to dart past Sauda, but Sauda's reaction was quick. She dropped her sword, and wrestled Red to the ground, putting her into a sleeper hold. Red struggled to wriggle free with her huge yellow incisors gnashing. Sauda dominated this one-sided fight, as Red lost consciousness lay limp on the floor.

Flynn scooped up Izzy, holding her limp body in his arms, and watched the wound close as her eyes slowly opened. "That hurt." Izzy managed to croak out.

Randall removed himself from beneath the loft and assessed their current predicament. Red was incapacitated by Sauda; two crossbowmen were held fast in the webbing, and were not an immediate threat. However, Musa was about to pull free, and would wreck total havoc on all of them.

Juliana stood looking toward Musa, held her free hand in a fist and made a hammering motion. "I call upon the power of The Mother to vanquish this foe!"

A mist formed in the air before Musa, who stopped his struggle in the web to watch what was unfolding. The mist slowly swirled, and within points of white light became brighter, coalescing, trying to take form. Their intensity grew, as the mists and light rapidly went from an amorphous form, to that of a feminine specter of an armored warrior, created from the divine powers conjured by Juliana. The form floated before Musa, who eyed it with curiosity, as it flickered in and out of view. It drew a ghostly mace and swung at Musa. His head was knocked to the side, crushing his eye socket. Musa drew his blade to parry.

"Please, come with me! The Mother's power will cover our escape, but we must go now!" Juliana pleaded with the others, as she ran to the front of the warehouse, sliding the door open enough to squeeze through.

The flickering form swung again at Musa, who evaded another blow.

"You are a dead man, Flynn! All of you are! I will cut out your livers and eat them before your dying eyes!" Musa would make good on his threats, if he was to catch them.

"I'm not giving him the chance." Randall said, looking to Flynn and Izzy, who was now alert and showing no signs of having a sword buried deep into her, other than her bloodstained clothing.

Izzy jumped out of Flynn's arms and ran to the door. Flynn followed close behind. Randall took another look at the scene above as Musa was struck again, breaking his collar bone.

Sauda stood over Red, who was slowly beginning to regain consciousness. Musa pulled free of the webs, but was beaten again by the spirit warrior until he collapsed.

"I think they're going to be mad at me for what I did for you." Sauda turned to Randall, with her glowing eyes. Sauda did not realize at this moment that Randall had bewitched her.

"Thank you. I'm sure that they will forgive you." Randall made a quick exit. He knew when the effect wore off, she would know she was under a spell. Best he put as much distance between himself and the assassins as possible.

Randall saw his companions already across the road, waiting for him. He wrapped his light stone and buried it in his book bag. They ran through High Port to the docks, with hopes to board the ship with Juliana. It was dark, and overcast skies provided cover from the moonlight, to evade the patrolling city guards.

Juliana found the ship docked where it was that morning. Izzy produced enough of the coin she scored from Thom Clarke's purse to buy them all a place on board in the cargo hold, with no questions asked. The captain didn't remember Randall from that morning, but that was due to the quantity of drink he and the crew had been enjoying in port. Events of the morning at the Custom's House, delayed the departure of the ship until the following day.

Juliana was quartered in a small room with a single bunk, and a chair and writing table. There was a chamber pot under the bunk, and a small portal to see the outside world. She hoped that Musa's pursuit was thwarted, at least for the evening.

Flynn, Izzy, and Randall had hammocks in the cargo hold amongst the many crates and barrels, that were still on board. There was noise from above deck, where the crew were quartered. Apparently, the crew were enjoying games of cards and dice by candlelight, with a bit of drink.

Randall thought of the events of the day, concerned with would be assassins, failure to clean out Geoffrey's private piggy bank, and worst of all, being aboard a ship. He was already feeling the effects of the boat rocking in the water, even though it was docked. He pulled a bucket nearby, just in case of an emergency.

19
Ada's Promotion

"You will find your quarters here quite satisfactory. I have no doubt they are far superior to anywhere you have lived before." Bennett's steward Umfrey, stood in the doorway with hands clasped together, waiting for Ada to enter the room. He was a tall man, with a gaunt face dressed in drab gray and black robes, with the only splash of color being a red chaperon on his head, its cornett tail hanging over his shoulder. He stood expressionless, as his dark eyes followed her as she stepped into the room.

"Thank you, sir. I am very grateful." Ada's room was a small servant's quarters, in the wine cellar and dry storage. There was a bed with straw mattress, on a simple frame, with clean blankets folded on top of it. A wood footlocker for storage was in front of it, and a three-legged stool sat in the corner, by a small table with pitcher and basin. The floor had a prayer matt, and a small carved medallion of The Mother mounted on the wall.

Ada felt a chill come over herself, as she waited quietly for whatever was coming next in this nightmare job orientation.

"Look at me child." Umfrey's deep set eyes stared, unblinking at Ada.

Ada slowly lifted her head up until Umfrey's eyes locked with hers. She was trembling as he reached to hold her by the chin with his thin hand. He turned her head from side to side, inspecting the delicate features of her young pretty face. He released her head only after he caressed her cheek with the tips of his fingers.

"Yes, you will serve His Grace well. There is a wash tub being sent down, along with fresh clothing. Before you report for duties, you will be clean of body and fed." Umfrey left Ada in the grim windowless chamber, lit by a single oil lamp.

Ada paced the room for a few moments, then kneeled on the mat facing the holy symbol of The Mother. She clasped her hands together and tightly, closing
her eyes to pray.

***

Later in the afternoon, Bennett was receiving a few high-profile citizens of Port Gwynn in the parlor. The wealthy visitors believed that a guaranteed place in the heavens, was influenced by the size of the tithe you bestowed to the church. They were sitting comfortably, enjoying freshly baked scones from the kitchen, piping hot spiced tea in delicate porcelain cups, all set on finely crafted silver platters. The furnishings in the parlor were very comfortable. Fine tapestries and paintings hung on the walls, imported woven rugs on the floor, and overstuffed tufted furniture and carved tables, inlaid with highly polished brass fittings. The good life was offered to those who followed the word of The Mother, and supported her with a generous tithing, as Bennett always liked to mention during these meetings.

"As always, thank you for your generous donation for renovations to the Port Gwynn Orphanage. This will help keep these most vulnerable of the city safely sheltered, and provide meals for another few months." Bennett rose from the davenport, with hands clasped together, smiling.

"Your Grace, we are always happy to contribute for the needs of the children." The wealthy contributors and their wives rose, and one at a time took Bennett's hand, kissing his ring in respect. They were escorted out of the manor by the butler, to their waiting carriages in the courtyard.

Grim Umfrey, entered the parlor, as Bennett poured himself another cup of the afternoon tea from the silver service kettle and stirred in a sugar cube.

"Yes, Umfrey. What do you have for me?" Bennett raised the cup to his lips and sipped with a loud slurping sound.

"Your Grace, letters have arrived, which I have left on your desk in the library." Umfrey said, with hands clasped behind his back.

"Very good, Umfrey. What else." Bennett took a bite of scone followed with another sip of tea.

"The new servant girl was shown to her quarters and is being attended to by the Housekeeper." Umfrey raised an eyebrow, relaying this last bit of information to Bennett.

Bennett took a long pause, and sipped his tea. He looked up at the expressionless Umfrey.

"Very good. Mrs. Hilde needs to stress the importance of the service she performs in this house, as equal to that of the cathedral in the eyes of The Mother." Bennet said, leaning back in the davenport.

"As to be expected, Your Grace. One letter bears the seal of Lord Mayor Geoffrey. I presume it is of importance. If nothing else is needed of me, I shall check in on the head gardener. The new pots you ordered arrived this morn, and he was setting them along the driveway into the courtyard." Umfrey stood, patiently waiting for his dismissal.

"A very skilled potter made those in Windy Dale. Remind him of that, so if anything is damaged, he will be responsible for replacing them, out of his own purse." Bennett stressed that point, while waving his finger.

"Yes, Your Grace." Umfrey turned and exited the parlor.

Bennett rose again from the davenport, brushing crumbs from his robes onto the floor. He adjusted the cap on his head, and took the grand staircase up to the second floor. He crossed a wide carpeted hallway accented by furniture and oil paintings hanging on the walls between doors to many rooms that rarely saw any use. At the end of the hall, were the doors to the library.

The library had wall to wall shelves filled with many leather-bound tomes, illuminated by hand. Religious texts and histories of the known world, could be found amongst curious artifacts that found their way into Bennett's possession. There were a few reading tables in the room with books stacked on them, not yet returned to the shelves.

The Bishop went straight to his writing desk and sorted the day's letters. Breaking the seal on Geoffrey's letter, he unfolded it to read with a brass magnifying glass.

Bishop Bennett of The Cathedral of the Merciful Mother,

While you are taking your leave in your country home, without concern of what transpires here in Port Gwynn, we are dealing with a situation. Captain of the Guard, Madok lead a raid onto the property of The Nightmen, that lead to a network of a criminal underground, which included lycanthropes operating in the city. The Captain, nor any of the men accompanying him that night, returned. As expected, there was an attempt to infiltrate and rob the Customs House in High Port. Thom Clarke was attacked and injured, but is now recovering back at his home. Thom reported that Randall is in league with said lycanthropes, and his current whereabouts are unknown.

One more important thing. The young woman that you had sent to the convent for safe keeping escaped, using witchcraft in an assault upon Sister Lucia and one of the church's own guards. She has not been seen since that night.

I don't believe our mutual investments will be secure, if kept for long in its new location and will need to be divided and transferred.

Paul Wolff

Bennett set the magnifying glass down on his desk and crumbled the letter in his hand. Moving their combined ill-gotten cash stores from the vault, into the tomb of Saint Lydia, beneath the cathedral was no easy task. Working undercover with short notice, using only a few trusted men on Geoffrey's payroll, increased the number of people in 'the know' and more scoundrels to pay off. Doing this was to be a temporary solution, but now Geoffrey had plans to remove his share, immediately.

One of the doors opened into the library, and Mrs. Hilde paused, seeing Bennett at his desk receiving his correspondence. Bennett looked up at the middle-aged woman, who was the head of upkeep of the manor house. The matronly Mrs. Hilde was in her uniform long black dress, with white head covering and white apron. Behind her, Ada stood to the side waiting, dressed in the same maid uniform.

"I apologize for the intrusion, Your Grace. I didn't know you were working in the library." Mrs. Hilde said, with a slight nod of her head.

"What is it Mrs. Hilde?" Bennett said, looking past her at Ada, then back to her.

"I was showing this new member of the staff the lay of the manor. We are just going over her daily duties and responsibilities. Sorry to disturb you, Your Grace." Mrs. Hilde did a small curtsy, and Ada mimicked the gesture.

"Mrs. Hilde, please do continue. I'm only going through today's correspondence." Bennett picked up the next envelope, breaking its seal, and began pretending to read its contents.

Mrs. Hilde led Ada through the library, describing the cleaning process and restrictions on touching any of the books, whether on shelves or the tables. Bennett watched the young girl with lecherous eyes, following her, then back to the letter when they faced him.

"Thank you, Your Grace." Mrs. Hilde and Ada curtsied again, then exited the library as Bennett acknowledged by waving them away with his hand.

Bennett sat back in his chair and breathed in deeply, after the door closed. He would ease his stress tonight with a private meeting, with his newest staff member, planned by Umfrey as always. He's been The Bishop's most loyal servant, through many years.

✳✳✳

Bennett used the small dining room, when not entertaining in the formal dining hall. This evening, he shared his table with Umfrey, which was not unusual, as he acted as his confidant. The two just finished their meals,

106

and were enjoying a bottle of Fermont brandy in their snifters paired with chunks of goat cheese, made in house from his manor's small goat herd.

"Thanks again, Umfrey, for having the courier deliver my response to the Lord Mayor so promptly. Dealings with him in our joint 'business venture' have been troublesome from the start. I believe my involvement has not been fruitful in revenues, with the addition of the other business partners and their own reckless endeavors. You saw this from the beginning, and I ignored your advice." Bennett held the snifter up to his lips and took a sip.

"Your Grace, you were already successful prior to this, in the blessings of The Mother from spreading Her word to your flock. I can understand how you would want to increase your most deserved compensation for doing Her work. Though, sometimes we can lose sight of Her blessings when challenged with the temptation of others, who have been corrupted by greed." Umfrey sat in his chair, without eating or drinking from the dessert spread before him.

"Very wise, Umfrey. I believe I will incorporate that into a sermon I'll write in the upcoming weeks." Bennett spoke, with a mouthful of cheese.

"Your Grace, I would remind you that your gout gives you trouble after a fine meal, as the one we had tonight after we finish with drinks and dessert," Umfrey said as he watched Bennett finish his brandy.

"Correct as usual Umfrey. However, life would be less enjoyable without a good brandy and such a fine cheese. I will need to remember to thank Mrs. Margaux for her cheese making skills. Keeping her family here to work, was a good choice." Bennett smiled.

"Mrs. Margaux passed away two months ago. Her son, Wil, has taken over that duty." Umfrey informed Bennett of the personnel change.

"Oh. I'm glad she had passed on her skill to him before her death. How did I not know about this?" Bennett seemed slightly confused by the news.

"You were away in the capital at the time. She had taken seriously ill several months before, and we had her payment compensation stopped until she was able to work again, so Wil began performing her duties since then." Umfrey said, matter-of-factly.

"Very good! I'm glad he was ready to step in for Mrs. Margaux. A fine young man." Bennett replied, nodding his head.

"Yes, at only age ten, he took over, and only took a half day away from his duties, when they buried Mrs. Margaux. We did give them a small plot on the edge of the property to use." Umfrey said, with his deadpan delivery.

"Very well. Remind me to schedule a visit, to console them during their time of grieving." Bennett said, rising from the table.

"I will consult the calendar and find a free time and plan it for you." Umfrey said as he, too, rose from the table.

Paul Wolff

Ada stepped into the dining room with large tray and began to load the dishes from the table. She did her best to be invisible, and not attract attention to herself. She was learning, from other members of the staff, that part of their job included being unseen. Waiting only a minute longer, she could have cleared the room after the two men left, but she was rushed by the kitchen staff.

Bennett caught a glimpse of her, as she leaned over the table with his eyes lingering to Ada's cleavage that was modestly covered.

"What are you doing, child?" Bennett asked of her, stopping and turning to face her.

"I-I'm clearing the table Your Grace." Ada stood up straight, with eyes looking down.

"No, no, no. This won't do at all. I didn't bring you here to be a scullery maid. I needed a chambermaid, that could also act as my valet. I thought I told you that Umfrey?" Bennett looked over to Umfrey.

"Sorry, Your Grace. I believe the valet is traditionally a young man's role. However, it is a good opportunity to offer the young lady, and break from traditions. A very important role." Umfrey nodded his head in approval.

"Thank you, Your Grace." Ada stood still, without making eye contact with either man.

"Good! I will send for you a little later, to personally go over your routines and expectations." Bennett exited with Umfrey, leaving Ada to contemplate whether to finish clearing the table.

As the evening progressed and more of the household staff left as their duties were completed, Ada was one of the few that was still on the property. She wanted nothing more, than to go back to her room and sleep. She had been picked up at dawn from her home in Port Gwynn and brought to the manor that morning. Only a few brief moments were allowed to break to eat. Exhaustion was setting in, but she still had to be briefed by The Bishop of what her other duties would include.

Ada stepped to the chamber door and knocked on it firmly. A moment of silence and she heard Bennett call to her. "You may enter."

Ada entered the room and closed the door behind her. Bennett was sitting at his secretary desk composing a letter, paying no mind to Ada entering the room. It was a magnificently appointed room, with oversized canopied bed and fine draperies to draw around it. A large ornate, polished, brass framed mirror leaned against the wall from the floor, standing taller than a man. A velvet chase lounge occupied the center of the room, which had layers of rugs spread to keep the floor warm. Over the fireplace, hung an oil painting of Bennett in full ceremonial regalia.

"Your Grace, I'm here." Ada said, nervously.

"I know you are, child." Bennett dipped the pen in the inkwell, then continued writing, as Ada stood waiting awkwardly by the door.

Some minutes passed, and Bennett had finished sprinkling the ink with pounce and shook most of it back into its bowl. The rest spilled onto the desk and floor. Slightly upset with his small mess, he frowned and then folded the paper, placing it in an envelope, and sealing it with melted wax, pressed with his signet ring. He looked over at Ada, who stood by the door, not knowing what to do.

"Why are you still standing there? You should have already set my night shirt out for me and unmade the bedclothes." Bennett said, with disappointment in the tone of his voice.

"Bedclothes, Your Grace?" Ada said, confused.

"Yes, the bedding needs to be prepared for me to sleep in. I can't be expected to sleep on top of all that." Bennett shook his head at Ada's ignorance.

"Sorry, Your Grace." Ada walked across to the bed and quickly removed the large number of pillows, then pulled back the fur blanket and silk sheets. She was surprised that the mattress was soft as it was, as she was used to straw stuffed in canvas, rather than the feather down like this one.

Bennett watched Ada from across the room, as she awkwardly prepared the oversized bed. She felt his gaze burning through to her soul, as his eyes lingered on her as she stretched and bent over.

"This isn't a bath night, so retrieve my nightshirt and cap from the closet." Bennett said to Ada.

"Closet?" Ada had never seen, nor heard of such a thing.

"I do forget, you most likely grew up in a one room hovel, and hung your clothes on a single peg. The closet is through that door. It is used for storage and hanging clothing. The blue one with its matching cap, will be satisfactory tonight." The Bishop was condescending, but correct with his assumptions.

Ada walked into the closet, and was shocked to see so many different pieces of attire owned by one person. Fine slippers, pantaloons, stockings, tunics, and there were a few articles of his formal wear for church, that were also here. Ada looked through the garments until she found a row of long night shirts. The blue nightshirt was fashioned from imported silk, as was the matching cap. She draped them over her arm and stepped back into the bedchamber.

Bennett was standing in front of the leaner mirror, already in a stage of undressing himself. Ada stopped and gasped, as he continued without acknowledging her return. She stood holding the clothes, looking away, as Bennett dropped every article of clothing to the ground around him, stepping out from it, wearing only a pair of slippers. His nakedness upset Ada, and she fought to hide her embarrassment.

"Bring them over, girl." Bennett stood in front of the mirror, quite the specimen of pale, wrinkly, sagging skin covered in bristly wisps of white body hair. Without his cap, the little bit of white hair on top of his head, did little to cover the liver spots. He cocked a bushy, white eyebrow, watching her, as he waited.

Ada walked over with Bennet's nightshirt, only looking at his slippers on his feet. She held out the silk gown and cap for him to take.

"Since you are new at this, to save time, I will dress myself. Just this time." Bennet grabbed the articles of clothing, and after struggling to pull it over his head, he managed to get it over his shoulders and down to his knees. He pulled the cap over his head and looked at himself in the mirror again.

"Will that be all, Your Grace?" Ada felt nauseated and wished to leave at once.

"No, you will need to gather these clothes, and place them in the basket in the closet. Mrs. Hilde has a woman that does the wash weekly." Bennett walked to the divan to sit, as she gathered the discarded clothing and took it to the closet.

"Will that be all, Your Grace?" Ada stepped back into the room, more than ready to make her escape.

"No. I wish to view you as you were when you were brought forth into this existence, unhindered by worldly clothing. We are all The Mother's children, and as we are each created as the fruit of our earthly parent's passion, I would like to make sure that there is no corruption in her design. Sometimes, wickedness of one's earthly parents, results in them being punished with children made imperfect by disease, deformity, or unhealthy mind." Bennett motioned for her to come closer.

Ada, trembling, stepped over between the mirror and the divan that Bennett was sitting on. Bennett stood and walked over to her, looking her up and down.

"Remove your clothing, child." Bennett said, circling Ada.

"Your Grace, no." Ada began to cry.

"Now!" Bennett spoke sternly, as he continued to circle her.

Ada slowly removed her clothing, and Bennett stepped back to the divan and seated himself. Tears ran down her cheeks, as she loosened the laces and dropped the top down to her waist, exposing her breasts. Bennett smiled and motioned for her to continue. The dress fell to her feet in a pile, and she stood shaking in the middle of it.

Bennett looked at her full frontal for a few moments, as Ada stared at the floor.

"Turn around." Bennett ordered and stared at her backside, as she now faced the mirror.

Ada looked into the mirror at herself and was filled with guilt and self-loathing. Behind her, she saw Bennett rise to his feet and slowly approach her from behind. He was inches away from her, and she could see that he was touching himself, while he looked upon in her vulnerable state. Her thoughts turned to the kindly woman she met the night before in the convent. Ada closed her eyes and prayed to The Mother.

"Be silent and open your eyes, child." Bennett said to Ada, as he looked upon her reflection in the mirror.

PART II

20
Redrock Castle

" All rise for His Royal Highness, Duke Archibald Payne." The herald made the announcement, followed by a pair of trumpeters in bright red and black uniforms, sounding their horns. The Duke was about to hear grievances of citizens, from around the lands he was sworn to protect. One of the things that The Duke dreaded to be bothered with. Ruling his Dukedom, under his idiot nephew, King Ernald III, was an inconvenience. He had to take on that duty when Archibald's older brother, King Ernald II, died after his long reign.

Duke Archibald was just south of eighty, by one year, and had no surviving heirs to step up and rule. The Duke and Duchess's daughter died at barely a year old, and two miscarriages left the Duchess barren and living life in despair for the past half a century. In the past few years, she had become ill and a recluse, rarely was seen in public. The Duke carried on with the King's business, collecting taxes in the Dukedom, and keeping the peace in the large swathes of land he governed. He enjoyed the benefits of being a royal with all the creature comforts, but would prefer to be left to his own private pursuits.

Archibald walked across the carpet, dressed in layers of fine clothing, which included a cape and pantaloons with tights. His upper body appeared larger under the doublet, puffy sleeves, ruff collar, and large black hat, but his thin birdlike legs told the true story of his frailty. He leaned on his walking stick for support, as he slowly made the trip across the red carpet to the waiting throne in the great hall of the castle. Those calling for audience with him rose and stood patiently, watching as he was escorted by his royal guards. The four towering guards, were clad in polished plate armor, and armed with halberds. The Dukedom's standard hung from the high stone wall above the throne; a long banner of a field half red and black.

Accompanying him, his most trusted advisor from his council, Osbert, who trailed the procession to the throne. Dressed in pale blue and white robes, with a tall white sugar loaf hat, he, too, was followed by the court scribe, who was carrying an armful of scroll tubes, paper, pens, and ink.

Archibald took a moment to maneuver into position, on the massive throne, as the guards took their positions on either side of him. Osbert stood to his right, and the scribe took a stool behind the small writing table, laying out his tools before him.

"His Royal Highness, Duke Archibald Payne, welcomes the petitioners of the dukedom to Redrock Castle. You may all take your seats." The herald made the announcement, after the small crowd took their seats.

"His Royal Highness is limited in his time today and will only be personally taking grievances from the ten petitioners, who out of all of you, drew the winning slates from the lottery when you entered the hall. The ten who are holding red slates, please rise." Osbert looked over the hall at the ten who rose, as sounds of groans and grumbling began to rise to a crescendo.

Osbert held his hand up to silence the crowd. The crowd complied and the hall fell silent.

"Call on the first petitioner, Osbert." Archibald said in a voice though aged, was spoken very articulately and of sharp mind. He leaned forward to listen.

One by one, the ten were called upon to bring to The Duke's attention their concerns, with hope that he would be able to right whatever wrongs they were experiencing. Property line disputes, brigands waylaying travelers on the Ironwood Forest Road, and of course, the pack animal dung polluting the congested city streets bringing the cursed biting flies. The Duke always had a quick answer or solution to remedy most grievances, except for that final one.

An hour into the meeting, a mustachioed olive-skinned man, was called upon by Osbert to speak as the time slowly moved forward. He greased a few palms to ensure he had a red slate to speak before The Duke.

"Your Royal Highness, thank you for hearing me on this day. I was sent as a representative of several merchant companies that conduct trade in King Ernald's kingdom and lands. Trade with the kingdom has always been lucrative and beneficial for those I represent. However, in recent times what was considered a fair tax levied upon imports brought in through the great city of Port Gwynn, have become a burden due to increases on the taxes. Profitability is being reduced, as excessive goods are seized on cargo inspections which are never recovered. Those I represent, have found that other ports of entry into the kingdom outside your Dukedom, have not sought higher taxation or seizures of goods from our vessels. We are looking to conduct trade as before, outlined in the agreement made in the treaties that King Ernald II signed between our nations decades before. Those I represent, wish to continue conducting trade with Port Gwynn as the main port of entry, however plans are being made to bypass it completely in favor of other ports outside of the Dukedom." The mustachioed man closed, with a respectable bow, and waited for Archibald's reply.

The Duke looked to Osbert, waving him over. Osbert bent over to The Duke, and the two exchanged words in heated whispers before the silent hall for a few minutes.

"His Royal Highness wishes to thank all that have come to seek audience with him today. He apologizes that he could not hear all the grievances today, but he will be available again this day in a week's time." Osbert announced, over a low grumbling from the attendees.

"Sir, The Duke does wish to continue the conversation of this most important and urgent matter in a private, more formal setting. You will be sent for this evening, to be his guest at dinner."

"Thank you for hearing me. I am positive that His Royal Highness will be able to find a fair solution to our dilemma." The mustachioed man respectfully bowed again.

The trumpeters sounded their horns, and the herald called for all to rise, as The Duke exited with his guard and Osbert, from the great hall. After the doors closed behind them, Osbert and Archibald carried on in conversation regarding the implications of the man's grievances.

"Archibald, that is Hakim Azad. He represents several of the major trading companies from the east that—" Osbert was cut short by The Duke.

"I am already aware of who this Azad is, Osbert. Just as I am sure that fool, Geoffrey is behind any plot that could disrupt trade for his own personal gain." The Duke said, as he walked with his entourage though the castle. "The High Sheriff is already in route, collecting tax revenues, so after the meeting you will send a courier with a message containing all the information we glean from Azad, for him to investigate. The auditors will need to spend a bit of extra one on one time with keeper of the accounts in Gwynn. If there is anything happening in Port Gwynn that is going to bring attention from The King into my dukedom, I want it dealt with proactively. I don't have time for any intrusions from my nephew here." Archibald stopped at a waiting open sedan chair, with a pair of servants dressed in black and red garb, to carry him the rest of the way through Redrock Castle to his chambers in the upper story.

"Your Highness, I shall make the arrangements for tonight's dinner and meeting with Azad and the others in his company. Will there be anything else you will have of me at this time?" Osbert asked as The Duke stepped onto the litter and slowly positioned his posterior onto the plush seat.

"No Osbert, that will be all. I will be taking my lunch in my chamber, with The Duchess this afternoon as usual. Then I'll be working in my library until the dinner is called." The Duke settled in the chair, as the men lifted the litter up and carried him along.

"Do you wish for me to make arrangements to have The Duchess join the dinner tonight?" Osbert asked, with a raised eyebrow.

"No, Osbert. In her weakened state, she will need to continue to take her meals in our bed chamber. Her nurse, has been tending to her whenever I'm away." The Duke replied, as the men continued forward leaving Osbert.

"Very good Your Highness." Osbert turned and headed to prepare for the evening's dinner and meeting.

The Duke was brought to the doors, leading to his royal bedchambers, he shared with his wife, Duchess Katherine. A footman waiting at the door, dressed in the black and red uniform, opened the door for him, as he stepped off the sedan chair using the walking stick as a third leg.

"Thank you, Raymond." Archibald said to the young man holding the door.

"Brandon, Your Highness." Brandon replied, with a bow.

"Hmmm? Oh, very well." Archibald shook his head, and continued into his chamber as Brandon pulled the door shut.

Duchess Katherine was seated in a finely crafted wheelchair, constructed of polished wood and brass fittings, facing a large fireplace that had a fire burning even though it was high summer. She was wrapped in a heavy fur blanket and rocked rhythmically in place, as her nurse read aloud to her from a tome filled with children's nursery rhymes and fairy tales. The silk scarf she wore covered most of her head, but allowed for some stray gray locks hang loose from it.

"Your Highness, Duchess Katherine has been enjoying the stories again. They seem to awaken something within her, when I read." She closed the book and set it on the table, next to the rocking chair she was seated in.

"Very good, Ms. Eleanor. That will be all for today. Perhaps tomorrow morning you can take her into the gardens. She does love the season's flowers." Archibald's smile revealed a few missing teeth and receding gumline.

"Duchess Katherine, doesn't that sound lovely?" Eleanor stooped over the duchess, smiling.

The duchess continued rhythmically rocking in her wheelchair, though she responded with an approving low grunt.

"Your Highness, I will have some fresh cut flowers sent up for your room as well, to replace the others. A mixed arrangement from the greenhouse?" Eleanor prepared to leave.

"That would be fine Ms. Eleanor. Anything to raise The Duchess's spirits, and good smells will help freshen the room as well." Archibald said, as he crossed the room and struggled to one knee, before his wife, taking her little skinny frail hand in his.

"Good day then, Your Highness." Eleanor curtseyed and exited the room, shooting a smile to Brandon as he held the door for her.

Archibald lifted Katherine's hand to his lips and after kissing it struggled to his feet.

"Katherine let's take in the sun on the balcony. Come!" The Duke held her hand, as she slowly rose to her feet the fur blanket fell to the floor, and she stood in a long off-white gown. Holding hands, they walked out to the balcony, overlooking the west gardens to the table setting under a canopy. "Please sit, my love." Archibald offered her a chair, before he took a seat himself.

Archibald leaned back in his chair to relax his body and mind, to enjoy a quiet moment with Katherine. He looked over at the west garden's sculpted hedgerows, the stone paths that traversed its lengths, water features, and beds of flowers. The Duchess sat in her chair, rhythmically rocking, resuming staring into space.

"This was always your favorite place to sit, when we took our breakfast with tea. You designed these beautiful gardens, and they were constructed and filled to your plan. They are still a sight to behold, even if it is now a struggle for us to walk together through them, as we did before." The Duke seemed resigned to a bit of sadness, thinking of a happier past before Katherine's debilitating illness.

He leaned on the stone balcony rail, taking in the warm sun on his face. He looked across at the gardens and beyond to the walls of Redrock Castle, that stood almost forty feet high. He turned again to Katherine, who continued in the rocking motion in her chair, seemingly oblivious to her surroundings.

"Do you wish to stay out on the balcony when we take our lunch today?" Archibald presented her with the simple question.

The Duchess stopped rocking and rose from the chair with a low grunt. The Duke looked into her eyes for a response.

Katherine's unblinking, cloudy, gray eyes were sunken, and the sockets appeared more pronounced with the darkening skin around them. Her mouth was pulled open from shrinking skin, exposing her teeth giving the appearance of a smile. Her marbled gray and green skin on her cheek had a fly land on it, which began to scurry across her face that she took no notice of.

Katherine turned and slowly shuffled back through the door into the bedchamber, where she returned to the wheelchair facing the fireplace. Archibald followed her into the chamber and with great, pain bent down and picked up the fur blanket and placed it over her. Kathrine gave an approving low grunt and began rhythmically rocking, staring into nothingness.

21
Sea Legs

Two days at sea and Randall wasn't feeling any better. He laid in his hammock below deck, rocking with the waves, as the *Lady Anne* sailed along the coastline. The captain had another port to deliver cargo to aside from Port Gwynn, that was outside of the dukedom. Randall had never taken a liking to any boat, whether a row boat or their current vessel. There was also no plan in place since his escape. Escape from the city he called home the past few years, with new companions he's known only for a week.

Currently, he was alone in the hold, losing track of the time. He would have to make a fresh start when they made it to the next port. Having no coin to start with would mean he couldn't make a break from his travelling companions now. He may have to rely on their talent of the "five finger discount" to survive a while, until he could find some kind of similar work as before. Maybe working for someone less dangerous than the Lord Mayor of Port Gwynn.

Sunlight and fresh air from the above decks came through the open cargo hatch. Randall thought it best to try to eat and drink something, even though he would probably immediately puke it up over the rails again. Somehow the others did not seem to have the same problem on board as he. Flynn had travelled on a sailing vessel many times before, and was a part of a ship's crew for a few years before settling in Port Gwynn. Juliana was treated well by the old salt of a captain, as she reminded him of one of his daughters. Izzy was always busy snooping around, and told more than once to stay off the rigging and crow's nest, as it was no place for a little girl. She was also making friends with the rats that hid in the decks below, that scavenged in the middle of the night. Flynn warned her to be extra careful on board to keep their true nature a secret.

Randall rolled out of the hammock and crashed onto the floor. Nothing broken luckily. He spent some time the first morning, before they had set sail, keeping his spell book securely hidden in case any of the crew came snooping along. Finding such a thing by a superstitious kind of person could possibly land him in deep water. Literally. The book was wrapped up in canvas and wedged in a space safe from prying eyes.

Randall made his way across the hold, climbing the stairs through the berth deck to the main deck. Most of the crew were performing their duties, as the captain was overseeing the operations from the vantage of the command deck. Juliana and Flynn were alongside him in conversation, as another member of the crew manned the wheel. Looking around for Izzy, he saw her scurrying about on the forecastle deck, fascinated by everything from the crew working the rigging, to the bow wave as it broke on the bow of the caravel.

Randall took a moment to lean on the taffrail and contemplate puking over the side again. He stared at the water breaking for a moment, then closed his eyes tightly until the nausea and dizziness subsided.

"Mr. Randall! Isn't this wonderful?" Izzy shouted down to him, as she climbed the rigging up the forward mast. The crew paid her no mind whatsoever. She took to climbing through the masts, ropes, and rigging like a crewman away at sea for years. She waved at Randall from high atop the forward mast's crow's nest.

Randall shielded his eyes from the sun to catch a glimpse of Izzy high above him. Quickly he turned to lean over the taffrail, attempting to empty his guts into the sea. Not quick enough.

"Bloody 'ell! I just cleaned 'ere!" An angry shirtless man, wearing a scarf to cover his shaved head stepped up to Randall.

"Sorry, sir." Randall apologized in a pitiful squeak of a voice.

"Looky 'ere you stumblebum. You're going to clean up your stomach chowder right now, or I'll serve it up to you with a tankard of bilge water for your supper." He took Randall by the arm and shook a meaty fist in his face.

Randall looked at the fist, his eyes rolled back, and then collapsed on the deck in a heap.

Raucous laughter erupted from all the sailors on deck. The captain looked down with crossed arms and shook his head.

"Are you okay, Mr. Randall?" Izzy shouted down from the crow's nest.

Flynn and Juliana hurried down to the main deck to Randall's aid. Flynn took his arms, and Juliana took his legs, then transported him below deck.

"I was only givin' the little feller a 'ard time. Meant 'im no 'arm." The big sailor said, smiling. He turned to grab the mop and bucket.

Flynn made a makeshift bed on the holds deck with some blankets, rather than place Randall back in a hammock. Juliana helped him into it and gave him a cup of fresh water to drink.

"Best thing for you is to drink lots of water and don't eat too much." Flynn said, squatting down by Randall's side.

"Izzy told me she has never left the city before, so this is quite the adventure for her. She taken to the sea quite easily. The crew are rather impressed with her climbing skills for such a small child," Juliana said.

"Well, I'm so damned impressed." Randall drank down the water, with a good portion of it running down his chin onto his chest.

"We are following the coastline to the next port, which is a week's travel. You should be getting over this sea sickness soon. I'm pretty sure that the captain is ready for you to keep your bile off the side of his ship." Flynn provided his words of encouragement.

"I think once we arrive in Sommer Harbour, I will offer my services to the church once again. From there I'll determine what The Mother would have me do. I don't think word of what happened in Port Gwynn will have spread there yet." Juliana took the cup from Randall's hands.

"Izzy and myself should be able to find 'work' of our own in Sommer Harbour as well. Peter's network of spies does not go too far outside of Port Gwynn. If you've crossed him and leave, you are permanently banished. Returning to Gwynn would be a death sentence." Flynn added.

"I think I'll be okay once we arrive, as long as the ground is not constantly rocking back and forth under my feet." Randall said, closing his eyes.

Izzy dropped through the hatch above and landed on all fours before the three. She looked over at Randall with a sad expression on her face.

"Mr. Randall. The nice captain told me, that if you watch the horizon from the deck while we're moving that it helps to settle your stomach. It helped me when we first left the city. You should try it too!" Izzy advised.

Izzy crawled over to the remaining cargo in the hold and squeaked at the large sacks of grain that were tucked in with barrels and a few crates. A large black rat squeezed its way out, with its nose and whiskers twitching furiously. It crawled up to Izzy's extended hand and then up her arm to cling on her shoulder.

"Mr. Randall, this is Arnold. He is one of my new friends. He has a lot of other family that live here too! You haven't seen them, since you've been sleeping most of the time. The captain said that there was a rat problem, and he was going to get a cat when they go to port. I think Arnold and his family should come with us..." Izzy was speaking so quickly, Randall could barely keep up.

"I-I don't think that would be a good idea Izzy." Randall said as Arnold sat on its hind legs balancing on her shoulder.

"I'm going to go back up and see if the captain will let me hold that wheel again. I think that is the most fun!" Izzy was getting ready to run up the steps.

"Izzy, better leave your companion down here." Flynn pointed at Arnold.

"Arnold, you better go back and hide. I'll talk to you later." Izzy set Arnold on the floor, and the rat scurried back to the cargo diving in between the grain sacks. After she was satisfied, he had made it into his hiding place, she ran up the steps to the above deck.

"Randall, we are all going to take our supper in my cabin tonight. Its small, but it would be more comfortable than sitting in the cargo hold, or sharing a table with the ship's crew. It would be better for you to come up again, after you rest a bit. We will discuss more about what to do when we reach Sommer Harbour. I firmly believe that we are all together for reasons that The Mother has not yet enlightened me of." Juliana smiled and brushed Randall's hair out of his eyes gently with her hand.

"I'll be there." Randall smiled, enjoying the gentle caress of her hand, and thinking more into it than she intended.

"I'll come back down and check on you a little later. If you want to try to come back up, I'll be there to help you up." Flynn patted him on the shoulder and left with Juliana.

Randall sat for a few minutes, leaning against the wall of the hull. The sounds of activity and some light coming in from the hatch above wasn't allowing him to fall asleep, and he was feeling better though weak. The nausea had left him, but his empty belly was now gnawing at him. To take his mind off it, he decided to retrieve his book to study.

He slowly rose to get acclimated to the gentle rocking of the ship. It wasn't so bad now, and his balance was better. Crossing the hold to retrieve his grimoire that was safely stashed, he spied some casks, neatly stacked toward the back in the shadows, he never noticed before. He stepped carefully across the floor, balancing himself against the hull wall with one hand, until he reached this cargo.

There were a dozen barrels, two rundlets, and a firkin secured with netting. Randall closed his eyes tightly for a few seconds, opened them again to adjust to the dark. Branded across the flat surface of the casks was the point of origin.

"Grummandy!" Randall felt a full recovery as he patted the firkin of beer, plotting how to smuggle it up for tonight's supper.

22
The Sick Room

Madok was awakened from a restless sleep as a damp cloth was laid across his forehead. The young Sister laid a hand across his cheek, feeling the heat of his fever warm on her palm. He laid atop a bed soaked in his own sweat, under a scratchy wool blanket.

"You're still burning with fever, Captain. Sister Lucia said your sickness can last a fortnight from the time of its onset." Sister Constance pulled the blanket down to Madok's waist to inspect the rose-colored rash on his chest. "You are very strong, and The Sister believes you will make a full recovery."

"How's Nigel?" Madok struggled to speak with a weakened voice.

"I would say almost as well. He also has a high fever; however, his breathing is very shallow. He has not awoken from his sleep today yet. You should not worry about him though. He is young and strong and is also being well cared for. You just need bedrest and drink lots of water. I must leave now to check on other patients." Sister Constance walked out the curtained doorway to visit her next patient.

Madok looked across the room with semi-blurred vision, and began focusing to the corner on the fat bearded figure with crossed arms, sitting on a stool. He realized it was Lord Mayor Geoffrey, who was paying him a visit. Madok groaned and laid his head back down on the pillow.

"Well Captain, I hope you are resting nicely under Sister Lucia's care," Geoffrey said, oozing with sarcasm.

"How long?" Madok asked.

"You've been here almost a week. Before you and your new Sergeant became bedridden, you did manage to report the bungled attempt to arrest those idiot gong farmer brothers. Let's see, your entire force was wiped out by rat men and a giant toad monster living in the sewers beneath the city. At least you took out Mark and Bert, and we have discovered an entire undercity that threatens Gwynn's existence." Geoffrey spoke frankly of the situation.

"What else?" Madok asked.

"Well, for starters the Custom's House was hit the same night you disappeared with your men. That idiot Clarke said it was Randall, with a pair of helpers. One of which was a wererat child. Of course, we already transferred all our accounts prior to that, so they got nothing. Currently, your First Lieutenant is in charge and has not determined if Randall is even still in the city. One more important thing of note, is now the rat-men are emboldened. At night there have been reports of them roaming in the shadows on the streets." Geoffrey stroked his long black beard with one hand.

"You will need silvered weapons to kill them. It is the one known way to put them down permanently. When we took out Mark and Bert, I realized that these creatures have allies among some of the people here in Gwynn. They have obviously had a network of helpers in Gwynn, that are not infected with that curse of lycanthropy." Madok propped himself up with one arm to sit up and face Geoffrey.

"We are aware of the need for silver against these creatures. I have conscripted the top silversmiths in the city to produce broadhead bolt tips for the crossbows, as well as silver mace heads. A new tax has also been levied to cover these costs, of course, for the protection of Gwynn." Geoffrey spoke while waving his hands.

"Of course." Madok replied.

"This is all happening as Bishop Bennett has decided to take a short sabbatical to spend time at his countryside manor. Obviously, he thinks that is the best way he can avoid the High Sheriff, who is due to collect tax revenues." Geoffrey wringed his hands.

"You are expecting trouble?" Madok laid back down on his pillow, after he drank water from the cup Sister Constance had left him.

"I'm not sure. Duke Archibald seems to always be aware of any business going on here in Gwynn, almost immediately. The incident at the Customs House and your botched raid will likely already have been reported to him. Having the High Sheriff here nosing around, will bring more unwanted questions and attention to my personal business. Yours as well, I might add." Geoffrey sat back, leaning against the wall.

"What are you suggesting?" Madok looked suspiciously.

"Obviously the truth. Mostly. Randall and rat men working in league together, raided the Customs House, plundering its coffers intended for the collection. I will exterminate these rats with the help of professional soldiers, sent with the High Sheriff, and the silvered weapons. Perhaps even finally put an end to the restless dead, that are still locked in the northern catacombs. It's only a short matter of time before the Lieutenant discovers another entrance into their lair, since that one you discovered was closed off. Thom has agreed with this story already. Bennett is not privy to this of yet." Geoffrey looked at Madok for a response.

"Am I missing something here? You had already removed your coin from the vault, which was obviously Randall's intended target." Madok covered his eyes with his hand to block the light that made his head throb.

"Yes, that and the coin from the safes in the Customs House, were transferred to another protected location. So, it will appear that the raid did yield Randall, and those creatures, the treasure they were seeking." Geoffrey continued watching Madok.

"I believe you are either mad, or I am completely delirious with fever and just imagined this whole conversation. Your greed has emboldened you to further scheme and endanger me, believing you can play the High Sheriff or The Duke for fools." Madok was irate, but unable to raise his voice in his weakened state.

"Captain, you are obviously unable to think rationally, falling ill from wading through all that filth and losing all those men. You best pull yourself together when there is an investigation, which will follow when the High Sheriff arrives. Perhaps by then you will have recovered, which for a man such as yourself, is a likely outcome." Geoffrey rose and pulled the curtain back, to exit through to his waiting guards. Pausing in the doorway, he turned and looked at Madok up and down.

"What?" Madok asked, turning his head to look at Geoffrey.

"You really do like shite. Perhaps the fever will take you." Geoffrey chuckled and left with his guards.

"Bastard." Madok said in a whisper. He forced himself to sit up on the bed, removing the blanket. Clothed only in a linen braies, he took a few pained steps across the small room to the chamber pot to relieve himself and look at his reflection in the small cloudy metal mirror hanging on the wall.

He was in a ragged state, brought on by the fever. His face was pale, and beads of sweat rolled down into his eyes and mouth. His hair was disheveled, and several days of going unshaven betrayed what was normally his image of a well-disciplined commander. He was also wracked with guilt, for being involved with the Lord Mayor's scheme.

"Captain Madok, back to your bed. You won't be allowed any visitors, even if it is the Lord Mayor, if you are not going to rest." Sister Constance took Madok's arm and led him back to his bed. Madok laid back into the bed, and Sister Constance pulled the wool blanket back up to his shoulders.

"Thank you, Sister." Madok squirmed in the bed, feeling aches all through his body and a sudden shiver.

Sister Constance dipped the cloth into the washbasin by Madok's bed, wringing out the water and wiping his face. Madok's eyes were closed, and he began to feel a calm come over him and relaxed under the sister's care.

"Captain, is there anything else you need?" Sister Constance asked, with true concern.

"Sister, I've never been a religious man. I've rarely voluntarily gone to a church service, nor read any of the Holy Texts. However, I would ask if you would say a prayer for me to The Mother. I feel that it couldn't hurt to start.

"Captain, we will say a prayer together." Sister Constance bowed her head and closed her eyes. Madok followed her lead.

23
Love Me

B ishop Bennett's sabbatical in his country manor, followed a regular schedule. Rising to a mid-morning breakfast served at his garden patio, complete with poached eggs, toasted bread with jam, and piping hot tea. Followed up with a walk, through the garden and fruit orchards. Religious research and study in the library before lunch. Lunch was served on the main balcony, shaded under the canopy, and visiting guests enjoyed a small ensemble of musicians performing for their entertainment with their meal. Other day's business with guests, was conducted in the opulent parlor with afternoon tea and cakes. Daily correspondence was received and penned in the library. Dinner, typically, was in Bennett's private dining room with Umfrey. If special guests were received, the banquet hall would be used, requiring an elaborate menu of several courses for dinner and the special reserve vintage wine from the cellar.

The close of Bennett's day had a dark routine as well. After performing her other duties in the manor throughout the day, as a ghost to the other staff, Ada concluded her daily toil in Bennett's bed chamber. Preparing his bed and clothes, drawing a bath, and enduring the ritual abuse.

As on her first night, this night, Ada was made to stand vulnerable and naked in her pile of clothes, as Bennett stood behind her as they faced the mirror. He pleasured himself, spilling his seed on the floor and splashed her backside, watching as a drop ran down her leg to her ankle. Bennett never touched her, convincing himself, he was committing no sin without contact. He took pleasure in seeing the girl's tears and her trembling in the mirror as he performed the act. She was sworn to secrecy, under threats to her person and family by Umfrey, who kept a watchful eye on her.

After Bennett dismissed her, Ada quickly gathered her clothes and dressed herself. She exited the room and hurried herself down to her cellar room.

Running away would be impossible, as a small group of the church guard were always on duty, patrolling the grounds in the background, doing their best to be invisible. She was shunned by the other staff, who gossiped behind her back, so there was no one to talk to in confidence. This would be her existence, until Bennett returned to Gwynn after his sabbatical, or grew bored of using her for his pleasure. Ada shuddered at the thought of enduring this for a year.

She knelt on the floor and said a prayer before bed. Laying under the covers wide awake, she thought of her family back home and wondered if they missed her

as much as she did them.

***

Bishop Bennett sat in the chair at his secretary desk, going over notes for tomorrow's scheduled appointments left by Umfrey.

"This is hardly a sabbatical if I can't have a moment's peace from visitors for even one day. I need a day in the clear, after tomorrow." He shook his head and laid the paper down to deal with the following morning.

Walking with lamp in hand to the bed, he paused before the mirror to adjust his night cap and stepped on the spot damp with his semen on the rug.

"Damned girl. That will likely be stained by morning." Grumbling, he set the lamp on the nightstand on which sat a small shrine. He knelt before it, saying a small prayer before extinguishing the light and crawling into the bed.

The waxing moon and starlight through the windows bathed the room in soft, silvery light and black shadow. Clouds, forming earlier in the evening, began to blacken and roll in thicker to darken the room, extinguishing the light of the moon. Large droplets of rain tapped against the windows, like fingers. The occasional flash of lightening created a strobe of blinding light, illuminating the room for a split second followed by the low rumbling clap of thunder.

Bennett tossed in bed, to be awakened by thunder each time he drifted off. The drapes around the bed were drawn, but provided no sanctuary from the crashing of the thunder which grew louder and followed closer each flash of lightning. The storm arrived and sheets of rain pounded the windows and howling winds added to the cacophony.

Bennett faced away from the windows and pulled the blanket over his head to muffle the sensory overload. Passing minutes felt like hours, as the storm showed no sign of easing its barrage.

He finally drifted off into sleep, feeling weightless and floating just above the bed on a cushion of air. His eyelids grew heavy and blackness washed over, as sounds of the storm faded into dead silence.

"Your Grace." Ada's voice, softly called out.

He peeked out from the covers, and saw the silhouette of the girl standing next to the bed pushing the drapes open with her hands. Her dark hair was hanging down, flowing over her shoulders, and she was only wearing her simple sleeping gown.

"What are you doing in here, child?" Bennett's heart raced and he felt as if the wind was knocked out of him.

"Love me." Ada called.

Bennett attempted to roll away, but found himself laying on his back unable to move. Ada grabbed hold of the bed clothes and slowly pulled them off the bed, uncovering him. She climbed onto the bed with catlike grace, as flashes of lightening illuminated the scene now devoid of the sound of thunder. She took Bennett's nightshirt, slowly lifting it up over his legs, then up to his waist, over his chest, then over his head, discarding it on the floor. He tried to speak in protest, but words could not escape his lips. Sweat beaded on his forehead and streamed down his face.

Bennett was paralyzed in place, unable to move and completely at the girl's mercy. She straddled Bennett's naked body, and with one hand reached between his legs and took hold of his flaccid member, while looking directly into his unblinking eyes. Involuntarily, he became erect, as it was manipulated in her hands.

"Love me." Escaped her lips again, as she maneuvered herself into position and slid him into her.

Bennett lay in place unmoving, as Ada rhythmically began to ride him, as the silent electrical storm raging outside, lit the room in flashes of blinding bright light. There was no sound other than heavy panting escaping from Ada's lips.

Bennett's unblinking eyes were unable to look upon anything other than the girl that was atop him, forcing her way on him. His heart was pounding in his chest, and his breathing became strained as she continued riding, bouncing, and grinding on his prone body.

The silent electrical storm that was raging outside the manor was coming to a climax, creating a strobe light effect. Flashes of light and then blackness made her movements take on an even more nightmarish quality, as they appeared in slow motion. He felt her tighten around him, squeezing and pulling, until it was causing him pain. Bennett felt as if the skin of his penis was being pierced with tiny, sharpened, metal hooks and was being pulled and held deep inside her.

The oil lamp sitting on the nightstand suddenly began to glow, and its light slowly increased with intensity. The rest of the room remained dark, except for the bed. Ada pulled the simple nightgown off, and cast it to the floor. Bennett's eyes focused on Ada sitting atop him, with her head tilted far back. Her once dark thick wavy locks of hair that flowed over shoulders were stringy, greasy, and thin with streaks of white. Her breasts sagged and hung low like empty sacks, and her belly appearing bloated and distended from the effects of starvation. Her skin darkened to a bruised purple coloration, and her fingers were elongated and skeletal, with sharp nails. Bennett felt the throbbing in his loins as a pained ejaculation gushed into her.

The electrical storm abruptly came to an end, casting the room in darkness, except for the silhouette of Ada sitting atop him. The sound of rain gently hitting the windows could be heard once again. Bennett remained paralyzed.

Slowly, her head dropped so Bennett's eyes meet her gaze. The face was now of an ancient hag with her yellow smile spreading across her face, as red rimmed eyes yellowed with jaundice, stared into Bennett's inches apart. Her suffocating, hot breath smelled like carrion.

Overcome with terror, he lifted his head to scream, but the hag put her hand over his mouth, then one finger to her lips and made the sound, "Shhhh."

She crawled backwards, disappearing through the drapes. Bennett was laying on a sweat soaked mattress now. He felt as if his heart were going to burst, wheezing, and gasping for breath, as he lifted himself up.

The drapes at the foot of the bed flung open and young Ada stood at the foot of the bed in her nightgown, smiling. She put one finger to her lips and made the sound, "Shhhh" as she walked backwards to the door. She opened the door, stepped through it, and slowly closed it until it gently clicked shut.

Bennett fell back on the mattress, pinching his eyes tightly shut, letting out a tormented scream of terror.

"Your Grace! Your Grace!" Umfrey stood to the side of Bennett's bed, shaking him to rouse him from his nightmare.

Bennett's eyes opened to bright daylight. He was covered in his blankets, still dressed in his nightshirt and cap. He sat up and looked around his room from the vantage of his bed, confused.

"She's a monster!" Bennett shouted at Umfrey, who had a very concerned look on his face.

"Who's a monster?" Umfrey asked.

"That girl. She was in my room last night! She..." Bennett stopped raving and tried to calm himself.

"It's almost the noon hour, and you appear delirious with fever." Umfrey put his palm against Bennett's forehead.

"Noon? I had just laid down to go to sleep and then the storm hit." Bennett pushed Umfrey's hand away.

"Storm, Your Grace? It was a clear last night. We haven't had rain in almost two weeks, if I remember correctly. This isn't like you to sleep so late. Should I send for your physician to come see you?" Umfrey's concern was genuine.

"No, Umfrey. You're right. I must sound mad. I am just exhausted. The dream felt so real." Bennett was shaking his head in disbelief.

"It would seem so, Your Grace. You have an important donor from the church that is meeting you for lunch today. The widow, Lady Elsbeth. Her carriage arrived and I realized you had not even come down for your breakfast yet. You will be receiving her on the balcony for today's lunch. She is currently waiting in the parlor, so I will tell her you will be down shortly." Umfrey exited the room hurriedly.

Bennett threw back the blanket on his bed, slid down to the floor, and put on his slippers. His body was aching, and his nightshirt was soaked with perspiration. He would need to take time to freshen himself. He walked up to the mirror, tossed his nightcap to the floor, and struggled to pull his long nightshirt off over his head.

Staring into the large brass mirror at his body, he saw fresh claw marks all over his chest and groin. Bennett gasped, then ran into his washroom where he threw his guts up into the privy. Sitting on the floor, naked, he studied the scratches on his body, that were inflamed, and burning.

He leaned against the wall, catching his breath while clutching his chest.

"The devil girl has bewitched me." Bennett closed his eyes and began to weep.

24
Arnold's Biscuit

The waters were calmer that evening, as the *Lady Anne* continued sailing toward an orange sunset with thin trails of purple clouds. They were following the wild frontier coastline, that a century before King Ernald I, commissioned adventurous explorers to map. These lands that bordered the kingdom turned out to be inhabited lands, but not with humankind.

Many warring tribes of humanoids lived in their own societies, outside of that in Ernald's kingdom. It is a land of minimal vegetation and water, treacherous terrain, but rich in iron ore and some precious metals. Small mining communities, on the border of the kingdom, have been in operation for years. They took their chances to scratch out a living bringing their bounty back into the civilized lands. These lands were the destination Bishop Bennett sent trouble makers. One way mission trips to preach conversion. These lands were commonly referred to as The Goblyn Badlands.

Randall felt better than the beginning of their voyage, and leaned on the taffrail observing the coastline. He tried to remember anything he could about these lands during his studies under his mentor, Master Williamson a few years back. Everything happening the past few weeks made him question his reasoning for abandoning the college, and breaking ties with his family.

"Mr. Randall, you look like you are feeling better." Izzy stepped on her tippytoes to look over the taffrail with Randall. Izzy had made herself a new dress from a cloth bag and discarded the little boys' clothes she acquired in Port Gwynn.

"Much better, thank you, Izzy." The color had returned to his cheeks and calmer waters settled his stomach.

Juliana stood on the forecastle, leading a prayer with a trio of sailors below on the main deck. The captain had retired to his quarters and awaited his dinner there. Flynn was on the quarterdeck enjoying conversation with the first mate, who was behind the ship's wheel. The remaining crew, were on the lower deck having their supper of biscuits soaked in beef stock and as it was a 'flesh day,' salted pork for their meat. Warm beer was always aplenty on their voyages, but the imported Grummandy cargo was off limits.

Flynn stepped down to the main deck, tapping Randall and Izzy both on the shoulder smiling.

"I see Juliana is attempting to make converts of this crew on this ship. I haven't the heart to break it to her that most of these men are faithful to the old gods of the sea. The Mother is barely known of outside the kingdom. I imagine they are more interested in her physical beauty than the beauty of her words. Perhaps we should get some food from the galley, and head to Juliana's quarters for supper." Flynn laughed, and walked down the steps below deck.

Randall looked over at the three men returning to their duties on deck, as Juliana completed her impromptu service. He imagined they were holding a conversation about who would be the one to win a night with her in her berth and show her the pleasures of a 'real man.' These thoughts gave way to his jealousy, and fantasies of summoning blue bolts from the sky to electrify the lot of them. Sadly, that was out of the scope of Randall's power and expertise at this moment. Their discussion was more mundane. 'Who was going to climb the rigging to keep watch in the crow's nest this evening?'

"I saw Flynn go below to get our supper. Would you help him while I get the room ready, Isabel?" Juliana walked up to Izzy smiling.

"Of course, Ms. Juliana. Mr. Randall said he's feeling much better now." Izzy skipped down the stairs.

"I'm glad to see you looking well, Randall. I would hate to have you taken ill during the entire voyage to Sommer Harbour." She smiled looking toward the fading light on the coastline in the distance.

"I guess I just never was on board any boat long enough to overcome it. Of course, there was no alternative means to escape Gwynn at that moment." Randall turned and leaned his back on the taffrail, crossed his arms, and watched the sailors working on deck.

"I have seen you call upon magic on the two occasions we were forced to fight along each other's side. This is different than what is granted to me by The Mother, when I call for her aid. I have heard of it referred to as 'dark magic' and the practice was outlawed long before we were born, yet you seem to be a master of it." Juliana was genuinely curious and wanted to keep an open mind.

"I learned quite a bit in secret; in the school I was boarded at for years. The headmaster, Theobold Williamson, had a secret library I discovered, and I read everything I could find. I discovered the grimoire during my late-night forays into his study, when everyone was asleep. I was able to learn the ways to harness the powers derived from elemental forces of nature, to those of supernatural design. It is all a matter of following the 'recipes' in the book. There were many failed tests and trials, until I discover how all the pieces fit together correctly. It's a combination of the words I speak, to the wave of a finger, and often a little material component I pick up along the way. The magic then can be used in many ways for getting oneself out of an impossible jam." Randall was hoping he sounded impressive to Juliana.

"I have witnessed you using that power as a tool that can be used as a force to do good in this world. I also think I could see how such power could corrupt one, when it is not used for a purpose other than one's own selfish wants. Randall, I believe this power is for a higher purpose, and like myself you don't know what that is yet. I'm heading to the room, to set it for us to eat." Juliana patted Randall on his shoulder and walked to her quarters.

Randall stood for a moment longer, watching the waxing moon in the sky as the sun sank into the sea. Izzy and Flynn came up onto the main deck, carrying old metal trays piled with the evening ration of food.

"Hey Randall, give us a hand here. You need to bring the drink." Flynn pushed by with Izzy and joined Juliana in her quarters.

"Yes!" Randall remembered the firkin of Grummandy beer waiting for him in the hold. He wasn't in the mood for the ration of watery swill that was served in the ship's galley to the crew.

Randall descended into the ship's hold, unnoticed by the men on the berth deck that were busy in conversation, having drink and a game of knucklebones played with human teeth of unknown origin. The hold was lit by a single lamp that was swaying overhead, making shadows dance along the walls. He pulled out his book that was stashed away in his satchel for safe keeping, for a little dinner time read.

He then decided to grab the cask, which proved to be his undoing. Randall found he was unable to lift it, instead he got a sharp stabbing pain in the small of his back.

"Augh!" Randall cried out and found himself stooped over, like an old man with his hand rubbing the strained muscles. The sedentary lifestyle, of a studious student and number crunching bookkeeper, did not prepare him for heavy lifting. No further attempts would be made to remove the cask from the hold, instead he got the evening's ration of watery swill from the ship's galley.

The four squeezed into the small cabin, enjoying a meal together. Izzy and Juliana shared her small bunk, and Flynn and Randall made do, sitting cross legged on a few cushions on the floor. Randall looked at the liquid in his wooden tankard and gave it a sneer before taking a sip. The others didn't seem to mind it as much. The conversation was relaxed, and there was the excitement of the unknown, pulling up stakes to explore a new place.

"I'm going to take this to Arnold. He likes these biscuits more than I do." Izzy took the one uneaten biscuit that wasn't soaked in broth.

"I don't think the captain will appreciate you feeding the stowaway." Flynn took the last gulp of beer from his cup.

"Stowa- a what?" Izzy looked confused.

"Stowaway - someone that hides on board a sailing ship, unbeknownst to the captain, getting a free ride." Randall answered, pausing from reading to look up at Izzy, as she stumbled across the room almost falling on him.

"Little girls probably shouldn't have that kind of beer. We always had a small beer with our meals growing up. No stumbling around after that." Juliana said, looking on at Izzy with some concern.

"I'm good." Izzy stepped out of the room and headed below deck.

Izzy passed through the crew's deck to the hold, using the handrail for a little extra balance. Perhaps Juliana was right about the drink. Typically, when she had beer back at The Nest, the young were served small beer, except on special celebrations when regular drink was available to all. The feeling of inebriation was not unknown to Izzy. However, it was one she was not accustomed to, and didn't enjoy not being her usual nimble self.

"Pssst, Arnold. I've brought you some dinner." Izzy then made high pitched chittering and squeaks perfectly mimicking Arnold. She walked across the hold continuing calling over to the rat.

Arnold climbed up on top of a small crate and stood up on his hind legs nose twitching and sniffing the air. He squeaked approvingly as Izzy held out the biscuit for him.

Izzy sat the biscuit on the crate. Arnold broke off a piece, holding it in his front paws, and began eating ravenously. Izzy laughed, as the rat continued enjoying the dry bread.

"You need to save some of that for your wife, Arnold. I'm sure she'd like that, instead of all that grain you eat from those bags down here." Izzy waved a scolding finger at the rat. It paused from eating for a moment, seeming to contemplate her suggestion.

Suddenly, a crossbow bolt struck the crate Arnold was perched on. The rat jumped off, disappearing into the cargo. Izzy fell backwards with a yelp, landing on her bottom and looked in the direction to the person who shot at Arnold.

One of the crew members was at the foot of the stairs, holding a light crossbow in hand and started laughing. His fat belly protruding out from his shirt and patchy beard, disgusted Izzy and her reaction changed from surprise to anger.

"See if you can get him to come out again. I haven't been able to hunt those critters since you lot have been on board. Captain's orders and all." The sailor set the crossbow down against the hull wall and hung the quiver on a peg. He looked up the stairs to the berth deck, looking out for onlookers and then began walking toward Izzy.

Izzy started scooting away on the floor backwards. "You better stay away from me!"

"I don't want that vermin getting fat off our food, filthy urchin." The fat sailor held out his meaty fist and waved it at Izzy. He laughed and then continued moving to her, picking up his pace until he had her backed to the wall.

Izzy started to scream, but the fat sailor slapped her across the face with an open hand, knocking her over flat on the floor. She tried to sit up, but he put his huge calloused hand over her mouth, pushing her head back to the floor as she began to struggle, flailing her arms and legs.

"I'm going to snap your skinny neck, and toss you in the sea." The fat sailor put his weight on top of Izzy, pinning her on the floor. The smell of beer was heavy on his breath. "Then I'll kill each of your friends in their sleep, and toss them overboard, filthy urchins."

The sounds of chittering and squeaks erupted around the cargo hold from all directions. The fat sailor looked up from Izzy, squinting as he scanned the area. The glow of many eyes reflected in the light from the single oil lamp swaying in the darkened hold. Slowly they advanced out of their hiding places, below from the bilge, along the rafters, and between barrels and crates. Arnold and a small hoard of ship rats were making their way, and the chittering and squeaks intensified.

"What in the nine hells is this?" The fat man shouted out at the small army of rats, his attention stolen away from Izzy trapped beneath him.

Izzy began shape shifting, as she lay trapped beneath the fat sailor. Fur sprouted over her face and body as her eyes changed to a glowing red, while the rodent snout elongated, and orange incisors pushed out. Again, she began struggling beneath the fat man, who suddenly looked down face to face at her hybrid rat form.

"A demon from the hells!" He screamed, as he attempted to roll off and away from Izzy.

Izzy screamed as she was freed, and launched herself on top of the fat man. She sank four sets of claws into him, then sank her sharp orange incisors deep into his hairy shoulder. She violently shook her head, as her jaw locked into the meat and blood flowed from the wound.

The sailor screamed in agony and grabbing both sides of Izzy's head, attempted to pull her off him. This only made her hold on tighter, with more resolve. The rats closed in, as the sailor thrashed about on the floor, unable to shake Izzy. Slowly, one by one, rats jumped on the sailor and then the whole rat hoard rushed in. He was buried under the swarm, as they were clawing and biting him. Izzy took a chunk out of his shoulder, bringing forth a crimson mist covering her face.

"Wot the 'ell is goin' on down 'ere?" A voice called out, as the sound of footsteps pounded on the creaking steps.

Izzy sprung off the fat man and crouched on the floor on all fours in her hybrid form. The sailor's blood dripped from her mouth, and she bared her incisors at the man at the foot of the stairs.

The rat hoard scattered in all directions, to their hiding places across the hold. The fat sailor pressed his hand on the gaping wound on his shoulder. Covered in bites, scratches, and blood, he struggled to his feet.

"The girl! She's a demon! She tried to eat me alive!" He pointed at Izzy. Izzy backed into the shadows, squeaking loudly.

"Hey you lot! Ere's a rat demon in the 'old with Fat Robb! The beast is tryin' to eat 'im! Call the Cap'n!" From the man's vantage he saw Izzy's red eyes and snout when the pendulum motion of the lamp swung, revealing her hiding place,

then oscillating back, engulfing her in the darkness.

✳✳✳

Randall closed his spell book, sliding it into the satchel before stretching his legs. His back was still a little tender, but he didn't feel too hindered to walk. Flynn consolidated dishes from their meal, to return down to the galley. Juliana cleaned her teeth using a small linen cloth with a pasty mix of herbs, acquired on her last shopping excursion for supplies in Port Gwynn.

Flynn stopped in the middle of his task and stood motionless, listening.

"There's trouble below deck." Flynn strapped on his sword belt as he rushed out the door.

Juliana dropped the cloth and exited with her mace, leaving Randall alone in the room. Randall waited for a moment and then stepped out under the night sky.

Looking across the main deck, up the quarter deck and forecastle he was shocked to see everything abandoned. No one was even steering the caravel.

"You down there! What's happening there?" A voice called out, from far above in the crow's nest.

Randall ignored the man, and followed the noise from below deck, which sounded like a rowdy barroom brawl. Descending the stairs to the berth deck, a few members of the crew were looking below, through the open cargo hatch to the scene below. Two more members of the crew, blocked the stairs to the cargo hold.

Randall crouched down beside the men and peered below. Flynn and Juliana were below, while the remaining five crew members were armed with whatever they could grab to fight with from the galley: cleavers, butcher knives, and even and iron pan. Izzy was on all fours, gnashing her teeth, menacingly sandwiched between Flynn and Juliana, who had not yet drawn their weapons.

The fat man had made his way over to the stairs, attempting to load the light crossbow despite his injury.

"Please, allow me to alleviate this situation. I can heal your injury with The Mother's power." Juliana pleaded with the man and the angry crew.

"Not a chance. That monster paraded around as a child with us all this time and now it shows its true self, as it set upon me and summoned vermin to kill me. Stand aside or I'll put the first one in your belly!" The fat man lowered the crossbow toward Juliana, who stood between he and Izzy.

"I will not!" Juliana said, defiantly.

He released the quarrel directed at Juliana only to have it blocked by Flynn, who jumped before her and took the shot into his own belly. The bolt plunged into his flesh, causing him to fall back a few steps bumping into Juliana.

Flynn winced in pain, but grabbed the end of the bolt with his hand and ripped it out from his gut, with blood gushing from the hole. The gaping wound rapidly sealed closed, leaving only a bloodstained hole in his shirt. He tossed the bolt aside and looked up at the fat man with glowing red eyes, as large orange rat incisors pushed out of his mouth and quickly transforming into his rat man form.

"They're all monsters! We're cursed!" The cook threw aside the iron pan and ran up the stairs, pushing the other crew out of his way.

"What in The Hells is going on down there, and why is no one on deck?" The Captain now stood over Randall in his nightshirt and slippers, with a club in hand.

"Cap'n theys rat people! I 'magine this is one of 'em too!" The man jumped up pointing at Randall and grabbed a chamber pot from the floor as a weapon.

"Oh no! I'm not one of them. I'm just an acquaintance." Randall attempted to rise, but the captain pushed the club between his shoulder blades, pinning him to the floor.

Flynn drew his blade and dagger, Juliana took a fighting stance with her mace, and Izzy rose to her feet stepping behind her friends. The fat man was busying himself loading another quarrel into the crossbow, as the remaining men nervously backed away, dropping their kitchen weapons.

The fat man pointed the crossbow again toward Juliana, readying to loose a bolt. Flynn with his lightning reflexes, threw his dagger, plunging it into the fat man's other shoulder. He cried out, dropping the crossbow, causing it to fire a bolt into the calf of one of the other sailors. Both men dropped to the ground, clutching their wounds.

"It looks to me like we have an infestation of wererats on board, men. Unless you can strike them with weapons of silver, we won't be able to hurt them. However, this little runt says he ain't one of them." The captain shouted down into the hold.

The three looked above to the captain overhead, who now planted a foot in the small of Randall's back to hold him down.

"Don't you hurt Mr. Randall!" Izzy shouted at the captain.

"I'll release him once the three of you are off the ship and swimming for the shore." The captain called down.

"I can't swim." Randall protested.

"Quiet your noise." The captain put more weight down on Randall, pushing his breath out of him.

The ship's movement abruptly stopped, with a loud crash and the sound of wood splintering below. Everyone standing was thrown to the ground, and the captain fell through the cargo hatch into the hold. Sea water began rise through the floorboards and then the caravel began slightly listing to port side. The lamp hanging over head broke loose and smashed, starting a small oil fire on the deck.

Randall was already in a prone position when the caravel ran aground, and was first to jump up, as everyone was confused and in shock. Flynn quickly rose up and pulled Juliana up to her feet, having to correct his balance leaning the opposite direction the ship was listing. The captain was on the floor, groaning with a broken arm, and the others were thrown against the port hull a few with freshly laid goose eggs on their heads. Izzy scrambled on all fours across the floor, up the stairs. Flynn led Juliana by hand to the stairs, stopping first to retrieve his dagger from the fat man's arm, who was whimpering slumped against the wall.

Red hot coals from the stove in the galley had spilled out across the decking and floor boards were beginning to smolder, as smoke rose to the ceiling.

Randall was already on the main deck, as the angle of the listing increased. He found himself sliding across the deck toward the ever-familiar taffrail, which stopped his descent. He heard a yell overhead as the man in the crow's nest fell, crashing onto the deck before tumbling into the sea. With only moonlight to guide him, he still held onto his satchel containing his book and reagents. He retrieved the stone and spoke the incantation, causing it to glow with a pale blue light.

Randall's companions came above deck and saw the light stone illuminating the way. The unmanned ship had struck large rocks that jutted out of the sea, before it became beached in the shallows. The body of the man that fell from the crow's nest, was floating face down in the water, drawn toward the shore in the distance.

Izzy joined Randall first, clinging onto the taffrail with her rat hands and feet, looking to the water and then out toward the shore.

"Izzy, the ship has run aground, we'll need to make it to the shore before the other's follow from below." Flynn called out to her.

Izzy looked at Randall with her red eyes first, then jumped into the water with a splash. The rat girl swam toward the beach.

"The backpack with supplies." Juliana wanted to make her way to her cabin, as smoke started to rise out of the hatch and noise from the shouts of the men below grew louder.

"We don't have time. We'll make do!" Flynn made sure his sword belt and weapons were secure, and with careful footing made his way down to join Randall at the rail. Juliana secured the mace to her belt, before carefully angling down the deck joining the others.

The angle of the listing increased as the first member of the crew pulled himself through the hatch.

"Give me your pack, Randall, I'll carry it for you." Flynn took the satchel from Randall and hung it over his neck. He grabbed Randall by the arm and flung him overboard.

It was a very short drop into the water, and his head dunked under the warm sea. He didn't go too far, before touching the sea floor with his feet. He pushed up and surfaced as Juliana and Flynn both jumped in. The blue light of the stone still glowed as it rested on the sea floor below, illuminating all the sea life around it, as well as the ship which had a large gash from the collision. The keel had dug a small trench to its resting place in the shallows.

Juliana swam to Randall, who was struggling to keep his head above the water and beginning to panic. Juliana was a strong swimmer and remained calm headed, as she reached out for him with one hand.

"Randall, you can make it. I'll help you." She spoke in calming and soothing words, that eased his fear. Moving behind him she wrapped one arm around him to keep his head above water, and with her free arm and kicking of her legs, swam with the waves to the shore.

Flynn was doing his best to keep the leather-bound tome and satchel out of the water, but it proved to be an impossible task. He swung it behind his back and swam from the wreckage just as the loud crack of the forward mast broke, dragging down the sails and rigging into the water and splitting the hull open. Flames and smoke poured from the ship, as surviving sailors leapt into the sea through the open hatch. The weight of the other two masts and sails finally turned the caravel on its side.

Flynn looked behind him at the crew splashing down into the water, while the rats on board also made their escape atop the now exposed hull.

He continued swimming, quickly catching up to Randall and Juliana, who were a short distance ahead of him.

"Once we get to shore, we're going to need to put distance between us and them." Flynn transformed back into his human form, as he continued swimming on top of the waves. "How is he?"

"He's all right." Juliana closed in on the shore and let go of Randall as soon as her feet could reach the ground.

Izzy was standing on the beach with her wet sack dress clinging to her body pointing at the *Lady Anne,* as flames engulfed the sails in an orange glow while black smoke rolled into the night sky. The soft blue glow of the light stone lit the sea beneath the waves. The sailors were doing their best to swim for shore, while the ship rats abandoned the ship as flames began spreading across the vessel's hull.

"Flynn, I lost my tools and knife." Izzy said, with disappointment.

"Yes, and Mr. Randall's book is a little wet." Flynn opened the satchel, pouring out seawater onto the beach.

Randall stumbled onto the shore along with Juliana and grabbed the satchel from Flynn's hands, and quickly inspected the contents. He pulled out the tome and was surprised to find that it was not wet, showing no signs of damage.

"This is odd. The book is dry. It doesn't even look like it was in the water." Randall shook his head, dropped it back into satchel, and slung it over his shoulder.

"Let's move inland before they swim to shore." Juliana urged, and trudged up the sandy beach to a terrain that became rocky and desert like, almost immediately.

"What did you do to cause all that trouble below deck?" Randall asked Izzy, as he followed Juliana.

"I didn't do anything. The ugly fat man with bad breath started it." Izzy snapped.

"Well?" Randall waited.

"He started a fight with me, so I bit him." Izzy answered.

"I see. What happens after you bite someone?" Randall asked, with curiosity.

"Hopefully he'll turn purple, swell up, and die!" Izzy said angrily.

"We should be so lucky." Randall said, looking over his shoulder at the burning wreck.

25
Ada's Departure

Awakening once again from a tormented, unrestful sleep, Bennett screamed. The morning sun had not risen, and he was resting on the davenport in the parlor. His assumption was by avoiding his bedchamber, he would escape the nightmares of young lustful Ada visiting him, only to transform into the fiendish hag in the climax of their depraved coitus. The entire week, since this first encounter, made the days pass in a haze of exhaustion and declining health after each recurring nightmare. His appetite diminished and his appearance was haggard and gaunt. The nightmares seemed so real and he often woke with fresh scratches and bitemarks on his body, as proof it was more than a dream.

Since the first nightmare he had made a made it clear that Ada was not to perform the duties in the house as before, and was removed from her quarters in the cellar to one of the communal cottages on the property.

"Your Grace, are you all right?" A church guard posted outside the door stepped into the parlor.

"No, I fear I am still being tormented with nightmares of which I cannot escape. Please bring Umfrey down. I must speak with him at once." Bennett wiped sweat from his brow with his handkerchief.

"Yes, Your Grace." The guard turned and exited.

Bennett struggled to rise from the davenport and then hobbled over to his chair to sit. His heart was still racing and breathing labored. Going the week without sleep, Bennett was weakened, blurry eyed, and seeing things from the corner of his eyes. His doctor was brought in from Port Gwynn to provide a remedy to allow him rest, which included a steady supply of small vials of opium, which provided the calming effect.

Umfrey stepped into the parlor, wrapped in a long blue housecoat and slippers. He too, had been experiencing exhaustion due to Bennett's frequent calls. He rubbed his eyes as he stood before Bennett.

"Your Grace, what would you have of me?" Umfrey stood with his arms by his side.

"Umfrey, the girl needs to be sent away at once. She is using her black magic to torment me for bringing her here." Bennett looked up at Umfrey with dark circles under his watery eyes.

"Your Grace, I'm glad you are heeding my advice. I'll have arrangements made later this morning, after the dawn's light. Would you have anything else of me?" Umfrey felt relieved by Bennett's request. An end to these sleepless nights would be a blessing.

"That will be all Umfrey." Bennett reached into the pocket of his robe and withdrew a small glass vial with cork stopper.

"Your Grace, the doctor mentioned to administer your medicine sparingly. The supply is very small and could make you dependent." Umfrey warned Bennett, as he removed the stopper on the vial.

"Right as always Umfrey. After she's gone, I won't have a need for it, I'm sure." Bennett pushed the stopper back in the vial and slipped it back into his pocket.

"Very good Your Grace." Umfrey exited the parlor.

Bennett retrieved the vial from his pocket without Umfrey's watchful eyes. He removed the stopper, and emptied the remaining contents of the vial in one swallow. The vial dropped from his hand to floor, and he sat back, fingers white knuckled, gripping the arms of the chair. Bennett stared at the small shrine, on a table top covered with the wax from candles that dripped over to the floor.

"Forgive me, Mother." Bennett whispered, and sank into a state of numbness.

$$***$$

Ada watched, as young Wil prepared the stomachs from unweaned baby goats, for rennet in his cheese production. He wore a soiled, oversized apron over his clothing, and was slicing the stomachs on the large butcher block in the middle of cheese barn. These were passed to Ada, for salting and hanging to dry.

Ada was relieved to have been removed from the manor house, even if she was still working on the bishop's property. However, she was still tormented by the memories of the nightly encounters she suffered in his bedchamber. Assisting Wil, and learning the cheesemaking process from the boy, was fun and he was becoming a good friend.

"How long have you been here Wil?" Ada asked, as she rubbed salt into the kid gut on the preparation table.

"All my life, I think. Before the Bishop moved here for sure." Wil paused, while he spoke.

"Do you ever think about leaving here? Now that your mum has joined The Mother in the Heavens?" Ada wondered.

"Only if my father would leave. He's been so sad since mum died. He visits her graveside every evening, after he herds the goats back in before supper." Wil's eyes welled up with tears, which he rubbed away on his sleeve.

"The kind lady I met at the convent told me she would come visit me here someday." Ada smiled.

"Juliana?" Wil asked.

"Yes. Now I think I would like to go see her first. Well, after seeing my mum and my brothers back home." Ada smiled.

"Well, you can't run away from here now. Not since you're helping me here." Wil snapped. He was growing very fond of Ada.

Work continued in the cheese barn through the morning, until a surprise visitor stopped in. Umfrey stepped through the open-door and cleared his throat to make his presence known to the two.

Ada and Wil stopped their work and stood side by side, heads bowed as to not make eye contact with Umfrey. He moved into the cheese barn, stepping carefully around tools and containers scattered about on the hay strewn floor.

"I bring you good news, girl. His Grace has decided to consider your debt, owed for destruction of church property, paid in full. With that your employment here at the manor is to be officially completed, and you are to return to your home in Port Gwynn. Transportation is being provided of course." Umfrey spoke, with a commanding voice. Ada was overcome with a feeling of relief, and felt a weight lift off her.

Wil grew upset at the news, his brow furrowing over his brown eyes. "Sir, Ada has been a big help to me here. She's learned a lot about making goat's cheese. She's going to be a good as me."

"Boy, you were not addressed and you will remain silent." Umfrey admonished Wil, then turned his attention back to Ada. "Today at the noon hour, you are to bring all the belongings that came with you to the manor to the carriage house. From there, we will depart immediately by coach. Be there promptly, so that I don't have to send someone to fetch you." Umfrey emphasized the importance of the order, waving his finger in Ada's face.

"Thank you, sir. I will not be late." Ada promised.

"Very good. I suggest you make ready, once I depart." Umfrey exited the barn and took the gravel path leading back to the manor house, through a shady copse of live oaks.

"I can't believe it. It is like you had a wish granted." Wil was shocked.

"The Mother has answered my prayers. I'm sorry I'm leaving you like this Wil. I had better go." Ada rinsed her hands in a bucket of water, then dried them on her apron.

"Take this for your trip." Wil retrieved a wedge of cheese with a brown rind, which he wrapped in a cloth for her.

"Thank you, Wil." Ada bent down to kiss Wil on the forehead, causing him to blush.

Ada gathered the few meager belongings she had brought with her. The brush for her hair, the cloth doll her mother had made for her with a painted wooden head, and the one spare change of clothing she owned. Gathering everything in a canvas bag with a drawstring, she carried it over her shoulder, on her walk to the carriage house for her noon departure.

The manor house loomed large over the garden courtyard, which was abuzz with activity as the gardener tended to the grounds. She stepped onto the cobblestone drive way, after receiving a scolding from him for 'trampling the grass.' Following the path around the backside to the carriage house, she found the gate open.

She stepped inside and saw that a horse was being hitched up to a two wheeled cart by the driver. Umfrey was beside him giving instructions and then turned to see Ada's approach.

"Very good. Prompt as instructed." Umfrey looked past Ada to member of the church guard, who was waiting just inside. Umfrey motioned to him and the guard slid the gate closed.

Ada was confused, but approached Umfrey. "I'm riding back home in the rubbish cart?"

Umfrey didn't answer, but looked over to another man, that was quickly approaching Ada from behind with a burlap bag. Ada turned to look behind her, just as the man placed it over her head and she began to scream.

"Quickly, before the witch can curse us!" Umfrey commanded.

The guard stepped forward with flanged mace and with a side swing crashed into the young girl's head, crushing her skull and immediately dropping her body to the hay strewn floor.

"Once more!" Umfrey ordered the guard.

The bag covering Ada's head already had the red stain of blood spreading across it as the guard raised the mace overhead and then smashed her head repeatedly. Umfrey ordered him to stop, after a third blow had left the bag a flattened red mess.

"You have done a great service to The Bishop, and will be rewarded for removing the curse this servant of evil had brought upon him. After you bury the witch's body, you shall receive your payment for this service. As I have already said, this is not to be discussed ever again amongst yourselves, or shared with anyone. His Grace wanted me to remind you that as servants of The Mother, She at times asks us to act on her behalf with acts of mercy, as well as brutality when the time calls for it. This was not a girl, but a witch, that was a tormentor who would have eventually poisoned the mind, body, and souls of all that live and work here, after she finished her evil work on The Bishop." Umfrey spoke, while stepping around the lifeless body of Ada, crumbled on the ground.

The driver and his assistant, carefully lifted the girl's body from the ground by the wrists and ankles and laid her onto a sheet of canvas on the stable floor, wrapping her in it and tying the ends tightly. Ada was tossed into the back of the cart with the bag of her worldly possessions, and covered with dirty straw. The two men worked quietly, each bared the feeling of guilt and sadness, though they were doing The Mother's 'bidding.'

The church guard slid the door to the carriage house wide open, and the cart exited with sound of the horse's hooves 'clopping' on the cobblestone pathway. They took the dirt path toward the secluded area off the property, where pit ready to receive Ada's corpse was already dug.

Umfrey stepped out of the carriage house onto the cobblestone driveway, as the church guard pulled the door shut behind them. The guard was dismissed and quickly departed. Umfrey stood alone in silence, in a moment of quiet contemplation.

He looked upwards, to the window of Bennett's bedchamber, where the Bishop stood looking down at him. Umfrey stood for moment, then gave a nod of confirmation. Bennett nodded his head in return, and then drew the tapestry to his bedchamber window shut.

Umfrey took a deep breath, then whistled as he walked the cobblestone path to the gardens to inspect the gardener's work.

26
Mirror Mirror

"Umfrey, you are truly more than a loyal servant. You are a true friend." Bennett's appetite had returned, and despite a week of sleeplessness, he felt slightly reinvigorated. They were enjoying an evening meal of roasted venison in a stew with potatoes and leeks.

"It's good to see your constitution restoring. I believe after a few nights of restful sleep, you will be as you were before. Then we can make plans for you to return to the city, to deliver the Summer's End sermon. It is only a few weeks' time from now." Umfrey consulted his calendar and schedules, which he always brought with him during their evening supper.

"I agree, Umfrey." Bennett reached for his wine, but knocked it over spilling across the table.

"It does appear you need to get that bedrest immediately after dinner tonight. I will have your bedchamber made ready, and a hot bath as well this evening." Umfrey called over for a girl to take care of the spill.

"I will follow that order, doctor." Bennett let out a pained laugh and wiped bread crumbs from his robes onto the floor as he rose.

Umfrey sent for Mrs. Hilde to prepare the bedchamber, as the two concluded their evening, behind closed doors in the parlor.

Umfrey and Bennett, each took a brandy before the fireplace hearth in their overstuffed chairs. It was a low fire, mostly unnecessary during the summer season, but Bennett requested it. He stared into orange flames as they transformed the split wood into red hot coals.

"Is something troubling you, Your Grace?" Umfrey finished his brandy and set the snifter down on the table between them.

"I wonder if the girl is a small part of a greater evil. Perhaps her mother is also of the same ilk. Maybe there is a coven of witches plotting to destroy me and the church." Bennett threw back his drink and set the empty glass on the table.

"Do you propose to send for an inquisitor to investigate? They do have creative ways of rooting out those, that practice the dark arts and shroud their true nature." Umfrey circled the edge of his glass with his forefinger.

"I should sleep on that, Umfrey. Tomorrow, once my body and mind have rested, I will be better able to plan the next course of action."

"Very good, Your Grace. I'm retiring to my chamber, if you have no further need of my services this evening." Umfrey rose and awaited Bennett's dismissal.

"That is all, Umfrey." Bennett waved him away, as he labored to rise from his chair. Slowly straightening his back from a bent position, Bennett sighed and shuffled out of the room.

Mrs. Hilde drew the Bishop's bath, adding salts, herbs, and flower petals, making the room pleasantly aromatic to aid in relaxation. Bennett dropped his clothes to the floor in front of the mirror, and took a moment to examine the marks left on his body from the nightly encounters from the witch.

"The damned devil girl. It was for the best." He shuddered, shuffling to the bath.

With some effort, Bennett eased into the warm waters of the tub and settled in to relax. He leaned back, resting his head with his body submerged, apart from his knobby white knees that broke the surface of the water. Soon Bennett drifted to sleep and slipped under the water as small bubbles rose to the surface.

Immediately, he sat up violently choking on the water. The room was now dark, with only silver moonlight shining through the open window, from which an icy cold wind blew sleet in. The water he was bathing in had also gone cold. He found himself shivering in the tub and when he exhaled his breath formed plumes of steam.

"Mrs. Hilde!" Bennett shouted out in distress. He drew his body into a ball, wrapping his arms tightly around himself and looked wildly about the room. The towel hung nearby, as well as his nightshirt and slippers.

He struggled out of the bath and called again for Mrs. Hilde with no response. Bennett fell to the floor, which had become slick with a thin glaze of ice. Crawling on all fours he grabbed the large towel and wrapped his body in it, and struggled to stand sliding his feet into his slippers.

"Umfrey!" Bennett cried out, fighting to shutter the open window. He locked the latch and shook in the cold. Bennett dropped his wet towel and pulled his nightshirt on.

Bennett opened the door to his bedchamber, but instead there was a thick forest with tangles of thorny briar undergrowth and dead leaves. Furniture was spaced about as it was in his bedchamber. The small shrine on the table that was covered in a mass of burning candles, sat next to the canopy bed. The large, brass mirror leaned against the trunk of a great tree, and the divan stood before it. The small desk and chair were wrapped in the vines of briar, at the edge of the light of the candles. Silvery moonlight filtered through the naked branches of the trees that creaked, as they swayed in the cold wind.

Bennett retreated to the bathroom, but it now occupied the same forest. The tub of cold water was the only feature that remained as well as the open door and its frame.

"Umfrey! Mrs. Hilde!" Bennett continued crying for help.

The wind gusted and sleet was stinging Bennett's face. The candle flames were not extinguished, but the wicks burned sideways with each wind gust. Bennett's fingers and toes were numb, his lips were turning blue, and his breathing increasingly pained from the cold.

Bennet sought shelter in the confines of his canopy bed, even as its curtains fluttered in the wind. Heart racing, he fought his way through the briars that pierced and scratched his ankles, as he stepped through dead leaves coated with an icy glaze.

He reached the bed, and found it seemingly protected from the unnatural environment he now found himself in. He pulled the warm blankets over his head and curled into a tight ball, shivering. Bennett struggled to catch his breath as he felt stabbing pains in his chest, which began constricting.

"Bishop!" The cracking sound of an old crone's voice, whispered through the forest and rang in Bennett's ears.

Bennett prayed to The Mother, under the 'safety' of the blankets, to rebuke the call of the hag. She continued calling out louder, causing him to stumble through the words of the prayer. He continued chanting louder and louder until the, sound of her voice was drowned out.

O Mother deliver us from evil
So that we may serve thee another day
Provide us with the strength
To drive away evil in the coming fray.

Bennett screamed the prayer from under protection of the blankets. Suddenly, he stopped and laid in the still silence, hearing only the sound of his beating heart and labored breathing. Slowly, he peeked out from under the blanket.

Gone was the forest, with cold sleet blowing through the branches. The floor was covered in rugs, rather than leaves and briars. The four walls were around the room once again, and a single candle burned on the pillar on the table. Sweat ran down his forehead and he wheezed with each breath, as he threw the covers off his head and struggled to a sitting position.

Quickly, he scanned the room left to right, nothing seeming out of place. Bennett tossed the blankets aside, planning to make his escape. Hanging his feet over the bed, he saw wet muddy leaves stuck to them and scratches covering his ankles.

"Bishop!" The voice of the crone resonated through the room from behind him.

Bennett spun around in shock, at the sight of the hag dressed in a filthy ragged gray dress. She stood hunched over, with the canvas bag holding the corpse of Ada, slung over her shoulder. The cackling hag threw the muddy blood-stained bundle across the bed effortlessly. Bennett fell off the bed and began crawling away.

Before he could reach the door, he looked up and saw the bundle now leaning against the door, blocking the way. Bennett stopped, and backed in the opposite direction. He rotated his body around and planted his hand on top of the corpse, that was now directly behind him.

He pulled his hand back immediately and clutched at his chest, as the corpse in the bundle lurched and wriggled about against the constrictive bindings. Bennett's wheezing breaths were shorter, feeling as if he were stabbed and the knife was twisting in his chest. He collapsed to the floor facing the bundle, which began to unravel as the corpse wriggled its way out of the ropes tied around it.

Ada's arm emerged from the canvas, fingers clutching into the air. She sat upright and pulled the bag off her head, revealing her crushed bloodied face, with blood-soaked hair hanging to her shoulders. Her lower jaw was missing, and one eye hung from a broken socket, fixed on Bennett, staring into his soul.

Unable to move, Bennet lay on his side frothing at the mouth, all color drained from his face. His eyes fixed on the corpse of Ada, dilated as his body went limp. Bennett exhaled his last breath, as Ada's body crumpled back to the floor.

The cackling hag approached Bennett carrying a large bag made from flayed human skin, stitched together with sinew. A face, with eyes and mouth sewn shut, was part of the patchwork nightmare. "Not so quick, Bishop. He awaits." The hag extended her skinny arm, with hand upturned and long boney fingers raised upwards. She made a clutching motion at Bennett, with her sharp black talons, and pulled toward herself repeatedly.

Bennett's fingers twitched and his legs kicked straight out. His back spasmed and arched, then his head was thrown back. Bennett's body began writhing on the bedroom floor, twisting unnaturally, arms and legs thrashed and pounded the floor, finally rolling onto his back. A bulge formed in his belly and grew larger, as yellow foam poured from his mouth down the sides of his face onto the rug. The bulge expanded his chest, then moved into his neck, and pushed forward, forcing his mouth open unnaturally wider. The top of the head of a creature within him crested.

Bennett's jaw dislocated, stretching apart as its head pushed out. The bald head had distorted features, resembling those of Bennett as a nightmarish caricature. Its bulging eyes opened wide beneath thick white eyebrows, and a bulbous nose flared its nostrils. The mouth of the creature opened as to speak, but words didn't come out. Only a swollen tongue protruded outwards, dripping with slimy drool. The creature closed its eyes tight, and strained as it continued escaping from the body. It twisted and pushed, as the head was followed by a sickly white segmented, grublike body with purple veins beneath its skin, pulsating as it moved.

The hag smiled and continued beckoning Bennett's wicked soul from his body. The living manifestation of Bennett's dark soul, continued pushing its way out, leaving a sticky yellow trail of slime as it inched along the floor. Bennett's body lay still now on the floor, eyes in a dead stare. For all appearances, he looked to have died from a heart attack.

"Into the bag, Bishop!" The hag shook the bag on the ground, summoning the soul worm. Bennett's head gnashed its teeth and inched its way into the bag, until all five feet of its putrid body was coiled up inside. The hag smiled with blackened jagged teeth, as she tied the bag shut, before tossing it over her shoulder. The morning sun filled the room and Bennett's corpse lay on the floor, as Ada's body dissolved away, as if a dream. The hag walked, unhindered by her oversized burden, toward the full-length brass mirror.

"Your Grace, will you be taking your breakfast in bed this morn'? I hope you got some restful sleep last night. We are all worried about you." Mrs. Hilde called out, as she knocked from the other side of the chamber door.

The hag paid no attention to Mrs. Hilde's voice and stood before the mirror. The hag's reflection in the mirror became clouded, as swirling silvery mists appeared and filled the entire mirror.

"You Grace, I brought the tea up for you if you, would like to have a cup before you eat." Mrs. Hilde called out again, from behind the door.

The hag chuckled and stepped into the misty portal, then disappeared into the silvery cloud. The swirling mists quickly melted away, and once again the mirror reflected only Bennett's bedchamber and his lifeless body sprawled across the floor.

"Well, I'm coming in..." Mrs. Hilde opened the bedchamber door.

***

A large mirror, with a frame of solid gold and silver relief sculptures of gargoyle-like creatures and serpents, intertwined about it, leaned against the stone wall in a round tower. The long red and black tapestry was parted on either side of it, as a figure seated back in the shadows stared at it, intently. This mirror showed the bedchamber of bishop's manor. Beyond the divan, the body of Bennett lay on the ground near his canopy bed. Mrs. Hilde entered the chamber, and dropped the tea tray to the floor as she screamed.

The mirror clouded and filled with silvery mists, from which stepped out the hag, with her bag slung over her shoulder. She dropped the bag on the ground as the mists in the mirror dissolved behind her, reflecting her backside and the tower room.

"I present to you, Bishop Bennett." The hag untied the bag and the frightened worm poked its grotesque head out. Its bulging eyes darted back and forth, scanning the room and grimaced, while uncontrollably poking out its enormous tongue.

"Ah, Bennett. Finally, you are a loss for words." Duke Archibald stood from his chair, with the assistance of his cane, and hobbled toward Bennett who was inching his way out of the bag, leaving a trail of slime on the tower floor.

"My payment, your Royal Highness?" The hag smiled and sniggered.

"Yes, yes. A job well done. His is now truly, an unredeemable, corrupted soul. This so-called holy man took the life of an innocent, and was too cowardly to do it by his own hand." The Duke pointed his walking stick to a wooden work table, covered in glass beakers and tubes of various shapes and sizes, mortar and pestle, brazier of smoldering hot coals and many labeled jars containing strange ingredients. In one cleared space, sat a wooden coffer.

The hag ran to the coffer, opening it and cackled with glee, as she ran her long taloned fingers through the gold coins that were loose in it. The Duke stepped up to the cowering soul worm. It grimaced and pushed its tongue out at The Duke, and made the sound of a vomiting cat. Archibald struck the worm on its bald head with his cane, causing it to shake violently and recoil from him.

"You've always been a loathsome fellow, Bennett. Not to worry though. I'm not keeping you for my amusement." The Duke stepped in the sticky putrid smelling slime trail, soiling his fine leather slipper. Becoming irate, the Duke reached out with his boney hand, grabbed the top of Bennett's bald head, and spoke an incantation. "Fulgur!"

Archibald's hand was covered with a crackling blue electric charge that covered the soul worm, lighting its insides up in a quick flash. The grotesque creature writhed about on the floor in agony, its tail end and head thrashing violently. A scorch mark in the shape of the Duke's hand was left behind, along with the smell of scorched flesh and ozone. The worm coiled itself into a pulsating ball of slimy white flesh, burying its face beneath its coils. Two bulbous eyes, barely reminiscent of Bennett's, peeked out in fear.

"Secure this foul thing in the cage. I can't have it leaving a disgusting slime trail everywhere it slithers." The Duke pointed his cane at an iron cage, that once held animals used for experimentation. The bottom was filled with rotten straw, and a few bones left behind by its former occupants.

Across the room on a finely carved wooden perch, a large raven made a low gurgling croaking noise and flapped its wings.

"No Barnabas, he is not for eating." The Duke shuffled over to the raven, patting its back, as the hag stuffed Bennett into a tight cage, securing it with a large iron padlock. "Bennett is going to be our guest here for only a short while. I intend to keep him safe and as comfortable as he deserves in the meanwhile."

Barnabas made a harsh grating sound, then spoke in a pompous voice. "Very well then."

27
Hostile Hospitality

"He's dead!" Juliana sat up screaming.

Randall and Izzy were startled awake, from their own restless slumber, beneath the deep scar carved into the side of the cliff face. Flynn looked in from the boulder he was hiding behind during his watch. They took shelter, after putting distance between themselves and the surviving crew of the *Lady Anne* that night. The only thing they had with them, was what they had on them as they swam to shore.

"Who's dead?" Randall asked, propping himself up on his elbows.

"The Bishop. I saw it in my dream. It seemed so real." Juliana was visibly shaken.

"Do you think it was more than a dream?" Randall asked

"It was different. I saw him tormented, by a hag with the corpse of a young girl, until he died. I believe the same girl I had met in the convent, before I escaped. She stole his soul in the form of those damned to the Hells." Juliana replied.

"Good riddance to bad rubbish. Bennett is one less prick that I must worry about coming after me." Randall arose with a little trouble. Sleeping on the hard ground, with a rock for a pillow, made for a stiff back.

"I'm hungry." Izzy yawned.

"Well, we may have some problems here. I climbed to the top to get a better look around at sunrise. here is nothing around as far as I could see, other than rough terrain, and little desert scrub. Attempting to travel across this without supplies will be impossible. Especially in the heat of the day." Flynn reported.

"What are you suggesting?" Randall asked.

"We will need to go back to the ship wreck and see if any supplies washed ashore. Then we follow the coast westward. I don't believe the crew will be a problem for us, even if they have objections." Flynn patted the hilt of his rapier.

Paul Wolff

"I agree." Juliana shook her head. She was only halfway paying attention, lost in thought over the vision.

"The fat man better had drowned. He was nasty." Izzy reminded the others.

"I'll take care of that one for you, Izzy." Flynn nodded.

"No, he's mine. He tried to kill Arnold." Izzy frowned.

"We aren't too far from the ship wreck, and I assume they set up camp near it to gather supplies. We should make our way there and work something out with them, before the sun is high overhead." Flynn suggested.

"Before we go, let's pray to The Mother for guidance and support. Please join me." Juliana asked the others.

"Okay, Juliana!" Izzy was the only one showing enthusiasm.

Flynn shook his head reluctantly.

"I'm going for a piss." Randall excused himself from the upcoming sermon.

Stepping out from under the cliff, he was at the bottom of a wide and deep rocky gorge. It was carved from several millennia of erosion, from an immense river that once emptied into the sea. A small stream of water was now all that trickled over its smooth rocks. Stepping carefully over the water, through some green scrub, and around a few dwarf-trees, Randall found a private area to take care of business.

The cliff faces exposed sedimentary layers of geological history Randall studied, as he relieved himself. Squinting, he was able to make out evidence of fossilized remains of ancient cephalopods imbedded in the rock. He thought to himself, it would be worth studying a little further in detail in the future, as he pulled up his breeches.

Turning, he looked up at the cloudless sky as the sun peaked over the jagged tops of the rocky ravine. To get a better lay of the land, he navigated his way up the path they had descended the previous evening.

"Randall, where are you going?" Flynn called out from below.

"Just wanting to look before we depart. I couldn't see much of anything last night." Randall's voice echoed through the gorge.

Flynn shot back a glare which Randall couldn't see, but somehow felt burning a hole through him.

Pulling himself to the top, he scanned the alien landscape. Pillar like rock formations, formed from years of erosion, stood at attention, while hills made of sheer jagged rock faces jutted straight up from the earth. Fairly flat expanses acted as pathways through the labyrinth of rock, that had minute traces of greenery in the form of short grasses, that thrived in the sandy, rocky soil.

154

The pangs of hunger were stating their case, as Randall's belly growled. Luckily, the small stream had provided a supply of fresh water, but a couple of eggs would've been nice to start the morning. Standing with hands on his hips, he scanned the area, wishfully searching for a vendor hawking loaves of freshly baked pandemain bread. Instead, he saw a scaley collared lizard with a tail longer than its body, sunning himself on a boulder. Possible breakfast? Maybe Flynn would know how to clean and cook it.

The lizard lazily looked over at him from his vantage point on the boulder. Randall squatted down behind a stunted shrub to hide, rather ineffectively. The lizard flicked its tongue and disregarded him as a non-threat.

He went through his spell repertoire to decide the best one for the job. In practice he had previously used one to take out a large hairy spider that was crawling across his window. It killed the spider, but smashed the pane of glass it was crawling on as well. Nothing to break out here at least.

He sprang up, and with forefinger pointed at the lizard and thumb raised upwards, he spoke, "Flatus illum!"

Three glowing darts of force simultaneously erupted from his fingertip, and took three separate arcing paths of which all three converged striking the lizard. The force of the impact blew the lizard apart, leaving a red stain on the boulder. Only the tail squirmed, as it rolled to the ground.

"Shite!" Randall proclaimed, as he examined the tip of his finger surprised.

He walked toward the boulder to examine the remains. Disappointed with the outcome of his hunt, he was quite impressed with the increased power of his spell. The sound of rocks tumbling to the ground caused him to spin, to face the disturbance.

Sliding down from a red rock formation, a humanoid no more than four feet tall and of slight build, landed on its feet and approached with a spear pointed at Randall. The goblyn's long ears protruded from his leather skull cap, listening for Randall's companions as his pointy nose sniffed the air.

"Weez needz to take him to zee Queen." Another goblyn called out, in a high-pitched voice.

Randall spun around, to see another pair of the creatures slink from behind another rock formation. One was wearing a great helm, that was sized for a large man, and armed with a nicked-up broadsword. The other approached with a flail, of which the ball of spikes swung freely at the end of its chain.

"Eez alone. Notz too smart." The goblyn armed with the flail, cheerfully proclaimed.

"Stay back! I'm a powerful wizard! I'll take you down like I did that reptilian beast on the rock!" Randall threatened, with his hands poised for spell casting to look threatening and fearsome.

"Heyz youz guyz. He sayz eez a weezard. Comez out andz help!" The helmed goblyn called out, and was immediately answered by a dozen screaming goblyns jumping down from their rocky hiding places, menacingly waving a variety of weapons. One pair of goblyns carried a net to subdue Randall.

Goblyns closed in around him, with their high-pitched maniacal laughter and shrieks of enthusiasm. They rushed from all directions, but in one direction there was only a solitary goblyn coming toward him, with a pair of hand axes hooting a goblyn war cry. Randall ran in his direction, then stopped to cast the same spell that had obliterated the lizard moments ago.

"Flatus illum!" He shouted the incantation, as he made the gesture with his hand once again. Three glowing darts of arcane force flew from the tip of his finger and struck their target. The goblyn's legs instantly locked up, and he fell face first onto the rocky ground, dead. Randall continued running again toward the opening, which was the opposite direction from the camp.

"Hez long legz makez him too fast!" Complained the one fat goblyn, lagging in the rear of the charge.

"Stopz him, youz!" The great helmed goblyn ordered a warty orange skinned goblyn carrying a bola, into action.

"Iz gotz him!" The orange goblyn said confidently, as he swung the weapon overhead. Squinting his beady black eyes, he timed his release of the bola. Flying across the landscape, it arced through air as it rotated.

The bola entangled Randall's legs, dropping him to the ground. Goblyns quickly converged on Randall, dancing around him in glee. Randall rolled over, holding his hands defensively, to block the beatdown by his cruel captors. Two goblyns tossed the net over, him as the great helmed goblyn pushed his way to the front.

"Youz iz prisonerz of the beautifulz Queenz Gronk and Brack." The helmed goblyn proclaimed, with his broadsword pointed in Randall's face.

"Queens Gronk and Brack?" Randall repeated the names.

A team of six goblyns hoisted Randall overhead, marching double time, away from the gorge. He was tightly entangled, and his captors were not being very gentle with their handling of him.

"Wait just a minute! You don't want to do this! I can-" Randall was cut off, as the helmed goblyn knocked him unconscious with the hilt of his sword.

"Theez weezard guyz talkz too much. Youz two stayz behind. Watch thoze otherz down therez. That dark skinz one mayz be troublez. I sawz him become big ratz." The helmed goblyn lead the foraging party back to the lair.

Two remained behind, grumbling while taking up positions up in the rocks once again.

***

Randall's head throbbed, as he struggled to open his eyes. How long he was out, he wasn't sure. Possibly hours. He was laying on the ground in total darkness. He was not alone, though, as he heard whispers of others talking amongst themselves. He lay silent listening to the muffled voices, discerning that he was not surrounded by the entire goblyn tribe. The voices were other humans and a few were familiar. It was the crew from the *Lady Anne*.

He felt about on his person, and his pouch was still on him. He carefully opened it up and took a quick inventory with his fingers. It seemed his reagents were still intact. The stupid goblyns probably didn't loot it, as he was carrying no coin upon himself.

"Hello... Uh, where are we?" Randall squeaked out.

"Eh, sounds like he's awakened." A voice in the dark whispered.

"We're in these little bastard's cave, in a holding pen. They captured us on the shore while we were setting up camp." Another voice whispered.

"How many of us are in here?" Randall asked.

"Including you, that would make eight. The others were killed on the beach as they tried to escape." He recognized this to be the voice of the captain.

"You made it to shore!" Randall said, surprised.

"Yes, broke my arm in the fall when the ship ran aground. We managed to get a splint on it before they attacked. We wouldn't be in this situation if it weren't for you." The captain was holding a grudge.

"What are they going to do to us?" Randall asked.

"I imagine feed us all to that queen of theirs eventually, like they did to poor old Nigel," called out another voice.

"They e-e-eat people?" Randall was beginning to panic.

"Well, that queen of theirs does, at least." The captain responded.

"We must get out of here! Do they not have any light down here?" Randall said, frantically.

"I reckon they see in the dark as well as we see in the light, the little creeps, those goblyns. When they brought us down here there was a large cavern that was covered in glowing fungus. It was lit up as if it were a purple twilight sky. That's where that queen was. She ate Nigel raw, after bashing his brains in." The captain said, glumly.

"Shite! Okay, we need some light." Randall felt around on the ground around him for anything he could cast his spell on. Finally, his fingers wrapped around a thick stick on the cave floor, and he fumbled around in his pouch for the material reagent.

"Et erit lux!" Randall found that what he though was a stick, was in fact a human femur bone, which now glowed with a bright blue light. Looking around, he saw the small chamber had many random bones strewn about. The captain and remaining members of his crew, leaned against each other and the walls of the natural cave chamber. All looked surprised, as they raised their hands to shield their eyes from Randall's magic light.

"He's in league with devils like that demon girl! A practitioner of black magic!" The fat sailor, that was responsible for all the trouble to begin with, called out. Surprisingly he had survived the shipwreck, and the wounds inflicted on him the previous night. Bloodied bandages torn from his shirt covered the bite and stab wound, which were healing quickly.

"Enough Fat Robb! What other tricks can you do that can help us escape?" The old salt of a captain was shocked, but hopeful.

"I'm not a common street performer! I am a wizard!" Randall stood up, proclaiming his professional title.

He held the glowing femur up to survey the chamber. The natural room had at one time had cave formations that were removed by the goblyns years ago. Stumps were all that remained on the low ceiling and floor of stalactites and stalagmites. The entrance was bricked up, and a thick door, of wood with reinforced steel bands, blocked the exit. Goblyns were quite clever, able to craft items from things they had scavenged or stolen in raids. This door was made from planks and hardware of a previous shipwreck.

Randall glanced out the barred hole cut in the door, and found there were no guards stationed outside. The passageway beyond looked to be a combination of natural cavern and worked stone, as goblyns also happened to be expert miners.

"No problem. I got this!" The crew all rose to their feet and watched Randall with curiosity.

"What are you going to do?" The captain asked.

"Recludo velox!" Randall spoke the incantation, causing the cell door's padlock to open and drop to the cave floor.

Randall pushed on the door and it squeaked open. The men looked at one another, then filed into the hall beyond. Randall held the light femur into the hall, which only cast dim blue light forty feet ahead, before fading into darkness. There was an empty guard post up ahead.

Randall led the way with the light, as the eight ran down the hallway double file. The unoccupied guard room had crude table and benches fashioned from driftwood and other materials, and the floor had filthy sleeping pallets scattered in all corners. An old barrel was filled with a mishmash of old rusted swords, warped spears, and spiked clubs. Each member of the *Lady Anne* crew claimed a weapon.

A small gang of goblyns stormed into the room with weapons drawn. The puny creatures backed away as they saw the men all armed, unlike when they ambushed them on the beach.

"Theyz escaped! Goz tell zee otherz!" A green faced goblyn, acting as the leader, shouted to one of the fellows in the back.

The captain ran forward, swinging a spiked club at the leader's head. The force of the blow sent him into the wall crashing into a heap, dead. The other men, emboldened by their captain, rushed in to engage the remaining three goblyns, while the fourth retreated down the hallway raising the alarm of escaping prisoners. Randall stayed back, holding the light aloft.

Two goblyns fiercely pushed their short spears deep into the belly of one of the sailors, and the other swung his short wildly at one of the men who ducked his swing. Fat Robb rushed the two before they could pull their spears out of the dying man. Crashing onto them, he pinned them on the floor, their ribs snapping under his weight. He finished them off, snapping each of their necks where they lay, broken on the floor. The sword wielding goblyn was quickly dispatched, with a thrust of a short sword into his chest.

"Get that little bastard!" The captain ordered, as the one goblyn was putting distance between them.

The entire group gave chase to the single fleeing goblyn. The gap was narrowing between themselves and the screaming humanoid, through the winding passageway that was widening as it ascended. The goblyn didn't attempt to duck down any of the many side tunnels that broke from the main path, to lose the group. Fat Robb, who was falling behind the group, was the first to hear footsteps behind him. Glancing over his shoulder he saw more pursuing goblyn's.

"More buggers are coming behind us!" He weezed, picking up his pace.

Randall stopped as the others caught the fleeing goblyn and pummeled it into a bloody mess. He withdrew the last bit of spider silk from his pouch and made the dramatic gestures with his hand, while speaking the incantation to complete the spell. "Aranea telam ingurgito!"

The sticky mass of webs formed across the cavern walls and several feet down the passageway, trapping some and blocking the rest of the pursuing goblyns. The crew men and captain looked on for a moment with awe, at the young man who they dismissed on the ship. The once helpless lad, proved himself again to be more than he appeared.

Angry goblyns struggled in the webs, as others backed out of the passageway to find alternate routes through the cavern. The men pressed forward, with Randall once again holding forth his magic source of light.

The tunnel opened into a massive cavern, that spanned hundreds of feet across and two stories in height. Randall's light did not illuminate the far reaches of the cavern, but large patches of bioluminescent fungi grew on the damp of ceiling, giving off an eerie green glow. A large body of clear water, fed by underground springs, had an arched stone bridge of goblyn construction allowing passage to the other side. Natural ledges around the perimeter of the cavern swarmed with goblyn, children watching the men with curiosity.

"Over that bridge is the way they brought us in here. There's another cavern past this one, where we were taken through, that their 'queen' was occupying." The captain said, catching his breath, ignoring the pain in his splinted arm.

"How hard could it possibly be to get past a goblyn queen? Does she have a large force of guards? We are all armed and these guys are puny, even to me." Randall felt confident.

"She is no goblyn. Damned, two headed giant. Craziest thing I have ever seen." Another sailor informed Randall of his false assumption.

"Yeah, and its more than twice as tall as any of us. It could easily kill all of us." Fat Robb added.

"Look! Across the bridge." The captain pointed with his club at a small group of goblyns crossing the bridge, approaching cautiously with weapons lowered.

The men raised their mismatched collection of weapons, preparing for more nasty fighting. Randall looked about the cavern and saw, that from the passage behind them, the other goblyns had made it through his web barricade. The goblyns pushed through looking a little crisp around the edges, having lit the webs up to burn them away.

"They're going to surround us!" Randall shouted, out as half the men turned to face the goblyns from the rear.

The helmed goblyn pushed his way to the front of others at the top of the bridge. He opened the rusty visor on the dented great helm and looked down on the men at the foot of the bridge.

"Youz guyz hold it right there." All the goblyns stopped advancing, and held their ground on his order.

"Uh, yes... sir?" Randall wasn't quite sure how to address the small humanoid, that had an unusual amount of hairy moles and warts on its face, even by goblyn standards.

"Weez make dealz. Youz help uz and weez let youz go." The helmed goblyn smiled a mouthful of sharp yellow teeth, and shook his head furiously.

The men all looked at each other, assuming any deal would probably end in treachery. Randall stepped forward with the light held aloft, looking around at all the creatures in the cavern. He too was not trusting of any goblyn that had captured him and planned on serving him up as the main dish to their queen.

"Uh, why the change of... heart? I'm not sure how you can expect us to help you after what you did to us." Randall looked around the cavern at the goblyns on the floor and the other hundred safely watching along the ledges.

"Weez needz beautifulz Queen gone. She tookz overz goblyn's homez almost one full moonz cycle ago. She killz our Boss. Stompz him flat like cavez cricketz. Toldz us she was Queenz andz that weez obeyz her, orz else. Weez catch fishez and crabz, then she makez goblyns go hungryz eating all our foodz. Weez see youz mighty weezard. Perhapz youz can turnz her intoz a fishez with your magicz?" The helmed goblyn's visor crashed shut. He quickly opened it, waiting for a response.

The men looked at Randall and whispered amongst themselves. Randall did not have the powers of transmutation, so the only thing he was sure of, was that he personally could be transformed into the Queen's lunch without the aid of magic.

"Well, boy? Tell them you accept. We won't get out of here alive fighting all of them." The captain ordered.

"You guys are backing me up, right?" Randall turned to the men, looking for their support.

"We will have your back, boy." The captain patted Randall on his back.

"Okay, we will do it. Before we do, did any of you bring a barrel of Grummandy beer back from the ship wreck?" Randall looked to the goblyns with hope in his eyes.

"Beautifulz Queenz drankz allz zee beerz weez findz. Shez drinkz from barrelz likez tankardz. Givez goblynz nonz." The helmed goblyn's visor slammed shut again.

28
Her Majesty

R andall led the crew of the *Lady Anne* through the subterranean passage by his magic blue light. Along the way goblyns ducked into the darkness of side passages, as the group advanced forward.

Goblyns are disgusting creatures. They lived in their own filth, with a total disregard of sanitation and their décor was equally grim and crude. The walls of the cavern were decorated with primitive goblyn art scrawled across the walls like bad graffiti. Bones of creatures that were past meals, were mounted on the walls and strung from the ceiling. Along the way, more than once, Randall trod through a fresh steaming pile of goblyn scat.

The smell of the place was sickening, but Randall concentrated on his current task. Ridding the place of their so-called queen. She must be something quite dreadful to behold, if she could take over an entire tribe of goblyns. Of course, these creatures are more of a nuisance than a danger, if you are even minimally armed to fight them.

The passage widened and around the ceiling patches of glowing phosphorescent fungus shed a dim purple light. Intermingled with it were strange glow worms that shed a twinkling blue light, as they inched across the ceiling like a field of stars. A giant glowing beetle darted across the passage in front of them and climbed the wall to hide in a crevice.

The captain motioned for them to stop. "We must be getting close to the cavern I was telling you about. The glow from all the strange critters and fungi light up its ceiling as if it were the sky at twilight."

"What is yer plan lad?" An older, white-haired member of the crew addressed Randall. The others turned and looked at Randall.

"I, uh... I have an enchantment that I will cast that should make her believe we are friends, and let us go without a fight." Randall felt confident of his mastery of the spell, which helped him escape from the assassins back in Port Gwynn.

"Ho, ho, ho! Those goblyns will be rather disappointed with their 'queen' remaining on her throne, after we walk out." Fat Robb chortled at the thought of a double-cross.

"Exactly!" Randall was not exactly sure how or if the spell would work on a non-human subject. He assumed it would be mostly human, aside from the two heads.

The group advanced cautiously through the ever-widening passage, illuminated by all the glowing organisms. Randall cast away the glowing femur. If need be, he could recast it on another handy object.

They reached an 'antechamber' to the 'royal throne room.' Goblyn guards were absent from their post. The tables and benches looked to have been quickly abandoned. Randall assumed they would return after the upcoming conflict was resolved.

Randall was the first to enter the 'throne room.' Just as the captain described, it was lit up like the twilight sky. The ceiling to the place was almost fifty feet above them and the cavern stretched out hundreds of feet. Glistening cave formations, running ceiling to floor, looked like supporting pillars for a palace. Goblyn miners had removed many of the formations, so that the remaining were evenly spaced and levelled out the floor in much of the cavern. Even with architectural improvements, it was quite the noisome space, since poor sanitation standards were the same in the 'royal throne room.'

"What I remember was there were several tunnels that lead out of this chamber, but the one we were brought through is on the exact opposite side of where we are. Their queen's 'throne' faces it. There won't be any way to avoid her." The captain filled Randall in.

"Yeah, the throne is carved directly from the rock in the center of this place." Another sailor chimed in.

"Perhaps we can sneak up behind her and I can get my spell off before she is any the wiser." Randall said, thinking positively.

"That would be most advantageous." The captain agreed.

"You go ahead first, and we'll follow at a distance." Fat Robb suggested. The others all immediately agreed.

"Um, yeah. That makes... sense." Randall looked over his shoulder at the men who waited behind in the ante-chamber. They waved him on, as he momentarily hesitated.

Almost dead center of the chamber, at the highest point, Queen Gronk and Brack's throne was carved from the remains of a white dolomite cave formation. It was a very large affair, that glistened and reflected the purple light of the glowing fungus on the cavern roof. Piles of fishbones, clam shells, and crustaceans were in tall mounds around the stone chair. The mound of garbage was at its highest by the throne, with a walking path leading down to the main floor.

The queen was currently being attended to by two of her goblyn subjects. One female goblyn was standing in the seat of the throne behind her, rubbing the neck of Brack, which was now dozing and snoring loudly. A male goblyn was at the base of the throne trying to massage a massive, wide, cracked, calloused foot and doing a poor job of it. Gronk grunted with displeasure, much to the masseuses' dismay.

"Sorryz beautifulz queenz. Iz tryz something elsez." The goblyn changed his attack, which seemed to improve the queen's disposition only slightly.

Queen Gronk and Brack enjoyed the life of luxury ruling over the goblyns, after taking over their home when she stumbled upon them seeking shelter in the cave. They gave up the fight, after she slew their 'big boss' and all his bodyguards in a battle in the throne room. The goblyn boss's smashed body still lay rotting on the ground where she slew him, as a warning to all the goblyns that she was now 'boss.' Their "beautiful queen."

If anything, she smelled worse than anything else in the cave. A warm curdled milk bouquet was noted when approaching within twenty yards of her. Her unwashed body appeared gray as those of her ilk never bathed. Her large engorged belly rested on her lap, and large breasts parted ways on either side of the belly. Each head had large tusks protruding from her jutting lower jaws. The long black hair was braided and tied back on Gronk's head and on Brack's head greasy hair hang loose and matted. Her only article of clothing was the vermin infested wrapping made of uncured animal hides, that acted as her queenly robes. Within easy reach were her two clubs, fashioned from the trunks of trees, wrapped with bands of iron spikes.

Gronk rested her head on her big meaty fist as Brack's head hung down drooling with her maw gaping open. Gronk was appearing restless.

"Gronk bored! Sing song!" Gronk gave the masseuse on the floor a light punt, that sent him rolling deep into a pile of fish bones.

"Yez beautifulz Queenz. Iz serenadez youz with famouz goblynz madrigal!" He brushed debris off his ragged clothing. Stepping forward, the goblyn pushed out his chest, held his spindly arms to his side, and threw his head back to spew forth the song.

Goblynz goez to warz
Breakz downz fortrez doorz
Killz the menz with ourz swordz
Wez delcarez ourselvez overlordz
La Lala La La

Fa Fala La La
Lo Lola La...

The madrigal was interrupted as Brack angrily crushed the singing goblyn flat, under the giant club with a loud thud. The goblyn girl massaging Brack's shoulders covered her mouth to stifle a scream.

"Why you do dat?" Gronk looked at Brack angrily.

"Noise wake me. Something so puny need be quiet." Brack spat on the dead goblyn.

"Yeah, you right. He no good sing." Gronk kicked away the dead goblyn into a pile of empty clam shells.

Randall had just sneaked within range of The Queen when Brack dispatched goblyn. He dropped to the floor, covering his face with his hands in a childlike attempt to hide. He peeked between his fingers toward the antechamber to see what his "comrades" were doing. The men had disappeared. Frantically, he looked around the cavern and saw no one else.

Randall wanted to retreat to the antechamber before he was noticed. Fat Robb poked his head from his hiding place behind a pillar with the glowing humerus bone. Randall furiously shook his head and waved his hands 'no' as Fat Robb lobbed it toward Randall.

The bone flew across the cavern end over end, crashing down a few feet from Randall into a pile of stacked bones. Brack looked over her shoulder hearing the noise, believing it was noisier goblyns coming to disturb her. Randall stood crouched over as still as he could, but Gronk spotted him immediately bathed in the bright magic blue light.

"Puny human!" Gronk roared, as she smashed the goblyn girl flat against the back of her throne.

The Queen grabbed a club in each hand, eyeing Randall, who stood shaking with fear. He saw the men were using the distraction to run for the exit. It worked well, as The Queen was oblivious to their presence and focused on him.

Both heads bellowed out a roar that shook the cavern floor, but Randall realized that his knees were buckling. She raised both clubs over her head, madly waving them, as she lumbered around the throne wading through the piles of refuse.

Randall gathered his wits and remembered his spell. He motioned the blowing of a kiss with his hand and spoke the arcane words. "Amicum gratissimum!"

The Queen halted her advance, both heads looked at Randall, then each other with confused looks on their faces. Brack shook her head, furiously attempting to rid her small mind of Randall's enchantment. Gronk furrowed her brow, then dropped the club in her hand.

Randall turned to run, but Gronk caught him in her big meaty hand. Randall struggled to free himself, but she lifted him up to get a better look at her prize.

Brack held tightly onto her club and her eyes narrowed focusing on Randall. "Yum yum, eat him up!" She licked her chops, making a 'thuup' sound, when she sucked her tongue back in.

Gronk held Randall up and away from Brack. "No, he my little friend. You eat flat goblyns."

"No, he taste better. Give me leg." Brack demanded Gronk stop playing with their food.

Brack threw down her club and grabbed for Randall, who was held out of her reach. Each head of The Queen controlled one half of its body independently of the other. Randall's enchantment was successful on Gronk, but proved failed on Brack. Now the creature that had always worked cooperatively regarding its own body, was at odds with itself.

The Queen spun around in circles, as Brack chased after Randall and Gronk held him out of her reach. Gronk's grip tighten around him, making it a struggle to breathe. Randall grew dizzy, as the spinning giantess acted like a dog chasing its own tail. He knew this would be the end.

Suddenly, Brack smashed her fist into Gronk's face.

"Now you gone and done it! I pound you into mush!" Gronk tossed Randall aside, and then punched Brack in her nose, flattening it and letting loose a flow of blood.

Randall fell on a pile of rotting crab parts, cushioning his landing. Bits and pieces of shells were stuck to him as he hastily made his escape.

"You dumb, dumb! Let lunch go!" Brack pointed at Randall, who was running to the exit passage.

"Friend, you come back. You rub shoulder!" Gronk called out to Randall, who ignored the order.

Randall was almost at the exit passage, when The Queen jumped in front to block him. He stopped just out of her reach and backed away. The Queen slowly approached him, with arms spread wide and the big sausage-like fingers wiggling.

"Yum yum, eat him up!" Brack smacked her lips.

"No, friend rub shoulder first, then eat him up!" Gronk made kissy sounds.

Randall stopped moving and looked at the exit passage between her legs. He spoke the incantation that got him out of a tricky bind on more than one occasion "Ut hic de mecum in infernum."

There was a brilliant flash that vanished, then reappeared at the edge of the exit passage with another flash of light. Randall looked over his shoulder at The Queen who was rubbing the spots before her eyes.

"Where he go?" Gronk was dumbfounded.

"You should have give me leg. Then he not run away." Brack was angry their meal had escaped.

Randall ran down the dark passageway, as the glowing fungus and other creatures with bioluminescence were encountered less frequently to light the way. He resorted to his light spell on a rock once again to light his way. The blue light showed him the way through, as he could feel the grade of the passage ascending more steeply than before. The air had also become fresher and the scent of goblyn filth was mostly behind him. Not much further, and then he'd be to the surface and could find his way back to the camp. If Izzy, Flynn, and Julianna hadn't left him behind.

The body of a goblyn lay on the ground in front of him, clutching a stab wound to the belly. The *Lady Anne* crew had passed this way. A little further on and he heard the voices of frantic goblyns and men shouting at one another. Randall sped up his pace and found the goblyns and the men, in a standoff in a large guardroom.

The men had the forethought to harvest some of the glowing fungus to light their way, so they weren't blindly feeling their way through. However, this final hurdle to make their escape was unexpected. These goblyns weren't part of the deal maker's group, and were loyal to their 'beautiful queen.' Another of the crew of the *Lady Anne* lay on the ground dead with several bodies of dead goblyns. The remaining guards were in position behind overturned tables, with spears pointed over them to defend.

"You bastards left me!" Randall shouted at the men.

"Look! Our wizard has rejoined us! He defeated your Queen! Let us pass or he will turn you all into slugs with his great magic!" The captain threatened the goblyns.

"Youz shutz up! Beautifulz Queenz will grindz youz all up intoz pastez." A goblyn taunted back.

"I told you; our wizard defeated her!" The captain repeated.

"Well, I, er um..." Randall didn't really want to break the news at this point, but there were the loud sounds of footsteps and the ground was shaking.

"Oh, shite!" Fat Robb's ears picked up on the sound about the same time as Randall. "Greatz Beautifulz Queenz comez to savez uz!" One goblyn cried out, and the others all joined in hooting with joy.

Queen Gronk and Brack charged to the entrance of the chamber, stopping abruptly to assess the situation. She was breathing heavily, had broken a sweat, pangs of hunger made her belly rumble, and a puny human had outsmarted her. Both heads looked around the room, where the men were now scattering for cover.

"You! Where you think you going?" Brack pointed a fat finger in Randall's direction.

"Hey! Where do all they think they going?" Gronk mentioned the other men to Brack.

"Right! All the yum yums try run away. You stupid goblyns don't let them go!" Brack commanded the goblyn guards.

Randall was down to one last spell that he thought may be effective in the given situation. He had studied it many times before and always kept it in his repertoire for emergency situations just as the conjured webs did. He reached into his component pouch and withdrew a handful of dried skunk leaves that were wrapped in linen.

He held the dried skunk leaves before him and waved them in one hand and pinched his nose closed with the other. Then he spoke the incantation to complete the spell's formula. "Artificium eul et facies nidore mea pedibus!"

The skunk leaves in his hand were consumed in a flash of green flame, disappearing into a puff of smoke. A huge thick cloud of green swirling noxious vapors was conjured, that enveloped, and obscured The Queen from his sight. The smell of rotten eggs, boiling cabbage, burning feces and the musky scent of a skunk's spray, hit everyone's olfactory sensory units.

The smell was horrendous, but did not harm all those catching a whiff. However, The Queen was in the center of the magically summoned cloud of enchanted stench. Sounds of her coughing, then gagging and wheezing boomed throughout the cavern. She then stumbled out of the cloud, hunched over, holding her belly with one hand as the other hand covered Brack's mouth. The magic even affected a creature as foul smelling as her.

"Ugh, me no feel so good!" Gronk was a little green in the face, as she started heaving like a cat coughing up a hairball. Suddenly, she puked up her guts on the floor.

Brack saw Gronk emptying her stomach, then immediately followed suit, coughing up chunks, that ran down her chin onto her breasts. She became weak in the knees and reached for the wall for support. Once again Gronk's jaws parted like a giant yawn and a fountain of stomach bile emptied over Fat Robb's head, who had the misfortune of taking cover in a crevice on that wall.

"Boys, let's get her!" The captain shouted to the others, and they all rushed the sickened giantess, as the green cloud of sickness behind her, swirled and billowed in place.

The men had the advantage in her weakened state and slashed, stabbed and bludgeoned her legs, until she could no longer stand. When she hit the floor, she struggled to fend off their attacks. Finally, the captain was able to push his way up to Brack's head and began striking her in the face with the spiked club. Another sailor drove a spear deep into Gronk's throat, leaning onto it, until it pushed it out through the other side. Gronk's arm went limp, and after several more blows into Brack's head, she was finished.

The men cheered their victory and looked over to the barricade set by the goblyns. The goblyns wisely abandoned their position, and fled down the exit passage.

"Well done lad! Sorry about that back there. We knew you would handle her." The captain started with the apologies. The other members of the crew followed suit, except for Fat Robb. He was quite upset, and picking out chunks of The Queen's final meal out of his patchy beard.

"Let's get out of here. I need to get back to my friends." Randall was very concerned that if there were to be any more trouble, he had no spell book with him to study.

"Looksee here. Them goblyns have some of our food!" The gray-haired sailor pointed to a small barrel and a crate that contained some of the rations recovered in the shipwreck. Salted and dried meats and ships biscuits.

"At least we have some food for travelling." The captain said.

"Maybe more washed to shore since that night." The gray-haired sailor replied.

"Something's coming down the hall!" Fat Robb ears pricked up, as he sniffed the air.

"Maybe those goblyns are coming back. Get ready!" The captain said.

"Hullo! You in there." A familiar voice called out of the darkness.

"Flynn!" Randall shouted happily.

A pure white light illuminated the tunnel. Juliana walked in, holding a glowing stone she had cast divine magic on. Izzy and Flynn stood on either side of her, taking in the scene in the room. The magic stench cloud was dissipating, and the Queen lay dead on the floor amidst the bodies of slain goblyns. The surviving members of the *Lady Anne* stood together with Randall. Fat Robb stepped back from the others in a glaze of stomach grease as Izzy looked at him. She drew her finger across her throat, which Fat Robb understood he would need eyes in the back of his head.

Juliana stepped into the room first and smiled at Randall. "When you didn't return to camp, we knew trouble must have found you. Flynn was able to track the goblyns back to the cave; after discovering quite the little fight you must have had at the top of the gorge. A few others came after us when we checked the body of the one you had killed."

"Yes, one managed to escape and we followed him back here. We spent hours watching the cave entrance and then we saw a bunch of those little bastards fleeing. That's when we knew you were in there causing them some trouble." Flynn said with a laugh.

"I ran in first Mr. Randall. I was wanting to sneak in to find you, but they made me wait." Izzy announced.

"Those rat demons are the reason we are where we are now. Keep away from us!" Fat Robb said, pointing his short sword in Izzy's direction.

"Lower that blade Robb. Now as I recall, there was no quarrel with these people, until you found yourself alone with the little one below deck." The gray-haired sailor shouted at him.

"We would be safer travelling together, until we get out of this wild territory. You will not have any trouble from any of my companions. I trust we could expect the same from your men?" Juliana addressed the captain, as she eyed his arm that was in a splint.

"Aye, I agree. Let's leave this hell hole before anything else comes after us. You two carry Colin's body out. We'll at least give him a proper burial."

Izzy was snooping around the body of the giantess queen, her nose turning up at her stink. She looked at the hides around her waist and discovered a crude pouch made of stitched animal skins on a rope belt.

"What did you find Izzy?" Flynn asked.

"Looks like she has something in her bag. Maybe some loot!" Izzy said excitedly.

Flynn cut the pouch loose and handed it to Izzy, who went rifling through it as the men gathered the barrel, crate, and their fallen comrade. Fat Robb made himself scarce.

"Oh look! Shiny things!" She pulled out a handfuls of gold, silver and copper coins stamped with the face of King Ernald I. There were interesting rocks, a large chunk of sea glass and a few trophy skulls that looked to be human. There was a fine curved dagger, with dried bits of meat stuck to it the queen used as the royal toothpick. The last item she retrieved was a long ornately carved stick, of which one end was covered in thick orange wax with a few hairs stuck in it.

"Yuck! I found her ear scratcher." Izzy was about to toss it away.

"Wait, what do you have there?" Randall called to Izzy, as Juliana was handing him his book and satchel she carried for him.

"You want this?" Izzy asked Randall.

"Maybe, you keep the dagger." Randall raised an eyebrow, as Izzy handed him The Queen's ear picker.

Randall inspected it under his blue light and noted that the carved stick was more than just a giant's tool for ear wax removal, even though it seemed to do a fine job of it. He scraped a gob of the orange wax off the end of it and saw the tip had a clear crystal stone set in the spiral carved, white wood stick. Along the spiral, glyphs were carved into it, which Randall recognized as magical script. The Queen had somehow acquired a wand.

Flynn looked at Randall with interest at his discovery. "Any idea what that thing does?"

"No, I will have to study it when we camp again. But first, I'll need one of those biscuits they're carrying off."

Juliana joined the three. "I was able to call upon The Mother's divine power to heal the captain's broken arm. He was very grateful for you saving their lives and wanted to apologize for abandoning you when they did."

"Right bastards the lot of them. I still don't trust them." Randall snapped

"That's right Mr. Randall. That fat one especially." Izzy agreed.

"Well, maybe we can lose them as soon as we break from the next camp. For right now, they do have some food we will need to share." Flynn said.

Flynn patted Izzy on the back, and the two headed into the exit passage. Randall looked at Juliana and made an 'after you' gesture with his hand, giving a slight bow. Juliana smiled, then took Randall's arm unexpectedly.

Randall let Juliana lead him into the passageway, arm in arm. Before they exited the cave it became hand in hand as friends.

29
Platinum, Gold, and Palladium

Osbert knocked upon the door to The Duke's bedchamber, bearing a message sent by a special courier. The message bore the seal of Lord Mayor Geoffrey Walters. It was well past the morning sunrise; however, Duke Payne did prefer to sleep in, despite his busy schedule. Brandon stood at the door awaiting The Duke's response.

"Who is it?" The muffled voice of the Duke called out from his bedchamber.

"It is Lord Osbert, Your Highness. You have been sent a message from the mayor of Port Gwynn." Osbert leaned in to talk to the door.

"Humph. Very well. Enter." The Duke called out.

Brandon pulled open one of the doors for Osbert, who politely gave him a nod as he entered. The Duke was already out of bed and his personal valet was dressing him for the day. The Duchess dressed in a long nightgown, stood motionless, facing a window that overlooked the gardens with her wheelchair behind her.

"Osbert, this must be of the utmost importance if a letter came before my morning tea." Duke Payne chuckled, then had a small coughing fit.

"A rider brought it in this morning. Do you wish for me to read it for you?" Osbert asked.

"Certainly, I'm sure if it's from that fool Geoffrey, it will require my immediate attention." The Duke said, as his valet helped him with the sleeves of his coat.

Osbert broke the wax seal on the envelope and withdrew the letter. Removing a pair of spectacles on a handle from his pocket, he looked over the page and then read aloud the letter written in Geoffrey's hand.

Your Royal Highness Duke Archibald Payne,

I feel it is my duty to inform you that I have discovered a conspiracy of the embezzlement of tax revenues that are to be collected this quarter. I discovered during my investigation that Thom Clarke had conspired with the keeper of accounts, a man by the name Randall. Thom Clarke murdered his wife and then committed suicide to avoid being brought to justice. The keeper of the accounts may have escaped the city, and is believed to have taken with him the bulk of the coin. It was found that he was involved with a crime organization made of villainous thieves, many of which are infected with the curse of lycanthropy and shape shift into rat men.

The city guard was unable to eradicate their force, which dwells beneath the city and moves using the sewers and catacombs. It is possible that there is a share of the tax revenues in their possession. I would ask that you send a small force of your professional soldiers to put an end to their criminal exploits against your citizens in Port Gwynn. I have put an order in for silvered weapons to be made, to use in their extermination. Port Gwynn's Captain of the Guard, Madok, is very capable and would be able to lead or assist in this task, as he made the discovery during his investigation.

There is also the matter of the restless dead in the catacombs, that we have previously asked for assistance in the destruction of as well. Their continued existence resulted in the deaths of a few of the guards, that gave chase to the keeper of accounts, when he and members of his gang sought refuge below.

I would request, considering all that is happening, that the High Sheriff's collection of revenues be postponed until the following quarter, at which time two quarters plus interest can be collected and paid.

Lastly, Bishop Bennett has passed away, while he was on sabbatical at his country manor. There will need to be an appointment made for his replacement by King Ernald III, as well as funeral planning. Currently his body is being tended to by the sisters at the Cathedral of the Merciful Mother. Preparations are being made for his interment in the catacombs beneath the cathedral.

Sincerely,

Paul Wolff

Lord Mayor Geoffrey Walters of Port Gwynn

"Leave us, please." The Duke dismissed his young valet, watching as he exited the room.

The two sat in the chairs before the hearth. Archibald took the letter and read it over for himself and sighed. He then smirked and laughed uncontrollably, which caused him to appear quite mad and made Osbert feel quite uncomfortable. Osbert forced himself to let loose a fake chuckle, not understanding The Duke's reaction to the letter with serious events that had transpired.

"Oh, Osbert I know you don't understand, but that's quite alright. Here is what is really going on in Port Gwynn. I have a special network of spies reporting to me, the goings on of The Lord Mayor and his criminal cronies. I've been keeping an eye on him and his scheming for only a short while now, but I've uncovered the corruption stretching from the church all the way to his own office and some points between. He thinks me the fool to believe that Clarke fellow would conveniently do himself in, so he could lay all the blame on him. I already know the location of the stolen funds and who was responsible for Clarke's death. The High Sheriff, who is due to arrive in Gwynn today, will arrest Geoffrey and his Captain of the Guard. We are actively tracking down the bookkeeper mentioned as well. Since the Church is also implicated, due to the corruption from its leader, orders have been given for its temporary closure and a thorough search for recovery of what is the Kingdom's property. That old bore Bishop Bennett got off light in comparison to what The Lord Mayor has in his future." The Duke went on his rant, waving the crumpled letter in his hand.

"What of the other things mentioned? The dead that have risen in the catacombs and the lycanthropes?" Osbert was in a state of shock, though fascinated with what was shared.

"Oh, those are minor nuisances that could have easily been dealt with by a child with a little training and a pointy stick. They were too preoccupied stealing from me, to cope with it. Regardless, I have far more important personal business to attend to than these distractions." The Duke tossed the letter into the fireplace.

"Your Highness, this is all very serious and the implications of speaking out against the church as well as shuttering it, even temporarily, could have great repercussions from throughout The Kingdom, including from The King." Osbert warned.

"My nephew will see that what I do, is in the best interest of his kingdom. Once everything is uncovered, he will probably see no alternative than to allow me to lead other investigations into corruption within the church. I guarantee you, that all its high-ranking clergy are as corrupt as that conniving Bennett." The Duke spoke unapologetically.

Osbert had no words. He sat silently in the chair. Archibald struggled to rise from his chair, with no success.

"Allow me to assist Your Highness." Osbert took The Duke by his arm helping him to his feet.

"My body may be frail, but my mind is still sharp, Osbert." Archibald shuffled to retrieve a walking stick from his collection. Today he chose a simple polished hardwood cane.

"I assume then, you will not be sending a reply to The Lord Mayor, in light what you have told me." Osbert asked, just to be sure.

"The High Sheriff will be my message. One more thing, I need my schedule for today cleared. I will be working on some of that forementioned personal business today from the tower. That is after my morning tea and breakfast is served." The Duke said, with the wave of his bony finger.

"As you wish Your Highness. I also received word that the Duchess's nurse had taken ill this morning. Shall I call for another to care for her today?" Osbert looked over to the Duchess, who had not moved from the window where she stood.

"Oh, no Osbert. She'll be fine. If need be, she will accompany me. You can take your leave Osbert." The Duke waved him on.

"As you wish Your Highness." Osbert made a short bow and exited the bedroom.

The Duke made his way over to his wife, who did not even acknowledge his presence when he stood next to her. He took her shriveled little hand in his and stood with her, looking out the window.

"My love, soon we will not be prisoners to these broken aged bodies of ours. You'll see. It will be like I was telling you." Archibald looked over to his wife, though she did not acknowledge his words, but let out a low groan.

He moved around to look her in the face and became upset that one of her yellowing eyeballs was slightly dropping out of its socket. Using his thumb, he pushed it back into place and pulled the eyelid over it to hold it in. He heaved a sigh and shook his head.

"You haven't moved from that spot since last night. Now take your chair to the balcony and we will have our breakfast there." The Duke said to the Duchess.

The Duchess slowly moved as she pushed her wheelchair from the bedroom through the doors to the balcony. Once she reached the dining table, she took her seat in the wheelchair. She began rocking in place slowly as she moaned.

A knock on the bedroom door shortly thereafter announced the arrival of the morning tea and breakfast. The young woman left the silver tray stacked with dishes of kippers, tomatoes, fruit and sweet pastries and the tea service. Upon her departure, The Duke enjoyed his morning tea as the Duchess sat motionless.

Another knock on the chamber door came just after the completion of breakfast. The Duke entered the bedchamber leaving the Duchess on the balcony.

"Enter!" Archibald called out.

A well-dressed middle-aged lady carried in a small plain wooden box with a padlock. Her armed escorts waited behind in the hall. The Duke's eyes lit up at the sight of the box.

"Lovely! I've been expecting you. My item is completed on time, and delivered to me in person, by the finest smith of precious metals in the kingdom! Please come in Lady Roesia." The Duke directed her to the table.

"You are too kind, Your Highness." Roesia set the wooden box onto the table by the hearth. She was dressed in clothes befitting her profession, but were not the ones she used in the forge. For a visit to Redrock Castle she wore a clean costume version of them, complete with boots, breeches and a vest with many pockets and compartments for a tinker's tools.

She handed a small key for the padlock to The Duke, who took it with much excitement. He opened the lid revealing a tufted red velvet lining to protect its contents. The Duke's eyes were wide with excitement, as he lifted out a small box crafted of pure platinum. He inspected it from all sides and angles. Strange glyphs fashioned in pure gold filigree were on each side of the exterior of the box. The press of a small button caused the lid to pop open, to reveal a palladium lined interior. Months of work were put into this special commission, that cost The Duke a small fortune.

"Splendid, splendid, splendid! Everything in its design is perfect to my exact specifications. You are truly gifted at your craft." The Duke smiled, revealing a few missing teeth.

"Thank you again, Your Highness. It was an honor that you called upon me for this. I will always be happy to craft any other fine art objects you request." Roesia gave a small bow.

"I may have work for your forge in the future, Lady Roesia. I will have funds transferred from the treasury immediately." The Duke said with great gratitude.

Roesia was about to turn to leave, but gasped when she saw Duchess Katherine standing just behind Archibald, motionless. Her thin white hair was hanging loose to her shoulders and her gray skin pulled tight across her gaunt face, with her yellow cloudy eye pushing out of the socket loose again.

"I-is the Duchess alright?" Roesia backed away slowly from the table, covering her nose and face with her hand to shield herself from the smell of decay. She had never met her before, but she knew she had been ill for a long time.

"Uh, yes. She's been recovering well. Thank you for your concern and again for the finely crafted piece." The Duke dismissed Roesia from the chamber.

Archibald returned to Katherine, looking at her with one hand on his walking stick, while shaking his head. The Duchess was slightly swaying, while she stood with her arms hanging to her sides. Once again, he used his thumb and pushed her loose eyeball back into its socket and pulled the lids back over it.

"My dear, I apologize that I was unable to do anything more for you after you died that night, almost a year ago. I just can't bear the thought of being without your companionship. Even if it is just the shell of your former self." Archibald took her hand to his lips and kissed it.

"I have work to attend to today, and your nurse is not available to tend to you. You will just have to stay in our room alone today." The Duke said.

He placed the platinum box back in the wood coffer and locked it shut. Placing it under one arm, he walked to the door. Katherine shuffled behind him, with her arms hanging, unmoving to her sides. The Duke turned, looked at her, and smiled.

"No, my dear. Stay." The Duke pointed to her wheelchair on the balcony.

Katherine turned and shuffled to the balcony and slowly sat down in her chair. She began rocking in place and making her low moaning sounds. The Duke exited his room, pausing at Brandon, who was in his position at the door with Archibald's guards.

"Brandon, I will be working in the tower. I have cancelled all appointments for the day, so no one else should be calling on me here. The Duchess seems to be more restless today and wanting to wander, so please be attentive and not allow her to leave." The Duke said to Brandon.

Archibald took a seat in his waiting litter, holding the coffer tight in his arms, as he was carried through the wide halls of Redrock Castle to The Tower. The ride was made in silence as he patted the box along the way.

30
Scrying Time

A rchibald's escorts dropped him at the door to his tower, which served as his office and private place to conduct research and experimentation. He commissioned a renowned architect and engineer to design and oversee its construction decades ago. Sadly, right after the construction was completed, both men died in a mysterious fire in their office, and the blueprints and secrets of the tower lost. Aside his office on the first floor, the other floors of his tower were forbidden for anyone to enter. Even Osbert himself, never ventured further than the office.

In Redrock Castle there was gossip, between the younger servants and even some of the younger guards, about what the goings on were beyond the tower door. The Duke at times would often enter and not leave for hours, or on rare occasions a few days at a time. The rumors were dealt with sternly by superiors that dealt out punishments for spreading gossip. For servants this would mean the loss of their jobs. Castle guards could be sent to the brig to serve a week in solitary confinement.

These same musings about The Duchess' current state, were also dealt with in the same way. This led to those in close contact with her, to act as there was nothing out of the ordinary. She was just 'under the weather.'

Archibald locked the door behind himself as he entered the dark office. He waved his cane slowly across the room and spoke a command and the chandelier, hanging from the ceiling, began to glow with a warm yellow light. The room was semi-circular, as it was divided in half by a wall with a single door in its center. Directly behind the desk portraits of a much younger Duke and Duchess hung side by side.

He shuffled past his desk, ignoring important documents spread across it requiring his attention. The door, to the other half of the tower, bore a small magical glyph on it, that glowed in gold light as he approached it. The security precaution would permanently deter unauthorized trespassers.

He passed through the door into the other semi-circular half of the tower along which a stone staircase hugged the circular wall. Above him, in the ceiling, was a circular hole with a corresponding circular tile on the floor, bearing magic script around its perimeter. He stepped onto the tile and the script glowed with a gold light beneath his feet. Looking upwards, he floated into the air and through the ceiling portal, continuing upwards through the different floors of the tower, bypassing the stairs his weak legs could not carry him up.

Reaching the top level, he stepped off onto the floor. The tower was the tallest structure in Redrock Castle, and from this vantage point he could also view the walled city of Redrock from the crenelated rooftop. Grotesque gargoyle statues were posed, as if watching over the tower, awaiting threats against it.

Again, he waved his cane and spoke the command word and light began to glow from a large chandelier. He shuffled his way through his crowded workroom. Within were worktables topped with glass beakers and test tubes, shelves with jars of preserved creatures floating in strange liquids and other rare reagents, rows of bookcases with cyclopedias for reference, as well as other texts.

Archibald looked over to the perch, where Barnabas typically waited for him and found it empty. "Barnabas! Where have you gone to?"

He scanned the room, then felt something brush against his leg. Looking down he saw a large hairy black spider, the size of a small dog, look up at him with its four eyes.

"Ugh! Barnabas, you know I find that repulsive." Archibald wacked the spider on its abdomen with his cane.

The spider recoiled and made a chittering noise. There was a small flash of green light and the large spider changed form into a raven. It then spread its wings and flew over to its perch.

"That hurt, Archie!" Barnabas croaked out.

"Don't call me that. I am The Master." The Duke was becoming cross with his familiar.

"Right, Boss." Barnabas never referred to The Duke as 'Master.'

"Bah, whatever. I have good news Barnabas. The platinum box has been completed. I can move forward with the contract!" The Duke was giddy to relay the news.

"Gee Boss, that means I won't have Bennett around to toy with anymore? He dislikes spiders more than you. He made the funniest sounds every time I sank my fangs into him." The raven said.

"I told you he was only our guest here temporarily. They can bring another filthy street urchin for you to play with. You broke the last one too quickly." The Duke removed the platinum box to show off to Barnabas.

"Oh yes! That would be nice, Boss." The raven eyed the platinum box held before him with curiosity. "That's nice and shiny."

"Now where are those crones?" The Duke looked around the room.

In the iron, cage Bennett was making a nasty gurgling sound, as his distorted face with bulging eyes looked at The Duke. It gnashed its teeth and its bloated tongue pushed out, but it was unable to speak. Puncture marks from spider fangs were all over Bennett's slimy grub body, but it didn't seem to cause him too much harm. Just pain and torment.

"Quiet Bishop. I'll be sending you away soon enough." The Duke pointed his cane at him threateningly. Barnabas laughed, bobbing up and down on his perch.

"Archibald, did you call?" The black-haired hag spoke up. She, the gray-haired hag, and the fat hag all appeared together with their hands clasped in front of themselves.

"I hate when you do that!" The Duke spun around and shook his cane at them. The hags cackled amongst themselves.

"Now, now, Archibald, I have acquired an item needed for scrying, to locate the last conspirator." The fat hag waved a thick finger with a long-broken nail at The Duke.

"Well, let's have it." The Duke pounded his cane on the floor.

"His residence was locked tight by the city guard, so many of his worthless personal items, aside from anything of value they looted, were still there. However, I found a brush with some of the lad's hair in it." The fat hag held out a simple wooden boar's hair brush, that had a few strands of Randall's brown hair in its bristles.

"Very good, Mama Matilda. What of that Captain?" The Duke looked at the brush in hand as he asked.

"He has recovered from his illness and was dismissed from the convent. He has returned to a light duty in the meantime. Do you wish for me to pay him a visit as well?" The gray-haired hag gyrated her hips, imitating sexual thrusting.

"Heavens no. You do get too much pleasure from that. I want the High Sheriff to arrest him. I want a few of these high-ranking conspirators taken alive, to make examples of, to keep order. Unlike what you did to Thom, and his wife."

"I thought the 'murder/suicide' angle was a nice touch!" The black-haired hag laughed.

Archibald shuffled over to the tapestries hanging on the wall, which the hags drew back for him, to reveal the large gold and silver mirror they concealed. He looked over to the fat hag. "What is the name of that bookkeeper again?"

"Randall is the name Thom gave, before I hung him from the rafter of his study. He thought that would save him and that wife of his." The fat hag said, proudly.

"Randall." The Duke repeated his name.

Archibald performed the ritual to have the large mirror act as a scrying device. He chanted many arcane words, as well as Randall's name repeatedly. The hair in Randall's brush aided in creating the conduit that would find him anywhere in the world he was hiding. The hags watched intently, as the swirling silvery mists in the face of the mirror had small blue electrical charges crackle throughout it and the light of the chandelier dimmed. As the ritual progressed, the motion of the clouds intensified, and the silvery mists changed to dark storm clouds, with lightning violently arcing across the mirror. With each crack of lightning the gargoyle and serpent relief sculptures seemingly changed their positions. Barnabas bounced up and down on his perch excitedly, and the trio of hags clapped their hands.

The dark storm clouds slowed their churning and the lightning gave way to small electrical charges. The clouds parted to reveal an arial view of a faraway beach. Slowly, the view began to center and close in in on a small group of people, looking like no more than ants moving about on the beach. The view quickly began to zoom in on the group, then focused on Randall.

Randall sat on a rock, with his spell book open in his lap. He held the twisted white wooden stick in his hand as he read.

"Ooh! The boy has a wand and a book of magic!" The hags were chatting between themselves, cackling.

"Quiet! You sound like a bunch of clucking hens. Bah, without a mirror on his side, there is no way to hear, or send any of you crones through. I'm going to see who is in his company."

The Duke concentrated, and the view changed.

The captain and his men were recovering useful items and cargo, from the wrecked ship that washed to shore. Juliana and Izzy were going through Juliana's recovered backpack, but the contents were soaked. Flynn stood overseeing, and keeping a lookout for goblyns.

"That boy, Randall, fancies himself a magician. Very interesting... He's lucky he was useful to Geoffrey, at the time. Otherwise, he would have been burned at the stake for heresy in the center of town. Well, Geoffrey is not too good at following the law." The Duke chuckled.

"The girl, she has that symbol around her neck. It appears she is a member of the clergy." The gray-haired hag pointed.

"Dressed like that and armed? Perhaps she was a member of the church guard. Regardless, it seems the boy's luck ran out as his escape plan sank. It's quite likely another ship will see their wreck and rescue them. He is a loose end to this matter that I just need wrapped up, no need to bring him in." The Duke speculated.

"What is it you are thinking, Archibald?" The black-haired hag asked.

"They are obviously along the coast of that ghastly wild territory. It wouldn't be too difficult to find him and take out this little apprentice. Barnabas!" The Duke looked over to the Raven.

"Me, Boss?" Barnabas croaked.

"Yes. I am entrusting you to take on this task. Fly out into the so called 'Goblyn Badlands, locate this boy and finish him off. You will wear the mirror necklace so we can communicate over the distance." The Duke tapped his cane on the floor, as he spoke.

"Gee Archie... er, Boss... A special assignment! Finally! I can take him out for you. It sounds like great fun. I haven't got to leave the tower in almost a year now. Stretching my wings and killing people would be great exercise!" Barnabas spoke quickly, without pausing, bouncing on his perch.

"Quiet, fool! I need you to do this without fail. I have more important matters to attend to while you are away. That book will need to be destroyed as well. However, that wand you could carry back easily. It might be of some use." The Duke's eyes slanted, while addressing the raven.

"Boss, I got this." Barnabas bounced violently on his perch.

There was a flash of green light again and Barnabas transformed into his true form. Leathery, bat-like wings sprouted from the shoulders of the small red skinned devil. Two long taloned toes on each foot gripped onto the perch, as he wrung his small hands together. Two tiny horns atop his head and a bulbous nose made his appearance comical, except for its tail that extended from his backside with a sharp stinger. His bright yellow eyes were pupilless, reflecting light like cat's eyes, in the darkened room.

"I welcome your enthusiasm Barnabas, but you will need to go without attracting attention to yourself. Are you sure you have this?" The Duke now questioned his own judgement.

"No trouble, Boss. There and back in no time. I'll even jab all the others and squirt them full of juice. They won't know what hit them."

"Look Archibald, the boy." The black-haired hag pointed to the mirror.

Randall was sitting on the boulder and now looking around himself and over his shoulder. He closed the book and stood up. He appeared nervous and apprehensive, as he stuffed his tome back into its satchel and slung it over his shoulder. He walked over to his friends and started talking as he looked around anxiously. He crossed his arms acting if he felt a chill. He had goosebumps, and the hairs on his neck were standing up.

"Hmmm. It appears he has detected the scrying. Bah." The Duke dismissed the spell. A bright light instantaneously flashed from the mirror. Now it only reflected the room occupants.

Everyone watched The Duke, as he seemed to be lost in thought.

"Barnabas, when you find him, you will not act until I give you the word. You will observe and report to me first. I want to know what he is up to. I don't want to underestimate his talents. He obviously has some knack for the art." The Duke thoughtfully rubbed his chin.

"Archibald, are we going to contact The Master next?" The fat hag clapped her hands, excitedly.

"He is my benefactor. No one is my Master." The Duke rapped his cane on the floor angrily, causing the hags and Barnabas to cower away, as the light of the chandelier changed and bathed the room in a blood red light.

31
The High Sheriff

"This is preposterous! You can't do this to me! I am the Lord Mayor!" Geoffrey stamped his foot, as the High Sheriff Guy Whitlee, stood before him rolling up the arrest warrant paper he had just read to him.

Geoffrey, the Lady Mayoress, and his daughter Madeline stood in the middle of the parlor arm and arm. Geoffrey cursed, as his wife and daughter cried and begged for them not to take him. The house servants all stood together watching, shocked.

A team of men were going through the house, removing items of value, and taking them to the caravan of wagons waiting in the courtyard below. Bookkeepers were taking inventory in ledgers, following the men, and pointing them to the 'good stuff.' Soldiers, dressed in mail with the red and black tabards of The Duke's colors, were everywhere in the residence keeping a watchful eye on the scene.

The barrel-chested Sheriff twirled the end of his large red mustache. "Geoffrey, you will be held here in the city jail, under The Duke's guard, until we depart for Redrock for you to face your trial."

"How long will that be?" Geoffrey was bewildered, as the guards locked the manacles on his wrists.

"Can't be too sure just yet, Lord Mayor. There are taxes to be collected, ongoing investigations to your corruption of this office, the need for proper leadership to be put into place in this city, which I will undertake in the interim. Possibly a few months. It is a very comfortable place you have made of your home, I must say." The Sheriff looked around the parlor with his arms crossed, nodding his head approvingly.

"What are we to do? Where will we go?" The Lady Mayoress barked out at the Sheriff, as she held tight to Madeline.

Two large guards lifted Geoffrey off the ground by his arms and carried him off to the transport cart, with his feet dangling above the ground kicking. The Sheriff turned to the two and sternly spoke. "You will be allowed to pack and take minimal personal belongings and some coin. That is all. Where you go, is not of my concern. Now get moving."

"Madeline, we can probably seek refuge at the convent for a short time. Until I can get word to my sister in Willowdale." Lady Mayoress was being hopeful.

"You will need to rethink that M' Lady. The Cathedral is also locked down, under orders from The Duke, pending an investigation into the misdeeds of the late Bishop Bennett who conspired with your husband, The Lord Mayor. Perhaps you two could find a little honest work at the bath houses in the High Port. I will be visiting one tonight." The High Sheriff laughed, and jabbed an elbow into one of the guards standing by him, who in turn started to laugh.

The Lady Mayoress and Madeline, acting quite offended, stormed off to pack the few belongings they would be allowed to take under the watch of the guards. The staff that were gathered in the parlor looked at each other with uncertainty.

The High Sheriff pulled a meerschaum pipe carved with the head and bust of a bare breasted woman from his pouch. He sat in down on a very comfortable, over stuffed, tufted chair and kicked his boots up on the matching footstool. Lighting up the tobacco in his pipe with a firestick, he proceeded to enjoy a smoke as the staff continued to stand and watch awkwardly.

"Oh, I'm sorry. All this travel and taking care of The Duke's business, does wear one out a bit. You folks go on with your regular duties. I am feeling rather famished though, so I hope that something especially nice, will be served for dinner tonight." The Sheriff eyed the crystal decanter filled with brandy on the marble top side table next to him.

"Sir any further orders?" The sergeant stepped into the parlor, asking a very relaxed Sheriff, that was now pouring brandy into a crystal snifter.

"Yes, there is. I am going to make this house my base of operations for the time we are in this city, so have the men halt the removal of any other items from the house. Also, inspect everything those two intend to take with them. Allow them some clothing and coin to get them by for a while. However, any jewelry or items of real monetary value will need to be confiscated." The Sheriff took a sip of the brandy.

"Will that be all sir?" The sergeant asked.

"Yes. Hmmm, Geoffrey does have some good taste in his drink." Guy tossed back the rest of his snifter and puffed on his pipe, as he rocked his feet back and forth on the foot rest.

***

Across the city, outside the Cathedral of the Merciful Mother, a crowd of onlookers stood and watched, as a unit of The Duke's soldiers set up operations. The captain of the operation, from atop his steed, was in a heated argument with Captain Ashdown of the church guard. Other members of the church guard stood before the closed doors with weapons in hand. Sister Lucia was on her knees with a reliquary in her arms before her, desperately pleading with the man on horseback, with tears running down her cheeks.

The captain on horseback held an official decree from The Duke, as he began addressing the gathering crowd and the members of the church guard. "It is by royal decree, that the cathedral is to be locked down and those that occupy it turned out until further notice. The late Bishop Bennett, was found to be conspiring to defraud the parishioners of the church and embezzling from The Kingdom for his personal benefit. This is a temporary closure, pending an investigation by the High Sheriff. Any resistance will be dealt no quarter under the order of Duke Archibald Payne. If the members of the church guard surrender their weapons, they will be allowed to leave peacefully."

A company of sixty of The Duke's men stood in formation, ready to act on orders by their captain, who sat patiently high in the saddle on the heavy white warhorse. Aside from Captain Ashdown and the four guards on the steps, another three held positions on the battlements above. The church guards nervously eyed one another, waiting for the other to act first.

A young guard walked down the steps unbuckling his scabbard and lay it on the ground before the mounted captain. Following his lead, one by one the others did the same, and eventually the men on the battlements also turned over their weapons. Captain Ashdown reluctantly lay his sword down and stepped back with his men.

"Very good. That was the honorable thing to do." The captain nodded his head to Captain Ashdown and his men. "Sister Lucia, my sergeant will assist you evicting the resident sisters from the convent. They will be allowed to remove their personal belongings and nothing more. There are arrangements being made to have them safely lodged elsewhere in town for the duration of this investigation."

"You can't do that! This is the house of The Mother and not to be occupied by common soldiers! The sisters will not be safe turned out onto the streets!" Sister Lucia stood, yelling at the captain, tightly holding the small, coffinlike reliquary to her chest.

The captain rolled his eyes. "Sergeant, please accompany Sister Lucia and help her vacate the convent."

"Yes sir!" The sergeant stepped forward.

"First, confiscate that item. She won't be taking anything other than her personal belongings with her." The captain pointed to the reliquary.

"No, you can't touch this, it contains the last mortal remains of Saint Esther!" Sister Lucia stepped back.

"Hand it over Sister." The sergeant stepped up and grabbed at it with his gloved hands.

Sister Lucia lost her grip and the wood box smashed on the ground. Gold coins spilled out of the broken coffer. Sister Lucia dropped to her knees, frantically scooping up the coins.

"Sergeant, assist Sister Lucia to her feet and get those women out of there." The captain shook his head.

"No! That belongs to me! You have no right!" Sister Lucia screamed, as the sergeant took her arm and pulled her along to the cloister entrance of the cathedral.

"Well, that one should probably be sharing a cell with the Lord Mayor. Ah well." The captain spoke, under his breath. He then looked over to the waiting members of the church guard and Captain Ashdown. "For the meanwhile, you will be spending your time in the barracks at the garrison with members of the city guard. They are now under the control of the High Sheriff, by The Duke's royal decree, pending this investigation."

The crowd around the cathedral was buzzing with conversations of the goings on. Many were appalled by the sacrilegious act done on holy ground by The Duke. Others were happy to see action being taken against a church that was enriching itself, with little benefit to the parishioners.

Two men in cloaks, with hoods covering the heads, did their best to go unnoticed watching the scene from afar and listen to other's repeating what was being said. Captain Madok was out of his armor and under the cloak, dressed in the clothes of a laborer, however armed with his longsword on his side. The newly promoted young sergeant, similarly dressed, stood beside him with his sword covered by his cloak. Nigel was a little pale in the face and had lost some weight while ill, after the attack on The Nest.

"What's happening?" Nigel asked Madok.

"The Duke has sent in the High Sheriff, and a small battalion of his soldiers, to investigate the goings on in the city." Madok responded.

"What has that got to do with the cathedral?" He asked.

"More than you need to know, sergeant. I think it would be best for us to move along." Madok urged the young sergeant along, with a tug of his sleeve.

The two pushed their way into the crowd, with Madok keeping the hood drawn around his face, avoiding all eye contact with other passersby. They headed through a main thoroughfare with heavy foot traffic, along with carts and wagons drawn by oxen and asses. A pair of heavily armed mounted soldiers baring the colors of The Duke and four Port Gwynn city guards were at an intersection observing the people on the street. All seemed to be looking for someone specific. Madok was immediately aware, that he was their intended subject.

"This way." Madok urged Nigel to take a detour down a narrow, litter filled alleyway between two shops.

Both men stepped into the alleyway, ducking down to watch as the procession of mounted soldiers and guards passed by. Each sighed with relief, as they were unnoticed by the small group of men.

"I'm going to have to leave the city, and I'll need your help." Madok put his hand on the sergeant's shoulder as he spoke.

"Absolutely, Captain." Nigel nodded.

"Every guard on the street is going to be looking for me, and all the city gates will have the Duke's men posted, as well as our own guards. I think my best chance will be to leave out of low port on a barge. With a little coin to grease a palm or two, I can get dropped off on a safer shore. I'm probably the most easily recognizable man in town, aside from the Lord Mayor and The Bishop, so getting there without being seen may be a tad... challenging." Madok rubbed the stubble on his chin.

"What do you suggest?" Nigel asked.

"The wainwright, Gerard, owes me quite a few favors and he's only a street over." Madok said.

"Yes, I know him." He replied.

"I will make my way there and wait until evening to head to low port. I have a stash of coin in my office at the garrison. You are welcome to half of it, just bring it to the wainwright's this evening. A floorboard under my desk is loose, and it's in there in a leather bag. Just in case of an emergency. Like this one, I suppose." Madok said.

"It sounds risky, me going there and into your office, if the guard is on alert with the Duke's men all over town. I'm supposed to be off duty recovering. I don't have any business to be there." Nigel said nervously.

"Just go pay a visit the other lads, then stop and pick it up before you leave. Maybe the lieutenant or any of the Duke's officers haven't taken over my office just yet." Captain Madok said, reassuringly.

"Ok, I'll just—" The sergeant looked past Madok with his mouth agape.

Madok sprang from his crouching position and drew his longsword from under his cloak. At the mouth of the narrow alleyway stood Musa. He stood before them barefoot, in his typical attire of loose airy breeches and vest to show off his tattoos and scarification. His arms were crossed, and his rapier and dagger in their respective scabbards.

"So, Captain, it seems you are found in an interesting position." Musa spoke, with a thick islander accent in his deep voice. "Do you wish to be a prisoner of the Duke and accept whatever fate awaits you in his courts. Or will you come with me and face the fair justice in the court of His Lordship, for the attack on our home and murder of our people. Of course, there is a final option, where I leave you dead with the rest of the garbage in this alleyway."

"Captain!" The Nigel cried out to Madok.

Nigel was captured by Red and Sauda. Each held one of his arms, and Red had the tip of her dagger pointed into his belly. Urine ran down Nigel's leg and puddled on the ground.

"The boy seems to have wet himself. Poor thing." Red kissed Nigel on the cheek and pushed the point of the blade into his skin, until a little blood spread across his shirt. Sauda covered his mouth with her hand.

"Shh, shh, shh." Sauda whispered in his ear as he struggled to pull loose from the two women.

"Who in the hells are you?" Madok growled, looking at the women and then Musa.

"Wrong answer." Musa nodded at the women.

Red drew the blade across the sergeant's belly, spilling his entrails onto the trash strewn ground. His eyes rolled back, then he fell into a heap in the alleyway. Musa drew his weapons and took one step forward.

"Captain, think before you speak. Which will it be?" Musa toyed with the thin dagger in his hand, twirling it in his fingers.

The scream of a girl pierced the alleyway, as she made the mistake of choosing this time to dump rubbish from her father's business there. Musa was distracted and looked over his shoulder.

The girl dropped the load in her arms and ran back into the street, dodging a wagon pulled by a team of oxen. Madok slashed across Musa's belly with his longsword, kicked him into the wall, and ran out into the street. He didn't see the three assassins leave the alleyway. They must have been following him for some time, waiting for the right moment to engage him. He sheathed his sword and pulled his cloak back over his head, as people rushed to the screaming girl.

Madok hurried his pace, deciding it best to take the most direct route to the harbor. He had enough coin on him to book him passage on a ship, but not enough to do much else where ever he may go. He looked back toward the alleyway, as he darted into the foot traffic and saw the women following from a distance.

Madok continued his push through the street, when he saw a man pointing to a rooftop shouting. "One of those beasts! On the roof!"

People on the street looked up and pointed. Madok drew his sword and spun around in time to see Musa, in hybrid rat form, running across the rooftops before leaping to attack.

Madok dove to the side and tumbled away, as Musa landed on the ground with a quick roll before bouncing back to his feet. Citizens scattered in all directions, ducking into shops, the driver of a cart nearly ran down pedestrians in his attempt to remove himself from the fray. Others continued watching as things unfolded before them.

Musa did not allow for Madok to fully rise, before he charged him to stab his uncovered left flank. Madok blocked with his longsword and regained his footing. The two circled another, looking for an opening.

Musa dove to thrust his rapier into Madok's chest. Madok blocked the attack, catching the blade on the hilt of his sword, but he plunged his thin dagger into Madok's shoulder of his sword arm, giving it a twist as he pulled it free.

Captain Madok cursed, as fiery pain shot through the length of his arm to the tips of his fingers.

"It hurts doesn't it, Captain? The difference is, your blade is only an inconvenience for me." The rat man taunted.

Madok felt the blood running down his shoulder, as the red stain spread on his clothing. Musa circled him, with his rapier pointing like a scolding finger. Madok traded his longsword to his left-hand, pointing it at Musa to return the taunt.

"Filthy rat, come get some cheese." Madok said, and spit on the ground.

"Kutomba punda!" Musa screamed. Madok understood it was not a term of endearment.

The two fought in the street, as people that hid in the shops came out to view the spectacle. Soon the busy street had filled with people encircling the two, as the clash from the steel of their blades rung out. Madok had the disadvantage.

The crowd became rowdy, seeing for the very first time, a lycanthrope on the streets. A rock flung from the onlookers struck Musa in the back.

The crowd chanted out loud, 'Kill it! Kill it!' As the two fought, a few brave souls would surge forward and strike at Musa with whatever was available: rocks, a broomstick and even a jar of grape preserves hit their mark.

Musa looked around at the mob, realizing the danger. Red and Sauda were deep in the crowd, watching from a distance. He knew they would not come to his aid and risk their own necks. He was left with no choice other than disengage, before the guard came down on him.

Musa leaped into the crowd, with his weapons at the ready, to dispense of any who would try and stop him. The people fell back, clearing his way as he ran to a store front. Quickly sheathing his blades, he climbed up the thick wooden post with his clawed fingers and toes. He made an acrobatic flip, and landed atop a slanted rooftop.

Musa moved up the roof, planning to make his escape, as the bolt from a crossbow struck his leg. The pain was searing; unlike any he had felt before. He reached down and pulled the silvered bolt from his leg. The wound was crippling and blood continued to flow.

Madok looked behind him and saw the two mounted soldiers riding forward, with the four members of the city guard armed with crossbows pushing through the crowd. Another guard raised his weapon and fired a bolt.

The silvered bolt struck Musa in the chest. Two other guards let loose their silvered bolts, striking him in the neck and side. Musa collapsed and rolled off the rooftop to the street, where he lay dead in human.

The mounted men rode forward scanning the crowd, as the crossbowmen checked Musa's body.

"Where is the man that was fighting this monster?" One mounted man, clad in the colors of the Duke, called out to the onlookers.

Madok cast off his cloak, swapping it for a wide brimmed hat and a fresh tunic, as he ran through the back door of a nearby tailor's shop.

He navigated his way to Gerard's workshop, through the back alleys and side streets. The dagger wound to his arm was burning, and blood was spoiling the new tunic. Passing through a large open yard filled with wood and metal scraps, he kicked the back door open to the workshop and staggered in.

A burly bearded man rushed into the storeroom with a wooden mallet in hand, ready to strike the intruder. Madok slumped against the wall, on which many woodworking tools hung and barrels of supplies and fresh cut lumber was stored.

"Captain Madok?" The man lowered the mallet.

"I need your help." Madok said, looking to his shoulder, of which the entire sleeve was now wet and red with his blood.

"Aye, we can do the quick fix to that. Kate, I need you here!" Gerard called through the open door to the front of the workshop.

A young woman, dressed in sawdust covered work-clothes and apron, appeared in the doorway. "Captain Madok?"

"Yes, it's me." Madok struggled to remove the tunic so Gerard could inspect the wound.

"I'll heat an iron." Kate immediately knew what needed to be done.

"You'll want some of my special spirits before we begin." Gerard retrieved a jug from a workbench.

Madok sniffed it, before putting it to his lips and taking several swallows. He looked at up at Gerard. "Distilled yesterday?"

"You'll want this." Gerard gave Madok a scrap of wood to bite down on, laughed and took the jug to pour the remaining contents on the wound.

Madok winced, but kept calm. Kate returned with an iron poker with a red-hot tip. Gerard held Madok back against the wall and looked back to his daughter. Madok nodded his head, and Kate pressed to tip to the wound. Madok blacked out.

* * *

Madok awoke on a small cot in a cramped office, with his arm wrapped in a fresh bandage Kate just finished dressing.

"I need passage out of the city." Madok looked over at Kate.

"The word is out all over about the High Sherrif hunting for you, as well as your fight with the rat man and the murder of the guardsman in the alley. I don't think they recognized you fighting that...creature." Kate rose from the bedside stool with scrap cloths from the bandages in hand.

"Well, word travels fast in this neighborhood." Madok sighed.

"Guards went door to door, but luckily didn't search the place. They took me for my word that a swordsman hadn't ducked in here." Kate smiled.

Gerard poked his head into the small office. "I've closed us for the rest of the day, Madok. What is it I can do for you to get you out of the workshop, so that I can go about business uninterrupted by nosy city guards?"

"I was telling Kate I need to leave Port Gwynn. I need to get to low port and board one of the barges." Madok looked at Gerard.

"Eh, I would think a better idea would be for you to just get yourself on one of the cargo ships sailing out of the High Port. The barges only go out far enough to dump garbage into the bay. The crew on one of those would take your coin and dump you, along with the rest of the garbage." Gerard responded.

"I agree with father. I can get you to High Port without a problem, as I need to drop off a cart we repaired there. You just need to buy your way on board a ship leaving out tonight." Kate said.

"I was going to acquire more of my own coin, but that plan seems to have gone awry." Madok said.

"Captain, you've helped me keep my distilling side business undercover for years, which I appreciate. I will gladly loan you some coin to help you on your way. I just hope whoever takes your place, will continue look the other way, for a mere monthly bottle tribute." Gerard chortled.

"I can't guarantee you that, but I will need to take one more bottle along to wherever this journey takes me." Madok said, peaking under the bandage at his new scar.

"I'll give you two." Gerard smiled.

32
By the Light of the Silvery Moon

I thought we were leaving these creeps." Izzy pouted at Flynn from their encampment.

The four friends were dozens of yards away from the rest of the *Lady Anne* crew, sheltering under a rocky cliffside overhang away from the beach. The wreckage of the *Lady Anne,* had much of its salvageable cargo and useful items brought to shore. Flynn laid claim to a fair share of supplies for their group, for their trouble.

"Before we set out on foot, it may be worth waiting to see if another ship passes by, as the captain said. This is a shipping lane along this coast, so it's quite possible we could be picked up by another vessel when they spot that wreckage." Flynn replied.

"I don't want to be on any boat with that fat man. He's been smart to stay away." Izzy said, as she studied her new dagger.

"Speaking of which..." Randall looked up from his studies at Fat Robb, who was approaching their camp alone carrying a cloth bag.

Juliana rose to her feet. "You're not welcome here. You should turn around and go back to your camp."

Fat Robb stopped and held up the cloth bag as a peace offering. "My apologies on my intrusion ma'am. I really meant no harm to the girl. I believe the drink muddied my mind that evening."

"What have you got there?" Flynn's eyes went to the bag.

"Oh, for the little Miss. There was a wheel of hard cheese recovered from the ship's larders. I thought she would, you know, being a mouse and all, like to have it." Fat Robb reached into the bag, breaking off a piece and eating it, to show it wasn't contaminated by anything other than his grubby fingers.

"I don't like cheese, and I don't want anything from you!" Izzy jumped to her feet, pointing the curved dagger at Fat Robb.

Robb dropped the bag and chunk of cheese, holding his hands up. With his nose twitching and teeth clicking, he stumbled backwards then ran back to his camp.

Izzy picked up the bag and broke off a piece to nibble. "Mmm. It's been a while since I've nicked a good piece of cheese."

"That does sound good. Break me off a piece." Flynn held out his hand.

Randall rolled his eyes before looking back into his tome. Juliana kept watch on Fat Robb, making sure he had rejoined the rest of the crew, before sitting down. Randall looked up from his reading at her and smiled.

"Have you learned anything about that wand?" Juliana asked, curiously

"Actually, that's what I'm preparing to do now. The inscriptions that are on it, will soon be deciphered and will allow me to learn what it does and how to use it. Well, so I hope." Randall reached into his component bag in a side pocket, and pulled out a cloth wrapped prism.

Juliana watched, as he held the prism in one hand and the wand in the other.

"This is the very first bit of magic I learned years ago. It was a necessity for being able to read anything written in this book. After I translate the magic script with the spell, I can understand the meanings of the magical writings, thereafter. Master Williamson's secret library had this spell's formula with special phonetic translations of the incantation, written down on papers atop his desk, along with the prism and how to use it. When I think back to it now, I realize he may have conveniently left it there for me to find." Randall felt a bit of guilt for leaving the school and stealing the book from the Master.

Juliana looked at him intensely. "Well, perhaps you can make amends with your teacher and ask for his forgiveness one day. I understand the law of the land regards practitioners of the magic arts, as being in league with fiends from the hells. I assume his intentions were not to corrupt you, but to encourage your talents and potential. He must have determined you were the one student with the talent and potential; he could share this special gift with."

"I think about that often too." Randall said, with a faraway look.

"Will you get on with it? I'm interested in knowing what your fancy ear picker does." Flynn chimed in

Juliana threw a disapproving look at Flynn, who smiled it away. Izzy moved herself over closer to Randall, who was a bit crowded by the others.

"Okay, just keep quiet and you all can watch." Randall laid the prism on the ground in front of him. He traced invisible words in the air with his first two fingers on his right hand, before touching the prism as he spoke the incantation. "Quid quod eius significatio."

Randall picked up the prism and held it before his eyes, to examine the strange glyphs inscribed all along the length of the twisted white wand. The three watched, as he slowly turned the wand in his hand and silently mouthed the words. After a few minutes passed, Izzy lost interest, and nodded off with her head resting in her hands.

Randall excitedly leapt to his feet and shouted. "A ha! This unassuming little twig holds great power! With it I can summon an icy wintery storm, bring forth a powerful freezing arctic blast of wind, or create a wall of solid ice."

"Well, whoever was its previous owner didn't seem to use if effectively against that giant. Perhaps it doesn't work anymore." Flynn suggested.

"One way to find out for sure. Time for a test." Randall stepped out from under the overhang onto the rocky beach. The others followed, but stood a distance behind him to observe.

Randall paced around a bit, looking along the beach as waves broke on the coast. He looked to the crew of the *Lady Anne,* who were passing time under the shelter of a makeshift tent from scraps of its sails. Holding the wand in his hand like a conductor's baton, he pointed it before him as an extension of his arm. Tracing a figure '8' motion in the air, he said the command word. "Glacies murus!"

The crystal glowed and a silver ray shot from it. As Randall moved the wand back and forth before him across his two chosen points, thick ice formed quickly in layers. Within a matter of seconds, the magic of the wand formed a wall of solid ice that was almost ten feet tall and sixty feet across.

"Amazing." Flynn gasped. They all walked to the ice wall, standing in the middle of the beach during high summer.

Randall had a smirk of triumph on his face. He impressed even himself.

"Where in the hell did that come from?" The muffled voice of a member of the *Lady Anne* crew could be heard from the other side of the ice wall.

Izzy ran up and touched it with her hand. "That's cold, Mr. Randall. Will you show me what else it will do?"

"I think it would be best to hold off on testing everything for a bit. From what I know of a wand, is they are of limited use. At least it still holds some power." Randall said, sliding it in his belt.

The captain and a few others of his crew stepped around the large ice wall, that glistened as it began to slowly melt.

"Very impressive young wizard." The captain looked at the wall and then to Randall. The other men touched, tapped, and even licked the wall in wonder.

"This is definitely an option for fending off any new threats." Randall eyed them while patting it.

"Oh, there will be none from us, young wizard. That I assure you." The captain called to his men to return to their camp, leaving Randall and his friends to themselves.

*** ✳✳✳

High above in the sky, the raven glided and then flapped its black wings, as it searched along the coastline for the young wizard/bookkeeper his master had sent him in search of. Barnabas had mostly been flying nonstop since leaving the tower at Redrock Castle. He took a short break to torment a goblyn, that had been separated from its foraging party to break up the monotony, and steal its dinner from his campfire.

Coming upon the scene below at the site of the shipwreck and melting ice wall, he circled above to monitor from a safe distance. Barnabas recognized everything from the view of The Duke's scrying mirror from the previous day. A closer look, as to what these ugly humans were up to, would be necessary. He began his descent.

He landed on the edge of the cliff face, unnoticed and peered over with one eye. Randall's wand was returned to his belt, and he and Juliana were inspecting the ice wall with the others. So many people were in his company, he knew it would be a challenge to get in close at this point. Waiting until nightfall, when humans slept, to grab the wand and the book would be his best chance. However, the Boss did want a little more information about what they were doing.

Barnabas straightened himself up and stepped back from the ledge, out of sight. There was a small flash of green light and he transformed back into his true fiendish imp form. He stretched out his wings and his arms, then let out a yawn. He cracked his knuckles on his little clawed hands, then snapped his fingers. In a puff of smoke, he became invisible.

The ice wall began crumbling and melting, as the four friends returned to their own base camp. Each took their selected spots on the hard ground. Juliana's recovered traveling pack and bedroll, was dry after laying out in the sun for hours. Izzy and she sat on the bedroll, while Randall and Flynn got comfortable on the rocks.

Barnabas glided down from the cliff face and landed a short distance away, before creeping forward. The small, mirrored pendant that hung loosely about his neck, was also invisible and provided the long-distance communication between the Duke and Barnabas. The hags were taking shifts, watching and listening, as Barnabas flew the distance to find the shipwreck site. Auntie Olga was on shift at this time. She was able to hear, as well as see the four friends, from the mirror in the Duke's tower. She kept quiet, as to not give away Barnabas's presence.

Barnabas crept into the campsite and positioned himself within a few feet of Randall. He watched as he flipped through the pages of his prized grimoire, toyed with the wand in his free hand. He listened as their mundane conversations turned to their destination of Sommer Harbour. The mention of the city of Redrock by Juliana, caused Barnabas's invisible ears to perk up. The young woman talked of offering her service to The Mother at Redrock Cathedral.

Barnabas grew bored as the conversation changed again to more day-to-day banter. So bored, that he began drifting off in the little pocket in the cliff face he had squeezed himself into. Soon he fell into slumber becoming visible.

"Well, I don't believe swimming in the sea counted as a bath. I will make a point of ordering one, when we finally get to Sommer Harbour." Juliana laughed, as she took a bite of a ship's biscuit.

Flynn was chewing on a piece of salted meat, shaking his head in agreement. "I concur. One of the simple pleasures I miss."

"Baths, baths, baths. I don't understand you guys." Izzy was happy with the new layer of dirt building up around her ankles.

The evening had come, and it would be the first night of a full moon. Skies were clear and there was a blanket of twinkling stars lighting the beach.

"On the first night of a full moon, Izzy and I can't control our transformation. I wanted to give you a warning that we will be unable to revert until the dawn." Flynn stated.

"Uh, should I be worried about anything?" Randall asked, concerned.

"Not at all, unless you find our animal form distressing. After so many years I have control in my bestial form, as does Izzy and does others of our ilk. It's just when you first acquire 'the gift,' the bestial urges do take control. I recall when Izzy first transformed, she would have no memory of events that transpired during the night, the following morning." Flynn recalled.

"I was a wild beast." Izzy said.

"Hey, listen. Do any of you hear that?" Juliana was looking around in their camp, from where she sat on the bedroll.

The rest went quiet and listened intently. The sound of whispering could be heard, from within their encampment.

Flynn rose slowly, and motioned for the others to sit still. He concentrated on the voice and silently as possible, crept toward its source. The others sat perfectly still, as Izzy drew the curved blade. Flynn spied the source of the sound only a few feet away from them, tucked in its hiding place.

Barnabas was visible, laying on his back using has wings as makeshift bedding. His little clawed hands were folded on his belly and his legs crossed. He made a low snore, that sounded like a cat's purr. Auntie Olga's voice from the pendant, was trying to rouse him up whispering, "Wake up, you idiot."

Flynn looked back toward the others, with a confused look in his eyes and shrugged his shoulders. He drew his dagger, then put a finger to his lips. Randall, Juliana, and Izzy each rose quietly and advanced with weapons drawn.

Flynn took the tip of his dagger and pressed it against snoring Barnabas's chest. "What the hell are you?"

Barnabas's eyes opened wide, and he let out a squeal. He quickly raised his hands in surrender. "I'm a friend! Don't hurt Barnabas!" The imp knew he blundered.

"You don't look like a friend of mine." Flynn held the tip of the blade in place.

"That thing is not of this world. It is a being from the Hells!" Juliana interjected.

"Let me see!" Izzy squealed, pushing her way in closer.

Randall looked over Flynn's shoulder at the imp who was trying to make a friendly smile, but its mouthful of pointy teeth appeared menacing.

"You there! The mighty wizard, Randall!" Barnabas shouted to him.

"You know who I am?" Randall was flattered. The other three looked over at Randall.

"Yes, your reputation precedes you! I've been looking for you!" The imp blabbed.

Randall's eyes narrowed, as he looked at the little devilish creature. "Looking for me?"

Barnabas paused for only a moment, before blurting out the next thought in his head. "Yes! To serve! You, boss!"

"Who sent you?" Juliana questioned, with a tight grip on her mace.

"No one sends me. I seek a boss to serve. I tell the truth! Barnabas would cross heart, but big man wants to stick that pointy blade in it." The imp held up one hand in a 'scout's honor' sign, while tapping Flynn's dagger with his clawed finger.

"Don't believe that thing. They are deceivers sent here to corrupt, then betray mortal men by their true masters in the Hells." Juliana warned.

"Well, it sure is ugly." Izzy wrinkled her nose.

"Thank you, Miss!" Barnabas was flattered.

"I think we should kill this wretched thing now. I don't trust it either." Flynn said, preparing to push his blade into the imp's chest.

The pale light of the full moon fell upon the campsite, illuminating the scene at their cliffside camp and along the beach to the *Lady Anne's* camp. Shouts, cries, and screams from the members of the *Lady Anne* crew, came out of their lean-to shelter. The captain and all the men ran out from under it, in all directions.

Flynn and Izzy began involuntary transformations into their hybrid rat forms with glowing red eyes. Flynn dropped his dagger during his transformation, giving Barnabas time to react and become invisible once again.

From under the canopy a very fat wererat emerged, with glowing red eyes and patchy black fur. It waddled out baring its orange incisors and flexing its clawed fingers, looking for trouble. His clothes were hanging in shreds.

"Bloody 'ell! Robb's a nasty rat beast!" An older sailor called out.

"That bastard was always a dirty rat!" The captain yelled, as he tried to safely maneuver on the rocky beach.

"Don't let him near you!" Another sailor threw a rock at the back of Fat Robb's rat head.

Back at the cliffside camp, the four searched for the fiendish interloper. Izzy and Flynn's rat noses were sniffing the air, and their whiskers were twitching wildly trying to catch the imp's scent.

"I can still smell you!" Rat Flynn called out to the imp.

"Meoooooow! Tee hee hee!" Barnabas mocked Flynn, as he swooped invisibly past his head.

"Little bastard!" Flynn spun around to stab at nothing with his dagger.

"Look over there!" Juliana pointed across the beach toward the fat rat man terrorizing his shipmates. Fat Robb was no more agile as a fat rat, than in his human form, allowing the others to keep a safe distance, as they pelted him with rocks and other debris.

"Yuck! He's even uglier than before!" Izzy rat stuck out her tongue in disgust.

The satchel, holding Randall's spell book, was suddenly lifted from the ground into the air. The weight of it appeared to be a struggle, for the invisible imp to become airborne more than a few feet off the ground.

"It's got my book!" Randall pointed to the floating satchel.

Rat Flynn grabbed the satchel, as Barnabas violently flapped his wings pulling it by the arm strap. Suddenly, the imp became visible, as it attempted to attack Flynn with his stinger tail that dripped with venom. With a quick reflexive reaction, Flynn snatched the imp's prehensile tail in his hand.

"Hey, let go you filthy vermin!" Barnabas squealed at Flynn, who held his tail tight with the stinger only itches from his face.

Juliana rushed forward and slammed her mace down on Barnabas's head, knocking him to the ground. What should have been a death blow to a creature his size, only appeared to momentarily stun him.

"That smarts lady! I didn't do anything to you." Barnabas released the bag and furiously flapped his wings to pull free from Flynn's grip.

Suddenly Fat Robb, the wererat, ran through the middle of their campsite on all fours, knocking over Randall and Izzy. Close behind him, his former ship mates were giving chase with rocks, and weapons taken from the goblyn cave.

"You let him get away!" The captain scolded, as they passed through.

"The little bastard is trying to stick me!" Flynn called out, as the imp reversed tactics and tried with all its strength to plunge its stinger into his face.

"Relax and hold still! It will all be over in a second." Barnabas strained with his dripping stinger.

Izzy jumped on the imp, and with a swipe of her curved dagger severed his tail, leaving only a stub on his posterior. Barnabas howled, as black ichor squirted from the stump.

Barnabas cried and pulled free from Izzy, flying overhead in circles. "You dirty rats! My beautiful tail! That wasn't fair! The Boss will punish you for this!"

Randall quickly swooped up his bag and checked his book. Flynn stood up with the severed tail in his hand. Izzy pointed at the imp with her dagger, as she danced about.

Juliana pointed her mace at Barnabas and shouted out. "I call on the power of The Mother to vanquish this foe!"

Barnabas angrily flittered about yelling obscenities, usually thrown about in casual conversation in the fiery pits of Hell. The ghostly mace, created from the divine power granted by The Mother, materialized in the air next to Barnabas.

"Definitely not fair, you rancid twat!" Barnabas squealed at Juliana.

The ghostly mace swung at the imp, who barely managed to dodge the blow. He continued to make maneuvers in midair to escape, but it followed him wherever he retreated.

"Screw you guys." The imp squealed and snapped his fingers, disappearing in a puff of smoke. The ghostly mace was dismissed, without a target.

Flynn tossed the tail to the ground in disgust. "What a foul-mouthed little monster. That thing didn't show up here by accident."

In the distance, the sounds of the *Lady Anne's* crew shouting and cursing, could still be heard echoing across the cliff faces along the rocky beach.

"Do you think it's gone?" Randall said, looking around nervously clutching his book tightly.

"That creature knew you by name, so it was obviously sent here specifically looking for you. However, I don't think it will be foolish enough to try and confront us again, after we thwarted its effort to kill Flynn and steal that book of yours." Juliana stated.

"Hey, look at this! This is pretty." Izzy picked up the small mirror pendant that had hung from Barnabas's neck. It had fallen on the ground during the struggle with Flynn.

"What is that Izzy?" Flynn's glowing red rat eyes looked upon the pendant with suspicion.

"Finders keepers. The little creep must have dropped it before I rescued you." Izzy held it by the chain and studied the mirror closely.

Randall held out his hand to Izzy. "Let me have a look at that."

"Okay, Mr. Randall." Izzy dropped the pendant from her little rat paw into Randall's hand.

Randall tried to studied it in the moonlight. "I have a feeling this is more than just a piece of jewelry that creature was wearing. Quite possible it is used to communicate with whoever its master is."

"No one is my master, dammit!" The voice of Barnabas squeaked from behind them and cursed, as he flew away into the night.

Randall laid the pendant on a rock and smashed another on top of it repeatedly, until it was in pieces. He carefully scooped up all the pieces, then tossed it into the sea.

"One thing is for certain; I don't think there is going to be any sleep for me tonight. I believe Juliana is right about that creature. In my secret night studies in a bestiary tome, I perused in Master Williamson's library, it described such fiendish creatures. Those that were native to The Hells." Randall sat on the ground.

"What was it?" Flynn asked.

"A small mischievous devil, that are sometimes sent to act as servants to evil practitioners of magic. A familiar spirit. It was very similar to the illustration I saw in the book. The book also mentioned, that these creatures can only be harmed by weapons that are silvered or even better, enchanted. That blade of yours Izzy. I think it may be the latter." Randall proudly stated.

"Magic?" Izzy's glowing red eyes opened wider, as she looked at the curved blade in her hand closely.

"Acquired by chance, much like this wand." Randall tapped the wand in his belt.

"I'm of the belief, that these things didn't just happen to come into your possession just by chance. Just as the four of us were brought together. The

Mother needs us to act for her to combat a greater evil in our world. She is providing us with the tools to do so." Juliana stated her case.

"You know, I think you are right." Flynn looked to her with his red glowing eyes.

"Company is coming." Izzy pointed to the approaching sailors.

"Thanks for nothing! At least we drove him off. He put up a nasty fight though." The captain said angrily, as he stepped into the camp with the other men.

"You know someone for years, then he changes into a giant rat, and turns all nasty on you." Another sailor said, as he stepped forward scratched up and bloodied.

All the other men bore bites, claw marks, and ripped clothing from the fight they put up against Fat Robb in his rat form.

"The son of a bitch even bit my broken arm you had healed with your magic Miss." The captain said to Juliana, as he held out his arm baring teeth marks.

"He's not a well-behaved rodent like you lot." The old sailor added.

"I will call on the power of The Mother to heal your wounds best that I can." Juliana stepped up to the men that were crowding around, showing their fresh wounds, and moaning about the pain.

Randall stepped away from the crowd and waved Izzy and Flynn over. "You know, I think it may be best for us to abandon camp tonight and make our way on foot."

Flynn looked over at the ship's crew and shook his head. "Agreed. I don't want to be around to watch over a whole group of new lycanthropes. They tend to act much like that fat one. Uncouth and ill mannered."

"Fine by me. This is exciting seeing more of the world! All I have ever known was Port Gwynn. Even that little guy was fun to play with." Izzy exclaimed, swinging the severed tail around, flinging more black ichor from it.

"Agreed then. Let's grab as much supplies as we can carry and go." Randall looked at the sailors and then to the silvery moon in the sky.

33

A Contract to Keep

The circular summoning room was dominated by the huge, inverted pentagram on the polished tile floor, surrounded by a perfect unbroken circle of salt. Each point of the star had a black pilar candle that glowed with a yellow flame. The walls of the chamber were bare, save for small ledges all around the perimeter, that held hundreds of flickering candles.

Archibald stood behind a small podium, upon which an open grimoire sat along with the items for the ritual. The censer was alighted with a foul-smelling incense, and the ceremonial dagger was in his hand next to a small brazier of glowing red coals. The gray-haired hag, Auntie Olga stood nearby, with the transformed Bennett cowering in fear on the floor next to her. The bulbous eyes on its distorted face, darted about the scene. Bennett's memories of his former life were lost. They were replaced with the raw emotions of guilt, regret, despair, and fear. His eternal torment in the afterlife.

"Place our guest in the circle." The Duke ordered.

The hag scooped up the fearful soul worm in her arms and carefully crossed into the pentagram, dumping him in the center. She quickly stepped out and took her position in the shadows, watching intently. Bennett stayed in place, pushing his bloated tongue out at Archibald.

With ritual dagger in hand, Archibald drew the blade across his left palm, squeezing blood over the coals in the brazier. He outstretched his arms and traced the 'infinity' symbol repeatedly in the air. with the dagger.

"Oh, great Dysvakar, I most humbly call upon you to accept my generous offering. Lord of Dis, heed my call, and accept my invitation to fulfil our contract, so that I may better serve you on this world for the eons." The Duke mustered his strength, to make his feeble voice sound forceful and commanding. He continued chanting a throaty mantra for several minutes, that resonated in the summoning chamber.

Bennett coiled himself tightly into a ball, leaving only a small space for his bulbous eyes to peak through, as the room began to tremble and items on the podium shook.

"He comes!" The hag cackled with glee.

The Duke continued chanting as the candles at the points in the pentagram's light intensified, while others around the room flared up then were extinguished. A large rectangular sheet of thick swirling purple mists appeared in the center of the of the pentagram, causing the soul worm to retreat to the edge of the salt circle. Blue electrical charges crackled throughout the mists, which then cleared away to reveal only a rectangular black void of a portal, that appeared to be only in two dimensions.

The Duke rested both hands on the podium for support, as the effects of the ceremony took a further physical toll on him. The already venerable Duke aged even more, and another tooth became loose, then fell out.

From the blackness, a statuesque angelic woman of unearthly beauty, stepped through holding a crystal flask containing a black liquid in her hands. Her large white feathered wings were folded behind her, and her voluptuous body was nude, save for a belt around her waist that held a sheathed dagger on one side, and a sword on the other. The blood red irises of her eyes and her intense gaze gave away her true fiendish heritage. She stepped to the side, standing at attention.

Another creature, nearly identical to the one before, stepped through and positioned herself to the opposite side of the portal and stood to attention with her hand on the hilt of her sheathed dagger. Bennett looked upon the two in fear, knowing the two were fallen angels sent from the hells. This piece of knowledge Bennett retained after its transformation.

From the void of the portal, a third figure stepped through. First a foot covered in a finely crafted curled toe slipper stepped into the protective circle, after which was followed by a bestial cloven hoof. Standing a full seven feet tall, the finely attired archdevil was dressed in a fine black silk suit and carried a walking stick in one hand. His handsome face could not hide his true heritage after tipping his fur top hat, since atop his bald head were two small horns, and his glowing red eyes filled one with dread.

Dysvakar scanned the room, then looked to the floor at Bishop Bennett. He stepped forward to the cowering soul worm and paused. Suddenly, he bent down and patted Bennett on the head. He backed away, then smiled ear to ear while stroking his black goatee. "Ooh isn't that just marvelous!" His deep voice was that of a cheerful dandy.

Archibald felt relief, managing a weak smile. "Lord Dysvakar, I present my gift to you, Bishop Bennett, former spiritual leader of the Cathedral of the Merciful Mother."

"Ooh yes, he was quite a naughty boy. He'll be the first addition to my new collection of self-righteous fools. Yes, just splendid!" He tapped his cane on the floor and the second fallen angel slinked forward.

The soul worm tried to move beyond the circle, but was trapped within by the magical protections. The feather winged devil, placed her foot on his body, causing Bennett to make a horrible croaking sound. She leaned in, applying more weight, causing him to squeal as his tongue and eyes bulged out.

"No, Naamah! I will not have that! There are plenty of others for you to torment back at the palace. Just pick him up and hold on to him. Not too tightly either." Dysvakar waved a finger at the offending devil, as the other continued to stand at attention with the flask in her hands.

"Yes, my Lord." The disappointed devil, Naamah, gathered up the worm in her arms and stepped back to her original position.

"Duke Archibald Payne, I am most pleased that you upheld your part of the contract, delivering this one to me. For this as you requested, I will grant you that which you desire. Eternal existence on this world for which you will owe me one corrupted soul every century. I assume you have prepared the vessel, with which to receive your life's essence as we last discussed."

"Lord Dysvakar, I have done this. I have also put into motion, the removal of The Mother's influence within my dukedom. Bringing stronger order to the dukedom, with the aid of your power, influence, and wisdom is what I desire. Then to the rest of the kingdom, your influence will spread." The Duke spoke of his ambitions.

Dysvakar tapped his hoof and rapped his cane on the floor at this development. "Ooh! That would be just lovely. You are in a position that you will be able bring more followers to me on this world. More will know the true glory to serve me here."

The Duke hesitated and then spoke. "Lord Dysvakar, one last thing I did mention before. My love, the Duchess, I used my magic to give her a semblance of life after she died. However, I was wanting her to join me, all the better to serve you. I would ask that you restore her as she was, before she left me."

Dysvakar's demeanor quickly changed and was irritated by this request. "That I cannot do, as her soul is beyond my reach. She served another, and her soul resides with her."

The Duke was disheartened and angered and pounded his fist on the podium. "The Mother failed her and left me with no living heirs."

Dysvakar pater's red eyes narrowed and looked down on the frail man behind the podium. "The souls of each of your lost children belong to me. Were you foolish enough to believe that the more power you attained to bring you where you are now would have no cost? I am The Master, and you are my servant."

The Duke buried his head in his hands with this new realization about his lost children, along with the overwhelming emotions of guilt and regret. The hag cackled behind him. Dysvakar tapped his cane on the floor. The first devil stepped forward with the crystal flask, and set it on the floor within the circle, then returned to her position.

"Enough of this Archibald Payne. Soon enough, you will not be troubled by those memories, after you gain the even greater power, I am granting you. For the final step you must take to exist in this world beyond a mortal's lifespan, I leave you with the elixir as promised. You must completely imbibe its entire contents, in the light of the first full moon with the vessel nearby ready to receive your soul. While the reliquary that holds your soul remains safe, you cannot be destroyed." Dysvakar reminded The Duke.

"Tonight, is the first night of the full moon." The Duke suddenly realized.

"Precisely. You should already be prepared to do what needs to be done, without delay. The potency of the elixir will not remain for the next moon cycle and would fail you, and you me." The arch devil emphasized that last bit.

Auntie Olga was amused by the exchange between the Duke and his Master, stifling her cackling with her hand over her mouth.

The Duke did his best to rise and appear strong. "It will be done."

"Lovely! Ooh this did end up going nicely. I very much look forward to receiving reports of the progress of removing Her influence from the kingdom, and most importantly the next soul you will bring to me. I've had my eye on Bennett for some time, but I assume the next one may not have even been born yet. So exciting!" Dysvakar was giddy as a schoolgirl, as he stepped through the portal, disappearing into the inky blackness.

The first devil followed next, disappearing through the portal. The second devil holding Bennett in her arms, squeezed him tightly in a bearhug. Bennett vomited up a foul-smelling yellow liquid, and even worse smelling black sludge was pushed from his anus splattering on the floor. Naamah smiled and entered the portal.

Moments after the last fiend left, the rectangular void was soon covered with a purple swirling mist. Blue electric charges crackled around it, and it blinked out of existence. Immediately, the candles at the points of the pentagram snuffed out. The summoning chamber was momentarily enveloped with darkness, then the hundreds of candles suddenly lit again at once.

Auntie Olga stepped into the circle and retrieved the crystal flask filled with the magic elixir. Archibald reached for his walking stick, almost losing his balance. The hag watched him closely, as he hobbled with the aid of the walking stick toward to door.

"Bring that to the roof and tell your sisters to come." The Duke said, as he exited. Ignoring the stairwell, he stepped over the open portal on the floor and looked directly above at the hole in the ceiling, after which he levitated to the top floor of the tower; his laboratory.

Archibald managed the rest of the way, without the use of magic, to the rooftop to wait for his hag minions to join him. The crenelated rooftop had a heavy stone bench, table, and a telescope for observing the starry skies above. The large lichen covered gargoyles hanging over the tower wall, appeared to keep watch over Redrock Castle and the surrounding lands. The Duke hobbled to the bench that sat toward the center of the rooftop and carefully seated himself to wait for the hags.

Within minutes the hags made their way to the roof, one by one. Auntie Olga carried the crystal flask to the table and set it before The Duke. Mama Matilda set the platinum reliquary on the table next to it. Grandma Gertie set a jewel encrusted chalice of gold on the table with the other items.

Archibald stared above at the full moon that bathed his tower in its silvery light. The wind was strong this evening, and the whisps of long white hair on his balding head were lifted by the breeze. He closed his eyes tight and sat for a long moment, as the hags looked back and forth to each other.

"Go ahead and pour it." Archibald said, as he took hold of the chalice and tapped it on the stone table.

Grandma Gertie pulled the stopper from the flask with an audible 'pop.' She tipped it to the waiting gold chalice and emptied the contents. The black liquid had an acidic biting aroma released in its effervescence, when it hit the air.

Archibald lifted the chalice to his nose sniffing the black liquid, as the tiny bubbles rose to the top as if it were boiling without heat. He took a deep breath and then placed the cup to his lips. The potion tasted of wicked pestilence and still he forced himself to quaff the entire drink. The Duke dropped the chalice to the ground and stared ahead blankly, as it rocked about on its side.

The hags stood silent and watched with anticipation what would be next to unfold. The obese hag bit her nails nervously, as the others wrung their hands.

The Duke screamed, and grabbed at his collar trying to pull it loose. His throat and belly burned, as if it were alighted with flaming oil. He tried to rise as he gagged, but instead fell backward onto the ground, splitting the back of his head. He convulsed and spasmed madly as his mouth foamed, his head felt as a hot brand were being pressed against his temples. His fingers clutched the air as his heart exploded in his chest. His bowels and bladder emptied for a last bit of indignity, before his final breath left him.

The Duke lay still on the ground in a puddle of blood and his own filth. His eyes rolled back into his head, then the lids of his eyes shut with his mouth agape. The three hags stood unmoving, eyes fixed on Archibald's lifeless body.

Mama Matilda pointed a fat finger at the corpse. "Look!"

Inside Archibald's mouth was a white glow, which grew brighter until it exited as a small glowing orb. The orb hung above his face for a moment and then shot through the air with a blue tracer trailing. It travelled in a wide arc, high above the tower and then returned at a high velocity, striking the platinum box, toppling it off the table.

The platinum box lay on the ground with cold steam rising from it. The gold glyphs that adorned it briefly glowed, then slowly faded.

Grandma Gertie clapped her hands together. "It is done."

"Hmmm, I didn't get a chance to mention to him that idiot Barnabas failed his mission. The little fool was discovered by that boy wizard and his companions." Auntie Olga said, crossing her arms.

"Archie may not return for some time, and that fool Osbert will be trying to nose around the tower if he is absent from court too long." Mama Matilda warned.

Grandma Gertie closed her eyes, and her form transformed from the gray-haired hag in the ragged dress into the visage of The Duke, dressed in his royal finery. She reached out a small frail hand and took hold of the walking stick that was leaning on the stone table, then hobbled around to stand beside the corpse of Archibald sprawled on the ground. "I'll take care of business of the court this time."

"You just want to eat all the sweetmeats that's served after dinner." The fat hag called out.

"Possibly. You two keep watch over him, so as those fools don't try to eat him." Grandma Gertie pointed the walking stick at the gargoyles.

All the gargoyles were now turned around, facing the body of The Duke.

"You there! Turn around!" Auntie Olga scolded all the statue like creatures, until they each reluctantly took their original positions along the wall.

Mama Matilda shook her head. "I hate when they do that. The most un-loyal guardians one could call into service. No brighter than a basket of turnips."

34
Madok Changes His Plans

Madok rarely ventured from the small cabin since he sailed from Port Gwynn. He already finished the bottles of Gerard's homebrewed spirits to dull his pain and memories of the past weeks. He enjoyed a strong drink on occasion, but now he was escaping into it.

Most of the coin went to booking passage and keeping his anonymity. He was not recognized as the Captain of the Guard of Port Gwynn by the crew on this foreign vessel. Other than the ship's captain, most of the crew did not speak his language. The crew's thick islander accents and appearance resembled that of the would-be assassin, Musa, but they paid him little attention when he ventured forth to the deck.

Madok had not taken a meal since the previous day and his drunk was wearing off, leaving him with throbbing headache. Food and possibly acquiring something else to numb himself, withdrew him from his cabin.

He stepped on the deck of the carrack, wrapped in a dingy gray wool cloak and old tunic Gerard had given him. Obviously, the old things Gerard wore in the workshop, as he was still shaking bits of fine saw dust out of them. His face was no longer that of the clean-shaven disciplined soldier. The beginnings of a beard had started during his recovery time in the convent, giving him a haggard appearance with unruly dirty blonde hair on top of his head.

The crew working ignored him as he moved across the main deck. The men wore only short breeches and bandanas, as they went about their duties in the afternoon sun.

"You there. I was beginning to think we were taking a body for a burial at sea." The first mate called down to Madok, then laughed.

Madok looked up to the quarter deck. "Not just yet."

"You should eat. The cook had prepared a wonderful meal of yam stew. It will give you strength." He urged Madok.

"I think I will, friend." Madok called back, struggling to smile.

The first mate pointed at him and returned a large smile. Madok found his way below deck and scrounged up a bowl of stew with a ball of rice in the center. Leaning against the mast pole he drank from the bowl, then ate the rice with his fingers. The first mate was right; he did feel better with a little food.

As Madok ladled out 'seconds,' a commotion was coming from above deck. He paid it little mind, more interested in the few pieces of chapati bread that was laying out. He never had eaten these foods before, but could see himself getting very used to the foreign cuisine.

The sound of the anchor dropping and the sails being lowered made Madok take notice that something was going on above. He slurped down the stew and took a flat bread in hand with him, as he climbed the steps back to the main deck.

The captain stood on the quarter deck with a spy glass, looking to the coast with the first mate, as the crew lowered the dinghy. The cargo net was thrown over the side of the ship in preparation for an excursion to the shore.

Madok leaned on the taffrail, straining his eyes to see the wrecked ship near the rocky coastline. He turned and looked up to the captain on the quarterdeck.

"Captain, why are we stopping here?" Madok shouted to him.

The captain looked down to Madok, as he passed the spyglass to the first mate. "We must stop. This is a shipwreck and there are survivors on the beach. They won't last long in the Goblyn Badlands, if we don't pick them up."

"It doesn't look like there's very much of them left. I count only six." The first mate said.

"You take four armed men with you to see what happened down there. Make sure this is not some kind of ambush, before we make an offer to pick them up." The captain ordered.

"Um, captain. Since you bring that up, perhaps we should just keep going. We could report this when return to port." The first mate said, nervously.

Madok climbed up to the quarterdeck, joining the captain and the first mate. "May I take a look?"

Peering through the spyglass, Madok saw the *Lady Anne* crew on the beach, waving their arms and the shirts off their backs back at the ship. He looked along the top of the cliffside for any signs of a hidden ambush. He passed the spyglass back.

"Let me accompany your men as an extra sword arm. The least I could do, for you allowing me to join you on board." Madok said.

"I was wondering if that sword you carry was just for decoration." The captain eyed the weapon on Madok's belt.

The men boarded the dinghy and the chore of rowing to shore began. Madok sat at the bow, the first mate was at the rudder as the other four rowed. There was little trouble navigating past the wreckage of the ship and the larger rocks, that jutted out in the path of the boat, before landing on the beach. The waiting men cheered and helped pull them to shore.

"Thank the gods, you've come! This land is not fit for man nor beast." The captain said excitedly, as the men exited the dinghy.

"What happened here?" The first mate asked, as he climbed out to the beach.

"We ran aground in the shallows while everyone was below deck. Half the crew have perished since that night. Just these lads and I are left." The captain said.

"Why was everyone below deck?" The first mate said with concern.

"The damnedest thing. We picked up some passengers in Gwynn, and a pair of them turned out to be wererats. A big fight blew up in the cargo between the crew and them. In all the excitement no one was above deck to mind the rudder." The captain explained.

"Wererats?" Madok's attention was piqued.

"Yeah, would've never guessed the little girl was one of those things. She was friendly with us all before that night too." One of the crew men chimed in.

"We wouldn't be in this mess if the pretty little lady didn't ask me to take her to Sommer Harbour. Quite preachy, but I believe her to be a good soul, even though she kept strange company." The captain said.

"Juliana?" Madok looked to the captain.

"Why yes! You know her?" The captain said with surprise.

"Did a bookish young fellow happen to be with them?" Madok asked.

"Why yes! He saved us when the damned goblyns attacked and captured us." The captain responded

"A mighty wizard he was!" Another responded.

"Yeah, created light from a bone, filled caves with magic webs to stop the goblyns, and even took down an ugly two headed giantess with foul smelling air he summoned!" Yet another shouted out, excitedly.

"He created a gigantic wall of ice out of thin air here on this beach too! Craziest thing I've seen in all my born days." The old sailor added.

"Okay, okay. He did all those things?" Madok was thinking all these men may have been in the sun too long. He thought that Randall was no more a wizard, than a street performing magician, pulling things from his sleeves to entertain children.

"I'll say he did. Performing magic in King Ernald's kingdom is a high crime, but I've travelled much of the known world in my years, and I've seen others call on magic before. For good and evil." The captain said, shaking his head.

Madok stayed on the beach, as the three members of the *Lady Anne* crew and boarded the dinghy, to be taken to the ship. The captain and the others remained behind waiting for them to return.

"So, were these friends of yours you are looking for?" The captain asked.

"Well, so to speak. I was an acquaintance of Juliana and... Randall. Where are they now?" Madok asked.

The captain shook his head, with a look of disappointment in his eyes. "They left us last night without so much a word. It appeared they didn't care to be in our company anymore."

"What direction did they go?" Madok scratched the hairs on his chin as he asked.

The older sailor pointed to the west. "I saw their footprints leading in that direction on the beach. They took some supplies with them, so I believe they plan on walking all the way to Sommer Harbour."

"I'm going to regret this." Madok spoke under his breath. Looking around he saw a few crates of foodstuffs about the crew's camp. There was a serviceable backpack with gear salvaged from the ship.

The captain watched Madok as he scavenged the preserved food items in the crates and stuffed them into the backpack. "Er, son what are you planning on doing there?"

Madok ignored the captain's question and continued stuffing salted meats and biscuits into the pack. He threw around scavenged items under the sail lean to. "Is there a wineskin here in this mess?"

"I hope you are not thinking of going it alone." The captain asked.

Ignoring the captain's comment, Madok found two empty skins and sniffed inside after popping the stopper. "Any drink?"

The captain pointed to a small cask that had a metal tap driven into it, without saying anything else. Madok hastily went to work, filling the skins with warm beer and spilling an equal amount on the ground. He put on the pack and slung the skins over his shoulder, then walked toward the three men who were watching his every move.

Madok pointed westward. "That way?"

The captain and the two men looked at each other and then to Madok.

"Yes, that way. It would be foolhardy of you to trek across here alone." The captain warned one last time.

Madok set off on foot. "This isn't my first time in this frontier land."

Captain Madok was well on his way, walking along the rocky shoreline before the dinghy returned for the remaining men. The summer sun wasn't too punishing this time of day with the wind blowing over the sea. There would still be some time before sunset, so he figured it would be best to close the gap, before he stopped to find a safe place to hole up. He couldn't be sure if they stayed on the same path along the coast, but he couldn't imagine they would venture inland through the rougher terrain.

Hours passed, and the western sky was awash with the purple and orange colors of the setting sun. The sun hung low and looked large in the sky. Madok determined he would have only an hour of light left and would need to find a place to shelter until morning. A pilar like rock formation had a decent crevice he could squeeze into for cover and possibly sleep with one eye open in. It passed inspection for being clear of spiders and other unwanted pests. However, a crab giving him a pinch in the night, was something to worry about.

He sat back into the crevice, which faced northwards toward the rocky hilly landscape. Madok dug into the pack and withdrew a bit of the food he had unceremoniously stuffed in it. He ate while he watched, as the light began to dim across the rocky scenery.

"Hello! Sir!" a man's voice called out addressing Madok in his crevice hideaway.

Madok leapt to his feet and drew his sword. His sword arm was causing him pain, but he ignored it. He stepped out and looked to the direction of the voice. "Where are you?"

A large figure, silhouetted by the setting sun, held his hands in the air to appear less threatening as he slowly approached. Fat Robb was shirtless, barefoot and his pants were quite frayed. "Sorry if I startled you. I somehow became separated from my friends last night, and I woke up this morning to find myself in the middle of this horrible wilderness alone. We were shipwrecked only a few nights ago. I haven't had anything to eat or drink all day. I was hoping you could spare something and possibly allow me to camp with you tonight for safety."

Madok was suspicious of the uninvited fat man, but tossed him a biscuit anyway. "I left your shipmates this afternoon. They were being rescued by the ship I was on."

Fat Robb had a genuine look of disappointment in his eyes, as he bit into the hard tack. "So, they have left me."

"There were four passengers on your ship that I was told were travelling this direction. Have you seen them?" Madok asked.

Fat Robb made a look of disgust. "Oh, them. The worst type of people. Especially the little girl. She looks innocent enough, but she and that islander man can transform into nasty monsters! Say, can I have some of that meat?"

Madok passed Fat Robb a chunk of salted meat and returned to his crevice. "I'm holing up here for the night and heading out at first light. You're welcome camp here, but I intend on finding them."

"Oh, do you have a bounty to collect on them? Criminals, all of them." Robb said, as he tried to squeeze into the crevice which proved too narrow for him to enter.

"No. I'm planning on joining them." Madok admitted to Robb's surprise

35
An Unfortunate Campsite

Juliana awoke with sweat beading on her brow and sprung to a sitting position. Her heart raced, as she looked around their encampment. The group had sheltered against another cliff side, a small way inland, after spending an hour putting distance between themselves and the *Lady Anne* crew. Randall was on the final watch, as the sun rose in the eastern sky. Flynn and Izzy were sleeping soundly and returned to their human forms with the dawn.

Randall took notice of Juliana and the distress she was exhibiting. He walked over and crouched next to her on one knee, offering a drink from the wineskin he had on his shoulder. "What's troubling you?"

"Another nightmare. A vision. I saw the performance of a dark ritual and contact being made with denizens from The Hells. An old noble man exchanged Bishop Bennett's soul in a pact with a powerful fiend. I don't feel this was only a dream." Juliana was shaken.

Randall sat down beside her and put his arm around her to provide some comfort. Juliana reached out and held on to Randall's hand and began to calm herself.

Flynn stretched and sat up on his 'nest' on the ground. "This is not good for my back, sleeping like this. I believe there was one little pointy stone I must have not cleared before falling asleep."

Izzy also sat up and yawned, as she stretched her arms. "Hey, what are you two doing?"

Juliana stood up, as Randall quickly dropped his arm from around her shoulder. "Randall was giving me a little support, after what I believe was a vision from The Mother of a dark event that has transpired. There are things in motion that will prove to be a great danger to all. I will say it again too. We have been brought together to prevent a diabolic influence from The Hells, to wash over and poison the peoples of the world. That creature that attacked us last night was obviously sent to prevent us from this mission."

"Okay, but can we have a little breakfast first?" Flynn produced a ration of some of the food they packed for the journey.

Izzy smiled. "I'm in too, Juliana. However, I'm hungry."

Juliana laughed and joined Flynn and Izzy to pick through the morning ration. Randall sat for a few minutes feeling dejected, but got over it to fill the empty spot in his belly.

After breaking camp, they began their march through the rugged lands. Randall was not feeling his choice of footwear was suitable for this type of travel, but then he observed how little barefoot Izzy was able to walk over anything without any trouble. A spell that would enable him to fly would be something worth researching in the future. Unfortunately, that wasn't already in the book he carried. He brought up the rear while Flynn scouted ahead in the lead as Izzy and Juliana walked together holding hands. Izzy truly looked up to Juliana as a big sister.

Hours passed, as the noon sun beat down on them overhead. It was becoming harder for them to continue their march across the terrain. Izzy was fatigued, and everyone's exposed skin was burning. Vultures with bald red heads and sharp beaks kept a distance from them, but followed watching from where they perched, on the large hoodoos they walked between. Finally, they all agreed to find a place to shelter and travel by night.

Flynn inspected an area that appeared suitably shaded for them to shelter, in a ravine with sheer cliff faces on either side. It looked that the little trench that ran through the center of it, had not had water flow through it for a year. A large flat boulder from a section of the cliff face that collapsed years ago, looked to be a good place to shelter under, and provided a view of anything that entered either side of the ravine.

Time passed quietly, and one by one they drifted to sleep until no one was left keeping watch, as evening crept in and the ravine was shrouded in darkness.

The sounds of many feet and voices of desperate goblyns broke the silence, as a large group of the humanoids marched in. Their leader wore a large pointed red cap, and all the others sported smaller similarly fashioned headwear. The 'Madcap Tribe' foraging party were fleeing for their lives, through the safety of the ravine.

Izzy was the first to hear the sounds, and she slapped Flynn awake with her open hand. He in turn roused Juliana and Randall. The four prepared themselves for anything. Under the cover of the flat boulder, Flynn assumed they would just pass them by unnoticed.

The goblyn sergeant stopped and turned to face the two dozen goblyns in his charge. "Iz thinkz weez lozt themz. Shhhhh...."

The goblyns all managed to quiet down, and all stood looking wild eyed in all directions in the ravine.

"Don't tell me it's more of those annoying little arseholes." Randall whispered, just itching to test out his wand.

Flynn motioned for him to be quiet and watched what was unfolding. Juliana on the opposite side of the boulder, watched as goblyns were crowding in the area surrounding them. Izzy's eyes glowed red as she and Flynn transformed into their hybrid rat forms, as the full moon of the second evening became visible above the ravine.

A lone goblyn scouted ahead further down the ravine, while the others watched him disappear around a bend. Juliana and Izzy watched the scene unfold from their vantage point.

The goblyn sergeant raised his sword and waved his fellows to continue following the scout. "Iz tellz youz Iz smartz! Trollz not findz us herez..."

Around the bend there was the cry of a goblyn, that was quickly silenced. The rest of the Madcaps stopped advancing and looked wildly at each other. An object flew from around the bend, tossed by a large, clawed hand attached to a long arm. It hit the ground bouncing twice, before rolling to a stop at the feet of the front line goblyns. It was the head of the scout, ripped from its shoulders.

The goblyns gasped in unison, as a troll jumped out from around the bend, with its long thin arms spread wide with long claws, ready to snatch the next victim. Atop the troll's head, rested the goblin's small red cap. A wide smile with razor sharp teeth spread across its warty green face, as it laughed madly. "Duh huh huh huh huh!"

The goblyns quickly about faced to run, but two more trolls were already advancing on them from the opposite end of the ravine.

"Hold it there you pip squeaks. Maybe, we not eat all of you. We let leftovers go." Said the largest troll, dressed in armor fashioned from the bones and hides of her many kills. She stood nearly ten feet tall, even though she was stooped over, and her knuckles dragged the ground.

"Mama, I wanna eat 'em all." The young troll said angrily, as his long tongue licked its lips and then licked off a thick stream of mucous oozing from its long nose.

"Shuddup! Mama bargain with food." Mama made a wild swing with her fist, punching the young troll in the head, causing him to crash against the ravine wall.

The troll wearing the little red cap snarled at Mama. "Sweetums, I like Junior's idea. Let's eat 'em all. I hungry from chasing them all day."

The young troll jumped to its feet, shaking dust and gravel out of the coarse black matted hair atop its head. It lurched forward, reaching for the goblyn sergeant with its giant clawed hand.

The sergeant was quick with his sword and with a lucky swing, severed the beast's hand. The troll jumped back looking at the stump. The sergeant stepped back into the pack of goblyns, that were now corralled tightly together with weapons pointed out in all directions, ready to defend.

Randall watched from his vantage what was unfolding, knowing trolls were impossible to kill without the aid of fire. Junior swiped up his severed hand from the ground. The hand's clawed fingers flexed and grasped as if it were still attached to his arm. Randall watched in the moonlight, as the young troll placed the severed hand to his stump and it quickly reattached itself.

"Holy shite!" Randall slapped his hand over his mouth.

The three trolls pounced on the pack of goblyns with fury, tearing and rending their limbs from their sockets with their bare hands. Goblyns fought back, but any wound made almost instantaneously healed. Goblyns that tried to flee the fray were quickly snatched up by a leg and then dashed upon the ravine floor. In little time the ground was covered in the spilled blood and body parts of the Madcap Tribe.

"Duh huh huh huh! Heads or tails?" The troll wearing the small red cap tossed a goblyn head high up into the air. It crashed to the ground, breaking off its jaw, sending it flying under the boulder, spraying Juliana with goblyn blood and teeth.

Mama turned and slammed her fist into the troll's face, breaking its long nose. "Dum dum, don't play with food."

The injured troll tried to bend its nose back into place, but bone and cartilage had already set. It was crooked, but looked becoming on a troll.

The three trolls gathered the goblyn corpses and parts into their own piles, before they started feasting on the gruesome meal. The armored troll pulled off a goblyn's leg and sat on the boulder, beneath which the four friends hid. She hungrily bit into and pulled away the flesh from bone, slurping it up without chewing. The other two followed her lead and soon all three were enjoying the grisly feast.

Table manners were frowned upon in troll society. Eating involved loud belching, farting, smacking of lips and licking fingers, as one chewed with one's mouth open. Swearing loudly and striking another troll reaching for the same goblyn arm you had your taste buds set on, would be considered courteous. The noise of the trolls dining hid any sound made from beneath the boulder.

"We should just wait them out, until they leave." Randall suggested.

Juliana shook her head in agreeance. "Yes, certainly they will return to their den after they're finished."

Izzy studied the goblyn jawbone in her hands, touching the little pointy yellow teeth with the tips of her rat-like fingers. "They need to go. I really want to get out of here and stretch my legs."

Flynn reclined as comfortably as he could. "Probably be able to leave soon. How much could those things possibly eat?"

The morning sun arose in the eastern sky, and its light cast long shadows in the bottom of the ravine. There was a noisome mess in the bottom of the ravine. The three trolls reclined, patting their distended bellies, filled with goblyn meat. Blood was pooled in the trench, and bones that were picked clean by the trolls were tossed about haphazardly. Large piles of fresh troll dung were swarming with flies enjoying a feast of their own.

"Should we go back home now, Sweetums?" The troll was still wearing the red goblin cap atop his head.

Ma troll didn't bother looking up, and she too now sported a pointy red goblin cap. "No, I'm stuffed. I don't want to move."

The young troll also had on a red goblyn cap and was squatting with its hands on its knees, straining to push out another pile of dung. The sound was not unlike a bucket of dead fish emptying onto the ground.

Horrible smells wafted under the boulder where the four sat beneath, angrily looking at one another. No one moved. No one said a word. All held their breath and covered their noses.

36
The Merger

Madok stretched, after a less than perfect rest. Early in the evening, he was roused from sleep by the sounds of a wild creature in the campsite. When he emerged from the crevice, there was no sign of it or Robb. Possibly dragged away by the beast? The rest of the night, he stayed on his guard, barely sleeping.

The sunrise gave him the motivation to move. Gathering his things, he stepped out of the crevice finding Fat Robb sprawled out asleep on the other side of the rock formation.

He gave to Robb a light kick in the rear with his boot. "You ran off without warning me. What came into the camp?"

Fat Robb shielded his eyes from the morning sun with his hand and rolled over to look at Madok. His hands and face had dried blood on them. Obviously, it wasn't his own. "I'm sorry sir, I don't remember anything about last night."

Madok backed away from Fat Robb, throwing him an untrusting look. "Whose blood is that on you? What happened last night?"

Robb was just as shocked as Madok, looking at his own hands and seeing the dried gore. His nose began to twitch. "I-I don't know."

"I'm not buying your horse shite. Apparently, you can hunt and eat your kill raw. So, no more of my rations will I share, as it doesn't look like you're in any danger of starving. If you want to follow you can, or stay here it doesn't matter to me. I'm not going to slow my travel." Madok shook his head in disgust and walked westward.

Robb followed after Madok, who was outpacing him. "I'm coming. You won't have any problems with me. You're right, I don't even feel hungry now. I must have slept walked last night. I've heard all kinds of stories about people who do the strangest things in the night when they are sleeping. Under a full moon especially."

Madok continued following the coastline, figuring this would be the most likely path Randall and Juliana took. He kept the hood of his cloak pulled over his head for cover from the sun, even though it was uncomfortably warm. Robb kept his pace behind him and though the rough terrain pained him to walk on, any scrape, cut or stubbed toe was instantly healed, due to the curse of lycanthropy. Fat Robb did not know this, of course.

After a few hours of trudging, Madok paused under the shade of a large hoodoo with a flat platform like top. He took a few swigs from the skin of warm beer, and watched as Robb stumbled his way toward him. He pulled a biscuit from the pack and laid it on a rock along with the extra wineskin for Robb to easily spot, and continued onward. Robb scrambled to the cover of the hoodoo, devouring the dry biscuit, and followed with a drink from the skin.

He grudgingly decided it was time to move, as he watched Madok continue to put distance between them. He picked up his pace as Madok found himself standing, pondering his next move, at a shear cliffside that sprung from the sea ending the beachside coastline.

Madok looked at Fat Robb as he closed in. He felt pity on his travelling companion. "You can have my cloak. The sun is very unforgiving on naked skin."

"Thank you again kind sir!" Robb accepted the cloak, snapped on the clasp, and pulled the hood over his head.

Madok found a pathway carved into the cliffside that lead to the top. Scores of footprints, large and small, were all over the beach along with many fish bones, shells, and scraps of crude fishing nets.

Madok picked up a red hat and chuckled before tossing it back to the ground.

"What was that?" Fat Robb asked.

"There are several different rival goblyn tribes that inhabit these lands. I remember the one's that called themselves 'The Madcaps' and all of them wore those ridiculous hats. When I was a sergeant at one of the frontier forts years ago, we had run ins with them. They raided caravans that deliver supplies to mining communities. Awfully poor raiders, but enthusiastically driven. Only a few well-trained fighting men are needed to drive them off." Madok said.

"I hate those nasty little green men! You don't think any are watching us?" Robb looked around nervously.

"Possibly. There are worse things to worry about than goblyns in the Goblyn Badlands." Madok chuckled again. "They must have gone up this trail. It looks like a well-travelled path, used by everything that lives here. I'm going to scout ahead to make sure, so wait until I wave you up to follow. I want to make sure nothing gets the jump on me, from your bumbling around."

"Uh, sure." Fat Robb said, nervously.

Reaching the top, after cautiously navigating the path, Madok looked across terrain. It didn't appear any marauders awaited to ambush them, which provided some relief. His attention was caught by vultures circling over something in the distance. He could tell there was a recent kill. Concern now was whether it could be the people he was tracking.

He gave the signal to Robb to follow, then he hiked a straight path toward whatever was attracting the carrion loving fowl. When he got closer, he could see that it wasn't Randall or any of his companions. A small number of goblyns were scattered in pieces over the area. They were already covered with flies, and ants were lining up to strip meat from their bones. A few vultures, already on the ground, ignored Madok as he observed the scene.

Counting little red caps scattered on the ground, he assumed it was four goblyns. There were tracks all over the area. Smaller ones that he deduced were left by a large group of goblyns and larger ones belonged to their attackers.

"Disgusting. Serves those little bastards right. Good on whoever did this to them." Fat Robb said, arriving on the scene.

Madok shook his head. "I'm sure the real threat is whatever did this to them. I'm hoping the ones I'm following haven't met this same fate. We should continue westward."

Madok walked on as Robb studied the death scene. Concerned about his lack of protection, he found a goblyn's weapon laying on the ground. "Better than

nothing at all," he figured, as he took up the rusty, pitted short sword.

✳✳✳

"Ma, look at what I done!" Junior proudly pointed a long finger at his artistic creation on the shear, rocky face of the ravine.

Using his own feces like cement, he had arranged and attached the freshly cleaned bones of several of the goblyns in decorative patterns. A grouping of several skulls was the focus of this piece. Troll art was generally underappreciated by non-trolls in the kingdom.

"Duh huh huh huh huh! He talented like his old troll, right Sweetums?" Papa troll said, proudly.

The troll, in her bone armor regalia, inspected the frieze as she held her chin in one hand. "Hmmm. Is nice. Need one thing to make perfect."

She snatched up several of the red caps, and placed them atop the skulls. She took a few moments with each, to make sure they were set just perfect. All three stepped back to admire the work, each holding their chins in hand.

"Gee, Ma. I guess that why you boss." Junior said, smiling broadly with all his pointy teeth exposed.

Papa troll punched Junior in the head, knocking him on the ground. "I head of this family!"

Sweetums turned to Papa, poised to slash him with long claws, causing him to instantly cower.

"I mean to say, Sweetums brains and boss of family." Papa quickly recanted.

Mama troll stopped her attack and stood perfectly still, while her pointed ears stood up. She looked around and sniffed the air.

"Shut up idiots. I hear something." Mama grabbed both trolls by their long noses.

The three stood perfectly still with their ears pricked up, twitching, and listening. Mama released their noses and motioned for them to hide. The three took positions in the ravine, doing their best to squeeze into crevices and behind rocks to prepare an ambush. Junior crouched behind the flat boulder, with his eyes and nose over the top, unaware of the four hiding beneath.

Juliana, Izzy, Randall, and Flynn sat motionless, as their hearts were ready to explode out of their chests. The lower half of the troll was all that was visible to them, and Junior's odor was overpowering. If more goblyns were heading down the ravine and they slaughtered them all, they would be trapped even longer, as the trolls lazily lounged for another day. Izzy was mortified by the sight of the troll's warty genitalia dangling freely, as these creatures shunned clothing.

Fat Robb and Madok walked through the winding rocky bottom of the ravine, mostly in silence until Robb couldn't keep quiet. "I don't understand it. If you believe those creatures went down here, why are we following?"

"It seems to be the most obvious path that Randall would have come. It's mostly shielded directly from the sun overhead and if there is any water to find it will mostly likely be down here. The unfortunate thing is everything else that lives in these lands will also travel it. Just keep quiet and alert." Madok explained again.

Coming around a bend, the smell of fresh troll scat and blood hung in the air, along with the sound of buzzing flies. Madok held his hand up for them to stop. Fat Robb covered his nose with his hand, and looked about the scene as Madok advanced. The newly created troll art exhibit immediately caught his attention.

"Trolls! Turn back!" Madok called out to Robb.

Fat Robb turned to run, but stopped as Papa leapt out of his hiding spot from behind.

"Duh huh huh huh huh! Lunch!" Papa laughed, as he held out his arms wide ready to receive.

"Peek-a-boo!" Junior leapt atop the boulder and licked his chops.

"Oh, a man!" Mama stepped out from her hiding spot, eyeing Madok as she salivated.

Madok drew his longsword and tried to keep from being flanked by Mama and Junior. Fat Robb backed away with his short sword pointed at Papa, who followed slowly.

Randall and Flynn watched from their side of the boulder, the events unfolding before them, as Juliana and Izzy repositioned themselves in the crawlspace.

Randall recognized the two men. "It's that fat sailor and... Captain Madok from Gwynn. What in the hells?"

Flynn was as surprised as well. "This may be our chance to escape while those trolls are occupied."

"Captain Madok is here?" Juliana asked surprised.

Papa troll slashed at Fat Robb across his belly, with one sharp black claw. Robb staggered back, as searing pain burned and a spray of crimson escaped the wound. The lycanthropic curse instantaneously caused the wound to seal, much to Robb and the Troll's surprise.

Junior leapt through the air at Madok, who tumbled aside leaving the creature to crash into the ravine wall. Mama reached at Madok with both of her long arms. Madok rolled aside with his sword in one hand and jumped back to his feet.

"We must help them now!" Juliana crawled from their hiding space with her mace at the ready. The other three also emerged, drawing the troll's attention from Madok and Robb.

"Looky there Sweetums! I knew I smelt something awful here all night! Awfully delicious!" Papa troll pointed to Randall and Flynn. Fat Robb used the opportunity to dart past him, to hide further down the ravine from whence he came.

Mama was busy looking over at Juliana and Izzy. "Much sweeter than goblyn meat! You idiots can have all the others; I just want to eat that little girl!"

Izzy's eyes opened wide and she let out a loud squeak. Juliana stood in front of her ready to defend. Madok was surprised by the arrival of allies from under a rock. Flynn was at the ready with rapier and dagger drawn, knowing that such weapons would be of little help against the trolls. Randall already knew what the best magical solution was in this situation.

Junior flung himself at Madok, with razor sharp teeth gnashing and wildly swinging with his long arms. Madok parried all attacks coming at him from the creature. It was young, but stood seven feet in height with a long reach. Madok slashed his blade across the troll's chest, and as it staggered back, the wound slowly closed shut.

The hulking mama swung her fist, knocking Juliana onto the ravine floor. She was knocked out cold when her head smashed into a rock. Izzy screamed and scrambled up the face of the cliffside. Mama troll ambled over toward Izzy and plucked her away. Mama held her up in the air, as Izzy kicked and screamed disturbing curses.

Papa swung and clawed wildly at Flynn, but the fleet-footed rogue dodged his attacks and quickly worked his way behind the troll. Flynn thrust the rapier and dagger into the monster's backside, piercing its kidneys. Papa howled, as Flynn twisted and pulled out his blades. The troll spun around to grab Flynn, but he already moved beyond his reach.

Randall had the wand in hand and decided to chance it. Not sure how effective it would be against his foe, he pointed it directly toward Papa and said, "Conus frigus!" The crystal glowed with a cold blue light, before the evocation magic brought forth a great frigid wind, that blew in a great conical blast, originating from its tip. Papa troll was caught in the center of the winds covering him in a layer of white frost, only narrowly missing Flynn. The troll appeared frozen solid, before tumbling forward and crashing to the ground. A large circular section of the ravine wall was covered in a sheet of glistening frost in the aftermath of Randall's attack.

Junior lumbered toward Madok, swiping with his claws. Madok ducked the swings, and fell to one, slicing his blade across its Achillies tendon. Junior fell face first onto the ground crying out. "Mama! Mama! Mama!"

The lead troll turned to face Madok and tossed Izzy aside. Izzy hit the ground and rolled with the fall. Izzy saw Juliana laying on the ground several feet away with a puddle of blood by her head. She sprang up and ran to her aid.

Mama troll lunged at Madok, as a blow he landed on her was deflected by the primitive bone armor she wore. Her long arms reached forward, grappling him and sank her sharp claws into his sides. Mama's gaping maw was open wide and the stench of her foul hot breath bore on Madok, as she drew him in for a bite.

Madok swung his longsword with all the force he could muster against Mama's thin rubbery neck, when he was in striking distance. The blade made a clean cut through bone, muscle, and sinew, severing the huge head with one blow. Mama dropped Madok to the ground, landing flat on his back. Mama's decapitated body walked around in circles, with its arms stretched out feeling about.

Before Madok could get to his feet, a sharp pain in his leg drew his attention. Mama troll's decapitated head sank her teeth into his leg through his leather boot.

Flynn's stabbed the severed head with his rapier. Mama unlocked her jaws, as Flynn held her head in place to so Madok could scoot away.

Junior rose after his severed tendon reattached. Enraged, Junior charged Madok where he lay on the ground.

Madok took his sword in both hands and swung low at Junior's thin legs. The skilled swordsman cleaved through its lower extremities, felling the troll like a tree. Junior lay flat on the ground again, and his severed feet lay twitching in a pool of dark blood.

Randall shouted to Flynn as he ran to his aid. "Quick! Put that head on the feet!"

Without hesitation he pushed mama's head off his rapier, onto Junior's severed feet. Randall said the incantation which brought forth a fan of flames from his palms, immolating the quivering troll parts, until the flesh melted away from the bone into a puddle of black tarlike goo.

Madok watched with amazement, Randall's command of magic for the first time. The distraction was brief, as he jumped up to his feet and blocked an attack from papa troll, that was intended to strike Randall from behind. He swung the longsword, laying a whirlwind of blows, slashing the troll's arms, creating deep gaping wounds that bled almost black with its dark blood. The troll backed away and Madok refused to let up his attack.

Izzy knelt by Juliana with her head on her knee, as she applied pressure to the cut on her head. She glanced up to see mama troll's body was walking around blindly, bumping into the ravine wall, and stumbling over larger rocks that lay in her path. They were in line to be trampled beneath the huge monster. Izzy left the unconscious Juliana on the ground, and darted straight into the path of the approaching behemoth.

Izzy shot between the headless troll's legs, then jumped on her back. She plunged the dagger into its back and used it for leverage to pull herself upwards, until she could reach and sink her fingers into the bloody neck cavity to gain a hold. She pulled the blade and continuously plunged it into the creature's back, between vulnerable spaces in the crude bone armor.

Mama's body spun in circles and the long arms tried to reach behind to grab the elusive girl, whose enchanted dagger was inflicting painful wounds that closed each time she pulled the dagger free.

Junior attempted to rise on the stumps on the end of his legs, but was unable to balance and fell flat on his face each time. "Ma! Stop dancing around with that girl and help!"

Flynn joined Madok in the fight with papa troll. Flynn slipped in and took up a position behind papa, as Madok kept him occupied with his swordplay. Again, Flynn thrust into the troll's back, landing well placed attacks to its vitals which served to distract it from Madok, who it faced head on. Madok had received a few slashes from the troll's claws to his arms, but nothing to hinder his onslaught. In one fluid motion as the troll reached for him with both hands, Madok jumped to the side and in a midair turn brought his blade down onto the beast's outstretched arms. It severed just above the elbows, removing both of papa's large hands.

Papa held up the stumps to his eyes, as a stream of dark blood pumped out with each beat of his heart. "Now you gone and done it! I kill you dead!"

Several glowing bolts of magic force struck papa troll in the face, knocking him sillier than before, making him stagger backwards before hitting the ground. Flynn looked across the ravine to Randall, who had just loosed.

Junior crawled over to hiss headless mama, who was still trying to reach Izzy on her back. Mama stomped down on his head, smashing it into the ground. As the headless troll tripped over Junior, Izzy released her grip and slid off her back. Junior lay pinned beneath mama with a mouthful of dirt.

Randall shouted to Madok and Flynn to follow as he ran to Izzy, who was back to Juliana's side. They all rallied together joining Juliana. He held out his wand again and pointed it at the ravine walls, making a figure '8' motion and then saying the command words "Glacies murus!" From the crystal, a silver ray shot forth and an ice wall quickly formed, as he built it up, back and forth to each side of the ravine.

"Wait! Don't leave me here!" Fat Robb jumped out from his hiding place. He ran across the ravine, hoping to make it before the ice wall was too high to cross.

Papa troll sat up as Robb passed. The troll's severed hand caught Robb's ankle and sank its sharp black claws deep into him, as it squeezed with a vice like grip. Robb tripped and hit the ground and the goblyn short sword slipped out of his hand. He pushed up and looked over his shoulder, as papa crawled atop of him.

"All is not lost! I've got a fat juicy one! Duh huh huh huh!" Papa laughed with glee, as he opened his maw and sank his sharp teeth into the meaty flesh of Fat Robb's buttocks.

Robb screamed, as his flesh was torn away and devoured. "No! Not like this! No, please!"

"Papa share!" Junior had pulled himself over to join. Robb turned just in time to look into the young troll's eyes on its warty green face, before it grabbed him by the head and twisted it off his shoulders. The two in a frenzy of hunger, began feeding.

The headless mama troll sat motionless on the ground with her legs crossed patiently waiting, as a growth of a new head began to form at the base of her neck. She drummed her claws on her knees, passing the time.

The ice wall sealed the ravine, at least temporarily, to prevent the trolls from following. Flynn and Randall knelt to check on Juliana, who was beginning to rouse. Madok stared at the giant wall of ice, that stood some thirty feet tall and spanned the width of the ravine. He looked back at Randall, who felt Madok's eyes upon him.

Randall looked up at the tall warrior, who was now bloodied by the claw marks, from the melee with the troll family. His short, dirty blonde hair was a mess and a beard grew on his square chin, his clothes were filthy and torn. He didn't appear to be the same man from Port Gwynn, that commanded the city guard and the respect of its most elite citizens. He appeared as another vagabond, just like the rest of them.

Flynn looked at Madok with suspicion. The man that led the raid on the nest, killing his friends and forcing him and Izzy to leave the only home they had known for years. He had been arrested and thrown in the Port Gwynn jail personally, by this man once upon a time, only to escape that same night in rat form.

Izzy looked at Madok and smiled. "Thank you for helping us!"

Juliana opened her eyes and moaned. She had a throbbing blue lump under the split on her forehead. Everything slowly stopped spinning, and she began to focus on everyone's faces around her. She looked to each of her friends, one by one, and smiled. Her eyes then shot over to Madok, who was standing over her.

"You. The Mother just told me you were to join us." Juliana whispered, just loud enough for all to hear.

All eyes turned to Juliana and then up to Madok.

Izzy sighed. "Well, the fat man was supposed to be mine."

All eyes turned from Madok to Izzy.

37
The Awakening

Barnabas perched on the stone table atop the tower, with his legs crossed and arms folded, basking in the afternoon sun. The stub where his tail once was, now bandaged. He watched impatiently, the crumbled frail body of Duke Archibald Payne, as it still lay where it fell days before. Putrefaction set in, and the body was bloating and blood had settled, thanks to the pull of gravity. Most of his face was a pale white, and the side touching the floor was purple. The dried bloody foam, that leaked from his nose and mouth onto the ground, completed the picture.

"He smells far better in this state. None of those perfumes are needed to mask the old man smell now." Barnabas's observation was only halfway sarcastic.

The hag, Grandma Gertie, waved a stick with a horse hair tassel attached to it, to shoo away the gathering flies from the body. "Oh, it is a sweet smell. Between the stupid gargoyles and these little black angels, I'm concerned if he doesn't rise soon, he'll be hobbling around with pieces missing and what remains filled with burrowing maggots."

One gargoyle looked over its shoulder and grunted, then returned its gaze watching over the city.

"Yes, I mean you!" The hag stood up to stretch, waving a disapproving finger at the gargoyle. She looked around annoyed. "Where are my sisters? It's time for one of those other bitches to stand watch over Archie."

Barnabas smiled. "I imagine they are leaving you to rotting corpse babysitting duty, while they wander the castle in the guise of Archie, drinking his wine and gorging on his food. Hopefully, no one sees two Dukes together."

"Bah! It would be like those fools to do something as ill-conceived as that. When they work together without my charge, something usually goes wrong." Grandma Gertie grew furious at the thought.

Barnabas's eyes opened wide and he pointed at the body of The Duke. "He moves!"

The Duke's frail thin fingers began twitching and his eyelids fluttered, then suddenly opened wide. His eyes were lifeless and cloudy, but a light red glow came from within them. He slowly rose to a sitting position and looked around the tower top through his lifeless eyes. He now saw things differently than the living. His eyesight, that was beginning to fail him in life, was sharper than ever and revealed auras from the energy that emanated from the others on the tower with him.

The Duke rose to his feet, without the aid of his cane. Something he was unable to do for years. When he stood, his soiled clothing peeled from the floor, encrusted with the bodily fluids that escaped him during his death throes. He stood up straight, no longer hunched over from the pains that had tortured him for so long.

The hag and imp watched silently, as Archibald took a few steps without his walking stick, picking up his pace and then walked the perimeter of the round tower. He was not hindered anymore by crippling old age.

Archibald smiled at his servants. "I made the right choice. My mobility has returned and I have life eternal! What could be the downside?"

"Well boss, I believe you won't need to sleep in that fine bedchamber of yours, nor eat or drink. That seems like a downside." Barnabas said, thoughtfully.

"The continuing decomposition of this mortal body will continue, thus making it a challenge to rule the dukedom." Grandma Gertie added.

The Duke looked at the afternoon sky, staring directly into the sun without a care. Then he became concerned. "How long have I been up here?"

"A little while." Barnabas responded quickly.

The Duke looked over to Barnabas, who turned invisible in a puff of smoke and ducked under the bench.

"I can see you, imp." The Duke said angrily. The Duke's unliving eyes could see through Barnabas's magic.

The hag cleared her throat. "Three days, Duke."

Archibald turned to the hag. "Oh my. I assume you and your sisters were taking care of business as discussed."

"Oh yes, Archibald. That man, Osbert, has been taking care of the day to day needs as he has for years."

The Duke nodded his head, encouraged by this news. "Good on Osbert. Always loyal. What of you, Barnabas? The mission I sent you on? What in The Hells happened to your tail?"

Barnabas stepped out from under the bench, with his wings tucked behind him, looking at the floor. "Well Boss, there was a minor setback."

The Duke's brow furrowed and the hag cackled. The Duke waved her to be silent and she immediately obeyed, but gave a yellowed smile of rotten teeth.

"Speak!" The Duke glared at the imp.

Barnabas gulped and then gave his report. "Boss, I swears I had the boy's book in these claws, when I was violently ganged up on and attacked by all of them. The big rat man cut my tail off with a giant enchanted sword and then tried to strangle me with it! The girl is a warrior priestess, that summoned a flock of angels from the clouds to smite me. I barely escaped when the boy tried to send me back to The Hells, blasting me with all manner of magics. Lucky I was able to make it back here to report, missing only my beautiful tail."

The hag cackled. "The worst liar from the second level of hell. Auntie Olga saw a little girl remove your tail, with the flick of a dagger, before you lost the scrying pendant."

"You old twat! That was a rat beast of great strength and size..." Barnabas screamed at the hag.

The Duke covered his ears. "Quiet, imbeciles! You failed this simple task, to thwart them from whatever ambitions they have, now their guard will be up. It was a mistake to trust you with this."

The hag flashed Barnabas a mocking smile, as the Duke paced the floor. Barnabas glared at the hag and sulked, defeated.

"Enough of this nonsense. I need ensure the affairs of my dukedom are in order, with no mayhem in my absence. Recall your sisters, I wish to see the duchess and walk the castle." The Duke said, as he descended into the tower.

"We should probably make sure the Boss is cleaned up and changes his clothes, before he makes his grand entrance." Barnabas said, thoughtfully.

Grandma Gertie shook her head. "Yes, I'm not sure how long he can keep up the ruse, with the sweet smell of death and decay surrounding him."

Barnabas flew alongside her, as they entered the tower. "He looks more like a walking corpse than before. He should check himself in that fancy mirror, and have a reality check."

Grandma Gretie cackled, as she barred the iron door behind them.

Hours passed, as Duke Archibald Payne was briefed by the sister hags, of the goings on in the dukedom, while bathing and dressing in fresh clothes. The passage of time no longer mattered, as the needs of a living body no longer applied to him. No need for sleep, food, drink, air, or protection from the elements, would concern again. His outward appearance was easily disguised with a spell, that allowed him to have the appearance as he was in life. One thing he decided he would not disguise was his mobility. No longer would he be viewed as the feeble old man, with escorts to carry him through his own castle. He would walk the halls without the aid of a walking stick. He would never appear weak ever again.

The Duke emerged from the tower into the hall of his waiting guards. He waved away the servants with his waiting litter and boldly walked ahead of his guards. They followed behind surprised, throwing quick glances to one another in silence.

The underlying scent of death was barely noticeable on his freshly washed body anointed with a strong perfume he often used in life. It was not unlike the scent of flowers, surrounding a shrouded body, awaiting internment. Unbeknownst to him, was the coldness that emanated from his body and caused chills in those in close contact with him.

Archibald entered the throne room, proudly climbing the steps to his throne and smiling, as he took his seat. His guards took their positions on either side of him. The hall was empty of other persons, save two women scrubbing the floors with hand brushes, and a bucket of soapy water.

His dead ears heard a cacophony of voices of person's he had passed sentences on, pleading for their lives in the hall. His dead eyes could see colorless, transparent, phantom images of each kneeling before him on the floor in chains. He looked over his shoulders at the guards and then to the cleaning women who did not acknowledge their presence. Scores of small orbs of light also floated in the great hall, only seen by Archibald's eyes. He was intrigued by his new senses granted in this existence.

Osbert's entry into the hall was unnoticed, until he stood at the bottom of the steps and cleared his throat twice. Looking up to the throne with hands clasped and one eyebrow cocked, he asked. "You sent for me, Your Highness?"

The Duke focused on Osbert waiting below. "I did. I want to have Lord Mayor Geoffrey Walters of Port Gwynn brought to Redrock, while he awaits trial. I want him here for safe keeping in the meanwhile. His co-conspirators have escaped justice by death or fleeing the city." The Duke stifled laughing at the 'death' part.

"I will send word to the High Sheriff for his transport immediately, under heavy guard. Your Highness, I would ask what you have decided on the course of action to take at the Iron Hills Mining Company encampment?" Osbert said with eyes averted.

The Duke was puzzled by the question. The hags had skipped over this in their briefing of what transpired during his absence. "Osbert, refresh my memory on this matter."

Osbert sighed and took a deep breath. "Your Highness, in my daily briefings the past two days, I have brought it to your attention. The miners have shut down all operations until their demands are met."

The Duke knew this was his blunder, entrusting the hags with any responsibility, other than performing special espionage assignments. The Iron Hills Mining Company's labor force was comprised entirely of nonviolent criminals, who were contracted out to reduce crowding in the prisons across the dukedom. Ten years of forced labor bought your freedom. However, this often broke the person in body and spirit and often death. Uprisings were not uncommon and quickly quelled by the mercenaries, hired to keep order. Often these mercenaries were criminal types, who themselves served time for violent offenses.

"Osbert, run it by me one more time please." The Duke sat back in his throne, listening intently.

Osbert held his hands behind his back and addressed The Duke with the same message he had previously relayed to the disguised hags. "An uprising at the southwestern mining camp broke out a week ago. The miners had killed several of the guards and now hold the encampment and mine. The Director and a few others are being held as hostages, and the few remaining guards that escaped were sent back with their demands. They want to be supplied with provisions and allowed safe passage out of the dukedom, in exchange for the hostages."

"Hostages? Bah. How do they have the upper hand? An unruly rabble of men armed with picks and shovels? The Iron Hills Mining Company should be hiring professional guards to keep order." The Duke was annoyed.

"Your Highness, if demands are not met, they will collapse the mine and bury the iron ore haul to be supplied to The King. The smelter in the capital is in short supply of quality ore for steel, needed in preparation for the inevitable invasion from the north." Osbert said, with concern.

"Ah yes, crazy Queen Cecilia declares herself Emperess of the world and threatens to invade once again, if my nephew, the king, doesn't swear fealty to her. This has been going on for the past decade, since she took over the throne from that senile husband of hers. King Aadam should not have married an ambitious young woman his late stage in life." The Duke snickered to himself, thinking of another's mortality.

"Archibald, that may be true, but King Ernald expects the shipments from the dukedom to arrive without delay." Osbert gave his council.

"Those miners have been breathing bad air too long deep within the earth, if they believe they will be granted clemency through extortion! We have more than enough fresh prisoners to replace these trouble makers. Send what they ask for. A few wagons laden with enough supplies to make their journey. Once they have moved a few leagues beyond the mining camp, a force of mounted soldiers can round them up and finish them off. Make the arrangements now." The Duke always formed a quick solution.

Osbert gave a short bow before turning to leave. "As you wish Your Highness."

The Duke watched as Osbert made the long walk out of the hall. Several minutes went by in the vast empty hall, as he sat with his chin on his hand. The guards were waiting patiently standing to attention on either side of him, wondering if they would be there until late in the evening.

"I wish to see the Duchess. Come." The Duke and his guards exited the throne room and made the trek across Redrock Castle to his bedchamber.

As they walked the halls people would bow, then gawk in amazement. The guards marching along with the him still didn't understanding the miraculous change in his condition, but kept their silence.

The sound of a loud scuffle, down the long hall to his chambers, caused the Duke break into a run, his guards double timed to keep up. Brandon was not at his station in front of the chamber door that stood wide open. From within the sounds of the nurse's screams, Brandon yelling, and a loud crash.

Archibald stopped at the open door and looked in at the scene. The Duchess lay on the ground, her head crushed under a small marble statue, furniture was toppled and a chair broken. Brandon comforted the nurse in his arms. He stepped through the door with the guards following on either side. The Duke screamed. "Katherine!"

Brandon released the nurse and held his hands up. The nurse was sobbing and frightened burying her face in her smock.

Brandon's voice was shaking. "Your Highness, I heard Ms. Eleanor scream and I rushed in to find the Duchess strangling her. I pulled her off Eleanor, and she attacked me."

Eleanor spoke, choking back her tears. "Your Highness, I'm sorry! I didn't mean to kill her! She started clawing Brandon and I hit her with that statue. There was evil within her. Her existence goes against nature!"

Archibald looked back and forth between his two servants, then pointed his forefinger at the two. In a strangely hollow, yet booming voice, he shouted the incantation. "Pessulum autem fulgur!"

A bright, forked bolt of lightning erupted from the palm of the Duke's open hand. The blue bolts struck Brandon and Eleanor in the chest, flinging them across the room crashing into the far wall. The loud sound of a thunderclap followed, shaking the room and the furnishings within. The smell of ozone filled the air, as the Duke stepped over to the body of Katherine and kneeled. Smoke rose from the charred flesh on the chests of his servants, whose bodies lay broken in a heap.

The four guards quickly exited the chamber and the sounds of their clanking armor faded down the hall. Archibald removed the statue from the Duchess's crushed skull, of which there was no blood, but desiccated chunks of brain tissue had spilled out. He took her hand in his and closed his eyes tightly, but no longer could he produce tears. The spell that he had cast to disguise his appearance faded and his true self was once again visible. He would not be able to bring her back with his magic again.

The Duke rose and clenched his small fists tightly. "No more distractions now. My real work must begin."

PART III

38
The Wheel

The five arrived in Sommer Harbour, after the two-week trek across the coastline. They were questioned at a border outpost of their wanderings in the Goblyn Badlands, and were released. They planned their aliases and background stories ahead of time, just in case. Word of the *Lady Anne* shipwreck hadn't reached the outpost, nor the stories of were rats, a wizard, warrior priestess, or a fugitive captain of the guard.

Sommer Harbour was smaller than Port Gwynn, but was the second largest port of entry into the dukedom. It was south of Redrock a week's ride by horse, or a few days travel down the Great Copper River. The city, as they discussed, would be a good place for a fresh start by pooling their resources and special talents. They acquired a fair amount of coin, from beautiful Queens Gronk and Brack, that afforded them a room in the city. The Barber Surgeon, Triston rented out the spare room above his practice to supplement his income. Haircuts, shaves, bloodlettings, tooth pulling, and the occasional enema rounded out some of the services offered. The five didn't employ any extra services.

The small room lacked privacy, furniture, or any comfort other than protection from the elements. However, the leaky roof and a draft that blew in from a hole in the wattle and daub construction, guaranteed this was a temporary living arrangement. Blankets on straw pallets made up their bedding, and a chamber pot topped with a lid sat behind a thin curtain in a corner. Izzy passed the time, watching Triston perform dental work on a harbor man the first morning through a hole in the floor. Most of the first day was spent about town to resupply and freshen up.

Flynn and Randall relaxed in the pool designated for men in the public bath house. The large building was a popular spot in Sommer Harbour and unlike the bathhouse they were accustomed to in Port Gwynn. It was a magnificent stone structure built during the time of an ancient civilization, predating the kingdom. It was one of the few remaining remnants in Sommer Harbour reflecting their architectural features, high arched coffered ceilings supported by ornate pillars, and colorful mosaic tile work. Many arched windows allowed sunlight in, and warm water was piped in to the pools from a heating room.

"Not what I was expecting, but I'll take it. The smell and grime, encrusted in me and my clothes, would have offended a shite eating sewer monster." Randall leaned with his back to the side of the pool, as was Flynn.

"I must agree with you there. Even in The Nest, I managed to enjoy a hot bath almost every week's end. Something others at The Nest didn't find to be a necessary endeavor. Putting new clothing on a clean body is welcome." Flynn said with eyes closed.

"Yes, they can burn my old garments to heat the waters here." Randall closed his eyes, as steam rising off the water put him into full relaxation mode.

"Our new companion made quite the impression on Izzy and Juliana." Flynn said smiling, without opening his eyes.

Randall tensed up and opened his eyes, looking over at Flynn. "What exactly are you getting at?"

Flynn opened one eye looking over at Randall. "Oh, it's easy to see Izzy is looking at him as a father type figure. As for Juliana, well, she obviously looks at him as something quite far from that."

"I was just beginning to relax. Thanks." Randall closed his eyes and submerged himself completely below the water, blowing bubbles as Flynn laughed aloud.

Finishing in the hot bath, the two dipped into the cold waters of the frigidarium pool before toweling off and dressing in their new attire. The pair left the bath house feeling revitalized.

Randall's share of the coin afforded him a new red tunic with gold thread embroidery, and a finely tooled leather belt with matching vambraces. He also acquired a new component pouch and sheath to conceal his wand. A gray cloak lined with fur with a silver clasp wrapped his body. Finishing the ensemble, a pair of poulaine shoes, and pantaloons. Atop his head, he had a green slouch cap with a peacock's feather plunged into it.

Flynn was more conservative with his outfitting, preferring not to attract attention to himself or appear foppish as his counterpart. A simple airy ivory tunic that laced in the front, a gray hooded cloak, and proper boots for travelling.

Exiting the bath house, there was a large procession of townsfolk heading to the city square. The two looked at each other and without speaking joined the crowd. The talk was of the surviving prisoners brought in from the Iron

Hills Mining Company uprising. Flynn listened to the excited conversations as they pushed along with the townspeople. The men who were brought in after the ambush set by the Duke's soldiers, were to face his justice.

The wide-open cobblestone square was crowded with people of all walks of life and vendors parking their food carts there were lucrative. A wooden platform had been freshly constructed, around which many soldiers stood at attention clad in mail and armed with halberds. Tabards bearing the colors of the Duke were worn over each of the men's armor, setting them apart from Sommer Harbour's city guard.

"I don't like the look of this one bit." Flynn said, as he looked across the throngs of eager spectators. Some held small children on their shoulders.

"I feel the people this reception is for, may share your sentiment." Randall responded, searching out the condemned.

The afternoon sun was beating down on the crowd, so the smell of body odor, mixed with food, and fresh dung dropped by passing pack animals, was overwhelming. Randall's new, out of season attire, was already drenched in sweat and he had to continually wave away a bothersome fly.

The procession approached from a wide throughfare. Mounted soldiers escorted a wagon with the prisoners. The two shackled men, dressed only in rags to cover their privates, held onto the iron bars as they peered out into crowd. Both were disheveled, dirty, and injured; fear filled their eyes as the wagon was drawn to the platform.

Climbing the steps of the wooden platform, a contingent of members of the city government of Sommer Harbour and a judge from Redrock took their places. Each of the shackled men were led to the top of the platform by a pair of guards, without any resistance.

Randall turned to another onlooker, a mature woman wearing a common dress and head covered in a plain scarf. "What's going on here?"

The woman sighed before speaking. "Milord, they are to be broken on the wheel."

Randall looked to the platform with disgust. "What crime did they commit to warrant something so extreme? This punishment hasn't been in practice well before I was born."

The woman shook her head sadly. "The Duke's official decree reinstated its use. These two were part of the uprising at the mine. Both are born of Sommer Harbour. Their sentence is being carried out here as a deterrent.

A tall muscular man and a woman of similar size and stature, climbed the steps carrying large clubs. Each wore a dark hood over their head to hide their identities and were clad in hardened black leather armor. Following them, several assistants hauled two oversized spoked wagon wheels and two tall poles.

One of the condemned men urinated on himself before the crowd, as the stage was set with for the spectacle.

A round man with a gray twirled mustache and goatee stepped forward. Dressed in a finely tooled leather doublet and white ruff collar, Lord Mayor Ralf Hughes spoke in a commanding voice. "Fine citizens of Sommer Harbour, we gather this afternoon, as witnesses, to the swift justice incurred for violent insurrection committed within the dukedom. From Redrock, Judge Bartholomew travelled to oversee the sentence carried out this day."

The Lord Mayor took a step back as the aged Judge Bartholomew stepped forward, with the aid of his gnarled walking stick in one hand and a rolled scroll in the other. His long white beard contrasted the plain black robes he wore. Unrolling the scroll, he looked across the large crowd. "Citizens of Sommer Harbour, the two men brought before you on this day, were involved in the rebellion at the Iron Hill Mining Company. This rebellion resulted in the murder of several people, as well as sabotage. The two before you, were justly tried in the high court of Redrock and the sentence passed of the savage, barbaric attack was deemed befitting an equal savage, barbaric punishment. Niles Tanner and Henry Cooper were sentenced to ten years of hard labor for crimes originally committed in Sommer Harbour, and thus their punishment will be carried out in Sommer Harbour. Let it be known, those who commit criminal acts of savagery in the dukedom of His Highness Duke Archibald Payne, will receive the harshest retribution. Bring them forth!"

The two men were dragged forward to the front and dropped to their knees before Judge Bartholomew. Both looked to the ground, avoiding the eyes of the crowd amassed in the square. Randall and Flynn, as the rest of the onlookers, watched in nervous silence.

The Judge rolled the scroll up and addressed the condemned. "Niles Tanner and Henry Cooper, do you have any final words to say to the citizens of Sommer Harbour before your sentence is carried out?"

Both men continued to kneel in silence shaking their heads 'no.'

Randall leaned to Flynn and whispered. "I would have said some final words in my defense, or at least curse that geezer of a judge."

Flynn whispered. "I believe those men no longer have tongues to say any words with."

Randall now noticed the dried blood around their mouth and chin. He was mortified by the thought.

"Their sentence will be carried out without further delay." The judge waved over to the assistants, who lead the two men to their respective wheels.

The silence of the crowd broke, as onlookers exhibited a variety of emotions. Some cheered, others gasped with dread of what was to come.

Paul Wolff

"Flynn, wouldn't it be customary in these instances, for a priest to be present to say some words of comfort to them?" Randall said with concern.

The woman leaned over to them, overhearing the conversation. "I assume you have just arrived in town?"

"Yes, only yesterday." Flynn responded.

"The churches were shuttered, by royal decree, a week ago. They say, they are under investigation for corruption. High ranking clergy were arrested. It's sacrilegious in my opinion, to do such a thing to those that serve The Mother and to Her house." The woman became emotional, as she filled Randall and Flynn in.

On the platform, Niles and Henry were each bound by their ankles and wrists to their wheels, rendering them helpless. All departed the platform, aside from the two executioners and their assistants, before the punishment was carried out.

Niles attempted to speak out, but couldn't form any words and made unintelligible sounds as he cried out. The female executioner raised her heavy club over head with both hands and brought it down in a crushing blow to his arm. The other executioner followed suit and struck a blow, cracking Henry's shin with the first strike.

Randall and Flynn grimaced, nauseated by the spectacle, as others in the crowd shared their feelings, and then others that cheered it on. Slowly and methodically, the blows were landed on different sections of the men's limbs, until bones were splintered and shards pierced their skin.

Time slowed. as the men moaned in agony when the assistants were called to cut their binds. Their broken arms and legs were twisted and turned in unnatural positions. as they were flipped on their bellies exposing their backs. The two executioners landed blows across each man's spinal column to complete the breaking.

The assistants threaded their broken limbs and bodies through the spokes of the wheels. After completing the grisly task, the wheels were lifted to display to the crowd.

Niles and Henry were unable to move, but their mouths could be seen moving and their eyes rolling in their agony. Each breath they took expanded their lungs, causing their cracked ribs and broken backs to act as skewers.

"They're still alive." Flynn said, appalled.

Randall looked away.

Both wheels were mounted on the ends of the poles, which were then raised and secured into the platform by the assistants, as the of executioners barked their orders. Soon the men were on display, high above the crowd atop the wheels, to be left to die slowly of exposure.

240

Cries from the crowd for a 'coup de **grâce**' for the condemned were ignored. Judge Bartholomew and the Lord Mayor returned to the platform, and the executioners exited.

Jude Bartholomew looked across at the crowd and made his final address. "The condemned will remain on the breaking wheels until there is no life left in their bodies, and thereafter for a month's time. Only then will they be removed to be quartered and dispersed, outside the city, for eaters of carrion to feed upon. Their heads will be placed on spikes at the city gates for a years' time, as a warning to those that would commit crimes against the dukedom, by order of His Highness, Duke Archibald Payne."

Flynn nudged Randall. "I've seen enough of this. We should be going. Something has changed since we fled Port Gwynn. Remember Madok telling us of the Cathedral being shuttered and your former employer, Geoffrey's arrest."

"Not just yet." Randall stared at the platform, with the men's broken bodies lashed through the wheels.

Looking around, Randall found the crowd was mostly distracted by the scene on the platform and others were dispersing. He held up his hand pointing his forefinger toward the breaking wheels, with thumb raised upwards and spoke. "Flatus illum!"

Four darts of force were conjured forth and shot over the heads of the crowd. Their paths split and arced wide, then converged on their targets. A pair struck Miles and the other Henry, ending their lives and their suffering. Randall was filled with guilt, but knew the merciful ending of their suffering to send them to their gods, was the highest form of compassion.

The Judge and Lord Mayor dropped to the ground and the Duke's soldiers took a defensive stance, protecting them with their halberds. They all scanned the crowd for the source of the magic bolts.

"Whatever that was, it killed those two." Lord Mayor Hughes said, as he looked up at the bodies on the wheels and then across the square at the crowd.

Judge Bartholomew raised his head up and looked to the Lord Mayor. "Not 'whatever,' but 'who.' A practitioner of the dark arts is here."

Flynn and Randall disappeared into the crowd exiting the square. There would be much to share with the others.

39
The Mob Rules

Juliana slammed her wooden tankard onto the table. "No, Randall did the right thing. The practice of public humiliation, torture and execution was wisely ended as The Mother's mercy spread across the kingdom. Learning places of worship have come under siege and members of the clergy imprisoned, is making things all too clear now."

Randall relayed the day's events to the others, as they shared a meal in a corner of the Raging Boar Tavern. Thusly named for the mangey stuffed boar head with large tusks, displayed above the hearth. Their chosen corner was not a private affair in the crowded common room. The conversation was the same amongst other patrons visiting this evening, and the five didn't stand out.

Madok sat back in his chair, crossed arms, and furrowed brow. "I'm saying it was foolish to pull your stunt in the middle of the crowd. If you had to, why not wait until the dead of night with less risk of being spotted.

"I would have to agree with the old bugger on this one Randall." Flynn said, as he slurped stew from his soup bowl, after taking a jab at Madok who was only a few years older than himself.

Izzy looked at the others without saying a word, drinking and dribbling stew on her new dress. Randall eyed the drink that filled his tankard, disappointed.

Randall called over the matronly woman lugging a tray of tray of dirty dishes. "Kind woman, I asked for a pint of Grummandy beer. Instead, I was served this dirty dishwater. Fetch me a fresh tankard of what I first requested. Please."

The woman slammed the tray on their table. "Look here you hoity toity, dandy boy. There is no Grummandy beer. The shipment we were expecting was on that ship that sank. So, don't ask for it again, you little twat!"

Randall sat paralyzed, mouth a gape, as she snatched his tankard and slammed it on the tray. She continued her journey to the kitchen for washing up.

"I like her." Izzy said, finishing her stew.

Flynn eyed the other patrons, to see if anyone noticed the exchange between Randall and the serving wench. "If they know about the sinking of the vessel, the crew must also be telling drunken stories about us in every tavern."

"Good point. Perhaps I should take my leave, before we receive any unwanted attention." Randall rose from his seat.

A familiar voice called out from across the tavern. "Well, I'll be! It's the wizard and his companions I told you about! You made it!"

The old salt captain of the *Lady Anne* staggered over with his burly arms open wide to embrace Randall. The bleary-eyed tavern patrons' attention was drawn to them.

"Oh, shite." Randall looked across the crowd with all eyes upon him, as a few rose to their feet.

The captain had Randall in a bear hug, lifting him off the ground, and patting his back. Juliana, Flynn, and Madok rose from the table with hands on the hilts of their weapons. Izzy dived under the table.

Over the captain's shoulder, Randall noticed the patrons talking amongst themselves and pointing at him. One young man stepped forward from the rest of the crowd and cautiously approached.

"That's close enough." Madok spoke forcefully, holding one outstretched hand to deter the man while the other gripped his sword hilt.

The captain dropped Randall and faced the crowd. The man stopped moving forward and held his hands up. He was dressed in stained and patched work clothes and his unpleasant odor was a giveaway. He worked at the tannery outside of the city.

"I mean no harm. Is it true? That you are a wizard? There's gossip about town that my brother, Niles was given mercy by a wizard, after what those monsters did to him." The young man's eyes welled with tears.

Juliana placed her hand on Madok's arm to lower it. Stepping forward, she looked over the crowd then to the mourning brother. "It was by The Mother's will that your brother was granted mercy and will find peace."

"Hey, wait a minute. I-" Randall was quieted by Flynn giving him a poke to the kidney.

Another man seated at the bar called out. "Those poor buggers are being left to rot in the square. This ain't right."

"Aye! Bloody 'orrible. A crock o' shite." A drunken patron slurred, before throwing back his tankard, pouring more down his beard than his gullet.

"I'd be grateful if I could give my brother a proper burial. Niles mutilated and on display, is pure evil. Mum was devastated when he was sent to the mines. This will kill her." The brother spoke to the group with hope.

The captain looked Randall up and down. "Certainly, you can help this lad out so he can bury his brother. You did take down that giant all by yourself."

"Well, I uh..." Randall stammered.

Madok looked at the others. "This is not exactly lying low. We should be leaving now."

Juliana stepped forward to address the crowd. "What happened in the city square today is an affront to The Mother. Her houses of worship are being shuttered across the Dukedom, and barbarity in the guise of justice is being dealt out to instill fear and obedience in the rising oppression."

The crowd became excited and the low murmur amongst the tavern patrons grew into a raucous of voices.

"Will you help me get my brother?" The young man said hopefully.

Juliana paused long, looking thoughtfully at the man. "Yes."

Izzy ran out from under the table to stand at Juliana's side, smiling. Flynn shrugged his shoulders at Randall, who grimaced back. Madok fell back into his chair and finished his tankard of ale.

The captain slapped Juliana and Randall on their shoulders, ruffled Izzy's hair, and let out a hearty laugh. "Well, it looks like you've got a task ahead of you."

Flynn leaned in to speak within earshot of Juliana and Randall." I just saw a man leave in a hurry, possibly to alert the guard. I'm going to head him off." Randall and Juliana shook their heads in agreement.

Flynn slinked away through the kitchen, exiting the back door into a garbage filled alleyway. Moonlight filtered through the cloudy sky, reflecting on dirty water pooled in the uneven cobblestones. Navigating his way through the muck, he stopped before stepping foot onto the street, to watch the few pedestrians out that evening.

He spotted his target wrapped in a hooded gray cloak. The man's boots clicked with every step, as he headed in the direction of the city square.

With leather lead filled sap in hand, he leaned back into the shadow of the alley. A single lamppost provided the only other illumination, as the moon became shrouded by the black clouds of the night sky.

Flynn leapt out and struck the man at the base of his skull, dropping him like a sack of potatoes. Flynn dragged his unconscious victim into the alley by his ankles. Propping the unconscious fellow up against the wattle and daub wall of tavern, he pulled the cloak aside to check for a purse for the trouble.

"This could be a problem." Flynn quickly backed away, seeing that the man he mugged was an off-duty city guard. The tabard bearing the yellow sun rising over the blue horizon was worn over a grimy suit of padded armor. Luckily, he wasn't wearing a helmet when he struck him.

Flynn retreated into the Raging Boar through the back, to find the patrons were all filing out the front doors to the streets. The table he had been sitting at with the others was empty, save the dirty dishes atop it.

Pushing his way out the front door Flynn saw his friends at the head of the crowd, leading the procession. Curious folk from neighboring 'watering holes' heard noise in the street and joined in.

Flynn pushed his way through to the front to rejoin his companions. "Well, that man was city guard and he may soon be waking from a nasty headache in that alley."

Randall looked down the darkened alleyway, as they passed, at the guard slumped against the wall. "This will at least give us the element of surprise."

"Not with this mob." Madok voiced his concern.

Juliana collected her thoughts before addressing the crowd. "These actions we undertake are not to be covert. This is a just fight in the eyes of The Mother. Today's events are an affront to Her, both cruel and unjust, as is the closure of Her house and the arrests of members of the clergy. Darkness is sweeping over the kingdom and The Mother has charged us to reverse it. We do this on her behalf."

The growing crowd, inspired by Juliana's words, cheered. Her companions also felt inspired by her words. Perhaps everything was happening according to a divine plan as she had often said.

The group entered the square, where only two Sommer Harbour city guards were on watch over the broken bodies on the wheels. The flickering yellow light of torches held in iron stands before each wheel, cast long monstrous shadows on the wall behind the platform. The guards looked to each other nervously, as the crowd now numbering almost fifty approached the platform.

The tall, lanky guard held out his halberd in a defensive stance and his shorter, plumper counterpart followed his lead. Peering across the square, he tried to keep his knees from knocking. Clearing his throat he addressed the crowd. "No one is to approach by order of Lord Mayor Ralf Hughs."

The plump guard then spoke with a bit of confidence, shouting out to the crowd. "Yeah, what he said!"

Juliana stepped to the front and looked at the two guards. "We have come to collect the bodies of Niles and Henry. There will be no violence if you leave now."

The guards fled down the dark empty street to the cheers of the crowd.

"Be quick and take them to their families. I expect they will return with more guards." Juliana addressed the people.

Immediately, several in the crowd swarmed the platform, breaking down the wheels and carefully removed the lifeless bodies of Niles and Henry. One man kicked over each torch stand onto the wooden platform and it quickly caught fire.

The people departed the square without lingering, leaving the five alone as the platform blazed, filling the air with smoke and glowing cinders into the sky. Madok, Flynn, and Randall watched the road the guards took as the sound of the mob faded. Juliana stood beside Izzy, stroking the girl's unruly hair.

Flynn was the first to speak. "I'm not sure exactly what the plan is now, but we should also depart."

Juliana looked to the others as she spoke. "Flynn, if you and the others wish to not take part, then retreat from here now.

Madok looked at Juliana then Randall. "Well Randall, what are you going to do?"

"I've got her back. I'm staying." Randall responded, breathing deeply.

"Me too!" Izzy squeaked and stomped her foot.

"Fine then." Flynn transformed into a hybrid rat man, as he disappeared into the shadows.

In the distance a whistle pierced the silence, followed by the heavy tromp of boots. Madok drew his sword, but Juliana motioned for him to lower his blade. The platform was engulfed in flames, bathing the whole square in the heat of its bright glow and the smell of acrid smoke.

Ten Sommer Harbour guards entered the city square, led by the sergeant in a mail hauberk blowing the whistle. The squad formed a line with the sergeant in the center and slowly approached the group with weapons at the ready.

The burning platform creaked loudly, then collapsed to the ground with a crash, sending a plume of flames and sparks skyward. The sergeant looked from the flaming display to the four before him. Pointing his sword at the four he gave the command. "Throw down your weapons and surrender! You are under arrest!"

Juliana looked at the guards and then their sergeant. "We are not here as an enemy of the people. We were called as representatives of The Mother to end this barbarity."

Randall looked at line of guards some twenty yards from them. They were young men like himself, who had enlisted to keep order, arrest pick pockets, and keep the random goblyn from sneaking through the city gates. They weren't part of the oppressive change spreading across the dukedom.

"Arsonists are what you are, from what I can tell. You will drop your weapons and come with us peacefully, or there will be no quarter spared." The sergeant pointed, with his sword directly at Juliana.

The sound of running feet were coming from the street behind them. Five more guards arrived in the company of the guard with a lump on his head. They positioned themselves to cut off an escape route. Shuttered windows from the apartments above the businesses in the square opened, and the residents watched the spectacle unfolding below.

"That's those bastards from the Raging Boar." The guard with the lump cried out.

Madok seeing they were flanked, readied his sword encouraging the guards from behind to not advance further. Izzy drew her curved dagger and transformed into her rat hybrid form. Juliana held her ground and pulled the mace hanging from her belt.

Randall took a few steps forward with empty hands outstretched. "Sergeant, I would ask that you and your men withdraw. We don't wish any violence against you or your men. We will be on our way. We will leave town. I'm sorry about them burning the torture stage."

The sergeant was preparing to give the order to for his men to advance, but it didn't come. Flynn had their sergeant's head pulled back and the blade of his rapier poised to slice across his neck.

"Give them the order to withdraw, or I'll pull your tongue out through your throat." Flynn hissed.

"St-st-stand down men. Let them go." The sergeant pleaded.

The guards looked to each other without making any move. The men were confused more than anything else, seeing a wererat get the upper hand on their sergeant.

"Do it!" The sergeant shouted out his order.

The guards backed away from the group, leaving Flynn holding the sergeant.

"Please don't kill me, I've got little ones." The sergeant begged.

"Not today." Flynn responded, releasing him with a kick to the rear.

Flynn ran past his friends, encouraging them to follow. The fire and the commotion from the square had drawn more onlookers out on their stoops, and soon people were bringing buckets of water to fight the blaze.

The sound of whistles warned of even more guards joining the pursuit. Flynn urged them to follow off the main road into a narrow alleyway, just as more guards tromped past them.

Paul Wolff

Madok angrily whispered to Juliana. "Well, what now? I assume this is not playing out as you envisioned?"

Flynn returned to his human form, speaking to Madok from the shadows. "I'll find us a way out of the city."

"The bath house is close by. We'll hide out there until you return." Randall suggested.

"I've already had a bath." Izzy snapped back, with a cross look as she returned to her human form.

"Won't it be locked up?" Juliana asked.

"I've picked up some new tools." Izzy produced a leather tool roll with a variety of picks, files and key blanks stuffed in it.

Madok shook his head. "Let's go then, before they circle back."

"What say you Flynn?" Randall asked, before realizing he already left them behind.

40
Bless Its Pointed Little Head

Izzy and Juliana huddled together on the marble floor, against the wall of the open-air pool. Randall had his feet in the pool, gazing at the stars in the moonlit sky. He occasionally glanced over at Juliana, to study the beautiful soft features of her face framed by short blonde hair. Madok paced the cloister surrounding the pool, anxiously

The sounds of guards moving through the streets and citizens fighting the fire in the square had died down to an eerie, still quiet. Randall hoped that Flynn would return with an exit plan, that didn't involve crawling through the sewers or chartering another doomed vessel.

Randall dried his feet and decided it was time for a bottle of wine noting earlier, patrons were served refreshments as they bathed. He slipped on his shoes and walked through an arched hallway, leading into the main building. Madok continued to pace, while Izzy and Juliana looked comfortable where they sat.

Moonlight filtered through the stained-glass windows, providing some light to navigate the place. Crossing through large rooms housing more pools, he found a series of promising heavy wooden doors with arched tops, matching the arches in the ceiling.

Choosing a door, he pulled the iron ring set in it and found it opened effortlessly. The chamber was furnished comfortably with a settee piled with cushions, plush rugs on the floor with even more cushions, and a tufted divan. A bureau with relief carvings of forest creatures and trees caught his eye.

Within, were several corked bottles sealed with wax, along with small drinking vessels. Randall soon had a chalice filled with drink and was sprawled across the divan. It was a shame he would have to leave the comforts of this bathhouse, after discovering the private rooms used for premium services.

The soft patter of rain drummed against the small stained-glass window. Randall was relaxed, staring at the window and listening to the gentle sounds of rain. The flash of lightning illuminated the room brightly for an instant,

Paul Wolff

followed by a muffled clap of thunder. The thought of leaving the comforts of this room to sneak out of another town, wasn't sitting right with him.

Why in the hells did he not talk Juliana out of pulling her misguided stunt in the square? He took several more sips from the chalice, while staring at the window as the storm started to put on a light show.

"Randall." Juliana's voice startled Randall.

Juliana stood in the doorway, arms crossed staring at him. She slinked into the room closing the door behind her. Her eye caught the open cabinet, then the chalice in Randall's hand.

"Oh, I was just trying to calm my nerves before we set out. Has Flynn returned?" Randall said nervously.

Juliana seemed to float to the divan where Randall was sitting. She took the cup from his hand and looked at the wine within. She swirled the glass and then sniffed the bouquet before sipping. "Ah, a hint of wood ashes. I assume from the Green Valley Winery. Good choice, Randall."

"Um, yes. W-would you care to join me?" Randall sat up, making room on the divan for her.

"I will take you up on that offer." Juliana sat next to Randall passing the cup back to him, then proceeded to remove her boots.

Randall nervously took another drink, watching as she stretched out her legs. She snatched back the chalice, drinking the rest of it, then passed it back to Randall. "I think we need more wine."

Randall took a second chalice from the cabinet and filled the two glasses. His heart was pounding and his mind was racing at what was happening. Perhaps he was overthinking Juliana's true intentions. He turned to return to the divan, when another flash of lightning briefly illuminated the room followed by a low thunder clap.

Juliana lay nude on the divan; her clothes piled on the floor. Randall looked from the tips of her long toes, slowly up to perfectly toned legs, and to her smooth hips and the triangular mound of hair between her loins. His eyes travelled along to her flat belly and then to her perfectly formed, small, perk breasts with erect nipples. His eyes met her blue eyes, that smoldered in the dim moonlit room.

"Love me." Juliana rolled onto her back; eyes locked with Randall's. She clutched at herself with one hand and sucked a finger on the other.

"I'll be right there!" Randall dropped the glasses and quickly made his way to the divan.

Kicking off his shoes and dropping his trousers, he removed the tunic creating his own separate pile of clothes next to Juliana's. Juliana moaned and her hips gyrated, as she touched herself watching Randall disrobe.

250

"Love me." She called to him again and spread her legs as her back arched.

Another flash of lightning lit the room as Randall crawled onto the divan. His slight build was a contrast to her athletic toned form. He soon was over her, on his hands and knees, staring into her eyes.

Immediately Juliana wrapped her legs tightly around Randall's waist, overpowering him and pulling him to her. The divan's legs seemed to struggle, keeping up their combined weight and movement. Randall couldn't believe this was happening. He believed that she was beyond his reach, but something had changed between them this night. Before he could overthink his situation, Juliana rolled them onto the floor with her atop him.

Lightning strobed through the window as the storm raging outside became more violent. Juliana straddled Randall, and held down his arms as she mounted him. Her movements began slowly and rhythmically, while staring deep into his eyes. Her firm breasts bounced together with the motion of her hips, as her movements became faster.

Feelings of ecstasy and a guilt were fighting within Randall, as was paralyzed in place while she had her way with him. Pleasure turned to pain, as friction was created with each thrust of the hips. He felt as if his member was wrapped in briar vines that were constricting tighter.

"Stop! Stop! Please!" Randall screamed aloud.

Juliana straightened her back and pulled Randall's hands up forcing him to cup her breasts. Tears from the pain rolled down the sides of his face onto the floor and she didn't relent. She laughed as Randall orgasmed with cries, in the searing pain.

He lay motionless as he felt his hands released. Slowly, he opened his eyes seeing only the moonlight room and crushing silence.

The cackling of an old crone broke the silence, and Randall's eyes met the gaze of Grandma Gertie. She stood beside the divan, upon which he lay fully clothed. She held Randall's satchel in one hand and his wand in the other.

Randall was soaked in sweat and weakened from the ordeal, but he forced himself off the divan. The hag backed out of the door that swung open as she approached it.

"Those are mine you disgusting old trollop! Stop!" Randall screamed and she responded with a cackle. He followed, but the pain in his loins reduced his movement to a stagger.

"You are a pathetic specimen, boy. Soon your soul will be mine." Grandma Gertie walked into the poolroom room toward her destination, a large mirror that was mounted on the wall on the far side. Swirling purple vapors filled the face of the mirror that was prepared to receive her.

Madok stepped into the indoor pool room from the long hall. He saw Randall staggering out of the doorway, but hadn't caught sight of the hag lurking in the shadows.

"Randall, what in the hells? You disappeared and are now making enough noise to bring the entire city guard." Madok spoke sternly, as he walked around the pool. Izzy, Juliana, and Flynn followed at a distance.

Randall pointed to the hag skulking in the shadows, making her escape to the mirror. "The old wench has my book!"

Juliana gasped. "She killed Bishop Bennett!"

Madok drew his sword and ran forward. Randall gave chase as the hag ran to the waiting portal. The others drew their weapons, joining the chase.

Grandma Gertie was within reach of the mirror, when Randall closed in and dove for the satchel. He clutched the strap and was now dragged toward the mirror, as the hag trudged along unhindered.

"Let go Mr. Randall!" Izzy cried out as Grandma Gertie stepped into the mirror, pulling him along.

"Randall, no!" Juliana shouted out, as he was dragged in.

Madok dropped his blade to grab for Randall's legs before he was completely pulled in. He found himself also being dragged. "Flynn! Juliana!"

Juliana and Flynn each grabbed a leg, as Madok was pulled into the mirror. A frightened Izzy covered her mouth, stifling a scream.

Randall found himself losing a game of tug-o-war, which brought him into the dimly lit workshop/laboratory of a tower. Grandma Gertie was holding the satchel by its strap with only one clawed hand, while Randall struggled to keep hold with his arms wrapped around it. Madok was halfway through the mirror with both hands gripped on Randall's ankles. Grandma Gertie looked down at Randall, eyes filled with rage.

"You stupid old crone! You weren't supposed to bring him here!" Barnabas's perch overturned, as he flew madly around the lab, squealing.

Madok looked around the room, from where he lay to the red and black tapestry parted around the mirror, he was halfway through. He immediately recognized the banner.

The strap to the satchel tore loose hanging in the hag's hand, as she fell backwards over a tall stack of books and smashing glass beakers and tubes filled with strange chemicals on a work table.

Barnabas snapped his fingers and disappeared in a puff of smoke, but could be heard flying about the room cursing Randall in his high-pitched voice. "Now you've gone and done it! The boss will make you pay, dearly!"

Grandma Gertie was lying flat on her back, but in a surprise feat of dexterity, kicked her legs up and in a fluid motion, sprung to her feet like a striking serpent.

Randall saw the white rune, encrusted wand lying on the floor. Freeing one hand from his book, he tried to reach, but it was out of his reach. Madok still held Randall's legs and both were being pulled back through the mirror by Flynn and Juliana, who held Madok.

Randall freed one leg and promptly kicked Madok in the face. "Sorry!"

Madok released Randall's other leg and was pulled back through the mirror to the bathhouse in Port Sommer.

Looking over his shoulder, Randall saw the mirror looked like a window into the bathhouse, and his friends were looking in. He quickly turned his attention to his wand and made another grab for it.

"Quick! Close the portal so he can't escape, fool!" Barnabas called out.

"Silence imp! You are just asking me to lock you in that cage again!" Grandma Gertie spoke into air, searching the room for Barnabas.

"Hey, he's got that-" Barnabas was cut off in mid-sentence.

Randall rolled under a work table for cover, waved the wand, and spoke the command words. "Glacies tempestas!"

An arctic blast of subzero winds blew into the tower laboratory, followed by a shower of hail stones, pounding everything in the room. Barnabas screamed, as he smashed into the wall, and hail stones pummeled him to the floor.

Grandma Gertie held up her hands over her for cover, as she tried to escape the indoor storm, but lost her footing in the 'white out' and slipped. Larger ice stones continued falling, burying her beneath them.

"Randall! Where are you?" Juliana's voice called out, as she entered after the winter storm subsided.

The room was freezing and the vapor from his breath was visible as he spoke. "I'm down here. I'm okay."

The air cleared in the room and the destructive forces brought on by the wand was evident. Randall crawled out from under the table and stepped through the hail stones that were over a foot deep where the spell was centered. The hag's bare feet were sticking out from under the pile, but he could see her clawed toes twitching. The sound of the groaning imp could also be heard.

Juliana grabbed Randall's arm, after he retrieved his book under a shallow pile of hailstones. She pulled him toward the mirror portal, which Izzy and Flynn were trying to prevent Madok from re-entering. "We must go now!"

"Hold it one moment! That arse of a little devil, and old crone both had their hands on my book. And that old crone she did a... bad thing to me. I'm not finished here." Randall pulled his arm free of Juliana's grip.

"Randall, there is a more powerful enemy at work here, who we are not prepared to confront just yet." Juliana tried to persuade him, unsuccessfully.

The hag's head lifted from under the pile of hailstones bloodied, confused and quite angry. "You are dead you little slug!"

Before any more words left the hag's cracked thin blue lips, five darts of force left the wizard's fingertips and unerringly struck her in the center of her forehead. Grandma Gertie's head fell back onto a pillow of hailstones.

Randall quickly scanned the room, briefly picking through the tomes that were knocked to the ground, pulling each from the mounds of hailstones. "No, nope. Naw. Nope. No."

"What are you looking for?" Juliana pleaded, as the hag snored from the concussion received from the blows to her head.

"Obviously, someone is collecting magic tomes and mine seems to be in high demand. That someone has a few magic tomes in their possession here. Ah, this looks promising!" Randall pushed his way through to a bookcase covered in a light dusting of frost. A thick leatherbound grimoire immediately gained all his attention. He pulled the heavy book from its shelf and saw that it had a locking mechanism on it, requiring a key.

"Is this one?" Juliana asked, looking at the tome bound in the leathery skin of an unknown creature with curiosity.

"Good enough for now. Let's go." Randall struggled with both his spell book and the new larger tome.

They turned to the portal as Madok, Flynn and Izzy stepped through, all with weapons drawn.

"Turn around, we're leaving!" Randall said to his companions.

"Well, you two didn't return. We thought you were in trouble!" Flynn spoke angrily.

"Mr. Randall, I was very worried about you!" Izzy stamped her foot.

Unintelligible words came from the floor, then the hag sat up cackling uncontrollably.

Madok lunged forward and slashed at her with his blade, removing her head with two strokes. Grandma Gertie's head rolled away as her body dropped to the ground.

"This is a problem." Randall said shaking his head, pointing to the mirror.

The portal was closed, and the mirror now reflected the room and the five companions.

"Tee hee hee hee! The boss is going to be very mad when he sees what you did! Methinks he'll turn you into oysters and feed you to the seabirds." The voice of Barnabas squealed, with evil glee.

Izzy stepped forward with her curved blade. "I know your voice. You're that little wimp."

"That's 'imp' you filthy rodent!" Barnabas protested. He threw a beaker at Izzy, narrowly missing her and became visible again.

"I see you!" Izzy squealed and made a running leap across the icy floor, snatching Barnabas.

The two crashed to the ground and a struggle ensued, as the imp tried to wriggle free of Izzy's hold. Without his poison stinger he had no way to fight off Izzy, who now held him in the air by his neck. Barnabas beat his wings madly to escape, but it proved futile.

"You know this creature?" Madok scowled at the little devil, that was cursing the foulest of words.

"We're old friends." Izzy squeezed Barnabas tightly to her body, and pat him roughly on top of his little horned head.

41
Business as Usual

"Your Grace, all your advisors and myself included, would like to call this meeting of the council to a close. May I suggest we reconvene tomorrow after the noon hour?" Osbert exhausted, slumped in his chair at the long table in the council chambers.

The table was in attendance by representatives from the Dukedom, as well as his highest ranking general. Everyone was at various levels of exhaustion, measured by how low they slumped in their chairs, heads propped up on fists, and even one snoring with his head resting on a pile of papers. Duke Archibald Payne sat at the head of the table, looking over the members of the council, not realizing that most everyone had long checked out from this meeting, that began ten hours prior.

"Oh, very well Osbert. It seems these young men don't have the stamina to address and work on the business of the Dukedom. We shall reconvene after the noon hour." The Duke waited for them to rise.

Around the table, the council struggled to rise from their seats, most needing to use the table for support. One council member snored, with his head on his papers. The man to his right reached to waken him, only to be stopped by The Duke.

"Leave him be. He'll now be the first one here once we reconvene." Archibald smirked, as the man withdrew his hand.

Osbert covered his mouth to yawn, then spoke. "This council meeting is closed and will reconvene on the noon hour... today." He rapped the gavel on the sounding block.

The Duke exited the council chamber through his own door, followed by two guards. The members of the council waited patiently, watching for the door to close behind him.

The snoring man at the table was awakened by the man on his right this time, with an open-handed slap to the head.

"Yes, Your Grace! A wise decision." The snoring man startled, sprung up, with a line of spittle from his papers to his lip.

"Oh, shut up, Leone. The meeting is over and he left. I suggest you be the first person in this chamber. We reconvene where we left off, at noon." The man gathered his papers as Leone rubbed the tender spot on the back of his head.

"I must apologize for His Grace. He would seem to still be distraught over the loss of the Duchess. He is immersing himself completely in his work for the kingdom. He does seem to lose track of time." Osbert offered.

The general of the dukedom's professional army, was the only one in attendance that did not suffer from fatigue. General Jaheem wore an ornate breastplate over his fine clothing that included a short cape. His short-cropped graying hair, contrasted his dark brown skin, on the old warrior's battle-weary face. He looked across at all the others of the council that were grumbling, as they gathered their papers from the table.

Clearing his throat first, Jaheem spoke with a deep commanding voice. "Osbert, I do think I speak what is on the minds of several others on this council. For more than a few years leading up to the death of Duchess Kathrine, the Duke has undergone some change. His mind has remained keen as ever, even as his physical health declined over his long life. However, now there is an immediate threat to the kingdom."

Other members of the council stood in silence, listening to General Jaheem, not daring to speak. They eyed one another and Osbert as he continued.

"In the short time following the Duchess's death and her interment, the Duke's once frail health has reversed. He now has the stamina of a man half his age. I wish nothing but the best of health for His Grace. However, this is not something that is possible, without the involvement of dark magic!" The General did not hold back.

Some members of the council gasped at the statement. Others were not surprised by the General's assessment.

"This coincides with oppressive measures and directives he has invoked across the dukedom, that do not align with King Ernald's rule. The closure of houses of worship and the arrest of the holy leaders was done on his own whim, and not a royal decree. Claiming that it was due to corruption does not make it true. This is turning the faithful, against the state. From across the dukedom, and from within the ranks of the military. From the common soldier, to its officers... myself included!" The general pounded his large fist on the table, startling the room.

The council members looked to one another nervously. Osbert eyed everyone in the room, deep in thought.

"What exactly are you suggesting, General Jaheem?" A well-dressed man in colorful robes and a crumpled hat asked, as he twisted the end of his thick mustache.

Another man with shaved head and long chin beard also chimed in. "Certainly, King Ernald has already been made aware of the current situation here in the dukedom. The Duke can't possibly think he can take these actions without repercussions from The King?"

General Jaheem sighed and leaned on the table. "The King has eyes and ears in Redrock and elsewhere in the dukedom, and the news has been delivered. We must agree it's in the best interest of the kingdom, he be removed from power, and a suitable member of the royal family or viceroy appointed to rule."

"Osbert, I respect your loyalty to the Duke after all your years of service, but I believe your wise council cannot influence his decision making now. This has already been set in motion. The Duke is to be placed under house arrest this evening. I am to assume control of power, until King Ernald appoints another to govern the dukedom.

"By the gods! Why wasn't this done before we were captive in this chamber with him for half of the day and evening!" The mustached man almost collapsed, but propped himself up on the table.

Others present in the chamber grumbled and made approving 'grunts and sighs' to his statement.

"This was contingent upon the arrival of King Ernald's guard and Lord Tristan who was delivering the arrest warrant. They were due to arrive this afternoon, but their travel may be delayed." General Jaheem offered.

"Personally, I believe they won't arrive at all." Leone said, stretching his arms as he arched his back.

"Why is that?" The mustached man looked to Leone with annoyance.

Leone cracked his knuckles. "Well, because their heads have been separated from their bodies. Just as yours will be General!"

"How dare you speak to me like this!" General Jaheem grew furious and was ready jump over the table to tear Leone apart. Three council members held him back.

The sound of hideous cackling erupted from Leone's lips, as he transformed into his true form. Auntie Olga clapped her hands loudly and the doors on both ends of the chamber flew open. The Duke's personal guard filed into the room, in full plate armor with halberds at the ready. Each member of the council had two guards hovering over them. Osbert and all the other council members looked wildly with fear at Auntie Olga, who now sat on the Duke's chair.

Duke Payne stepped back into the chamber, followed by Mama Matilda, who carried a covered basket in her arms. The Duke glared at Auntie Olga, who immediately relinquished the seat.

The Duke motioned at Mama Matilda with the wave of his finger, and she dumped the basket atop the table. Lord Tristan's bloody head rolled out onto the table, startling the council.

The Duke held out his hand toward the severed head. "I presume everyone knows Lord Tristan? I think we may have been cousins through marriage."

Osbert looked frantically to the Duke. "Your Grace! What have you done? Who are these... women?"

The Duke waved over one of the guards. "Please see Osbert safely to his bedchamber for the evening. He will need plenty of bedrest for a big day tomorrow. The council and I have further business to conduct."

General Jaheem and the other men of the council shouted protests as Osbert was led out and the doors barred behind him. The Duke held up his hand again to call for silence.

"I'm a reasonable man. No need for everyone to fear a feeble old man. Now sit!" The last words from the Duke's mouth resonated across the chamber.

The men of the council, quickly took their respective seats, without a word. The guards stood behind each man at attention, unmoving as statues.

Duke Payne studied each man in turn, though none dared to make eye contact aside from General Jaheem. Most eyes were on the table's new centerpiece, wondering if they were next. Only the General stared at the Duke with defiance in his eyes.

The smell of rancid decay filled the chamber, as The Duke dropped the magics that concealed his true state. An unnatural aura of chill cold emanated from his undead body. The hags standing on either side, had wide smiles of rotten yellowed teeth as his visage was revealed. His sunken eyes were replaced by glowing red points of light in their dark sockets. His putrid flesh had a splotchy green color, and his nails appeared to have grown, as the skin receded on his fingers. The clothing he wore couldn't escape staining from the remaining bodily fluids that oozed from his decaying flesh.

General Jaheem knew that a pact with an extraplanar being of great power, was made to grant him an autonomous undead existence. Jaheem arose, pointing an accusing finger. "Your existence is an aberration! An affront to The Mother!"

The others slowly lifted their eyes to the Duke, then shrunk back in fear. Duke Payne laughed as all cowered, apart from General Jaheem who was now held down on the table, face to face with the head of Lord Tristan by the guards.

"Everyone comfortable now? If so, I won't waste too much more of everyone's time. General Jaheem, has correctly deduced that things are different now." Duke Payne addressed the council.

Mama Matilda cackled uncontrollably, even with her hand covering her mouth. Duke Payne looked at her and the red points of light in his empty eye sockets burned with fury. She silenced herself and looked at the floor.

"For years I have kept order in my dukedom with only minimal intrusion from the King. As long as tax revenues are collected and materials for his war machine provided, life remains prosperous, and my subjects are easy to keep in line. Those who cheat me or bring in outside interference will receive special treatment. Shall we start by foregoing the lengthy show trial?" The Duke turned his gaze to the armored guardsmen holding General Jaheem.

The council men watched in horror, as Jaheem was pulled from the table and pushed to his knees on the floor. The General didn't flinch; he looked defiantly at Duke Payne, then shouted, "You damned yourself for eternity in the hells, on a selfish whim! Unlike you I don't fear death. I will spend eternity in-"

General Jaheem's head was severed with one stroke. The council members' faces turned white, a few soiled themselves, and one vomited.

"Now that is out of the way, I would like to say that things can go back to the way they once were. However, we all know that is impossible. I have one question for everyone on the council. Is there anyone that feels they are unable to fulfil their duties to me or the dukedom?" The Duke looked across the table at all the frightened men.

Auntie Olga spoke up. "Well, obviously the General, Archie."

The Duke glared at Auntie Olga.

Mama Matilda cackled and added. "Oh yes, Leone as well. Remember he was tossed in the dungeons a few days ago, before this meeting was called."

The Duke glared at Mama Mathilda, then shrugged his shoulders as he sunk back into the chair. "Oh yes, I somehow forgot. I believe he is sharing a cell with another thieving scoundrel. That idiot mayor from Port Gwynn, Geoffrey."

The Duke sat lost in thought for a long moment, which to those seated was closer to half an hour.

The Duke spoke again after a long while, to the hags. "You crones, remove General Jaheem and Lord Tristan from the chamber. I need the members of this council to answer the question I posed, before I was distracted by your banter."

Mama Matilda placed both heads in the basket, Auntie Olga threw the General's lifeless hulking body over her shoulder effortlessly, then both exited the chamber.

The large doors closed behind them with a booming slam. The men all looked at one another nervously, as The Duke sat unmoving in his chair. The armored guards all stood to attention, motionless around the table. The visors of their helms all closed, not allowing anyone to read their faces.

"I'll call for some tea and scones for you. It seems that the first light of morning is coming through the windows and there is much to discuss." The Duke offered breakfast amidst the blood that had been spilled.

"Will fresh butter be provided?" The mustached man asked, with concern in his voice.

42
Feeling Boxed In

"I'll ask you one more time or else I'll skewer you on the point of my blade. Who do you serve, and where are we?" Flynn kicked the cage that Barnabas was stuffed into, while toying with his dagger.

The travel through the mirror felt as if they had just stepped through a door at the bath house in Sommer Harbour. Randall knew powerful magic transported them to wherever they were now. Madok guarded the lab door, and Juliana watched the stairs to the rooftop. Both kept an ear on the interrogation of the imp.

Barnabas stood up and brushed away rotten straw and animal filth. Taking hold of the bars, he briefly studied the lock on the cage door, then looked up at Flynn and Izzy with the most pitiful look he could muster in his pupilless red eyes. "You would lock me in here and leave me to starve."

Izzy felt sorry as he tugged her heartstrings. Flynn rolled his eyes.

Randall continued scavenging the room for more items that could prove useful. He found a finely crafted leather haversack that felt light, even as he stuffed his books and other items in it. This item was obviously the creation of a powerful wizard. Perhaps the one who's laboratory he was looting.

"Well, you won't have to worry about starving." Flynn swooped down to shove the dagger through the bars into Barnabas. He stopped with the tip just touching the imp's chest.

"No! Wait! I'll talk!" Barnabas fell back and scooted away from Flynn's blade.

Izzy clapped her hands. "See, Flynn! He wants to help us."

"You can't trust a creature from the hells to be true. It will mix truth with lies and twist its words. It will only say things to benefit itself and the one it truly serves." Juliana warned.

"Listen here, toots, I never lie." Barnabas turned to lie, directly to Juliana. He then spoke directly to Flynn again. "I give the wisest of counsel to Archie.

This is his tower you intruded uninvited, and the ugly broad on the floor you murdered, was one of his lackeys. Oh, he won't be happy with you at all, when he sees this mess. Especially, that fool stealing all his belongings."

Randall looked over at the caged imp puzzled. "Archie?"

Madok spoke with a distressed tone in his voice. "Archibald. Duke Archibald Payne. His colors are on the tapestry around that... mirror."

Barnabas touched his finger to his nose. "We have a winner!"

"He was the one I saw in my vision. Consorting and dealing with devils. It makes sense now. The Mother brought us here to end this." Juliana stepped toward the cage.

"No way, sister. You were brought here because that pipsqueak wouldn't let go of that book. I saw it all. Dragged through that mirror by the headless old twat." The imp pointed at the body of Grandma Gertie.

"Redrock. We are in Redrock. We need leave now." Madok walked over to the mirror and placed his hands on the silver surface. It was solid and only reflected Madok.

Barnabas chuckled at Madok's frustration. Juliana also approached the mirror studying it and the nightmarish gold frame, with the silver relief sculptures nightmarish creatures intertwined around it.

"How can we return through this mirror?" Madok asked the imp in a commanding tone.

"Well, the proper ritual must be done to work the magic, with one who has the knowledge to perform it. The old dead prune on the floor can't do it for you. However, you could just wait for Archie to return and ask him. Say 'pretty please with a cherry on top!'" Barnabas laughed at his own retort, slapping his knobby knee.

Flynn stabbed his dagger through the bars of the cage and Barnabas narrowly dodged being impaled. He squeaked out a gasp, then snapped his fingers disappearing in a puff of smoke.

"I know your tricks. You're still in the cage." Flynn said angrily.

"Piss off!" The voice of Barnabas squeaked within the cage.

Juliana called for the others' attention. "We must destroy this mirror. This has been used to send those creatures through and spy upon us."

Randall inspected the mirror. "I agree. This mirror, just like the locket that imp had, and is somehow used for scrying."

"Let's get on with it then. Keep an ear on that door Izzy." Madok waved Izzy to the door.

Madok found that the large mirror was surprisingly easy to pry from the wall and topple to the floor. Juliana used the flanged headed mace she carried, to land several blows to it. Pieces of gold framing broke off, the silver surface creased, bent, and cracked. The silver creatures surrounding the frame broke off and lay scattered across the floor. Within minutes the mirror was reduced to pieces of scrap metal. Valuable scraps as they were, no one dared pocket them.

"Oh boy. He's not going to be happy with you for that." Barnabas was once again visible and shaking his head.

"I don't hear anything, sir! I think we're clear." Izzy pulled her attention away from the door to address Madok.

Randall pointed at Barnabas, who was eyeing everyone from the cage. "What do we do with... it?"

"It must be destroyed. It is not of this world, and if left alive it will continue to be an evil influencer and corrupter of souls. That is its only purpose for being sent here." Juliana spoke sternly, pointing her mace at the cage.

Barnabas desperately engaged in dialogue with Juliana. "Whoa there hotsy totsy! Let's not be hasty, getting all murdery here. I'm not ready to be sent back to Hell for another freakin' century, to wait in line for a new assignment! I promise I'll-"

Five magic bolts of force struck Barnabas, cutting him off in mid rant. Barnabas' body lay in the bottom of the cage and quickly melted away into a bubbling, tarlike ichor, leaving a tiny skeleton atop it. Within moments, the skeleton crumbled to dust and the ichor evaporated away leaving no trace. Randall was still pointing the finger he had launched his spell with as everyone turned their attention to him.

"Well, that's that. I hated that little guy." Randall pulled the haversack over his shoulder while the others looked to one another without a word.

"What do you know of Redrock, Madok?" Flynn asked, as he sheathed his dagger.

"I do know that we are now some ten leagues to the north of Port Sommer, some two days of travel on foot. This tower is within the castle walls, and from atop it a perfect lookout to see the lands for miles around. The city of Redrock is just outside the castle, and should provide us a place to disappear into temporarily. Of course, we must make it past a garrison of soldiers, and the guards in the halls below." Madok spoke bluntly.

"If only I was able to return sooner to the bathhouse, this could have been avoided. Speaking of which, how did it come to pass you were alone with that... witch?" Flynn eyed Randall, as he stepped toward him.

"Er, I just went looking for a drink, while we were waiting for you. She caught me from behind and attempted to steal my book. Lucky you returned, when you did." Randall took a step back.

Juliana stepped between the two. "We have no time for this. I don't know exactly what we are up against right now, giving Duke Payne's pact with a Duke of the Hells. I may receive further guidance from The Mother."

Izzy studied the empty cage and spoke without looking up. "Why don't we wait for that Duke guy to just come back here. We could beat him up and stop running away. Everything we have done is bringing us to him. Juliana keeps saying it's 'happening for a reason.'"

Everyone was silent for a long moment.

Madok smiled. "Ambush him in his own tower. That's something he wouldn't expect. I feel even if we succeeded, there would be no escape. It would be suicide."

Juliana got on her knees next to Izzy, putting an arm around the girl. "Madok, I believe the Mother would not abandon us to that fate, doing Her work."

Madok thought for a moment. "Funny, I seem to recall there are a lot of Saints martyred doing Her work."

Flynn and Randall nodded their heads to Madok's point.

Flynn rubbed his chin. "Perhaps a bit of subterfuge would improve our chances. Randall used his magic to disguise himself as Thom Clarke rather convincingly."

Randall chimed in. "Not that convincingly. Clarke just happened to be at the Customs House, causing that scheme go south."

"Yes, but this time it wouldn't likely work out that way." Flynn pointed at the corpse of Grandma Gertie.

"Using the same deception on the Duke as she did on me?" Randall shook his head disgusted.

"What do you mean?" Juliana asked concerned.

"Uh, nothing." Randall quickly answered.

Flynn continued. "I imagine he will be returning soon enough, as these creatures were spying on us. Catching him before he gets to his ransacked laboratory is imperative."

Madok thought for a moment. "We could tie off a rope and scale down from the roof top for our escape."

Randall thought for a moment. "I have a spell in my book that could help with that. I'll need a little time to study it. If we leap from the tower top once its cast, we will drift gently to the ground light as a feather! I made use of it one time to make a quick exit from... a 'friend's' balcony."

"Flynn and Juliana come with me, let's check the layout of the place, and make sure no one else is lurking about." Madok drew his weapon.

"What about me?" Izzy felt left out.

Juliana patted her shoulder. "Protect Randall, so he can study."

"Sounds boring." Izzy crossed her arms, annoyed.

"Just do it Izzy. We'll return soon enough." Flynn reassured her.

Madok cautiously opened the large wooden door, exiting the wizard's laboratory onto the landing where stone steps descended to the lower floors. All exited and closed the door gently behind them. Flynn noticed the circular hole in the floor and alerted the others to it. After a quick inspection, he deduced it went all the way to the ground floor.

"This looks like a quick way to the bottom; however, I suggest we use the stairs." Flynn said, pointing into the round portal.

The way was dimly lit by wall sconces with enchanted soft glowing red light, rather than candles. Flynn took the lead, and the three descended the stairs single file, hearts racing, and breathing labored.

Randall poured over his tome and inventoried his bag of components. "Good! I still have a few feathers buried in there."

Izzy studied the hag's severed head, frowning as she pulled open the mouth to look at its rotten blackened teeth. Losing interest quickly with that, an irregularity in the stone wall caught the attention of her keen eyesight. Dropping the head with a 'thud' to the floor didn't distract Randall from his book.

Small nimble fingers felt around the stonework, as she tapped with one fist on the wall. There was something odd about that small section of the wall. "Mr. Randall, I think I found something."

"Quiet!" Randall hissed, without looking up from the book.

Izzy stuck her tongue out at him and went back to inspecting the wall. Much like back home in The Nest, doors disguised as a wall were common place and the denizens there could easily learn to recognize them as such. This was no exception. Running fingers between the stones, she found a small latch. Giving it a pull, there was a light click and small square section of the wall pivoted open.

Izzy gasped, excited by her discovery. No more than a one-foot square space was revealed behind the small door. Inside were scrolls of rolled parchment and a book bound in an unknown leather. Lastly was a plain wooden box with a small padlock.

Ignoring the other boring things, Izzy pulled out the box. Taking a seat on the floor by the dead hag, she inspected the box before picking the lock. "Oh, this is pretty!"

Inside, on the red velvet padding, the platinum box sat. Izzy's eyes opened wide at her find. She lifted it out of the wooden box and inspected every face of it. The gold filigree runes that covered its surface intrigued her. No matter how she tried though, she found it impossible to open. She felt an uneasiness and sense of dread, as she ran her fingers over it, then a chill washed over her.

"Hey, Mr. Randall..." Izzy said again.

"Not now! I'm almost done. This is important!" Randall snapped back.

Growing frustrated, Izzy placed the platinum box back in its coffer, locking it before stashing it in her bag. Now increasingly impatient, she kicked the hag's head across the laboratory.

43

Exploration

This room was in my vision. I saw him consorting with the devils here." Juliana was shaken and would not step through the threshold.

Madok and Flynn were startled as they walked in, and the hundreds of candles about the room ignited. The summoning room remained as it was when The Duke sent Bennett with the trio of devils. Flynn examined the ritual dagger, dried blood, and podium. The human tooth on the floor was spotted by Madok.

Madok approached the thick salt piles circling the pentagram on the floor, but dared not cross over them. "Let's move on. I've seen enough."

The three retreated from the summoning room, descending further down the stone steps. Another landing with a large thick wooden floor stood before them, with another circular hole in the floor. Flynn pressed his ear to the door, as Madok watched the stairs that continued downward.

"Well?" Juliana whispered to Flynn after a long moment.

"I'm not entirely sure. I hear... whimpering." Flynn said with his ear pressed to the door.

Juliana sniffed the air. "What is that smell?"

Flynn scrunched his nose. "Something cooking? It doesn't smell... right."

Madok stepped toward the door, speaking in a whisper. "How many in there?"

"Possibly one." Flynn whispered.

Madok and Flynn readied their weapons. Sweat ran down Juliana's brow as she gripped the pull ring, looking to Flynn and Madok. Madok took a deep breath and gave Juliana a quick nod to open the door.

"What in the hells?" Madok lowered his blade.

The three studied the room for a long moment, before Flynn stepped in.

The large semi-circular room covered this floor of the tower, save the landing. The fire within the nightmarish, stone hearth carved to resemble stacks of human skulls and bones bathed the room in a dim red light. Warming over the hot coals, was a sickening stew in an iron cauldron. Cluttering the floor were piles of children's clothing and shoes. Mixed within the mess, the bones of their previous owners.

The cutting block in the center of the floor had tools for butchering and another table was covered with flower, mixing bowls, pans, spoons, and meat grinder. A pie of unknown filling, covered with a flakey crust was cooling. Links of sausages were draped from the rafters overhead.

Three unmade beds with filthy bedclothes were pushed against the wall, as well as a small round dinner table with three mismatched chairs. Open cabinets overstuffed with all manner of junk and other work tables were covered with rubbish.

Flynn pointed out a small cage, tucked away in the shadows. "Over there. A child!"

Juliana pushed through and knelt on one knee. Imprisoned within, a young boy five years of age, lay sucking his thumb. Large brown eyes acted as windows to his traumatized soul. He was well fed, but there were signs he was a victim of torture.

Juliana looked at the padlock on the cage. "I'm going to get you out of there. Don't be frightened."

A few well-placed blows from her mace smashed the iron lock, while the boy covered his ears. The iron cage's door squeaked as Juliana opened it, and offered her hand to the child.

The boy was hesitant at first, but took Juliana's hand and squirmed out of the cage. Wrapping his arms around her neck, he buried his face in her shoulder.

"Whoever is responsible for this, does not get to live." Flynn fumed. The boy reminded him of his beloved nephew far away in his homeland.

Madok looked about the room as Juliana lifted the boy in her arms. In a fit of rage, he flung the meat pie off the table. "We will get the chance for that. Juliana, take him up to Izzy to watch over him and bring Randall here."

The three left the bed chamber. Juliana carefully climbed the tower stairs with the boy in her arms. Flynn and Madok watched her disappear around the curve, before continuing the exploration of the tower.

"Who is that?" Randall was surprised at the child in Juliana's arms.

Juliana spoke, saddened. "He was a prisoner, and hasn't said a word since I freed him. I fear he has seen horrors no child should witness."

Randall saw the boy's troubled, faraway stare. "Don't worry, we'll get out of here."

The boy remained non-responsive.

"I took a quick look around on the roof. There is nothing up there, except some stone furniture and ugly statues. This tower is on the edge of the castle walls, atop high rocky hills overlooking the city. When we make our escape, we don't have to worry about landing within the castle walls. The rocks are red too! I've never seen red rocks before. Do you think that's why this is called Redrock Castle?" Izzy spoke excitedly, without taking a breath.

Randall was amused at Izzy's enthusiasm. "You have it figured out. If all goes as planned, we float to the bottom and make a run for it. If not, we fall to our deaths."

"Mr. Randall, that won't happen. Don't be so neg- nega-" Izzy stumbled on her words.

"Negative." Juliana helped.

Izzy smiled shaking her head.

Juliana gave the rundown to Izzy one more time, before she and Randall departed. "When you hear a skirmish below, head to the rooftop. When we take out the Duke, more guards may follow that could overwhelm us. If we don't return, you must be prepared to go on your own. Transform and climb down the wall to safety."

"What about him?" Izzy said, concerned.

Juliana took a deep breath. "Disregard what I said. We will all go together."

Juliana grabbed Randall's arm and dragged him to the stairs. They continued downward, bypassing the floors already explored, to Randall's objections. His curiosity was piqued by treasures they may be missing out on. Then they heard a fight. It was metal on metal and only the voices of Flynn and Madok carried upwards.

Juliana left Randall, hurrying down the stair with mace in hand. When Randall reached the others, everything had gone silent, save for their heavy breathing.

Madok and Flynn looked at the two opponents they dispatched on the floor. The shining full plate armor of the guards bore creases and punctures on their steel shells, yet there was no blood.

The three were scratched and bruised, but not badly hurt. Randall crouched down at one of the fallen guards intrigued. Opening the visor of the helmet, he discovered it was empty.

"Amazing! Whatever manner of magic used to bring that armor to 'life' is beyond anything I studied. What happened?" Randall looked to the others.

Madok sheathed his sword and knelt. "The armor was piled on the ground. When we stepped into this room, it pulled together and attacked. Each fought us unrelentingly, until we destroyed them."

Flynn pointed to the door on the wall. "I believe this is the ground floor and that is the exit."

Juliana looked at the door. "We haven't looked beyond that door yet."

Randall grabbed Juliana's arm, preventing her from touching the pull ring. "There is a ward cast on the door, possibly deadly."

A small magical script glowed on the door when Randall put his hand near the pull ring, and dimmed when he pulled away.

"What would happen?" Madok asked curiously.

Randall scratched his chin. "Hard to say. Powerful forces could be released to thwart an intruder. Fire, lightening, extreme cold."

Flynn pointed to the rune inscribed circle on the floor and hole in the ceiling directly above it. "What would that be then?"

Randall walked over to the circle, and magic glyphs began to glow. He studied them for a moment and the ceiling overhead. "My assumption is this is for levitation. A quick way to the top, rather than climbing all those stairs for a feeble old man. This is amazing."

Randall stepped into the circle as the rest of the group let out a collective gasp. Looking upwards, Randall ascended through the round portal in the ceiling.

Madok hissed in protest. "Fool, we don't have time to play around in here."

Randall's voice called down the stairwell. "I was right! This is superior to taking the stairs."

Flynn looked at the piles of armor. "I'm going to return these suits of armor to the same state we saw them in, when we walked in here. Maybe we can still get the jump on him."

Madok looked at the magic circle, and then the hole in the ceiling. "Like Randall said, he will use that rather than the stairs. We wait above and take him out when his head pokes through."

Flynn nodded his head. "I like the way you think."

Juliana looked over to the others. "We are out of time. I hear someone on the other side of the door."

"Up the stairs!" Madok ordered.

The three climbed the stone steps, joining Randall on the landing by the hags' chamber before the door opened. Randall watched through the hole, as the large wooden door slowly creaked open and stopped before opening wide.

44
Best Laid Plans...

"Well, what of my cousin and the good general?" The Duke asked his companions that walked alongside him, followed by the line of guards.

Mama Matilda waddled alongside him, extra cheerful. "Their heads will be placed on spikes at the city gates this afternoon with the other traitors to the Dukedom. It should be quite the event!"

Auntie Olga was quite chipper herself. "Oh yes, Archie. The general's quartered body has been sent on the wagons, with the others, to the far reaches of the Dukedom for display! It will be a wonderful deterrent against future usurpers to your throne."

The Duke also had a bit of pep in his undead step, and didn't negatively react to being addressed as 'Archie.' As the procession of guards, hags, and The Duke passed through the halls of Redrock Castle, frightened servants stood to attention, looking to the floor avoiding any eye contact. All were completely ignored.

"Very good. However, I have other plans for the heads. Something special. I have promoted a new loyal general, one known for being a strong commander and brilliant tactician. It is unfortunate I must deal with my nephew, after my cousin's little threat. I need your sister to return her attention to the King through the mirror, and learn more about plans to send others to 'punish' me. Ernald's attention should be more focused on threats from the northern kingdoms than here." The Duke waved a boney finger ending in a long yellow nail at Auntie Olga.

"As you wish Archie." Auntie Olga performed an exaggerated curtsey, and with one finger touched her chin with a wink.

The Duke suddenly paused and the entourage stopped. He grew furious and his sunken eyes glowed red. "The platinum box is being molested! To the tower!"

The Duke and his guard double timed it, across the castle to the tower. Mama Matilda and Auntie Olga entered first followed, by the dozen guards.

"It's not The Duke. There's more of those old crones and walking suits of armor." Randall whispered to the others, as he moved away from the portal.

Auntie Olga appeared on the landing in a flash of light, and charged Randall with her long talon-like fingers. Randall fell backwards before she reached him, hitting his head on the wall and crumbling to the floor.

Madok swung his longsword with both hands, slashing at Auntie Olga. Instinctively, she evaded the swing of the sword, tumbling away before Flynn could attack. She pointed her forefingers at Madok and Flynn, screaming the magic words. "Flatus illum!"

Eight magical darts of force shot from the tips of her fingers, striking Flynn and Madok. Flynn was knocked back into the wall and Madok staggered, as it knocked the wind out of him.

Mama Matilda cackled and appeared on the landing, as Juliana held the symbol of The Mother in one hand with her flanged mace in the other. In an unfaltering, commanding voice Juliana's words rang out. "Mother I ask you to protect your servants and help vanquish these unholy foes!"

Auntie Olga shouted to her sister. "Stop the bitch before she finishes!"

Mama Matilda focused on Juliana, pointing her beefy forefinger at her. "Flatus-"

Madok slammed into Mama Matilda, knocking her off her feet, disrupting the spell. Both crashed to the ground with Madok pining her.

At Juliana's feet, a whirlwind encircled her, increasing in velocity and expanding outwards. Soon it reached to the ceiling and expanded, until the landing was filled. The whirlwind slowed, revealing semitransparent apparitions of angelic figures wielding swords, ready for battle.

Their colorless forms had the faces of beautiful young women with long flowing hair, clad in long robes that tapered into nothingness. Gliding on feathered wings, the ghostly forms darted through the room, encircling everyone in serpent like fashion.

Mama Matilda pushed Madok off her and arose, as Auntie Olga was encircled by the strange spirits. Flynn backed away, as ghostly angels swarmed him, though they did not cause him any harm. Randall groaned, lifting his throbbing head to view the scene. The benign apparitions also flew around him, unthreatening.

Auntie Olga cried out first, as the ghostly angels struck her with incorporeal swords. The blades did not draw blood, but every blow caused excruciating pain, draining her vitality. "You let the bitch complete her conjuring!"

Mama Matilda was also swarmed by the angelic spirits. Seeing Flynn blocking the archway, she made a break for the levitation portal in the floor, near Juliana. Mama Matilda dropped feet first through the portal screaming, "No more!" The hag landed on her feet and shouted orders at the guards.

Randall crawled toward Juliana, away from the vicious fight ensuing between Auntie Olga, Madok, Flynn and the summoned spirits. Auntie Olga's long talons ripped into Flynn's chest, as he tried to flank her. Madok already suffered wounds to his shoulder. Auntie Olga shrugged off the attacks from the spirits swarming her.

Randall saw through the portal, Mama Matilda pointing the twelve guards to the stairs. "The big witch is sending more suits of armor our way!"

Juliana charged forward with her mace into the thick of the fight with Auntie Olga, who was holding her own against Madok and Flynn. The hag was surrounded and unable to defend against the three friends and the conjured spirits. Juliana's mace connected between Auntie Olga's shoulder blades, with a blow that would have crushed a normal man. The hag was staggered by the hit, but spun to face Juliana.

Flynn took the opportunity to lunge with his rapier, plunging it into the small of her back. Auntie Olga reeled in pain, as the rapier pushed all the way through. Flynn put his boot to her rear, for leverage to pull it free. Madok put all his strength into his attack. The sword cut through flesh, sinew, and bone, severing her arm above the elbow.

Auntie Olga howled as her arm hit the floor and the stump bled out smelly, inky, black blood. She reached into the folds of her dress, retrieving a small black gemstone from a hidden pocket.

Juliana raised her mace to deliver a finishing blow to the hag's head, but before it met the target the hag became incorporeal, then disappeared from their sight. Her severed arm still lay on the ground.

The sound of clanking metal on the stone steps grew louder. Madok shoved past Flynn and stood on the stairs at the ready. "We can hold them off in the stair well, fighting them two at a time. Those things are mindless!"

Flynn took up his position next to Madok, advancing down the stair well enough for Juliana to step behind them, followed by the conjured angelic apparitions that circled them.

Juliana called to Randall. "Watch the portal! She may return through it!"

Randall nodded as Madok and Flynn engaged with the first ranks of the guards. Juliana had her mace in hand and the protecting spirits that flew around her.

"YOU?" A booming voice echoed through the tower, as if it were calling from deep within a forgotten crypt.

Paul Wolff

Shaken and heart racing, Randall turned to see the Duke himself, levitating through the portal. The fiery glow from his empty eye sockets intensified from laser fine points, that grew until they were like beacons bathing the room in red light. Randall cowered at the horrid visage of his putrid, rotting flesh and his thin white hair, flowing as if in a breeze.

"Juliana!" Randall cried out, but she had already stepped back into the room followed by whirlwind of spirits.

Juliana's conjured spirits swarmed the Duke, as the sounds of battle from the stairwell grew louder. The angelic apparitions swung at him with their ghostly swords, seeming more nuisance than hinderance.

The Duke stepped onto the floor raising his thin arms above his head, then dropped them to his sides as his voice again boomed. "Inrita monens magicae!"

Juliana's conjured spirits vaporized, leaving the scent of ozone in the air. Juliana gasped, while the undead nobleman stepped toward them.

The Duke's attention turned to Randall, filling him with dread emptiness as their gazes met. The Duke spoke again in the unworldly voice. "Very clever of you to bring yourself to me. Far more convenient than hunting you across the countryside. You will surrender... NOW!"

Madok and Flynn were still fighting the 'living' suits of armor, pushing their way downwards on the stairs, with each pair they destroyed. The long reach of the spear tips and axeblades of the halberds made the going difficult. Flynn's wounds from the steel had little effect on him, as he had assumed his wererat form and found them only a painful inconvenience, as they instantly closed shut. Madok was not as fortunate, only the adrenaline kept him from slowing with each wound.

Half the metal foes were taken down, and now they struggled with their footing on the pieces of armor that littered the stone stairs. Madok's boot slipped on a greave, and he fell backwards onto the steps, atop more armor pieces. Flynn deflected the halberd blade that was swinging down to cut into Madok's groin.

"Your future kids will be grateful for that!" Flynn quipped, as he now found himself on the defense as Madok struggled to pull himself up.

Flynn found himself fending off attacks from four guards. The two guards directly in front of him swung the axe blades, and the pair in the rear, stabbed with the spear tips of their halberds. Flynn changed strategy and finding an opening, leaped headfirst into the belly of the first armor guard.

There was a loud clatter, as Flynn's head connected and he tumbled down the stairs, bowling down the remaining guards. Madok followed, destroying each where they lie as he went.

On the ground floor Mama Matilda and Flynn faced off, circling with eyes fixed on the other. Flynn's glowing red rat eyes burned with rage. The hag's red rimmed black eyes appeared fearful. The sounds of Madok smashing the remaining guards rang out, and then he appeared on the bottom step as a pile of armor crashed to the floor before him. The hag retrieved a black stone from the folds of her dress and disappeared, after becoming incorporeal.

Juliana drew forth the symbol of The Mother from its chain around her neck and held it forcefully toward the Duke. "You are an affront to the light of The Mother. You will be damned to the pits of hell!"

The Duke flew forward, laughing maniacally. Then with an open slap of his boney hand, knocked the pendant from Juliana's grasp across the floor. The burning cold from his hand felt as if she had submerged in an icy river. The burning red in his empty sockets began to shimmer and turn to green flames, as Juliana's eyes fixed on them.

Juliana was overcome with an unnatural dread, then a tingling numbness spread through her entire body, beginning at her fingers and toes. Her knees buckled as she collapsed to the floor pulling her arms over her head to shield herself from the supernatural terror.

Floating above the floor, the Duke spun to face Randall, who had backed himself against the wall. "Foolish boy, I shall end this madness now!"

The Duke began the gestures and chanting to rain down death upon Randall and Juliana.

Flynn took a running leap as he arrived on the landing, and head butted the floating Duke. Randall barely dodged the two, as they crashed into the wall where he had stood.

Flynn rolled away and returned to his feet with weapons ready. He charged again, but was stopped as a brilliant flash of light strobed and the room filled with an electric charge. The deafening clap of thunder rang out, after the summoned bolt of lightning had already struck Flynn. Flynn was thrown backwards to the ground; his shirt had a circular scorch burned in the chest and his fur was smoldering at that point. He reverted to human form, as his body went limp.

"Flamma Illum!" Randall screamed the incantation in retribution.

From the tips of Randall's fingers, flames shot forth and fanned out at the floating Duke. The extreme heat of the magical flames ignited the Duke's fine clothing and melted the rotting flesh on his face and hands away to the bones.

Madok raced up the stairs, stopping in the archway to access the battle. Before him, the fiery form of the Duke was flying madly through the room, attempting to extinguish the flames consuming his flesh. Juliana raised her head from the floor looking to Madok for help. Flynn's body lay curled on the floor unmoving. Randall raised his arms to shield himself from the intense flames that engulfed his foe.

The Duke raised his arms to the air, then dropped them as he chanted. "Inrita monens magicae!"

The magic flames immediately were snuffed out. He had now been reduced to skeletal form, covered in charred flesh and his clothing turned to ash.

Madok charged, swinging the longsword in two hands with enough force to split a man in two. The weapon struck the Duke across his waist, but did not cut into him. He floated to the ceiling out of Madok's reach.

Juliana reached for her pendant as the skeletal Duke swooped toward her. The fiery red points of light in his empty sockets intensified, fixated on Juliana. Madok placed himself between Juliana and the Duke and again attacked with his longsword. The blade skated off the Duke, as if it had hit stone.

The Duke floated back a few feet again, then pointed a blackened skeletal finger at Madok, shouting the incantation that shook the tower walls. "Inrita monens magicae!"

From his finger, a black beam struck Madok's face and washed over his entire body in an instant. The Captain staggered backward, as his strength was drained by the Duke's spell. He felt as if his feet were stuck in thick mud, and struggled to keep his balance as he dropped his sword.

The Duke's attention turned to Randall again as Juliana went to Madok's aid catching him in her arms as he collapsed. Randall looked to Flynn's body then Juliana and felt the situation was hopeless.

"Boy, there is no escape and there will be no quarter for any of you." The Duke prepared the grand gestures of another spell.

Juliana cried out, looking to the ceiling. "Izzy, No!"

Through the levitation portal in the ceiling, Izzy made her entrance into the room in hybrid were rat form with her curved dagger held in her teeth. Swinging in, she threw herself onto the Duke's back, wrapping one arm around his neck and her legs around his skeletal body. Now with the enchanted dagger, she wildly stabbed at her prey.

Unlike the failed attacks from Madok, the enchantment allowed the weapon hit its mark, and the Duke felt the blade sink in.

"You killed Flynn! I hate you! I hate you!" Izzy screamed, as she stabbed the blade into him repeatedly.

The Duke again flew backwards and crashed into the tower wall, smashing Izzy into it. The rat girl held on, determined to fight to the end.

Randall pointed a finger at the Duke and spoke the familiar incantation. "Flatus illum!"

The darts of force launched from his finger and arced in several directions, before all converged and struck the Duke. The magic attack Randall launched against him, seemed to anger him even more and again he flew back into the stone wall with more force, crushing Izzy between he and it. Izzy lost her hold and crashed onto the floor.

The Duke cursed, and his scorched form again raised to the ceiling, out of the reach of Izzy. He prepared the spell Randall recognized, to summon a bolt of lightning.

"Run!" Randall screamed and darted through the archway. Izzy bolted out after Randall on all fours with her dagger in her teeth, as Juliana and Madok struggled around the corner up the stairs.

The loud clap of thunder followed, as the electric bolt passed through the archway missing Juliana and Madok. Chips of stone were blown from the tower wall and a circular scorch mark was left in its wake.

Izzy darted up the helix of stairs past Randall. Juliana and Madok struggled upwards, arm in arm. The Duke wasn't behind them, yet.

Madok pulled Juliana's arm off him. "Go on. My strength's returning."

Juliana nodded, then ran up the stairs, quickly catching up to Randall and Izzy. "Madok is following. Keep going!"

They reached the laboratory floor, after rounding the stairs past the summoning chamber. Izzy was peering through the levitation portal as the others arrived.

"I don't see him!" Izzy reported.

Madok reached the top of the stair, breathing heavily and fatigued. "He didn't follow. He had us. I don't understand."

Juliana pushed open the door to the lab. "We will need more help. I feel this is something that The Mother isn't expecting us to do all on our own."

"Great, to the roof and we can make the leap." Randall stepped into the laboratory.

"Little boy! Come on! We're going." Izzy transformed back into human form, while the others headed up to the rooftop.

Juliana spotted him, cowering under a cluttered work table. She held out her arms to coax him out. "Come with me. I'll protect you."

The frightened child reluctantly crawled ran to Juliana's arms, burying his face into her shoulder. Izzy was despondent, her eyes glazed, staring down the stairwell as the others made their way to roof.

Randall called out to her. "Izzy, there's no time to waste!"

Izzy turned to Randall, with tears running down her cheeks. "Flynn, he's gone."

Randall took a deep breath, seeing Madok at the top step, opening the rooftop door. The warm light of the morning poured into the windowless tower. Feeling the same pain, he did his best to comfort her. "Flynn sacrificed himself to save us. We will avenge him, but we need to survive today to fight tomorrow."

Izzy wiped her tears and joined Randall on the rooftop.

Madok was at the edge of the crenelated tower wall, planning the escape route from the elevated vantage. The Duke's tower on Redrock Castle overlooked a cliffside. Beyond that, farmers working the fields bordering the great Iron Forest.

Juliana was doing her best to comfort the boy and keep her balance, with the strong wind gusts blowing across the rooftop.

Randall surveyed the tower, top noting the nightmarish statues of the winged creatures perched along the wall overlooking the castle. Izzy took his hand and held it tightly.

"This will now be the end of your intrusion!" The Duke's voice carried across the rooftop, above the sound of the wind gusts.

They found Duke Payne behind them, in his form as he was in life, dressed in his finery once again, hands clasped behind his back. The four gargoyles atop the crenelated tower wall turned, and stretched out their wings, as they rose to a standing position. Their eyes were fixed upon their prey.

Randall looked over to Madok and Juliana, who returned fearful glances to him. Madok was seriously injured and disarmed, Juliana held the boy in her arms and Izzy cowered behind Randall.

"There is nowhere for you to go. I can end this for you quickly, or my servants can make this a very messy and drawn-out affair." The Duke was a reasonable man.

In his hand, Randall held a feather. He spoke the incantation as he looked at his friends. "Pluma quasi lux!"

Each had the strange tickling sensation in their bellies, as if butterflies were fluttering about. Randall knew that the spell had taken effect. The Duke sensed Randall's spell and grew furious.

"Rip them apart!" The Duke commanded his gargoyles, in an unnatural booming voice.

Randall pulled Izzy along. "Everyone over the wall!"

Trusting Randall unquestioningly, they made the running leap, and hurtled over the tower wall. Izzy squeaked as Randall tossed her over the side. They found themselves drifting gently downwards, toward the ground. Gusts of wind carried them on a course away from the tower and rocky cliff face, toward the fields.

All looked around, amazed by the sensation and viewing the surrounding lands from this perspective. The sprawling capitol city of Redrock, was just to the west. The towering canopy of hardwood trees of the Ironwood Forest, was to the south. The Great Copper River that flowed south, bisecting the land, was fed by the snows from the peaks of The White Mountains that lay far to the north.

Izzy was the first to notice that Randall had not followed them on their descent and called out to him. "Mr. Randall!"

Randall stood atop the wall, hesitating his leap. The four gargoyles spread their wings, taking to the sky, circling Randall.

The Duke pointed at Randall. "Kill him first!"

The stonelike monsters dived to rend him into pieces. Randall took the wand from his side and pointed it toward the oncoming attack.

"Conus frigus!" Randall pointed at the oncoming gargoyles.

A blast of arctic air shot forth from the wand's crystal, fanning out to engulf the monsters on their descent. Layers of ice and frost formed on three of the beasts, as the fourth dodged the arctic blast. Losing their mobility, they hurtled downwards out of control.

The first crashed through the rooftop into the laboratory. Another hit the crenelated wall before continuing its descent to be broken apart on the cliffside below. The third hurtled unimpeded to the farmlands below.

Randall looked about feeling better about their chances, until he saw the fourth circling back toward him, and the Duke was preparing a spell to extinguish him from existence.

Randall leapt from the tower and drifted slowly to the earth. Below in the fields Madok, Izzy, Juliana, and the boy watched his descent. The farmers and their field hands were now attracted by the scene of flying creatures and floating people.

Randall gently touched down, feet first, onto the wheat field unharmed. The rest were only a short distance away. He jogged toward them, hoping to leave the tower, hags, gargoyles, and an angry little Duke far behind.

Madok wildly waved his arms in the air and Izzy jumped up and down screaming. Juliana had her mace in hand and was chanting. Randall then realized what was happening, as the gargoyle swooped in and grabbed him.

The vile creature couldn't lift Randall, because the last gargoyle sprang up from the wheat field held Randall by his ankles. Unable to take flight with its wings and legs broken, it played a deadly game of tug-o-war with its brethren, hoping to win Randall as his prize.

Randall felt as if he was going to be torn in half, as he cried for help from the others. Juliana's prayer to The Mother was answered, and the spectral weapon was summoned forth to attack the airborne gargoyle.

The ghostly mace bludgeoned its target repeatedly, until it released Randall. The winged beast retreated into the air attempting to evade the unrelenting attack of the disembodied weapon.

Randall fell to the ground, only to find the crippled gargoyle setting upon him. Splintered bone pierced outward of its skin, preventing it from standing. Randall struggled to wriggle out from underneath its great weight, but was pinned. The beast pulled itself up, face to face with him and opened its salivating maw, revealing rows of razor-sharp teeth and foul hot breath. Randall and the creature's eyes locked, as it prepared to bite into his face.

Juliana swung her mace, dealing a crushing blow to the small of the gargoyle's back. Two of the men tending the fields, also arrived to aid in the fight, stabbing with pitchforks. The creature attempted to stand, but collapsed on its broken legs.

"Mr. Randall! Juliana! Look out!" Izzy screamed before Madok covered her and the boy under his body.

Atop the crenelated wall of the tower, The Duke released a small ball of fiery light from his forefinger to the battle below. Before striking the ground, it exploded into a huge ball of orange flame, heating the air and scorching the fields within the blast radius. The farmhands and gargoyle, were carbonized in its blast.

Randall and Juliana escaped the full brunt of the attack, diving out of its range. With singed hairs, burns to exposed skin and smoldering clothing, both clambered up. Madok pulled Izzy and the boy from the ground and Juliana encouraged all to follow her.

Exhausted from a sleepless night and fatigued from battle, the four continued undeterred, until they were out of sight of Duke Payne's tower. Only after taking cover under the canopy of the trees of the Ironwood Forest, would they attempt to rest. The chaos they stirred up was only the beginning.

By a shallow stream, Juliana tended to Madok's wounds, invoking the Mother's name and channeling the healing power through her hand. Slumped against a tree, Randall looked at the scorched leather on his shoes and inspected the hole burned through the seat of his breeches. Izzy shared water from a skin with the boy, before taking a drink herself.

Izzy looked at her friends and managed a small smile. "His name is Mosi, and he wants to go home to his mama and baba."

45
The Visitation

"Master Osbert, his Grace requests your presence in his council chambers immediately." The young guard, respectfully delivered the Duke's invite to Osbert.

Osbert stood at the open door to his bed chamber, hesitating momentarily. He had not left his bedchambers for two days, since the council meeting and the subsequent attack on the Duke in his tower. News of goings on from the outside was second hand from servants that brought his meals. A guard was posted at his door with orders to confine Osbert to his quarters.

Osbert was horrified by nightmarish display of evil perpetrated under the Duke's orders, the surprising reveal of his true form and the diabolical creatures he consorted with. The Duke was an eccentric and private man, but he never imagined this. He was duped and betrayed by the man he served for a decade, keeping his true nature hidden behind a façade of cordial exchanges and pleasantries.

"I'm coming, I'm coming." Osbert placed the tall white sugarloaf hat on his head, checking his appearance in the mirror before departing.

The castle was on high alert, after the intruders made their assault on the tower and the dramatic escape. More soldiers patrolled the castle's halls and walked the battlements. For the first time in many years human guards were stationed atop the Duke's tower, while workers were brought in to perform repairs. The ant hill had been kicked and it was full of activity.

The door for the council chamber was opened for Osbert by his escort, while two other guards stood at attention on either side of the large heavy doors. When Osbert entered he found himself alone in the large room. All evidence of bloodshed a few days before had been removed.

He crossed the floor to his usual seat, to the right of Duke Payne's throne. Taking his chair, he sat nervously drumming his fingers on the table. The other set of doors soon opened and the Duke entered. Once again, magic gave the illusion that he was his living self. The doors closed behind him and he took his throne.

"You look well, Your Grace." Osbert struggled to act as if everything was back to normal.

"Thank you, Osbert, as do you. My apologies for the events of the other day in this chamber. It was necessary to remove the threat to my dukedom with a firm hand. There were further threats since we had last met. They have not been eliminated, yet. A small group of assassins invaded my tower. They sadly evaded justice and escaped after wreaking a bit of havoc." The Duke relayed news to Osbert, waving his small hands as he spoke.

Osbert listened to the Duke's words intently, and paused for a moment. "Who do you suspect?"

The Duke leaned forward. "I already know who these would be assassins are. They have been known to me for some time. They are part of yet another conspiracy to sabotage my authority in Port Gwynn. They are quite clever though, but they shall not succeed, even though they have managed to eliminate some of my spy network. Only a minor setback."

Osbert wiped the sweat beading on his brow with his hand. "Your Grace, I feel I am unable to provide you council on these matters, being sequestered in my chamber these past few days. I was not privy to any information."

"Osbert, war is soon to be upon us! My nephew is planning on removing me and sending assassins out, while disrupting the dukedom's commerce with thievery to bankrupt me! Come with me now! I'll show you how deep this runs and what I am dealing with from within my borders!" The Duke rose from his throne and motioned for Osbert to follow.

The two were accompanied by a pair of heavily armed bodyguards in black and red garb, as they traversed the halls of Castle Redrock. An iron portcullis was raised at the top of a stone staircase that led to the dungeons. The further they descended into the darkness, the heavier the air felt to Osbert. He carefully watched his footing on the damp steps, narrowly missing a rat that scuttled just before him.

Smoky torches, in their iron sconces along the hall, cast their yellow light on the rough mason walls, low ceilings, and the damp uneven floor stones. It proved a stark contrast to the opulent setting of Castle Redrock's ground level.

Osbert removed his tall hat to prevent it from touching the wet ceiling, carrying it in his hands in front of him. The Duke waved Osbert on, to not fall behind, as he met with the gaoler.

They passed several barred cell doors overcrowded with prisoners, most living, a few dead, and rotting. The awful unclean smells and tragic moans of prisoners suffering in their cells were not unknown to Osbert, but now it began to overwhelm his senses. He recognized their destination, the interrogation room.

The gaoler pushed open the large oaken door to the landing, where more stone steps descending into a large chamber. The ceiling was vaulted and too high for the light of the few torches and braziers around the room to illuminate it. In the shadows of the room, shackles were set into the wall, tools for extracting information were neatly laid out on a large wooden table. 'Man shaped' gibbet cages hung in the upper reaches, suspended by thick chains on a pully system. A round well in the center of the room had a pully and harness system, to lower victims headfirst into its depths. A large wooden chair covered in nails and thick restraining straps sat unoccupied.

Osbert nervously scanned the room, as the Duke walked down the steps and the gaoler pushed the door closed. Osbert hesitantly followed, as the Duke turned to wave him on.

"Oh, Osbert. I have some very interesting caged vermin. I presume you already know this one." The Duke motioned over to the gaoler.

The gaoler worked the wench and slowly lowered the first gibbet cage. The torchlight illuminated the backside of a large naked man. He was in a forced standing position within the cage. The Duke frowned, and motioned the gaoler to rotate the cage to face them.

The man was covered in many festering wounds, forced to stand in his own filth. Slowly he lifted his head to look at his visitors. The once thick black hair of his beard and head, was thin and graying, due to the stress of his incarceration.

Osbert gasped and covered his mouth. "Geoffrey Walters..."

The Duke smiled from ear to ear. "Oh yes, the 'Lord Mayor.' Such a naughty lad. He was the lead conspirator in Port Gwynn, as you already know. I decided to keep him and let him rot down here. No need for pesky trials, he's already forgotten. Now here's a rather interesting specimen, also from Port Gwynn."

The gaoler moved to another nearby gibbet, and slowly lowered it into view. His Lordship of the Nest, Peter, was crammed tightly into a cage naked. He held onto the bars of the cage tightly with his fat fingers, angrily eyeing Osbert and The Duke.

The Duke walked around the cage, examining Peter as he spoke. "This one is a nasty fellow. A cursed shapeshifter. Turns into a filthy, giant sewer rat when he pleases. His shape changing brethren are causing all kinds of mayhem in Port Gwynn as of late. Well, until I sent in proper soldiers to eradicate them. Surprisingly, this is the one that they chose as their leader. He put up a pretty good fight from what I was told, but now I have him here to study and experiment on. The whole lycanthropic condition is quite interesting. News from the south is that more of these rat men have been infecting people in Sommer Harbour. More mayhem that I will have to eradicate. Best to find if this condition is reversable by some means, or if it will just come down to curing them all, one by one, with silvered weapons."

Peter hissed at the Duke angrily, and spat at him.

"Fulgur!" the Duke spoke the incantation and touched the metal cage with one hand.

Immediately the gibbet was engulfed in crackling blue sparks that transferred their charge to Peter's body. Peter cried out and went limp, but still standing in the tight cage.

"Filthy beast that one. It will give me great pleasure to dissect and study it." The Duke motioned for the gaoler to lower one more gibbet.

The last cage was lowered into view. Flynn was stripped naked in his cage, though appeared to be in far better condition than the others. His wounds healed, save for the scar left from the lightning bolt that struck his chest. He also was crammed into his man shaped cage, unable to move and the bars were too narrow to make his escape in rat form. He listened in silence.

"Now this one here, is another one of those nasty shape changers. He managed to let himself get captured as all his companions abandoned him, after their assassination attempt on me! He is yet another Port Gwynn conspiracist and denizen of that 'Nest.' Thievery and murder, that's all that seems to come from Port Gwynn. We plan to glean more information about his co-conspirators. So far, he has not been forthcoming. What I do know, all three of these dishonorable wretches are solely driven by their love of coin." The Duke shook his head and stepped away from the gibbets back to Osbert, who was distressed by the show of cruelty.

"Your Grace, is this the reason you requested me to join you down here? Interrogations are not in my field of expertise." Osbert was growing more upset.

Duke Payne chuckled a bit. "Oh no Osbert, I wasn't going to have you take any part in that. I just merely wanted to show you that the growing threat in the dukedom is being dealt with and order restored. However, this you will find more interesting."

Duke Payne and Osbert crossed the chamber past the rack, which had traces of dried blood spattered on it. On the far side of the room in an alcove, illuminated by a single torch, spikes were set into the wall with several severed heads mounted upon them. Osbert immediately recognized Lord Tristan and General Jaheem, as the freshest additions to the collection.

Osbert looked away from the ghastly display. "I don't understand, Your Grace."

"Watch this, Osbert." The Duke reached out and slapped the heads of General Jaheem, then Lord Tristan.

The eyelids of the heads fluttered and slowly opened. The whites of their eyes were first revealed, and then they slowly rolled straight ahead toward the Duke and then Osbert. Alarmed, Osbert stumbled losing his balance, falling backwards to the ground.

"Oh, do get a hold of yourself, Osbert. These two can't hurt you." The Duke chuckled, as he patted the General's head with his hand.

"Your Grace, why?" Osbert rose to his feet, leaving his crumbled hat on the floor.

The Duke smiled. "I was needing some questions answered and thought, what better way to get them, than going straight to the source. It appears that the General wasn't acting on his own in this matter. It seems that the plot to usurp my throne had other co-conspirators. Someone that I had trusted for years, to advise me and assist in carrying out the administrative duties in the rule of the dukedom. Someone that was acting as a spy for the king, relaying messages to him. I purposely allowed for some of them to get through and others were intercepted, in hopes of them revealing all of who were involved. I have found that these two in death, were able to reveal more names. However, there was one I never suspected."

The Duke turned his attention from Osbert back to the heads of Lord Tristan and General Jaheem. The mouths of both hung wide open and the eyes had rolled back. The Duke clapped his hands in front of the faces of both, causing their eyes to roll forward again and focus on him.

"Tell me again, who is the one behind the conspiracy to remove me from my throne?" The Duke asked, as a mother talking to her children.

Both head's eyes slowly shifted their gaze from Duke Payne to Osbert. Struggling to form the words with their mouths, each whispered the same name softly. "Osbert..."

"Your Grace! I only meant to do what is best for the kingdom. Since the Duchess's long illness and her death, I know you have been distraught and distanced. I never meant for you to be removed, only to keep King Ernald informed. Jaheem became overly ambitious..." Osbert backed away from The Duke and the alcove of heads.

"Osbert, it's okay. I know you believe you are doing what is right and have allowed the teachings of that 'Mother' to beguile you. It just won't be allowed to happen anymore, from this day forward." The Duke smiled.

Paul Wolff

"What do you intend to do to me?" Osbert looked around desperately at all the implements of torture.

"Oh no Osbert. Not any of this nastiness. I consider you a friend, even now after this betrayal. Those things are reserved for my true enemies. You have served me and the dukedom well for years. However, you won't go unpunished. I introduce you to Naamah." Duke Payne looked past Osbert, signaling the figure lurking in the shadows.

The female devil slinked forward across the room with her feathery wings tucked behind her back. Her tall and perfect naked form moved with catlike grace toward Osbert. Her red eyes unblinking, were locked with his.

She stood in front of Osbert with her breasts almost pushed into his face, looking down into his fearful eyes with her unblinking red stare. Osbert turned now, facing the Duke. Slowly he dropped down to his knees, with despair in his eyes. Naamah ran her fingers through Osbert's hair with one hand.

The Duke nodded his head. "Do it."

Grabbing a handful of hair, Naamah pulled back his head and slowly sawed at his throat with her dagger, as she spread her feathery wings. The blade's cut opened his throat, spilling blood down his front and bathing his killer's hand in crimson. Within moments, she cut through bone, muscle, and sinew.

Osbert's body fell forward to the ground, still pumping blood out of the neck stump. Naamah folded back her white feathery wings, holding the head of her prey, while blood spattered her body and onto the cold stone floor. The Duke smiled, nodding approval.

Naamah plunged Osbert's head onto an empty spike with the others. Licking the warm blood from her fingers, she turned to The Duke. "What now, Archie?"

The Duke rolled his eyes and shook his head. "Firstly, clean yourself up and get some clothes on. You can't walk the halls like that. One more thing, for the last time don't call me Archie!"

"By all means, Your Grace." Naamah walked with a sensuous slink up the steps and exited the interrogation room.

The Duke looked at the head of Osbert for a long moment. His mouth hung wide open and the open eyes rolled upwards. The Duke gestured with one hand, as he chanted an incantation. Suddenly Osbert's mouth closed, and his eyes met with the Duke's.

"Ah good. Nice to still have you with me, Osbert. Perhaps I shall move you into the tower later. We could still chat from time to time that way." The Duke was pleased with this turn of events.

The Duke also exited the chamber, and the gaoler with the assistance of another removed the headless corpse of Osbert. The three gibbets remained lowered, their occupants forgotten.

Flynn looked over at Peter and Geoffrey, in their respective cages. Both were unaware of what transpired before them. Unable to sit, Flynn leaned back against the bars trying to wrap his head around it. He had no idea how he could escape without outside help.

46

An Uneasy Truce

"I'm going for a piss." The grizzled soldier stood up from the light of their campfire and accidentally kicked over his empty tankard.

"You're being a right cunt, stepping out before I have a chance to get my coin back!" An equally rough looking soldier shouted, as his comrade stumbled through a tangle of tree roots.

Two other soldiers laughed, quenching their thirst, drinking warm beer out of leather jacks. Each tossed another silver coin in the pot for their next wager. They rolled the bones as the grizzled soldier disappeared behind a large gnarled tree, dropping his breeches along the way.

Patrols scoured the fringes of the Ironwood Forest and farming hamlets, hunting Randall, and his companions. This patrol set up camp, just off the forest road, not far from their own camp.

Madok and Juliana lay in the underbrush undetected, watching this undisciplined rabble for almost an hour. Madok determined as poorly trained as they appeared, they were well equipped. Randall and the others were instructed to stay hidden at camp until they returned.

Not one to follow instructions, Izzy also kept a watchful eye from up high in an ancient oak tree in giant rat form. There was a dozen soldiers encamped with an equal number of horses. She was tired of eating the one thing that seemed plentiful in this forest the past few days, those damned tough and bitter tasting black squirrels. She now eyed the unattended tent where their food supply was stored.

Madok eyed the soldier relieving himself on the tree, only a few yards from them. The soldier's sword on his belt and the mail hauberk he wore would be a nice little prize, as he was utterly defenseless losing his.

Randall pressed up against Izzy's tree, unable to see her high in the upper branches. Peeking around the tree, he figured most of the patrol was sleeping, aside from these gamblers. He could easily conjure an ice storm from the wand. However, Juliana made him promise no unnecessary killings as, 'These poor souls were just normal men, played as pawns by the Duke.'

Juliana spoke in a soft voice. "By Her power you are rigid! Hold fast!"

The guard continued with his piss, until the stream shortened to a dribble on his boots. Frozen in place, he held the hauberk up in one hand and his 'Johnson' in the other.

"Be quick!" Juliana patted Madok on the shoulder.

Madok dragged the guard away, and stripped him of all his equipment down to his undergarments. He strapped on his sword belt, donned the open face bascinet helmet, then tossed the mail coat over his arm while Juliana had eyes on the campsite.

"It won't take them long to miss him." Juliana reminded Madok.

"Thanks again, sir." Madok said to the stripped-down soldier, just as a large black beetle crawled across the man's face from the forest floor. The man did not flinch or blink, under her spell.

Izzy climbed down the tree without a sound or moving a branch. She looked to Randall, and then looked at the food tent.

"Not a good idea, Izzy! Let's head back before Madok discovers we left. I don't want him rattling on." Randall scolded the rat girl in a whisper, while he held her clothes and dagger.

Ignoring Randall, Izzy lurked in the shadows darting between trees, as she made her way to the back of the food tent. Randall knew he couldn't keep Izzy in line, so he prepared to back her up if trouble started.

The game continued until one inebriated gambler emptied his jack. "Aye, there must be a hole in this. This is the third time its run dry."

Laughing the other passed him his empty tankard. "Well, get us another round, Eric. You're a genius swiping that firkin of Grummandy from the captain's personal supply. Pretentious arse. Sending us out here while he's back in Redrock. Probably getting his knob polished by your wife."

The three laughed, as the man struggled to his feet feeling very wobbly, then staggered toward the supplies tent. The others finally came to the realization their other comrade hadn't returned from his break.

"Terry is still out there. Think he's passed out in his own filth?" The soldier squinted, looking into the dark forest.

"Better get him. Perhaps I should empty my bladder as well." The first said, as he struggled to his feet off balance from the drink.

"Careful there, Michael. I'm not dragging both of you out of there." The burly soldier kept his seat and tossed another small log onto the fire.

Eric stepped into tent and eyed the small cask branded 'Grummandy.' Holding his leather jack unsteadily under the tap, he filled the first drinking vessel. Out of the corner of his eye he saw a giant rat on its hind legs, sniffing around the provisions oblivious of him.

Eric's eyes opened wide, and he dropped the jack while the cask continued to empty its contents to the ground. Izzy spun around with links of sausage hanging from her mouth. Her red eyes met his, then she darted out of the tent with sausages trailing behind her.

Eric scratched his head, backing out of the tent. He slowly walked backwards toward the campfire. "John, we've got rats. I just saw the biggest bugger ever in the food tent."

Michael called out while dragging Terry into the campsite. "Everyone up! Terry is bewitched! Quick now!"

Randall dropped Izzy's gear preparing to act, when a hand covered his mouth and the tip of a blade stuck his back.

"Remarkable luck I would say finding you." A female voice whispered into his ear. Randall raised his hands to surrender.

Within the camp, the men were springing out of their tents from their bedrolls and equipping themselves. Michael dropped Terry and drew his sword, when he was struck in the face with an arrow. More arrows flew into the camp, striking men as they pulled on their mail and tied sword belts.

A figure leapt upon Eric's back, who was struggling with an arrow lodged in his flank. The wererat was clad in battle worn leather armor and wielded a dagger. Eric crashed to the ground, as he was repeatedly stabbed in his exposed neck.

Three more wererats sprang into the campsite, brandishing swords. Within minutes the violent chaos wreaked havoc on the Duke's men. The small force of wererats left no quarter and the horses were driven off.

The leather clad wererat wiped blood from its dagger on Terry's underclothes, as the spell ended and he looked about frantically. The wererat plunged the dagger under Terry's chin.

Once again, the leather clad killer wiped the blade on the dying man's underclothes, as she reverted to human form. Red surveyed the carnage in the encampment. "Bring in those voyeurs."

Randall was led into the camp by Sauda at the tip of her sword. Madok and Juliana entered with hands raised, followed by three men in clad in leather with bows drawn. The three stood together with hands raised as Sauda disarmed them.

Red looked around the perimeter of the camp, sheathing her dagger. "Izzy, I know you're out there. Come here right now. I won't hurt you."

Red and Sauda, along with the rest of their gang, stood motionless staring into the woods. Madok, Juliana, and Randall each threw glances at one another, wondering if the other was going to make a move.

Sauda stepped to the edge of the campsite. "That's fine Izzy. You just stay there for now. We're just going to talk."

"Where's Flynn, and why do you travel in the company of this murderer?" Red pointed at Madok.

"Murderer? You slaughtered a dozen men without provocation." Juliana snapped back.

Red moved up to Juliana's face, their eyes locked. Juliana stood defiantly, unmoved.

"Yes, murderer. That man led the initial assault on our home, murdering many of my brothers and sisters before we drove him out." Red hissed.

Madok lowered his arms. "What do you mean 'initial?'"

Sauda stepped forward. "The Duke sent soldiers in to clean us out. We are all that escaped during the onslaught."

Randall cleared his throat. "So, you tracked us down to kill us?"

"I found Izzy skulking about." A dirty woman clad in leather armor with greasy long black hair stepped into the campsite, tugging Izzy along by her ear.

Izzy had dressed so quickly her clothes were on backwards. She held the sausage links and her dagger hidden by the folds of her skirt.

Red smiled, kneeling, putting her hand on Izzy's shoulder. Izzy backed away to Juliana, who pulled her close. Feeling the rejection, Red huffed as she stood up,

"Now, where's Flynn? Did this one kill him?" Red drew her dagger and placed the tip to Madok's throat.

"Don't you hurt him!" Izzy tried to kick Red, but Juliana pulled her back tightly.

Red pulling the dagger away from Madok's throat, she asked again. "Then tell me where Flynn is."

"The Duke killed him!" Izzy screamed out, as she welled up with tears.

The gang of rogues all looked at each other, whispering among themselves. Sauda waved her hand for them to be silent.

Sauda looked Izzy in the eye. "Was he killed in a fight with one of the Duke's patrols. We've seen patrols like this one all along the Forest Road."

Randall spoke up. "No, it was The Duke himself. We were in Castle Redrock's tower and our ambush failed. He is a powerful wizard, and we found ourselves outmatched."

Sauda was shaken. "How is it you escaped and not Flynn?"

Madok quickly responded. "Flynn sacrificed himself to save us."

"It is true. He was selfless in his actions." Juliana added.

Red looked her prisoners over and seemed lost in thought for a moment. "You are still guilty of the assault on The Nest, as any dogs that wear the Duke's colors."

Red drew her dagger and swiped at Madok's throat. Madok dove away and grabbed her arm on the follow thru. He twisted her arm around behind, while she fought to keep hold of her blade.

"Ut hic de mecum in infernum!" Randall spoke the incantation and in a flash of light he disappeared from the camp. Madok spun around using Red as a shield just as the three archers released their arrows, striking her instead of the intended target. Izzy drew her hidden dagger and stabbed Red in the thigh, as she transformed into hybrid rat form.

Juliana faced off with the three swordsmen, as she called upon the divine powers of The Mother and spoke the word. "Sleep!"

The attackers fell into a magically induced slumber, each dropping to the ground and curling into a ball.

Red fell to the ground, struggling with the arrows and the wound from Izzy's enchanted blade, which did not heal. Madok disarmed her, taking the dagger and sword from her belt to face the archers, who now drew their short swords. The stringy-hair woman transformed into a greasy wererat and advanced on Juliana to prevent more prayers of divine favor from The Mother.

"Flamma Illum!" Randall cast the spell from behind the three advancing on Madok. The flat fan of flames shot from the tips of his fingers and bathed the three in the magic fire. The intense heat ignited the gray cloaks they wore over their leather armor, causing them to flail about on the forest floor. The magically summoned fire continued to burn the bodies of his victims, after they succumbed to the flame. Randall turned his attention to the three sleeping on the forest floor, and summoned forth a sticky mass of webs to restrain them before they woke.

The greasy wererat lunged Juliana. Madok threw Red's dagger with such force and accuracy, it sank all the way to the hilt between its eyes. The wererat was dead before it hit the ground and reverted to human form.

"Don't try it, Sauda!" Izzy threatened, as she faced the tall warrior woman, whose eyes were on Madok.

Red struggled to sit up, three arrows remained in her body and the dagger wound continued to bleed out. She grasped an arrow lodged in her right shoulder, but failed to pull it free and fell back.

Madok held Red's own sword to her throat and looked up at Sauda. "We have the upper hand, yield!"

Sauda lowered her sword, eyeing the four who easily overpowered them, even after they were disarmed. She tossed her sword to the ground in defeat. Red lay on the ground, struggling with the pain of her wounds.

"Hey, give that back!" Randall recovered his special satchel that was dumped on the ground, and retrieved his wand that was tucked in Sauda's sword belt.

The other rat men began to stir from their magic slumber, only to find they were now trapped beneath Randall's summoned webs. They cursed and struggled to pull free, but they were held fast.

Randall curled his lip in disgust, grabbing the hilt of the dagger lodged in the dead woman's head. He looked away placing, his free hand on her bloodied forehead for leverage to pull it free. He wiped the blood from his hands onto the dead woman's cloak, before joining the rest of the group.

"This dagger is silvered. I suppose you carry this in case one of your brothers or sisters becomes a nuisance." Randall inspected the weapon, before passing it back to Madok.

"I suppose you will kill us now?" Sauda asked, amidst the carnage.

Randall tugged on the few hairs on his chin before responding. "No, I think not. I want to know what brought you all the way out here, so far from Port Gwynn."

"Yeah, I want answers!" Izzy pushed out her chest and crossed her arms.

Juliana knelt before Red, looking over her wounds and arrows protruding from her body and gave her a chunk of tree bark to bite down on. "Let me help you."

Sauda watched Juliana, as she pulled the first arrow from her shoulder allowing the wound to close immediately. Red passed out from the pain. Juliana continued to the next.

Seeing Juliana was true to her word, Sauda answered Randall. "Shortly after the High Sherriff arrived in Gwynn, things took a worse turn. The Lord Mayor was arrested, cathedral closed, then their attention turned to The Nest. They discovered more of our hidden entrances and sent a force of heavily armored men with silvered weapons. It was a slaughter. Even the children weren't spared. His Lordship lead us on a counterattack, but there were too many. He surrendered to their leader, hoping to get them to spare the others as me and Red escaped into the sewers. Once out, we found the few others that escaped and hid in plain sight around Gwynn, while our home was destroyed. We only learned that Peter survived the attack after news spread that he, as well as Geoffrey, were transported to Castle Redrock under heavy guard. We followed the caravan, looking for an opening to rescue him, but we never had one."

"So, what are you still doing here?" Randall asked

Sauda sighed. "We were spying on the castle. Watching the sentries on the walls, searching for alternate points of entry."

"Planning a rescue? Why not choose a new leader and move on." Madok said, while shaking his head.

"He is my father!" Red spat out the tree bark and a little blood. Juliana pulled another arrow from Red, and once again she lost consciousness.

Sauda looked to her comrade, then to Randall. "We heard the news around Redrock of intruders in the castle and their escape into the forest. They identified the four of you in detail, including your names. That's when Red wanted to find you first."

"What, for? Payback?" Randall asked angrily.

"Yes." Sauda responded.

Juliana pulled the remaining arrow from Red and watched the wound seal shut.

Madok got into Sauda's face before saying his piece. "Your home got all the unwanted attention from The Duke by involving Randall in the scheme to rob Geoffrey. Payne already knew about Geoffrey's plot and all involved."

Juliana completed her spell, healing the stab wound on Red's thigh. Stepping back, she looked across at the dead that lay in the campsite as the light of the campfire burned low.

Juliana addressed everyone. "This barbarity ends now. The common enemy is Duke Payne. He serves a power that is a danger to the world. Somehow, he continues to live after death, as we witnessed in his tower. His rule is tyrannical, and the master he serves desires a foothold here from The Hells. I call for a truce now. Injustices done to one another can be righted later, including what happened this evening. Let's come together to remove this monster."

Red rose to her feet and nervously eyed Madok. Randall looked over to the three trapped in the webs, then dismissed the spell. Izzy sheathed her dagger. Juliana retrieved Sauda's sword and returned it to her hand. Madok passed Red her sword and dagger.

Juliana looked around at the carnage one last time. "Gather the dead together. I will say some words of The Mother over them."

Without speaking, everyone went to work.

47
The Ritual

Four horses pulled the carriage down the abandoned low road into the vale. The new moon provided no light, as they traversed the overgrown trail, over decades old wheel ruts. Either side of the trail was alive with the sounds of chirping frogs and insects; the only living things thriving in the peat bogs. These marshlands, near Whistling Pass between the Redrock Mountains, were avoided by most, and only the occasional traveler risked this shortcut. Typically, ones that were prepared for its dangers, or those ignorant of the risks.

The driver's face was shrouded by the hood of their black mantle. The lanterns mounted on the front the carriage lit the way ahead for the horses on the treacherous stretch of road, which was built up just above the marsh. Just ahead, a long crumbling stone bridge crossed over a slough of brackish water that sliced through the wetlands.

The driver stopped the horses just short of the ancient bridge and threw back her hood with her one hand. Auntie Olga looked at the bridge, then frowned. "You're not fooling anyone! Get out from under there and show yourself."

Beneath the stone bridge, a long green warty nose came up and then the rest of troll emerged. The creature pulled its lanky body up and stepped onto the road. With one hand it scratched the nest of filthy black hair atop its head, as the other arm dragged the ground. It looked Auntie Olga up and down, then held out its huge hand to collect. "Gimme shiny pretties, stupid!"

The voice of The Duke called out from within the carriage. "Why have we stopped?"

Auntie Olga jumped down from the driver's seat onto the road. The stump of her recently severed arm was wrapped in a fresh dressing and didn't inhibit her actions. "This fool of a bridge troll wants to collect a toll."

The carriage door flung open and Naamah stepped out first. Her body was clad in plate armor made from blackened steel with a longsword and her dagger on her side. She stretched out her wings and her arms for relief after the ride from Castle Redrock. The Duke, in turn exited the carriage. He was dressed in flowing black and red robes that covered his skeletal body and a red felt cap atop his skull. The red glowing points of light in his sockets burned as pin points

The troll watched the three with his hand outstretched, as the skeletal Duke approached. The Duke stopped in front of the huge monster and crossed his arms, surveying the slough ignoring the troll's existence. Confused, the troll continued to hold out its hand, expecting a shiny pretty.

The Duke nodded his head approvingly and turned to the others. "Perfect! This is the location of that centuries old battle. The northern barbarian invaders attempted to retreat through Whistling Pass after their failed raid on Redrock. The bottleneck at this very bridge is where they were met by my great, great grandmother Lady Cecilia Beatrice Payne, who was quite the sorceress. No one remembers her these days. She is said to have summoned a powerful storm, slowing the invader's movement as hundreds of them crossed the bridge. She summoned lightning from the turbulent black clouds overhead, striking all on the bridge. It is said to have been an amazing slaughter! Those attempting to avoid death by electrocution, perished by drowning when they dove into the slough, whose waters rose in the storm."

The troll continued to hold out one hand, while picking its nose with the other.

"Okay, Archie. The history lesson was very nice, but will this work?" Auntie Olga stood beside the Duke, also paying no mind to the troll.

"Absolutely! The bodies of those barbarians remain where they fell. Those cluttering the bridge were tossed into the slough and swallowed by the bog." The Duke recalled the book in his library of his family's history.

Naamah set up a brass brazier on a folding tripod, at the edge of the stone bridge. She turned to the hopeful troll, that still held out its hand. She placed her hand on the hilt of her sword, spread her feathery wings, and shook her head disapprovingly. The troll backed away, then shambled off with its knuckles dragging the ground, disappointed. Naamah folded her wings back and continued to prepare for the ritual, adding special coals and incense to the brazier, which spontaneously ignited.

"It is ready, Archibald." Naamah backed away from the smoky brazier as the glow of the coals provided a sinister underlighting to her face. She disappeared into the darkness, returning to the carriage.

Duke Payne and the hag approached the brazier, and their nightmarish visages were enhanced by the glow of the burning coals. Auntie Olga began a droning, humming deep from her throat, as the Duke pulled back the sleeves of the robe, stretching out his skeletal arms into the sky swaying. Thick fog overflowed from the brazier to the ground, crawling across the marsh, filling depressions along its way. The slough up to the bottom of the stone bridge was obscured, as everything was slowly taken over by the fog on its advance across the vale.

All the sounds of nature went silent. Then the Duke's voice boomed across the marshlands. "Oh, great Dis Dysvakar pater I, your most humble of servants, call upon your blessings and help once again to better serve you. Spies have reported a military force from King Ernald to sabotage all the work I have done in your name. You have provided me the gift of immortality, and a general to command my forces. I now ask that you give me an army that never rests, and will fight without mercy, to send the king's troops to The Hells as your slaves."

The red-hot glowing coals in the bowl of the brass brazier were replaced by a green glow and like flames rose high, licking at the sky. Within the flames, a spectral semi-transparent face of the arch devil Dysvakar, took form. The devil's eyes looked down on The Duke, who stood before the brazier, with his arms outstretched. The hag's throat noises continued without interruption as they stood knee deep in the thick soupy fog.

Dysvakar's eyes, on his disembodied head, shifted focused now on Auntie Olga and narrowed. "Archibald, do you think you could get her to stop that awful racket? It is truly not something I ever need to hear again. If you must insist on bothering me you, could you possibly bring along a musician with talent that could play a cheerful ditty on a fiddle?"

The hag immediately went silent, humiliated she stepped away from the brazier disappearing into the darkness. The head of Dysvakar turned and the eyes focused on the undead Duke. "Okay, enough with the flattery and flowery speech requesting your little army. This was bargained for already. Do you have the payment for this? Sending you Naamah to serve, was already a large request in such a short span of time for what I have already done for you."

The Duke dropped to one knee before the image of Dysvakar in green flames of the brazier. "Yes, my Lord. I apologize for petitioning for-"

"Oh, stop that. You'll get your robes all muddy. Stand up and let's get on with this." Dysvakar's eyes rolled, as his disembodied head shook disapprovingly in the green flames.

The Duke returned to his feet, calling Naamah waiting by the carriage. "Bring her forward."

She opened the carriage and helped the last occupant exit. Gripping tightly on to one arm, she pulled along the captive, who struggled to walk barefoot in shackles along the overgrown track. Her head was covered by a cloth sack, hands in manacles and dressed in a dirty linen chemise.

Naamah pushed the woman to her knees and pulled the sack from her head. The woman breathed in deeply; her disheveled gray hair had been clipped during her short imprisonment in Redrock Castle and her face bruised and swollen. The woman looked up with her blackened eye to the brazier and Dysvakar's image, that was smiling back ear to ear.

Dysvakar addressed the woman. "Well, a pleasure to meet Bishop Caitlan, former spiritual leader of that former Mother cult in Redrock. I understand that there was quite the resistance from the church guard to prevent the cathedral from being shut down. So sad that it had to end the way it did. Cathedral doors battered down, looting and fires damaging that fine piece of architecture. All surviving members of the clergy rotting in the dungeons. The others have their heads decorating spikes around Redrock's gates."

Bishop Caitlan spat in defiance, looking over at the skeletal Duke. "You sold your soul for this existence? You're betraying and destroying the lives of so many of your own people for your 'Lord.' Whatever you do to me will not change the fact, you are damned eternally to burn in The Hells as his slave."

"Bishop, your words are as wasted on me now, as the dreadful pontificating of your sermons you performed for the sheep. Purging my dukedom of you and all the other feebleminded members of the clergy that serve Her, has been a long time in the coming. You should be interested to know that many of The Mother's former faithful, will soon be serving my Lord. They will be easily swayed to leave Her, to join with my Lord, who is diametrically opposed to all She stands for." The Duke gloated as he taunted Bishop Caitlan.

"You are a fool, Archibald. You will soon find yourself to be a prisoner in The Hells, just as the Lord that you serve truly is. I resign to my fate, but I would have you know that I will join The Mother in paradise in The Heavens. Your moment here is only temporary. You will soon be destroyed and forgotten. However, your torment in The Hells will never end." Bishop Caitlan closed her eyes, held her head up and squared her shoulders.

Dysvakar r smirked and his eyes fell on The Duke, watching his reaction. He was amused as the Duke fell into a rage, as Bishop Caitlan failed to show any fear.

"Well, get on with it Naamah!" The Duke ordered.

"With pleasure." Naamah smiled and drew her dagger from its scabbard.

Naamah stepped behind Bishop Caitlan, pulling her head back against her body, to slowly slit her throat before quickly sheathing the dagger. Blood spilled from the wound down the front of Caitlan's gown and her breath escaped from the gaping wound. Naamah held Caitlan's head tightly, until all color drained from her face. She let Caitlan's lifeless body drop to the ground. She smiled, while licking the blood from her fingertips.

Green flames slowly spread across the corpse of Bishop Caitlan. The green glow of the flames bathed the Duke and Naamah in the nightmarish light, as it quickly engulfed the corpse. The flames consumed the body, leaving no trace, other than the iron shackles from where she lay moments before.

"You shall have your army with this most suitable sacrifice. It is quite laughable that Bishop Caitlan did not realize, that in death, her soul was stolen away from 'paradise' to be my guest in The Hells for eternity." The head of Dysvakar turned to look over the bridge and the slough.

The fog continued to melt away, uncovering the black waters under the bridge. First a few small bubbles rose to the murky surface of the stagnant slough. The bubbling water became more turbulent, appearing as a cauldron coming to a rolling boil. The Duke, Naamah, and Auntie Olga stepped onto the stone bridge, walking to its center almost fifty yards distance. With silent anticipation, they watched the waters below.

Auntie Olga pointed to the water. "Look, they rise!"

The first of the long dead barbarian invaders, rose out of the peat bog waters and marched out of the slough. A dozen others, clawed their way out of the peat and marched to the drier ground. The dead warriors' water-logged bodies were well preserved, emerging from the peat with their naturally mummified skin, tanned a leatherlike deep chestnut and their clothing and equipment mostly intact. More of the barbarian bog mummies, marched out of the slough and fell into a semicircle formation, evenly spaced around the brazier under the eyes of Dysvakar. Soon the bog mummy formation stretched outside of the light of the green flames, disappearing into the darkness. Those that were closer, glistened and reflected the green light. Within the hour their numbers grew, and the ranks filled until they numbered almost two-hundred.

The Duke crossed back over the bridge, closely followed by the hag and Naamah. He inspected the undead warriors, that stood to attention without any motion or a sound. Many held axes or broadswords in hand, with a round shield on their other arm. Many were without helms and had long manes of mud caked, matted hair and beards. Their armor consisted of animal hides, though some wore rusted mail.

Dysvakar grew impatient during the inspection. "My time is very valuable and I have given much of it to you once again. Do not fail with this task, as I want no further interruptions from you, contacting me with news of another failure and more requests of my power. Furthermore, from this night forward, you will provide a suitable sacrifice at the height of the next twelve new moons to repay your debt to me."

The Duke was unable to show any expression of emotion, lacking all flesh, but the glowing red points of light in his empty eye sockets glowed brighter with his rage. Dysvakar's insult and demands made to him, before Naamah and

Auntie Olga were unacceptable. However, he didn't dare protest. "It will be done, my Lord."

"Good! Just what I needed to hear! Oh, this is just going to work out swell. Now make that next sacrifice someone special. I will say Bishop Caitlan was quite a nice catch. Imprisoning the soul of an uncorrupted mortal that was devout to The Mother, is almost as nice as acquiring that truly vile Bennett fellow." Dysvakar smiled, ear to ear.

"My Lord, I will make it my mission, to deliver to you the souls you requested, over the next year with each new moon. There will be no failure." The Duke made a low bow.

"Until the next new moon then." Dysvakar ended the conversation abruptly, and his image in the large green flames, winked out over the brazier. The tall green flames quickly diminished and then snuffed out, leaving the dim orange light of the glowing coals.

The small army of the dead stood before the three, unmoving and at attention. The sounds of insects and chirping frogs, once again sang their songs to the night. A gentle breeze blew over the marsh, rustling the tall grasses that grew along the bank of the slough.

"Naamah, you will march your company to set an ambush. This force will be enough to deter the King's men from marching into Redrock. Striking fear into their hearts and demoralizing them as the dead slay their brothers in arms, should be enough to make them retreat. I will then petition the King with my demands of the dukedom gaining independence from the kingdom. His intrusions will be dealt with increasingly, harsh retribution."

Naamah looked over the waterlogged army of mummified barbarians. She then addressed the Duke. "King Ernald sends a small battalion of foot soldiers and knights on the High Road. We will meet them at Whistling Pass and prevent them advancing on Redrock."

"I am more concerned with those that intruded in my tower, than King Ernald's continued meddling. Patrols in the Ironwood Forest have turned up nothing in the days since they escaped. One group has not reported in, leading me to believe that they came to an unfortunate end when they found them." The Duke tapped a skeletal finger on his boney chin.

Auntie Olga chimed in, holding up the bandaged stump of her arm. "Yes, retribution! Those are the ones that should be a suitable sacrifice for your Lord on the next new moon."

"That is one thing we can agree on. However, I believe they have fled halfway around the world by now with my property." The Duke responded, with a nod of his skull.

Paul Wolff

Naamah drew her sword at the approach of a large creature spying on them in the high grasses along the river banks. She shouted out an order with a hiss. "Show yourself!"

The bridge troll stepped out of the tall grass and held out its hand. "Gimme shiny pretties."

The Duke grumbled and reached into his purse, withdrawing a single silver coin in his boney fingers. He tossed it at the troll falling short to the ground. The troll reached down with its long lanky arm and held it to his eye for inspection. A smile of sharp teeth spread across its maw.

"Shiny Pretty!" The troll jumped into the slough with a splash, disappearing under the bridge.

The Duke shook his head, shrugging his boney shoulders. "I never understood why trolls are so insistent on collecting tolls. I've never seen one shopping in the market square."

48
Out of the Dungeon

Flynn lost track of the days, fed stale scraps of food and brackish water drawn from the well in the middle of the 'interrogation chamber.' The bars were too narrow for him to squeeze through, even in giant rat form. He was given only enough sustenance to keep him alive, and weak with hunger. Fighting to keep his sanity, he distracted himself from the hunger and fatigue, reciting poems and stories from his youth. This was followed by counting aloud forwards and backwards to one-thousand and then repeated in the three other languages he was fluent in.

The other 'guests' were not fairing as well. Geoffrey was locked in his cage for weeks, and his mind, body and spirit was broken. He mumbled incoherently and often let out a loud groan. Peter was quiet in his cage, staring down to the floor the normal rats who were making forays in search of anything edible.

Flynn was approaching the end of his backwards countdown for the third time within the hour. "...Tano, nne, tatu, mbili, moja."

"Flynn, I beg you, please stop." Peter uttered his first words in days, in a soft pained voice.

Flynn was surprised to hear His Lordship's voice for the first time since he was locked in his gibbet. "Peter, I thought they had removed your tongue."

"It's hopeless. All is lost. He means to keep us in this wretched existence, to slowly waste away." Peter didn't move as he softly spoke, eyes fixed on the floor.

"You deserve no better, sending Musa after us." Flynn snapped.

"Perhaps you're right. I failed everyone, bringing unwanted attention to our home. Greed got the best of me. That fool over there is truly the most deserving of what he gets." Peter pointed at Geoffrey's cage.

Geoffrey didn't stir, but continued babbling so softly that even Flynn's sharp hearing couldn't discern anything intelligible.

Paul Wolff

"I'm not resigning myself to this, as you are so quick to do. There is more to this than punishment for our robbery gone bad. You've spent so much of your time hidden away, concerned only for yourself and The Nest. You've lost the full picture of the world outside. You have no choice now, other than to take notice." Flynn laid it out.

Peter looked over at Flynn. "What exactly are you talking about, Flynn?"

Having nothing but time, Flynn filled Peter in on the goings on, since his escape from Port Gwynn and his new companions. Emphasis was put on the biggest threat to everything and everyone in the Kingdom. was an indestructible undead wizard, pretending to be doddering old Duke Archibald Payne.

The one-sided conversation ended at the sound of the interrogation chamber door unlocking. The grim gaoler pushed the heavy wood door open with one hand, while holding an iron ring of keys in the other.

Two assistants lead in a prisoner. The tall, muscular man's head was covered by a heavy sack and his hands shackled in front of him. The man's clothing was ripped and stained with blood. Possibly, most of it was not his own. One of the assistants urged him forward with a club pushed into the small of his back, as the other assistant guided him down the steps with a hand on his arm.

On the floor the gaoler pulled the bag from the man's head. "All right, this one goes in the chair for questioning."

To Flynn the man looked vaguely familiar, though not in his current state or this setting. The two dirty assistants clad in worn leather armor, each had an arm of their prisoner, leading him over to the 'interrogation chair.'

The sound of unruly prisoners, from the open door atop the steps, drew the attention of the gaoler. He pointed to his first assistant that gripped a club in his free hand. "You, shut that rowdy lot up!"

"Aye!" The leather clad assistant trotted up the stairs and out to the hallway of crowded cells, to quiet the unruly captives.

The gaoler grinned with the few yellow teeth he still had and patted the chair that was covered in small metal spikes. "All right, good cap'n. I've reserved the best seat in the house fer ya."

The assistant was caught off guard, when the seemingly downtrodden Captain Ashdown sprang into action. He pulled his arm free and clubbed the guard in the head with his shackled fists, followed by a kick sending him into the well headfirst. The sound of the splashdown came after the screams on the way down.

The gaoler's bloodshot eyes were wide with fear, as he called his other assistant. "Ee's loose! Elp! Get down 'ere!"

302

The gaoler drew his dagger from his belt, pointing it menacingly at Ashdown. Ashdown pulled the closest burning torch from its sconce, with his shackled hands. The gaoler's eyes darted about the room, looking for an opening as Ashdown closed in on him.

Flynn and Peter watched the actions unfolding below, as hopeful voyeurs. Peter filled Flynn in. "That bloke looks like the captain of the church guard from Port Gwynn. Well, former captain now, I suppose."

Flynn looked to Peter for a moment and then to the scuffle below. Captain Ashdown and the gaoler were circling the floor. The gaoler made a dash for the door, but Ashdown quickly blocked his path, swinging the torch at the gaoler's face. The shouts and splashing from the well, added to the cacophony of chaos.

Ashdown's torch connected with the gaoler's hooded head, sending sparks flying. As the gaoler stumbled backwards, Ashdown swung the torch again, striking the hand holding the dagger. Losing the grip on his blade, it dropped onto the stone floor.

The gaoler looked first at Ashdown, then dove for his lost dagger. The gaoler reached for the dagger, but Ashdown was already atop him, wrapping the chains of his manacles around his throat. A short struggle ensued, but Ashdown's knee planted firmly in the gaoler's back, provided the leverage needed to break his neck.

A determined Ashdown removed the iron ring of keys from the gaoler's belt. He quickly ran through the keys to find the one to free his wrists of its restraints. One hand was free and he was frantically trying to unlock the other.

The other assistant returned, stopping on the landing to access the scene below. Ashdown was still busy with the lock on the second cuff.

Flynn's voice shouted from the darkness. "Hey! The guard is back!"

The manacle fell off Ashdown's wrist, and he quickly armed himself with the gaoler's dagger. Ashdown stood tall and defiant, at the ready to do what was necessary to defend himself.

The guard retreated out of the chamber, raising a cry of alarm.

"Hey you! A little help here! Before he brings the entire castle guard down here!" Flynn shouted from his cage.

Ashdown looked up into the darkness at the cages. He followed the chains that lead from them to the wenches. "Who's there?"

"My name's Flynn. I can help if you, just unlock this damned cage!" Flynn felt his chances were improving.

Ashdown studied the wenches that controlled the gibbet cages and lowered the one Flynn occupied. Ashdown found the right key and with the clicks of the tumblers, Flynn felt hope. The cage door opened with a creak and Flynn stumbled out.

Paul Wolff

"Flynn, my boy! Don't leave me here!" Peter called out from darkness.

Flynn took the keys and lowered the other two cages occupied by Peter and Geoffrey Quickly Flynn went to work freeing Peter and Geoffrey from their confinement.

Ashdown was already making his way up to the door and Flynn grabbed a device from the torture rack that would work as a weapon. The long club covered with short nails, was intended for dragging across the bare flesh of a person during interrogations.

Ashdown crossed the threshold, into the dimly lit hall that ran past rows of cells, overcrowded with prisoners begging to be freed. Flynn looked down the torchlit hall, expecting reinforcements, but they were in the clear.

"Best we create as much chaos as possible and let everyone out." Flynn suggested.

Ashdown looked at the men in the cells. Many appeared to be the criminal sort, more than eager to be freed and wreck mayhem upon anyone between themselves and freedom. Peter made his way into the hall, startling Ashdown in his fat wererat form, wielding the club the man in the well dropped before his plunge.

"The Hells! He's a rat man!" Ashdown backed away, with his dagger pointed at Peter to keep his distance.

"Don't worry about him. He's mostly okay. Peter, open the cells!" Flynn tossed Peter the ring of keys, then transformed into his humanoid rat form, and looked over Ashdown with glowing red eyes.

Peter unlocked the first cell and the occupants backed away from the lycanthrope acting as their rescuer. Soon they pushed their way out of the cell, crowding into the hallway. Peter moved to the next cell, repeating the procedure.

Ashdown looked at the men crowding the dungeon halls. Few appeared to be hardened criminals, deserving their fate to be locked away forever. Most were regular folks, subjugated under Duke Payne's authoritarian rule of recent times for whatever petty offense brought them under his scrutiny.

Ashdown shouted out over the crowd. "The Mother will give us Her guidance and strength to escape to freedom. We must stand strong together. When we reach the hall, arm yourself with whatever you can improvise as a weapon. We won't be well armed, but we outnumber the castle guard. May The Mother protect us."

Ashdown's words reminded Flynn of someone else he knew quite well.

The naked Lord Mayor Geoffrey Walters staggered into the hall, using the wall for support. He continued babbling incoherently to himself, and went unnoticed.

At the top of the stairs, several men had picked up spare clubs from the guard room and others were lined up at the lowered portcullis. Attempts to lift it were unsuccessful, as the escaping guard locked it down.

Flynn pushed through the throngs of men to reach the gate, with Ashdown close behind.

A muscular man with a shaved head and arms covered in crude tattoos, looked to the two as they got to the landing. "We can't raise it."

Flynn looked at the bars of the portcullis. The narrow bars looked wide enough for him to squeeze through, if he were to undergo one more transformation. Flynn tossed the spiked club through the bars and then underwent the transformation to a giant rat form. The men gave him a wide berth, with looks of wonder in their eyes. In moments Flynn squeezed through the bars and into the lower hall of Castle Redrock. Sitting up on his hind legs, he listened and sniffed the air. He could hear the reinforcements heading for the dungeons.

Ashdown pushed his way to the gate, as Flynn returned to hybrid rat man form. "Can you raise the portcullis?"

Flynn nodded his head and pulled the bar locking the mechanism and cranked the wheel to raise the barred gate.

Men piled out of the dungeon into hall, as soon as there was enough clearance for them to pass. A seemingly endless stream of men poured out of the dungeons into the lower castle hall. The men in the front with Ashdown were armed with clubs and stretched across the breadth of the hall.

The mob lead stopped their forward movement, when the line of a dozen castle guards clad in mail and open bascinet helms blocked the path. The guard's formation had long spears pointed at the approaching mob and their black and red heater shields formed a shield wall.

The sergeant in plate armor, who stood behind his men gave a command to the mob. "Stand down! Drop all weapons and turn back! No quarter will be spared to those who take up arms against The Duke or his soldiers."

Ashdown pointed his dagger toward the line of soldiers, behind their wall of shields. "The Duke has betrayed The Mother and all the people of his dukedom. Yourselves included! I was wrong to surrender my command when he sent troops to occupy Port Gwynn and desecrate The Mother's house. Don't blindly follow The Duke, only to perform evil acts on his behalf!"

"Forward!" The sergeant barked his order to the line of spearmen.

Spears lowered, the soldiers marched forward. The front line of prisoners had no way to retreat from the approaching spearmen. In unison guards thrust their spears forward, plunging the sharp heads into the bellies of a dozen men.

The first men in line fell to the ground, as Ashdown made a defensive move to prevent himself from being impaled on the end of a spear as well.

The spearmen continued forward, stepping on and over the men on the ground as the sergeant put his sword to the wounded. The next in line fell, as the guard continued to push forward. Ashdown was pinned between a soldiers shield and the next line of prisoners.

Flynn made his way to the front of the mob, sprinting across the tops of their heads and shoulders. He dove over the castle guards, landing on his feet behind them.

The sergeant swung his longsword, but the rat man rolled away. The steel struck the stone floor with flash of sparks. Flynn's glowing eyes locked with the sergeant's, as he held the spiked club in both of his clawed hands ready to strike.

Flynn sidestepped the thrust of the longsword, but the sergeant countered with a swing, slashing the rat man's chest. The sergeant's weapon was not silvered, and Flynn's wound closed.

Ashdown pulled a spearman's shield down enough for an opening. The guard fought to protect his vulnerable neck, but Ashdown thrust the dagger under his chin, felling the man. Ashdown pushed through the opening and the line of guards quickly fell to the overwhelming numbers of men.

The sergeant retreated, raising a cry for help, as he was pursued through the dark lower halls of the castle. As the freed men spread out, smashing through storage room doors they gathered stockpiled weapons, preserved foodstuffs, and raided the wine cellar. The sergeant continued to evade his pursuers and alert the rest of the castle of the prison break.

Flynn and Peter left behind the mob and were followed closely by Ashdown, who scavenged a heater shield and longsword. The freed prisoners were now wreaking havoc on the main floor of the castle. Off duty guards were called from the barracks and suiting up to join their comrades.

"Flynn, let's make our escape through the sewers while the guard is occupied. We just need to find the privies." Peter paused in the hall and his pointed rat nose sniffed the air for the scent.

"The last time I did that, I could smell the foulness on me for a month." Flynn shuddered the thought.

Ashdown caught up to the two rat men, as the mob behind them destroyed furniture and the Duke's banners that adorned the great hall, while others fought incoming guards ill-prepared for an attack within the castle walls.

"Look!" Ashdown pointed his sword to the far end of the great hall.

Eight guards in full plate armor, armed with halberds, marched down the steps toward the three. Behind them, standing in front of the throne, was the

Duke dressed in layers of fine clothing, appearing as he did in life, with his thin stingy white hair hanging to the tip of his shoulders under a green velvet muffin hat.

"Those three! Kill them first!" The Duke pointed at Flynn and his companions as the bodyguards hastily descended the steps.

Flynn gripped the spiked club tight in both hands and charged. Peter transformed himself into a giant rat and scurried into the shadows, leaving his weapon on the ground. Ashdown got into a fighting stance and said a quick prayer to The Mother.

Flynn dodged the bodyguard's halberd blades, leaping step-to-step between his foes, focused on the prize at the top. It was a suicide mission, knowing his attacks were ineffective on the Duke. However, it may be possible to disrupt his spellcasting to buy some time, going toe to toe with him. To what end it didn't seem to matter.

The Duke appeared genuinely frightened, as Flynn made it past his guards unscathed. "Fools! You let him through!"

He backed away from Flynn and gestured with his hands in preparation for a spell. His lips parted to utter the words to finish the incantation, but Flynn was quicker, leaping from the final steps at the Duke. He was narrowly missed, as the blades of the bodyguards' halberds cleaved for him.

The spike club connected on its target with a midair overhead swing, smashing the Duke's head like a melon. Flynn rolled away, as the bodyguards rushed to the aid of the fallen Duke. Flynn dashed for cover behind the large wooden throne, but the pursuit came to an end.

"What witchery is this?" A cry from one of the Duke's bodyguards could be heard over the chaos in the great hall.

Flynn pressed up against the back of the throne, as silence fell across the great hall. He reverted to his naked form, and tore a section of a low hanging banner to cover his nakedness, and stepped out.

All stood with weapons lowered in silence, crowded around the fallen Duke. Flynn pushed his way through fellow prisoners and former combatants alike, to see what had changed the course of the conflict.

Sprawled on the ground in a pool of blood and gray matter, lay Mama Matilda in her ragged dress. The hag had reverted to her true form, following Flynn's killing blow. The hag's fingers twitched, then slowly closed with her eyes in a death stare.

"Where is Duke Payne? Why was this witch woman masquerading in his stead?" The leader of the Duke's bodyguard raised his visor, addressing the others under his command.

Ashdown looked at the dead hag for a long moment, also taken aback. "Duke Payne is in league with one that seeks to destroy the good works of The Mother. I suspect there are others, aside from this creature aiding him."

Flynn spoke up. "I have seen the others. I was with friends fighting him in his tower. We were pulled into it through a magic mirror by another of these hags. That one was killed as this one, but another escaped."

The lead bodyguard threw his helm to the ground. "Other evil roams these castle halls. I suspect Osbert has been put to the sword, as was General Jaheem. Payne is now attended by his new advisor, Naamah. I believe her to be a fiend from the pits of The Hells."

Flynn nodded in agreement. "Yes, I saw her when I was locked in the dungeons. I watched as she killed this Osbert you spoke of."

Ashdown kneeled over the corpse of the hag. "If she is acting as The Duke, where is he?"

"That I don't know. Duke Payne has been even more mysterious in recent times. He disappears for long periods into his tower, and it is whispered throughout these halls, that he traded his soul for an eternal 'unlife.'" The lead bodyguard responded.

Ashdown shook his head. "I was arrested and brought here, as were others of The Mother's church guard and members of the clergy, as this cult has been spreading through the dukedom under his order."

The lead bodyguard looked over to Flynn. "There are bounties on the heads of your comrades that escaped. Patrols have been searching the Ironwoods for them ever since."

"They survived?" Flynn's spirits lifted.

"They did. The Duke was very adamant in his orders, that all should be killed with no quarter given. Especially the young wizard, who was the most dangerous." The bodyguard stated.

"Randall." Flynn whispered his friend's name.

"However, the young woman in their company, is to be taken alive and brought back to him." The bodyguard added.

"Juliana?" Flynn's voice was filled with concern.

"Juliana?" Ashdown said her name, looking to Flynn with surprise. "You travel with her? She escaped from the convent and disappeared without a trace. I would never imagine her consorting with the likes of you."

Flynn on any other day, would have carved out Ashdown's liver with his dagger for his words. However, he recalled the words Juliana often repeated: 'This is happening for a reason...'

The calm that had taken the great hall broke, as twenty castle guards rushed into the hall, forming a line with spears lowered and shields linked. From the top of the steps looking down on the crowd of liberated prisoners and fresh soldiers, the lead of the Duke's bodyguard drew a deep breath and raised his hand.

"Stand down, men! There is much to discuss this night, while it appears Duke Payne is away." The lead bodyguard began his address to the uneasy crowd.

49
Cabin Fever

Izzy passed half of the dark loaf of bread to Mosi. They were enjoying the warm stew in a more comfortable setting in the abandoned ramshackle cabin, than their former camp. The boy was feeling comfortable with his new companions, days following their escape. Food won from the Duke's men, made this boring game of 'laying low' slightly more bearable.

The simple cabin was a one room affair with a stone fireplace, rustic table with two wooden stools, and a single bed with a dingy, straw filled mattress. A small iron cauldron of pottage stew, warmed in the fireplace. Sunlight filtered in through a gaping hole in the roof over the table where the three were gathered.

Randall sat on one of the stools, studying the book he had stolen from the Duke's laboratory. He inspected the different reagents spread across the table in neat rows. Izzy and Mosi shared a stool on the opposite side, watching Randall as they ate.

Izzy spoke with her mouth full of bread. "Mr. Randall, you've been looking at that big book and all those things-"

"Reagents! Components needed for the 'recipe' to make magic work." Randall corrected her, as he tapped his finger on a glass vial filled with yellow brimstone. Another jar contained balls of bat guano, a wooden box held desiccated insects, and a cloth wrapped up lead shavings.

Izzy wrinkled her nose at the items laid across the table. "Re-a-gents?"

"That's correct. We've gone over this many times before. These are special materials that are part of the 'recipe,' for the rituals needed for magic. Just as much as the words that I speak and the motion of my hands. All combined, they harness energies needed to cast the spells, turning the odds in our favor, of the many challenges we face." Randall responded in a haughty tone.

Randall smacked Izzy's hand away, as she reached for the jar of guano balls. Izzy wrinkled her brow and frowned before sliding down from the stool. She stomped out of the cabin, slamming the door that barely hung on one rusty hinge. A heavy layer of dust fell from the rafters overhead, covering Randall's head and shoulders. Mosi hunched over to protect his bowl of stew.

Randall growled and Mosi snickered.

Izzy stepped out onto the forest floor from the rotten floorboards of the front stoop. The ground was thick with undergrowth and the cabin was camouflaged under a tangle of briar and ivy. There was no discernable path leading from it, and after Izzy walked only twenty yards the cabin all but disappeared. Only the thin stream of white smoke, rising from the crumbling chimney into the canopy of trees, gave a clue to its existence.

Izzy sneaked through the underbrush, ending her movement upon hearing the whispered conversation of Juliana and Madok. Crawling closer, careful not to rustle dead leaves or snap a dry twig, she found the pair sitting together on a wool blanket laid across the ground. The two were sharing what they believed was a private moment, holding hands and leaning against each other shoulder to shoulder.

Izzy's nose scrunched up and she grimaced. Not wanting to disturb the two, she began to back away, but standing over her was Sauda.

Sauda stood over Izzy with her hands on her hips, looking down on her. She then turned her attention to the pair, who hadn't noticed the voyeurs. Sauda smiled and nodded her head approvingly.

"Everyone, Colin, and I have returned from the reconnaissance at Redrock. Come!" Sauda left for the cabin. Colin stood nearby, watching with his face hidden under his hood.

Madok and Juliana jumped to their feet, both slightly embarrassed. Izzy stood up, shrugged her shoulders, then skipped after Sauda. Juliana and Madok looked into each other's eyes other for a moment, then followed the others into the cabin.

Colin pulled back his hood, freeing the greasy black hair that framed his gaunt face. He eyed the group before clearing his throat to speak.

"There was an uprising in the dungeon below Redrock Castle and many prisoners escaped to the city streets, before the full force of the castle guard quashed it." Colin looked to each person as he spoke.

Juliana sat with Mosi on her knee and Izzy by her side. "Where are the others and what of The Duke?"

Colin's eyes met with Juliana's. "They remained behind when they heard that a pair of wererats aided in the uprising. It was also said The Duke has been absent during all this and an imposter covered for him."

Izzy squeaked joyfully. "Flynn?"

Colin shook his head in acknowledgement. "Peter too. They are among the few that escaped, according to a few others."

Randall was packing his books and magic components back into the enchanted haversack. "I assume they are hiding out now?"

"Well, not hiding out, rather they are trapped. There was much ensuing chaos and many of the castle guard deserted, as word spread of the imposter. A witch woman, that transformed herself into his likeness through magic. Those that remain, are blindly loyal or serve out of fear." Colin said looking over to Randall. "Peter and Flynn joined some of the deserters, that took over a guard house in the city. They're barricaded in and are surrounded by many of the remaining loyalist castle guards."

"What's keeping them from taking the guardhouse?" Madok asked.

"Hostages. The Duke's stooge mayor of Redrock, Frederic, happened to be there, when that guardhouse was overrun with others serving on the Duke's council. Apparently, they interrupted a meeting with captain of the guard." Colin rubbed his stubbly chin as he spoke.

Madok shook his head. "I don't understand any of this. Where is Payne? Away on holiday while this is happening?"

Juliana set Mosi down and rose. "We need to return to Redrock immediately. Flynn helped make it possible for us to escape, and The Mother watched over him during his confinement. It is my belief that she has united us, and charged us with the removal of Duke Payne."

Randall closed the haversack, after stowing a jar filled with animal eyeballs. "You may recall, that our visit with the Duke ended with him running our arses out of his castle. He was unaffected by everything Madok hit him with. I'm guessing he is currently putting together something especially nasty, as the patrols hunting us have not been all that competent."

Izzy drew the curved dagger. Light glinted off the blade from the hole in the roof "He didn't like it too much when I stuck him with this!"

Randall smirked. "Yes, he is protected from weapons that are not imbued with magic. That is something that I do not possess the knowledge or skill to create. Well, just yet."

Juliana took a deep breath. "The Blessed Sword of Saint Vittoria. Her sword was interred with her many years ago, after her martyrdom. Her crypt lies beneath Redrock Cathedral. She wielded it, defending against an onslaught of northern invaders centuries ago. She saved lives of many innocents, before her capture and murder, at the hands of the northern invaders. The sword was a divine gift and gave her favor in battle."

Madok's interest was piqued. "How was it she came to be captured then?"

Juliana looked away from Madok's eyes. "She was distracted by earthly lust and betrayed by a lover, that served the enemy. If recovered, this sword would provide more means to help us fight the Duke."

Sauda eyed Madok and Juliana. "That cathedral you mention is now in ruins. If there was a weapon you mention, it would most likely have been stolen when it was looted and burned."

"No. A weapon blessed by The Mother, would not allow itself to be handled by one that did not serve her." Juliana stated this as fact.

Colin and Sauda threw curious glances at each other. Izzy grimaced. Madok was unsure of what exactly 'would not allow itself to be handled' meant.

Randall threw the strap of the haversack over his shoulder and looked over everyone. "I'm with Juliana on this. The Duke is not going to give up on hunting us down, until we are all dead no matter where we hide. It won't be long before he sends something other than a patrol of soldiers after us. That annoying little imp bastard, those hideous hags, 'living' suits of armor and gargoyles are just the taste of things to come. He is vulnerable to magic, so the more things we can throw at him the better."

Madok nodded in agreement. "He has a personal vendetta against Randall and myself; I don't see him letting go. Gathering more allies in this fight is crucial. Payne was never well loved and always a weak ruler. Those serving under him do it out of loyalty to the kingdom, or Payne's coin purse, not just to him. Since his rule has taken a drastic turn to oppressive in recent times, the uprising in Redrock will only grow and spread across his dukedom. We should return now, and save Flynn."

Juliana's eyes lingered on Madok for a long moment. Randall looked back and forth at each of them, noting Madok's eyes meeting Juliana's during the long pause. Longer than it should have gone on for Randall.

Sauda broke the awkward moment, slinging her pack over her shoulder. "It's half a day's travel from here back to Redrock. By the time we get there, a day will have passed since their escape. If Duke Payne hasn't returned to take charge, either the troops surrounding the guardhouse will have retaken it, or Red may make an ill planned suicide mission to save Peter. We were holed up in an abandoned building across from the guard house, watching as things developed. She was growing impatient and especially angry, when left to get you. You have talents that could make a successful rescue possible."

"Do you have a plan to get us into Redrock, before we are spotted by everything that has been out searching for us?" Randall asked.

Colin nodded his head. "Yes, the way we did; a secret way in through the city sewers, bypassing city gates much like Port Gwynn. We go in that way to take them by surprise, rather than announcing our arrival at the gates."

Madok and Randall shuddered from thoughts of their recent experiences in city sewers. Izzy perked up and smiled. Juliana just nodded her head.

"The boy can't come with us. It was a mistake for you to bring him with you." Sauda looked over at Mosi, whose expression changed from calm to fear.

Izzy stomped her foot and waved a small finger at Sauda. "Mosi is my friend, and I've promised to get him home to his mama and baba! One of those hags stole him away from his family, and Madok already cut off pieces of the other! I bet Flynn killed another one! It will be safer now for all the kids, not worrying about being stolen from home."

Randall looked at the little boy with unruly, kinky hair and smirked. "Does he even know how to find his home, or even what his parent's names are?"

"My baba is a soldier! He was away when the hag took me. If he was there, he would have killed her!" Mosi spoke out for the first time, catching everyone by surprise.

Madok smiled at Mosi. "Well, that's helpful. Do you know where your father was posted?"

"Redrock." Mosi replied.

"A member of the city guard?" Madok asked, with a raised eyebrow.

"No sir, at the castle." Mosi quickly answered.

Madok scratched his chin and looking Mosi in the eye. "So, he was a castle guard in the garrison?"

Mosi shook his head. "No sir."

Madok became more curious with each answer Mosi gave him. "He wasn't a castle guard? What was it he did in the castle then?"

Mosi crossed his arms and frowned at Madok. "He was the general."

"General Jaheem? Commander of Duke Payne's armies?" Madok put both hands on the table, leaning in toward Mosi. The others looked at each other, shocked.

Randall leaned over to Madok whispering. "I imagine the general he has fallen out of favor with the Duke, considering how and where we found Mosi."

Juliana threw Randall a look. He immediately knew it would not be best to speculate about Mosi's father's fate in front of the boy.

Sauda began to lose her patience, feeling precious time was being wasted. "Enough of this. We need to travel back."

Juliana nodded her head. "Agreed. We've wasted too much time hiding, while Flynn survived and was imprisoned. Before we go, we must say a prayer of thanks to The Mother, for watching over Flynn and to help us reunite with him to finish our mission."

Colin and Sauda rolled their eyes, as the others closed their eyes, bowed their heads, and held onto each other's hands. Juliana led the prayer, as Colin leaned against the wall and Sauda pulled her pack over her shoulders.

Paul Wolff

A dusty piece of rotted shingle, fell from the hole in the roof, on top of Izzy's head while Juliana prayed. Opening one eye, Izzy looked at the ceiling while no one else took notice. Perched overhead, peering sideways through the hole, was a single raven. Izzy made eye contact with the jet-black bird, which seemed to be listening in.

Izzy pointed at the raven. "Hey!"

The bird croaked before flying away.

Without saying a word, Colin kicked the door down and dashed out with his longbow and quiver.

Randall startled by the sound, ducked under the table with Mosi. Madok, Juliana, and Sauda drew their weapons, looking to where there was once a door.

Izzy scrambled out of the cabin, waving to the others to follow. "Come on! Colin is tracking a bird spy!"

Izzy trampled off into the underbrush tracking Colin. She followed the sound of his footsteps on the dead leaves, plodding deeper into the woods, when the sound stopped. She heard the others in the distance. The sounds of their voices were fanned out, calling for her to return.

Izzy slowed her pace, but continued to press forward, hoping to catch up with Colin and the elusive raven. Izzy held her breath and peered around the trunk of a giant gnarled ironwood tree, when she spotted Colin.

Colin crouched down behind a great fallen tree with his gray cloak drawn about him and hood pulled over his head. The raven roosted on the lowest bough of an ironwood tree. The ink black bird was facing away, paying no mind to the figure in gray. Colin nocked an arrow and drew back the long bow to take aim. The bow creaked, as the thick sinew string drew tight and Colin focused on a point between the raven's folded wings.

Izzy fixed her eyes on the raven.

Colin suddenly spun his entire body to his right, loosing the arrow at a new target. The gangly troll leapt from its hiding place in the underbrush, camouflaged by its green warty hide. The arrow lodged deep into the troll's shoulder, but it considered it a minor nuisance like a mosquito bite. Colin dropped his bow reaching for the sword on his belt, but was tackled from behind by another one of the giant humanoids.

Izzy held in her scream, as the two trolls quickly pulled Colin's body apart in their giant clawed hands. Colin fell silent, as his head was smashed flat under the fist of one of the attackers.

Covered in warm blood, the largest of the two trolls rose, as the other devoured their fresh kill. It sniffed the air with its long bulbous nose, and its pointy ears twitched as it listened. It spotted Izzy as she tried to slip away.

"Lookee! There's one of their pups. I hear the rest on their way too!" A string of drool hung from the troll's toothy maw, as it pointed at Izzy.

314

"I'll swallow that one whole!" The other troll arose and launched itself at Izzy.

Izzy squeaked as she transformed into her hybrid rat form, and dove between the lumbering troll's legs as it reached for her. She rolled away, just as the troll tried to stomp her flat.

Izzy made a running leap to an ironwood tree, quickly scurrying up its thick trunk.

"You come down from there!" The larger troll stretched out its long arm, grabbing for Izzy's leg. She scampered just out of its reach, climbing into the higher branches.

"Move out of the way! I'll get it!" The smaller troll pushed the other troll aside and dug its claws into the huge tree to pull itself up.

The larger troll grabbed his comrade's leg, pulling him from the tree and slamming his body to the ground. "My turn! You get the others I get her!"

"I'll bite off your dangly bits for that!" It yelled, as it rolled over from its back and got up on all fours.

The larger troll got in a stance to face off with his companion. "Just you try that! I'll rip your nose off and shove it up your smelly arse!"

The smaller troll let out a deep guttural growl, then lunged at the other. The two tumbled to the forest floor, smashing headfirst into a rotting log, sending pieces of wood and bark flying. The larger troll threw the other off, then sat up with its head swarming with ants and wood splinters. Shaking its large head furiously, he did not see the next attack coming. The smaller troll latched its teeth into the other's groin, and bit off his dangly bits.

The larger troll shrieked as the other pulled its head up, face dripping in blood. The smaller troll held his partner's severed organ in its hand waving it around. "Mine now!"

A ball of fire exploded, centered on the two trolls. Flames and intense heat spread outwards twenty feet in all directions from the blast. The trolls' skin burned and blistered. Their fingers and toes fused together, as they melted and the hair on their heads singed away. The two laid out on the smoldering forest floor, struggling to stand, as they shouted curses from the searing pain.

A second ball of fire exploded on the two trolls, finishing them off. The underbrush in the blast radius was blackened and smoking. Their charred bodies were reduced to blackened flesh stretched over bone.

Randall stepped into the blast radius, rather pleased with himself. He stamped out a small burning twig beneath his boot, as the smell of smoke and burned troll flesh filled the air.

Izzy climbed down from the tree as the other's arrived. Madok scanned the area for more trolls lurking about. Sauda stooped over the remains of Colin. Juliana remained farther back, holding Mosi's hand as she approached.

Izzy returned to human form and stood next to Randall, imitating him crossing her arms inspecting the scene. "Did you do cast those spells using those new 're-a-gents?'"

"Yes indeed." Randall nodded his head.

Izzy kicked the blackened leg of a troll, which crumbled into a pile of gray ash. "That spy bird got away."

Madok spoke with concern in his voice. "Randall called this one. He's going to send more creatures, to hunt us and ravens to spy for him. However, I don't understand how these loathsome trolls could be convinced to do his bidding."

Izzy crouched down, prodding the carbonized trolls with a stick. "Oh, look at this!"

Juliana stepped closer her curiosity piqued. "What do you have Izzy?"

Izzy presented her find to the group, brushing away the ash. "This one had a shiny silver coin!"

50
Return to Redrock

Auntie Olga hitched the small team of horses back to the carriage and loaded the brazier. The red morning sun rose over the marshlands, as Naamah marched her undead army off to Whistling Pass. Payne stood aside the carriage, watching the bog mummies until they disappeared into the mountain pass. The flickering of the red points of light in his empty eye sockets burned intensely, and the Duke felt confident his nephew would give up these lands for him to rule autonomously.

Paying the bridge troll the silver coins the previous evening had attracted all the creature's brethren to the Duke, with their grubby hands extended for an easy payday. Payne paid a dozen of the creatures to search for Randall and his cohorts, assisted by his raven spies. Perhaps the loathsome trolls would be successful in inflicting casualties on them and demoralize the troublemakers. Trolls were just not very good at following direction, were quite dim and would most likely fail their mission. This was good enough, as it would send the message that Randall and company would never be safe, and the ravens could return with word of their location.

"Archie! Shall we depart now?" Auntie Olga stood at the carriage holding the door.

The Duke looked away from the mountain pass and now fixed his gaze on the hag. "Do you really expect me to ride back to Redrock with you engaging me with your inane chatter? I've been gone far too long, and entrusted your sister to run things. I should have put Osbert's head in charge instead. Keep to the High Road and take extra care that my carriage and horses are returned safely."

The hag slammed the carriage door angrily, and climbed onto the driver's seat cursing under her breath.

The Duke stood on an overgrown path next to the carriage, seemingly losing himself in thought. He concentrated and began to visualize his laboratory, on the top floor of his tower at Castle Redrock. He spoke the magic words of the incantation aloud, with his skeletal arms outstretched. "Lanuae ad turrim officinarum!"

An intense bright white light flashed from where the Duke stood. Auntie Olga cursed and covered her eyes too late. The Duke was gone from where he once stood, and the smell of ozone hung in the air. On the ground, blue electrical sparks fizzled out into small puffs of white smoke, from where his feet were once planted.

"That sorry son of a bitch." Auntie Olga rubbed her eyes for several minutes, before taking up the reigns and journeying back to Redrock.

＊＊＊

There was another bright flash of white light and instantaneously Duke Payne stood, with arms outstretched in his laboratory. Everything was as he left it, before they departed to the marshlands. Repairs to the tower roof were completed and his laboratory was once again in order after the intrusion. It appeared Mama Matilda hadn't snooped around during his absence. Payne was happy, imagining she was too occupied, acting on his behalf to get into trouble in his laboratory.

The Duke paced the room for a moment, before deciding he should recall Mama Matilda and get a briefing of the goings on during his short absence. Undoubtedly, it's been business as usual.

Payne lifted his hands to the air, then brought them down to cover his skeletal face as he spoke the incantation. "Mutare forma iunior!"

His boney hands underwent the illusion appearing as they were covered with flesh. When he parted his hands, he once again appeared as he did in life as the aged Duke Payne.

Duke Payne called out to the hag throughout the tower, hoping she would be nearby. Failing to get a response that way, he attempted to reach her concentrating telepathically. He touched his fingers to his forehead for a short time and again nothing.

"Bah! The old witch is wandering too far from my reach. I'll just see how she's been handling things for myself." Payne descended from the upper levels of his tower, to his private office on its ground floor, through the warded door.

The office had been turned over by the escaped prisoners from the dungeon break. The desk smashed, papers strewn about, and the door battered down. The wards he had cast on the other door to enter the tower had held. Three bodies lay where they were struck down by a lightening trap, days prior.

"What in the Hells?" Payne shouted out in a fury, slamming the door behind him. The light outline of the magical glyph, that was cast on the door, was still in place with a dim glow. It would be ready to be set off again, by any future intruders into the tower.

Payne stepped into the halls of Castle Redrock, with growing concern over what insanity had transpired in a short time. Throughout the halls of the castle, were the signs of the uprising that transpired. His collections of oil paintings slashed, statues smashed, antique furniture broken, and tapestries burned. Bodies of guards and prisoners alike lay where they fell. The smell of death filled the air.

He continued to the "grand" hall, where he once held court, addressed petitioners, passed judgement, and sentenced criminals. It had not withstood devastation, and bloated bodies of the dead lay all around. His eyes were drawn to the dais, where his throne sat with the chair Osbert used to occupy.

He walked up the stone steps to where the body of Mama Matilda lay with her head crushed. His throne which was occupied by the only living person in the hall.

Geoffrey sat on the throne, wrapped in a regal purple robe, raided from his wardrobe with a fine mink cap atop his head. These were the only articles of clothing he had on. In one hand he held a goblet of wine, and in the other hand a roasted lamb shank he was eating off the bone.

Duke Payne paused for a long moment, taking in the former Lord Mayor of Port Gwynn. The Duke sighed and took the seat that was formerly Osbert's and continued watching, resting his chin on his fist. Geoffrey had a wild look in his eyes and turned away from the Duke to hide his food.

"Lord Mayor, would you be so kind as to tell me what happened here?" Payne asked, patiently awaiting Geoffrey's answer.

Geoffrey swallowed a mouthful of lamb and gulped down the red wine, with most running down his long beard. "Your Grace, it was quite the fight! I was freed from that cage you put me in, by the rat man you brought me here with. Not my kind of folks, but it was kind of him to let me out. Come to think of it, they let everyone out and then we all marched through the castle. It seems that things took a strange turn when she came out disguised as you with your bodyguards. After she was killed, everyone abandoned this place."

"Anything else?" Payne contemplated the horrible manner of Geoffrey's death he would bestow, as he asked the question.

Geoffrey wiped is mouth on his sleeve, leaving a streak of meat juice. "Yes, there's a captain that drove the traitors out of the castle into the city, where there's a standoff." Geoffrey burped and gulped more wine.

Duke Payne walked down the steps, leaving Geoffrey sitting on his throne.

"Your Grace, will there be anything else?" Geoffrey said with slurred words and dropped the goblet on the floor.

Payne continued walking out of the hall without turning. "No, you just make yourself comfortable until I return."

Payne found a few of his castle guards remained, as he crossed outside to the bailey. All the men looked upon him in shock, then quickly stood to attention. A sergeant, showing signs of fatigue stepped forward.

"Your Grace! You are here with us!" The sergeant's mood seemed to improve.

The doors of the barbican were closed and barred and, on the battlements, the few guards on duty turned to look at The Duke, as he inspected their defenses.

"Yes, I'm here. There was an imposter that took advantage of my brief absence from court and the resulting chaos needs to be quelled quickly." Payne looked into the eyes of the young sergeant.

"I am under orders to hold the castle, until the captain returns. We are all that remains of the garrison." The sergeant said, as he pointed out the few men remaining on the ground and walls numbering only ten.

"I see. Where is your captain?" Payne asked, angrily.

"He has the larger remaining force of men surrounding the Central Guardhouse in Market Square. Some of the guards, that joined in with the revolt from the dungeons, are barricaded in there with hostages. The mayor of the city of Redrock included!" The sergeant relayed the information to Payne.

"Well, what is stopping them from storming that guardhouse and putting a quick end to this?" Payne responded, angrily.

"Well, the hostages sir, and its heavily fortified." The sergeant was unsure about Duke Payne's apathy for the wellbeing of the mayor.

Duke Payne shook his head. "Well, I have to see to this myself then."

The sergeant looked at his men, confused by the Duke's words. Duke Payne pulled back his robe and spoke the incantation. "Sursum et auferet!"

The Duke floated inches above the ground of the bailey. The onlooking men gawked in amazement, as he shot into the air above the castle walls, then flew over the sprawling city. Rumors of Payne delving into magic, and dealing with devils and his hag companions were the gossip of many of the guards and citizens around Redrock, but only a few witnessed it.

Soon the Duke was hovering high above the stone guardhouse, overlooking Market Square. What was normally bustling with the activity of merchants selling their wares, was now a military encampment. Trade and commerce, in this hub of the city of Redrock, was brought to a standstill as Central Guard Tower was surrounded by heavily armed troops.

The fortifications were not impossible to breach, but the important hostages within, caused the captain to take the utmost caution. Negotiations for safe passage from the city, after which hostages would be released, were thrown about. Neither side was trusting enough to come to any agreements.

✳✳✳

Flynn found himself as trapped as the others. Silver tipped quarrels were carried by the archers for their crossbows. The lycanthropes barricaded in the tower, would not escape so easily. Peter discovered this when one such bolt was fired through a window; he had peeked out the day before. There were stores of food and drink in the guardhouse, but not enough to sustain everyone inside, hostages and hostage takers alike.

Ashdown took charge and had all the doors barred and windows shuttered. Talks between Ashdown and the captain, were communicated by shouting from the rooftop to the ground.

Red and her two wererat archer companions, kept watch in shifts from the windows of the abandoned warehouse. The structure was damaged by fire months before, but survived destruction. The owners, however did not. Their burned bodies were found bound together in chains, next to one another inside, when the fire brigade came to the scene. Victims of the crime underworld existed even in the Duke's capitol city. The current occupants took advantage of the reputation of it being haunted, making it their base of operations.

Skulking through the city via the sewers, Red was determined to find a way to rescue her father, Peter, rather than wait on Sauda to return. The guard tower's privy emptied into the city sewer; however, the way was too narrow to squeeze through in rat form. There was a race going on to widen the drain, before the inevitable storming of the tower. The work was unforgiving in the dark, stench, and filth.

Upon discovering Red was tunneling through, during a chance visit to the basement privy, Peter forbade any use of them thereafter, by the others holed up in the guard house. He told the others, giant poisonous centipedes were crawling out of the privies, and he didn't want to chance any coming into where they were holed up. He planned to slip out before the guard house was breached.

Unfortunately, everyone shared the same chamber pot, that was almost full and fouling the air in the guard tower.

Red continued carving away, enlarging the tube leading into the privy. The ancient masonry surrounding, it was easy enough to pry away, to dig into the underlying earth. Trowels and picks, lifted from the site of a nearby excavation, made the job easier. Working nonstop through the night, they were going to break through in minutes.

Duke Payne's flight, above the city over Market Square, did not go unnoticed by citizens and soldiers alike. People in the surrounding neighborhoods watched from their windows, balconies, and the streets, pointing him out as he circled and hovered overhead. Payne descended into Market Square, as the astonished guard backed away. The diminutive Duke Payne gently touched down, eyed the tower, then addressed the crowd.

"Will the captain of the guard please come forward. Now!" The Duke gave the command in a booming, hollow voice.

The captain, in full plate armor, stepped forward and bowed to the Duke. "Captain Miles, your Grace. The situation is under control. The hostages-"

"Oh, do shut up Miles. I don't understand how you managed to allow the prisoners to escape, and these traitors take refuge in one of your guard houses." Duke Payne scolded the hulking captain like a child.

"Your Grace, we dared not risk a full assault because the hostages-" Captain Miles was cut off again.

"Enough! No more excuses and bargaining with these people after the destruction and chaos they have caused in Castle Redrock. I don't care who is in there. There will be no bargaining to escape justice. I will deal with this." Duke Payne waved the captain away.

Duke Payne cut through the line of men that surrounded the guard tower. Alone, facing the heavy oak door, he looked up and down the structure with his hands on his hips. He clasped his hands behind his back, before addressing those who were sheltering inside.

"I will allow you one chance to walk out the guard tower that you are unlawfully occupying, lay down your weapons, and surrender to me. Captain Miles will give you to the count of '10' and if no one exits your, sentences will be carried out immediately." The Duke turned to Captain Miles. "You are able to count to '10,' Miles?"

"Yes, your Grace." Miles bit his tongue.

Flynn and Ashdown watched Duke Payne through an arrow slit. The men that once served as Payne's bodyguards, listened to the threat, and contemplated surrender. The mayor and other hostages looked at each other fearfully, contemplating their fates, having witnessed the way General Jaheem was relieved of duty.

"He will kill everyone, whether we surrender or stand our ground. Retreating here has made this our tomb!" One of the former bodyguards spoke, defeatedly.

The mayor of Redrock pleaded. "Duke Payne is a reasonable man. If you allow us to leave as he said, he'll be merciful and just."

The other council members nodded and made agreeing grunts. The lead bodyguard knew this would not be a possibility for him and his men, after all he witnessed and once perpetrated on behalf of the Duke.

Ashdown whispered to Flynn. "I haven't seen Peter in some time."

Flynn had a sudden realization. "The basement! The bastard has been plotting something. Quick!"

Flynn and Ashdown rushed to the wooden stairs leading to the guard house's basement. The others ignored them, as the Mayor and other hostages pleaded for their release.

Flynn turned and shouted back as a man aimed his crossbow at Duke Payne through an arrow slit. "Your weapons are useless against him! Follow me!"

Flynn's words were ignored. Ashdown gave him a push to keep moving.

The Duke stood apart from the crowd before the stone tower with hands clasped behind his back, as the captain began his slow countdown. A crossbow bolt struck Duke Payne's body and shattered. Payne shook his head with disappointment. Captain Miles paused the count, looking to Payne, astonished.

Payne frowned. "The number '5' follows '6' captain."

The captain resumed the count, stuttering as he continued.

Flynn reached the dark basement first. The door to the privy was closed, though all the planks that were nailed up by Peter to keep it shut, lay on the floor. Ashdown arrived shortly thereafter, with a lamp.

Flynn pulled the door open and Ashdown held the lamp through the door. The wooden seat that sat over the hole to the sewers was removed, and the hole in the floor had been widened enough to allow fat Peter to make his escape. Peter's clothes lay in a heap. The foul smell of the sewer caused Ashdown to feel nauseous.

"This is where he went through. Someone has been helping him!" Flynn looked down into the black void.

"3, 2, 1." The captain finished his countdown, while the Duke patiently waited.

Duke Payne levitated upwards, until he was level with the second floor of the guard tower. The men within, watching through the arrow slits, saw his face revert to its true form. The red points of light glowed bright from the skull's empty sockets.

Payne stretched his arms outwards and began making a slow, circular, windmill motion, with the bony palms of his hands facing the tower. In a booming voice, he spoke the words of the incantation. "Mea pedit fœtor quando ego avias brassica pulmentum!"

A large billowing cloud of opaque green and yellow swirling vapors was summoned forth, slowly moving toward the tower away from Payne. The tower was enveloped and obscured from the sight of everyone observing, from the surrounding the square.

From within the tower, all the sunlight that poured through the arrow slits, was blocked from entering by the thick, soupy vapors, leaving only the light of a few candles to illuminate the large round room. Everyone backed away, as the noxious smelling cloud began to slowly pour through the openings all around the guard tower and settle to the floor.

"He means to poison us! You have killed us all!" The mayor screamed at the leader of the guard.

"Quick to the roof!" One of the guards quickly climbed the ladder to the rooftop and pushed open the trapdoor.

The cloud of poison vapors poured through the open portal, engulfing the man on the ladder. He attempted to push through and immediately began gagging. Suddenly, he went silent and his body crashed to the floor. His skin turned purple, eyes were bulging out of their sockets, and his swollen tongue protruded from his mouth.

The thick swirling vapors rose like flood waters. Men swallowed by the deadly cloud cried out before they were silenced, asphyxiated by the deadly gas.

The floor was completely covered, and gas was rising to their knees. The stairs were clear, as the heavy gases were flowing down to the ground floor.

"Better to go out fighting, than die like this!" The leader called the few remaining fighters to follow. The hostages all fell silent, as the room soon filled to the ceiling with vapors.

The ground floor wasn't flooded by the gasses yet, but they were flowing down the stairs, like a thick rug and slowly spreading across the floor. The men went to work pulling away the barricade and bar that was blocking their avenue of escape. When the door opened and the few survivors poured out, they were dropped by a volley of crossbow bolts. Those laying wounded on the ground, were given a quick 'coup de grais' from the advancing spear men.

Ashdown heard the sounds from above, of the lives being snuffed out. He stripped to his braies and peered into the darkness. "That horrible opening looks tight."

"I'll go first, and you follow. If Peter squeezed through this, you won't have any problem." Flynn transformed into rat man form and took a deep breath, before going in head first into total darkness.

"Shite!" Ashdown looked at his hand, smeared with feces, when he crouched to the floor. He pointed the lamp down into the hole and saw Flynn's backside and feet as he disappeared into darkness. Setting the lamp on the floor, he closed his eyes following headfirst.

51
Princess Danica

The horses of the calvary on the High Road were followed by wagons of supplies, drawn by oxen and the infantry. All outgoing, unauthorized communications from Payne's dukedom to King Ernald, were intercepted for weeks. The fate of Lord Tristan was a mystery to Ernald's court, and this larger force was accompanying another emissary to Redrock.

Princess Danica, King Ernald's older sister, rode alongside her troops, saddled on her gray stallion. She wore plate armor bearing the imperfections of creases from deflected mace blows and scrapes from the blade of an enemy sword. Short graying brown hair framed her sun weathered face, that bore thin scar from along her cheek, from a decades old wound. The princess was not a lady accustomed to the comforts of royal living, as her brother.

Danica's lieutenants, Simon and Fulke, were keeping the company of one hundred troops moving. Scouts returned with reports of 'no activity' on the road for miles ahead. This troubled Danica, as this route was normally travelled by caravans from the dukedom to trade in other parts of the kingdom. The large metal cage on one supply wagon held several homing pigeons. Lord Tristan failed to send any messenger birds before his disappearance.

The Whistling Pass, bisecting the Redrock Mountains, was named for the sound the northern winds made as they blew through it. Military outposts also dotted along the road. The stone watch towers housed guards, assigned to patrol and protect those that travelled the road, into and out of the dukedom. These posts were filled by King Ernald's soldiers, but now the occupants were gone and the armories emptied. Though Danica's uncle, Duke Payne, was a strange and distant man, she always believed him to be loyal to the realm.

The Redrock Mountains shear, red, granite faces loomed high above the narrow winding pass. Before long Danica's company would be clear of the mountains and able to hasten their march to Redrock Castle. This was not a military overthrow, but a show of muscle to encourage Duke Payne to peacefully step down. She now wondered if one hundred soldiers would be enough for this assignment.

The final tower in Whistling Pass was the same as the others. Nothing left behind, to tell the fate of those that were posted. Logbooks gone, armory emptied, and the former occupants gone without a trace. Danica and her lieutenants walked the tower as they did the others, speaking no words during the inspection.

"Fetch my writing kit and a bird." Princess Danica ordered first Lieutenant Simon, as she pulled a stool to a simple wooden desk beneath an arrow slit.

Within a few minutes, the lieutenant returned with the box, that contained small scrolls of paper, ink, and pens along with a homing pigeon. Princess Danica carefully detailed her findings, before securing it in the bird's message carrying capsule.

"Go ahead and release the bird from the rooftop lieutenant. It's best to let my brother know that things are worse than expected, in case we disappear like Lord Tristan. My gut tells me; we won't find my uncle welcoming us at Castle Redrock." Danica handed the bird back to Lieutenant Simon.

Lieutenant Simon gave the princess a respectful nod of the head, while holding the pigeon in both hands. "Yes, Your Highness."

Danica exited the tower and returned to her mount. Looking to the top of the crenelated tower, some thirty feet above, she watched as the pigeon was released. Instinctively the bird found its course and flew in the direction of the capitol city.

Danica climbed into the saddle, reckoning the open road leaving the Whistling Pass, may be where they encounter the real dangers within Payne's dukedom. Her men had the same sense of dread when, yet another lookout tower turned up, seemingly abandoned. The whispered conversations amongst themselves, seemed to conjure up everything from plague to the northern barbarians invading again.

One of the mounted soldiers pointed toward the bird disappearing into the distance. "What is that?"

Another responded. "It looks like a large eagle."

The homing pigeon was pursued and overtaken by the larger avian creature. The smaller bird was unable to outmaneuver the larger, which snatched it up in flight. The men gasped collectively and Danica knew immediately, this creature was not an eagle.

Naamah flew a wide circle back toward Danica's small force. The troops watched in awe as Naamah descended, with her white feathery wings fully outstretched, gently holding the frightened bird in her hands. She touched down gracefully before Princess Danica, as her troops backed away and the mounts grew fearful. Princess Danica calmed her mount and held her ground.

Naamah folded her wings behind her and looked over Danica's troops with a wry grin. Her black plate armor fit her like a second skin, that accentuated her feminine form, unlike Danica's traditional armor. Naamah removed her helm allowing her long hair to flow past her shoulders.

Danica's mounted soldiers moved forward, back into line after calming their steeds. All were intrigued by the mysterious, beautiful, winged woman, unsure whether she was an angel from the heavens.

Danica's eye's narrowed, as she sized up Naamah. "Who are you, and where are the guardians of the High Road?"

Naamah stroked the head of the messenger bird she cradled. "I am General Naamah, supreme commander of His Royal Highness, Duke Archibald Payne's armies. Protector and the enforcer of justice in his dukedom. These outposts, along the High Road, are an intrusion on his sovereignty over his domain. Those guards have been relieved of their duty."

Danica was angered by Naamah's words, but calmly responded. "Duke Payne is not the sovereign ruler of this land. He serves King Ernald. These words you speak, on his behalf, are treasonous."

Danica's men looked upon General Naamah nervously and whispered among themselves, this creature was a fallen angel.

Naamah smirked and gently removed the message attached the bird's leg. She quickly read it, then discarded the paper. "You will compose a new message for your king. His Uncle Archibald wishes to meet with him and discuss the formation of a new country from these territories he holds, that are now independent. You will then accompany me to Castle Redrock, where you will be an honored guest of your uncle, King Archibold while we await your brother's response."

Danica looked over to her lieutenants on either side and gave a nod. Naamah calmly stood her ground, as Lieutenant Simon had ten soldiers surround her with swords drawn. Several men on horseback, on orders from Lieutenant Fulke, rode forward and once in position, targeted her with light crossbows. The remaining men kept watch, along the High Road and to the mountains, for the coming ambush. The winged warrior's confidence was unnerving, as she stood alone against Danica's men, without drawing her weapon.

Danica rode up to Naamah and drew her longsword. She stared back at her with her red eyes, still patting the pigeon on its head. "General Naamah, whatever treachery you have planned, you are first to die."

Naamah shook her head and smiled. She kissed the small bird on its head and then slowly twisted its head off in her hands. She dropped the dead bird to the ground, as Danica's men looked to her for a visual cue.

"Princess Danica, your men are dismissed." Naamah chuckled.

Naamah snapped her fingers and disappeared, with a whisp of gray smoke that dissolved in the air.

There was a collective gasp among the men that had surrounded her and then panic set in. Danica searched frantically around for Naamah, turning her gray steed around with reigns in one hand and her sword in the other.

"She's using magic to hide herself! She is still here! Be on your guard!" Lieutenant Fulke shouted out to the men.

The first of the bog mummies burst from the earth, clutching its axe in its skeletal hands. Others followed its lead, climbing out of their shallow graves along the road. No longer saturated by the centuries of being buried in the peat of the slough, their brown skin appeared as dry paper drawn over their bones. Their long hair and beards were matted and filled with dirt, that shook off as they rose. Their black eyeless sockets had no sight, but the dead were drawn to do the task of which they were commanded by their general.

They set upon the foot soldiers, cleaving them with axes and slashing with swords. Merciless and without fear or thought, the undead barbarian hoard, that was two-hundred strong decimated the troops. Dancia's men were flanked and soon the horses fell with their riders, as they too were eviscerated and dismembered. The undead barbarians shrugged off crossbow quarrels that stuck deep in their bodies, and continued fighting, even when limbs were hacked off.

Danica fought furiously amongst her men, as their numbers dwindled. Lieutenant Simon was first to be overtaken, as he was swarmed by the mummified barbarian warriors. They continued butchering him with their axes, as he lay dead on the ground. Lieutenant Fulke moved in closer, with his few remaining men, to protect Princess Danica. All were bloodied and wounded, unlike their foes who continued the onslaught.

Danica's gray steed reared back, throwing her off to the ground. Danica looked up to see her steed drop to the ground. Naamah reappeared in a puff of gray smoke, pulling her sword from the neck of the dying horse.

"Protect Danica!" Fulke shouted to the few remaining men and moved in to engage Naamah.

Naamah held her longsword in both hands as she charged Fulke. Their swords clashed with sparks flying as they struck. Immediately Fulke was put on the defensive, as she was faster and her blade swung with blinding speed. Obviously, she was toying with him, as he was now retreating to where Danica struggled to her feet, as the last remaining man was cut to pieces by the undead hoard.

Naamah thrust her longsword through the lieutenant's breastplate as if it were tin foil and gave it a twist before pulling it free. Lieutenant Fulke dropped to his knees, as blood flowed from his wounds over his plate armor. Naamah spun on one foot and cleanly removed Fulke's head in one swipe, as he fell forward.

Danica stood alone now. The undead hoard stood motionless, as Naamah wiped her sword before sheathing it. The air became still and then deathly quiet. Folding her wings behind her, Naamah approached Danica, trampling the bodies of dead and wounded in her path.

Danica saw nowhere to retreat and her sword was well out of reach. All other weapons, lost on the field of battle, were already in the hands of the undead.

Danica reached for the hidden dagger in her boot. She drew it preparing to plunge it into her own throat. Before she could make the cut, a skeletal hand grabbed her wrist. The icy coldness from the hand, ran up her arm and left her feeling weakened as she turned, and her eyes met the dead man's empty black eye sockets. The dry skin was drawn back around its mouth, revealing its yellowed teeth, as if it were smiling. Her dagger dropped, clattering onto the High Road, breaking the heavy silence. The coldness enveloped her entire body.

Danica felt faint, and her legs buckled as darkness washed over her. She fell limp to the ground.

Naamah looked upon Princess Danica lying prone for a few moments. "Strip her of her armor and see that she has nothing else hidden."

The undead followed Naamah's command, removing each piece of her armor, down to the padded gambeson she wore beneath it. Danica was bound, at her ankles and wrists, with iron manacles and placed on the supply wagon with the remaining, caged homing pigeons. The scores of undead, working in pairs, carried the bodies of the slaughtered men further down the High Road, through the Whispering Pass. The dead warhorses were also dragged from the field, in a long procession, overseen by Naamah, who flew overhead. The wagon that carried Danica was pulled by undead barbarians in place of the horses.

Not much further, after exiting the pass, the army of dead left the High Road with the grisly trophies of the battle. They travelled down the overgrown track of the Low Road into the marshlands. The sun fell to darkness and the sounds of chirping insects and belching bullfrogs sang over the silent dead, as they trudged along the muddy path. The wagon bearing Danica was in the center of the marching army of the dead barbarians. She regained consciousness, and sat manacled, unsure what torment awaited her. The light of the waxing moon and stars shined brightly, and the crumbling bridge crossing the stagnate waters of the slough were ahead.

Naamah circled overhead, then landed in the wagon standing over Danica. She folded her white feathery wings behind her and placed both hands on her hips. "I took it upon myself to write the message to King Ernald. No need to bother yourself with that now."

Danica looked at the undead warriors carrying the bodies of her men as they crossed the bridge. "If you think the King is going to give in to your demands, you are quite mistaken. How foolish is Duke Archibald to believe the king would sacrifice the kingdom, taking me hostage?"

Naamah sat down in the back of the wagon, next to Danica, to stretch her legs out. She pulled another of the frightened pigeon from the cage and gently stroked its head. "Oh, he is quite foolish. However, whether King Ernald agrees to any demands doesn't matter. Perhaps he will send in more of his forces to remove Archibald, but they will be dealt with just as your little excursion was. King Ernald is stretched thin with his wars in the north. A small kingdom, ruled by his favorite uncle, is the least of his worries."

Naamah suddenly squeezed the pigeon between her hands. The bird's bones made a cracking noise as it struggled to escape, but it soon went limp as life left its body. Danica looked away disgusted, as Naamah tossed the pigeon out of the wagon.

"This is far enough! Throw every one of them into the slough!" Naamah shouted her orders to her undead warriors.

The sound of the bodies of the dead and horses alike, splashing down into the waters below, haunted Princess Danica who watched helplessly, as Naamah oversaw their disposal.

"Why are you doing this? You are leaving nothing for their families." Danica pleaded.

Naamah grew annoyed with Danica's plea and looked down at her with her glowing red eyes. "I'm preparing for the future. Who knows, maybe one day you will march alongside them again, fighting for King Archibald."

52
Unwanted Company

The return to Redrock was made without any further sightings of Duke Payne's men. The trolls and raven spotters, sent by Payne to track Randall and company, proved easy to evade, since trolls are quite moronic and easily distracted. The ravens keeping the trolls on task, were eventually devoured by the ravenous monsters, annoyed by their constant croaking.

The walled city of Redrock was in view, and a sliver of the waxing moon was partially obscured by the cloudy night sky. The Duke's tower was a black silhouette, looming high above the castle. Sauda led them to the foul-smelling stream flowing out from the city connected to the sewers. Refuse and worse organic matter, would eventually float out to the Copper River.

The iron grate, that was in place at the sewer's exit from the city, had been modified to allow secret access to city. It was obvious to Sauda, that the city of Redrock has a criminal underworld that used these as a means of egress.

Randall clutched his haversack, holding his books and reagents, close to his body. Madok helped Izzy keep her balance, and Juliana carried Mosi. The brackish water, they all stood in, teamed with mosquitoes, biting flies, and other unpleasantness.

"The releasing catch is underwater." Sauda whispered, before submerging in the stream.

There was an audible 'click' and the iron grate shifted. Rising out of the water, she waded over to the grate and pulled it open. Randall held his light stone and cast the spell to bathe the muck filled tunnel with blue light. Juliana, Mosi, and Izzy followed Randall in.

"When I found myself travelling through the sewers of Port Gwynn, I fell ill with fever for a week. Minimizing our time in this filth would be wise." Madok cautiously stepped into the tunnel.

Sauda glared at Madok as he passed her. She pulled the grate closed, causing it to once again 'click' and lock in place. "Yes, for those of lacking in stalwartness and vigor, I understand it could prove problematic."

Madok hissed at Sauda, as she pushed past him to the front of the group. "Cease with the insults. We will finish this in the future."

Sauda slowly drew her sword from its scabbard. "Why wait?"

Izzy panicked, while Randall looked for cover in the narrow tunnel. Mosi squeezed between the two.

Juliana addressed the foes exchanging glares across the tunnel. "You two will hold it together! There's so much at stake here. We need to be united to complete the task charged to us by The Mother."

Sauda and Madok stared at one another, as Juliana held firm. Mosi clung to Randall peeking out from behind him. Izzy crouched on the ground, with her dagger at the ready.

Sauda smirked and pushed the blade back into its sheath. She turned and continued further into the tunnel, which had a gentle incline up and out of the water, until there was only a thin stream in the center. The others breathed easy again for the moment and followed.

"I'll protect you from her Madok." Izzy whispered, as she ran past to Randall and Mosi, who were not well-versed navigating the sewers.

Madok stayed silent, as he kept his eyes to the rear.

The further into Redrock's ancient sewer system they ventured, the larger, more complex, and grander the design was. Drainage and wastewater were channeled in the center of a large arched tunnel, with wide, smooth stone walkways on either side. Randall's light stone bathed the area in the pale blue light, but it wasn't enough to illuminate the entire complex. Just forty feet outside of the spell was darkness. The upper reaches were home to the many spiders, that fed on other vermin thriving below in the filth. Scores of black rats scurried from Randall's light as they advanced down the passageway.

Smaller side tunnels that branched from the main passage, fed the main water channel with waste and runoff, from the gutters and privies from above. Sauda pointed to one of the smaller arched tunnels ahead.

"That one there. There are rungs to climb up to an alleyway, near the square. We'll join Red and see what she learned, before our next move." Sauda looked at each of them as she spoke.

Randall moved to the tunnel to look for himself. "Well, it's just as she said. Who's first?"

Izzy piped in. "I'll go! I'll take a quick peek and make sure it's clear."

Juliana patted Izzy on the shoulder before she trotted off. Looking upwards, the rungs disappeared into darkness, out of the range of the light stone.

Water droplets from above splashed her face as she reached for the first rung. She sensed movement above her, just before the large weighted net fell, trapping her.

Izzy screamed, as she struggled for freedom. The more she fought, the more entangled she became.

Sauda drew her sword, Randall fumbled for his wand, Mosi clung to Juliana as she tried to advance to the side tunnel. Madok spun on his heels into a defensive stance, with his longsword in hand to face the darkness behind him.

Many pairs of glowing red eyes advanced toward Madok. The same approached from the opposite end of the passageway. A lanky wererat dropped to the floor from above by Izzy.

The wererat only wore ragged breeches and was wrapped in a gray cloak. Drawing a thin sword, he quickly thrust it into the net under Izzy's skinny throat. Izzy stopped struggling and whimpered, as he lifted her head up with the flat of his blade. Sauda lowered her weapon.

More glowing eyes advanced from all direction, and the passage was filled with the sounds of their squeaks and chittering. They were surrounded and outnumbered.

Randall held his wand boldly in hand, and pointed it toward the largest group still shrouded in darkness. He tried to be intimidating as possible, but he stuttered. "D-don't you come any c-closer or I'll bring the icy h-hand of death upon you!"

Juliana wanted a diplomatic solution. "Randall, I don't think using threats is the proper course of action."

Madok backed up to the others, as the wererats continued toward him. "I don't think 'diplomacy' is in their vocabulary."

Randall bumped into Juliana, giving himself a little startle. Quickly composing himself, he continued to threaten with his wand.

A lone wererat stepped forward from the darkness. She wore a dingy tattered dress with once vibrant colors. Her weapons, however, were well cared for. In one hand she was armed with a rapier and parrying dagger in the other. She transformed to human form; Her long mop of graying, black hair fell down her back and thick, black eyebrows furrowed over dark, brown eyes. The matronly woman grinned, revealing a gold incisor as she eyed Randall. "Well, well, well. This little one likes to wag his tongue a lot. I think he can put that tongue to a better use in my bed, before I eat him for my supper."

Randall gasped. He waved his wand at the woman, while shouting the command. "Conus frigus!"

The gemstone at the end of the wand glowed with a blinding white light that flooded the entire passage, illuminating a score of wererats surrounding them. Powdery frost starting at the stone, ran up the twisted white wood to Randall's hand. The cold was so intense that Randall dropped it, shattering the gemstone into fine shards, snuffing out the light.

Randall looked to the floor in horror, then to the woman who stood before him in the pale blue light laughing. Randall spoke softly over his shoulder to the others. "M-my wand has finally been expended."

"Perfect time for it." Madok snapped, threatening the advancing rat men with his longsword.

Juliana stepped between Randall and the woman to attempt a diplomatic solution. "I am Juliana, servant to The Mother and protector of Her children. We apologize for our intrusion to your home, but we only wish to enter the city without drawing unwanted attention. We will gladly pay a tribute for safe passage."

The woman scrunched her nose up, as she grimaced looking over her shoulder to her wererat companions. "What do you lot think?"

A man called out from the darkness. "Send them floating. They look like trouble."

A woman's shouted, from Madok's end this time. "Too many trespassers here of late. Especially with so much havoc around Redrock now."

The gravelly voice of an old man called out from another side tunnel. "They are responsible for the chaos. Trouble follows them."

Izzy was led by her captor, at the point of a sword, to the wererat leader.

The leader looked at Izzy and then to her captor, raising one thick eyebrow. The rat man pulled the net off the girl, but did not allow her to return to her companions. The leader smiled at Izzy and tousled the girl's locks of dirty brown hair. Izzy attempted to pull away, but the rat man dug its claws into her thin arm.

"Ouch! Not so tight you creep!" Izzy snarled and elbowed him in the groin.

"I like this one." The leader chuckled.

Juliana spoke again with her calm voice of reason. "Yes, we are the ones that were in the tower, but we were not there on our free will. We were brought there by one of three hags, that serve him by powerful magic."

The leader listened and thought for a moment. "Perhaps, yet you return to Redrock, invade our home, and turn his attention to us. We aren't quite as brazen here, as the fool from Port Gwynn, who managed to get captured and thrown into the Duke's dungeon."

Sauda took one step toward the wererat leader. "You're speaking of Peter. I brought them to help free him."

The woman laughed and her wererat companions followed in suit. "Well, you are too late for that. He and the others are our 'guests.' He escaped death, unlike the other unfortunates in that guard tower. They would have left a path directly here in their escape, except we discovered them from all the noise that Red bitch made tunneling."

The voice of the old man spoke from the darkness of the side passage. "I crawled up that unpleasant tube and set things right in that privy. I could hear the Duke's men right above me, as I pulled the box back over the hole."

Madok spoke to the more vocal of the wererats, as he kept his eyes to the rear guard. "What happened at that guard tower?"

The leader became serious. "You don't know? We kept eyes on the events as they unfolded. The Duke himself, used powerful magic to create a giant cloud of poison to kill everyone within the tower. Those fleeing, were put to the sword as they made their escape. None were left living, other than the ones that found their way here."

Izzy felt hopeful. "Flynn?"

The woman nodded. "Yes, he's with us too, along with the self-righteous prick, Ashdown. We caught that bitch, Red and that real scurvy fellow, Reg, when we got Peter. There was one more feller, but he tried to put up a fight. He floated his way out of Redrock."

Juliana was surprised by the familiar name. "Captain Ashdown?"

The woman smirked. "Captain? If you say so. When we caught him, he was naked and covered in filth. Didn't look like one to give orders."

Another woman spoke out from the darkness. "I don't trust them. I reckon they have more business in Redrock than a reunion."

Randall cleared his throat and stood straight, attempting to look in charge of the situation. "We do. I plan to even the score. Payne's been sending assassins after me, and I know they won't stop coming until one succeeds. You can make this easier for us, by releasing Flynn and the others."

"Or what? You planning on threatening me with a little glow stick again? Choose your next words wisely, boy." The leader pointed her rapier at Randall.

The wererats slowly closed the gap between them, entering the cool blue glow of Randall's light stone. Madok faced the enemy approaching from the rear. He twirled his longsword in one hand, before taking hold of it in two. He swung it with blinding speed before him, forcing them to retreat into the darkness. Little Mosi fell to the ground in a ball, burying his face in his hands. Sauda and Juliana also held their ground, with weapons at the ready. The wererat on Izzy's arm, dug in with its claws.

Randall made a quick assessment of the situation. These dwellers under the city were not unlike those from The Nest. Randall needed to choose these next words wisely. "Um, will you release our companions and let us go, please?"

Juliana and Sauda looked back at Randall, then to the advancing wererats.

The leader pondered for a moment. "Planning on 'settling a score' with Payne? Big talk for a young lad like yourself."

"I-uh, its just-" Randall struggled.

"Okay, you lot come along. You convinced me." The leader laughed, sheathing her weapons with a twirl, then motioned for the others to stand down.

Izzy was released and then all the wererats slinked into darkness. Soon the glow of the red eyes also disappeared. The leader turned and began walking, then stopped to turn and look at Randall and his stunned companions, urging them to follow.

"I am called Esma. Lad, you walk with me. You seem to be a most interesting young man." She called to Randall, almost seductively.

Randall attempted to keep calm, as the thought of being ravaged by Esma flashed in his thoughts. Madok gave Randall a firm push, to urge him forward. "I-I was just going to keep watch on the rear passageway."

The wererat's lair wasn't an impressive affair like The Nest. They all stood with Esma in the center of the large circular chamber, hidden beneath the city. Thick timbers, that supported the high dome ceiling, were crawling with rats. No privacy was offered to the wererats that dwelled here. It was all communal and bleak. Stolen goods and foodstuffs lay strewn about, amongst their shoddy furniture. Oil lamps and candles provided dim illumination in the shadowy chamber. Piles of dirty linens and old clothing, acted as bedding for their entire community. Randall tried to shake the thought of Esma taking him.

The main thing was everyone was together again. Flynn was reunited with Madok, Izzy and Randall. Sauda joined Peter, Reg, and Red. Juliana knelt by Ashdown, who was on the floor away from the others.

"Juliana?" Ashdown looked at Juliana's familiar face with surprise.

Juliana looked over the former captain, whom she served under. His hobble restraint didn't allow for him to walk. His hands were manacled in iron cuffs. He was filthy and miserable, but didn't appear harmed.

"Captain Ashdown. Finding you here in Redrock, would not seem to be something that would be of pure chance." Juliana mused.

Ashdown held up his cuffed hands and looked hopefully at Juliana with the slightest smile. "It was Her will that brought us together."

"There he goes again, with that talk. I brought you here after fishing your shite covered arse out of the muck." A slender man with pencil thin mustache, stepped up to the two.

He dropped the key on the floor, at Ashdown's feet and walked away. Ashdown rubbed his wrists and ankles after Juliana removed the restraints.

Peter, wanted to make a quick exit from Redrock. He felt starting over in another city outside of Payne's reach would be best. Flynn reunited with Izzy and his friends, was eager to give Payne much deserved payback. Especially with all he witnessed, within Castle Redrock and its dungeons. He knew the reach of Duke Payne, was not something that could be evaded, by putting a little distance between him. Ashdown and Madok were well acquainted with each other and the positions they held, serving as captains of the city and church guard in Port Gwynn. Now they would be joining together with Randall, instead of hunting him. The young boy, Mosi no ties to anyone, was nervously silent.

Esma eyed Mosi. "Who is the boy?"

Juliana put her hand on Mosi's shoulder. "He says he is General Jaheem's son. I intend to keep him safe, until we can find any family he may have left, that will take him in."

"That is very noble of you. I heard the general had fallen out of Payne's favor, and when he disappeared there was whispers of the abduction of his wife and boy." Esma said.

"My Mama?" Mosi looked up at Esma.

"Yes, after she was taken into the castle, that was the last anyone had heard of or seen her." Esma rubbed her chin.

Randall was intrigued by the story of Flynn caged, talking heads on spikes, and the winged woman. However, news of his former employer, Lord Mayor Geoffrey Walters in the dungeons of Castle Redrock, far from the comforts of his mansion, gave him a little pleasure.

The wererats provided their guests with a small ration of food and drink from their own stores, and allowed Ashdown to pick from their collection of stolen gear. The sword and ring mail coat, were not what a professional soldier as himself would go into battle with, but it would suffice in the interim.

Esma wasn't just being charitable, she wanted some share of the spoils. She had knowledge of much that went on in the city, as Peter once had in Port Gwynn. She just didn't have a network of accomplices in the city. However, her knowledge of the vast sewer system would be useful to get around Redrock, covertly. She could lead them through the sewers outside the cathedral, but there was no direct way in. Juliana's focus was recovering the sword of Saint Vittoria from the crypts below, so this would be their best chance.

Randall set his spell book away from everyone and opened it up. He wished the wand was still in his possession. It was a bad time for such a useful item to be expended. He had a good understanding of its power and had transcribed on the blank pages possible magic formulas to work as spells.

Peter made his way to Randall, who was nose deep in the tome with quill and ink. "Well, my boy. I'm very impressed by the stories Flynn told me of you and these companions of yours, up until he was hanging in a cage. Sauda and Red filled me in on the rest. I knew you are a lad with talent. It's a shame you travel with that murderous captain. It's unforgiveable what he did to The Nest. You could do well to work for me again!"

Annoyed with Peter lurking over him, Randall's nose was still in the book. "It's unforgiveable you sent assassins to murder me, when your plans for the robbery at the Customs House was botched."

"Now my boy. That was a misunderstanding. Certainly, you can see that. You made peace with my girls just fine. Perhaps you can do the same for me?" Peter pitifully pushed out his lower lip.

Randall's eyes stayed in his book. "You haven't offered Madok or Juliana the olive branch. How would it benefit me to get involved in any schemes you cook up. It was foolish of me to get caught up in Geoffrey's activities, then getting hauled away to be killed just for bedding... er courting Madeline."

"Perhaps it was the discovery of the trollop you had visited in that 'fine bordello' along the docks in Port Gwynn, that really turned him against you when you were seeing his young lass." Peter wasn't being judgmental.

Randall was angered with Peter's words; however, they were true. Randall egocentric, and not very empathetic. That was until travelling with a group of companions that felt more like family than just friends. Peter made him reflect on this at that moment. He felt ashamed for his past behavior.

"Eh, but who can blame a young lad, when the opportunity for dipping one's wick in some lovely young lass is presented to him." Peter shrugged.

Randall exhaled heavily and sulked a bit. "Okay, Peter. I got your point."

Peter scratched his stubbly chins and looked over at Madok and Juliana. "You know, perhaps I should 'extend the olive branch' as you say. Let bygones be bygones. Everyone that is here, from the orphaned boy to that disgraced captain as well as myself, need a new beginning. The past wrongs, each of us endured or caused others to suffer, can be overcome by making things right with them."

Randall did not expect those words from Peter's jowls. Then again, Peter lost everything and had time to reflect, locked away in a cage for weeks. Peter left Randall to himself and joined the others. He spoke with Madok and Juliana out of Randall's earshot. He appeared to make peace with them, when each took Peter's big hands in their own.

Randall went back to his studies, then felt a tug at his sleeve. Mosi looked at him with nervous brown eyes. Randall smiled and put him in a chair beside his. "You are studying magic?"

"Yes, just as before. I always prepare for the unexpected. Magic gives me an edge." Randall said, proudly.

"Can you teach me?" Mosi asked, hopefully.

Randall was intrigued. He pondered the thought of a young apprentice. His mind would be like a sponge, ready to absorb whatever bits of knowledge that were put forth.

"I would be honored. However, before you could learn to do what I do, you will need to learn other basic things. To read and write, mathematics, the sciences and history of the natural world and humanity. I'll see to it you and Izzy both are educated. Perhaps, by my old master, Theobald Williamson, where I was once boarded..." Randall looked over to his other side at Izzy, who also pulled up a chair.

Izzy curled her dirty little nose and shuddered at the thought. "Why would I want to do any of that? I bet he would try to make me wash up too."

The conversation about the virtues of education and bathing continued. A much different discussion, on the other side of the wererat lair, revolved around The Cathedral crypts where Vittoria's sword resided, Castle Redrock, and Duke Archibald Payne. Esma suggested they rest, while her people did reconnaissance around the cathedral. This was welcomed by Juliana. Madok and Ashdown agreed with one another, to sleep with one eye open. Neither trusted Esma, or the dozens of wererats that resided here. However, she and her entourage could have taken them out with their ambush, but she didn't.

Randall continued working, while Mosi slumped off to sleep leaning against Randall. Izzy curled up next to Juliana, who made a comfortable spot for the two of them. Madok kept a watchful eye over Juliana, smiling as she and Izzy fell asleep. Ashdown snored, finding comfort, released from his bonds. Red and Sauda watched in shifts, as Peter and Reg dozed without a worry. Only Esma and a few of the other wererats remained, as the others left to forage in the city.

Randall's eyes began to grow heavy, and he knew he needed to rest. The touch of a warm soft hand on the back of his, neck began squeezing and rubbing moving to his shoulders. Randall let out a satisfied groan. "Oh, that's nice."

He looked over his shoulder at Esma kneading his shoulders. She winked and continued the massage.

"Oh no..." Randall gulped.

53
Be Our Guest

Naamah circled over Redrock, with her prisoner held tightly in her arms. High above the city in the night sky, her arrival went unnoticed, by the few citizens making an exodus.

The once beloved city was suffering a crisis. Many citizens had boarded up their shops and homes to flee the disturbing changes of late. The public spectacle, Duke Payne committed in Market Square, was the turning point. Witnesses spread the word, of the dark magic The Duke unleashed on the occupiers and hostages, alike during the siege.

Naamah observed people in the streets with loaded wagons, fleeing under the cover of night. The desertion of most of the city guard, left the gates open and unwatched. Naamah's small force of undead warriors were on the outskirts of Redrock, just out of sight. Their orders were to remain there until she called for them. Citizens fleeing the city would not be in danger, unless they wandered too far off the High Road.

Naamah remained silent since taking to the air, seemingly lost in thought. The flap of Naamah's wings and the creaking of her armor, was all Danica heard, as they circled Redrock. Danica's wrists and ankles were feeling raw from the irons that restrained her, but she was consumed by thoughts of dread.

Naamah dropped Danica on the tower rooftop, as she herself gently touched down. The lone surviving gargoyle turned its stony head and licked its lips.

"She is not for you, idiot!" Naamah hissed.

The gargoyle slurped its long tongue in, leaving a long thick string of drool, from its chin to the crenelated wall, upon which it perched. The disappointed creature returned to its watch.

Danica lifted her head to see Naamah standing over her. "What do you intend to do with me?"

"Duke Payne requested you to be his guest, as I already stated." Naamah grew annoyed.

Naamah removed Danica's shackles and pulled her to her feet. She walked her down through the tower to the hags' chamber. "Make yourself comfortable here. I will let The Duke know you have safely arrived."

Danica felt anxious, as Naamah closed the door, leaving her alone. The hags' room had not been touched since Mosi's rescue and the ensuing fight. The smell of the spoiled stew in the cauldron filled the room. The rotting meat pie, flung to the floor, was covered by weevils. Her eyes narrowed, spying a small, shriveled finger amongst the bits of rancid meat that were part of the gory feast of the insects.

Almost an hour passed and there were no sounds of activity. She was unarmed and wearing only her gambeson. The butchering tools, the hags had used to cut meat, were still scattered about the worktable. She pulled a butcher's knife that had been stabbed into the bloody block, and hid it in a hole in the padded under armor.

Danica visited her aunt and uncle since she was a child into adulthood, but never set foot in the tower. The place was a mystery to her. Brought here as a prisoner, after ambushing the King's soldiers, was treason against the kingdom. If she met with her uncle, perhaps she could plunge the knife into his heart, before his bodyguards could react. She would die trying at the very least.

The door opened easily, cracking it enough to peer outside. There was no guard posted, so the winged woman wasn't concerned about her leaving its confines. She stepped onto the landing and debated on the stone stairs before her. Danica decided better to descend, rather than confront the creature on the rooftop. The scorched wall, from the blast of Duke Payne's lightning bolt, remained etched in the wall. Danica noted this, not knowing its significance.

She entered the room housing Payne's living armor guards. The battle-damaged pieces of armor were neatly sorted into piles of breast plates, greaves, helms, and the halberds lining the walls and weapon racks. Duke Payne had not re-enchanted the armor, so they harmlessly stayed where they lay. Naamah failed to pull the door all the way shut to The Duke's office, so the deadly protective ward did not reset.

Danica stepped into Payne's private office. The large door that accessed the castle was closed, so she pressed her ear to listen through the thick wood. She detected a strange gurgling sound, but it was within the office. Slightly startled, she tried to listen at the door again.

Once again, the gurgling sound grabbed her attention, from the cabinet behind the desk. She slowly crossed the office as it went silent again. Stepping around the desk, she stopped before the finely crafted cabinet and waited for a long moment. Her heart racing, she reached for the pull rings on each door. Danica held her breath, as her fingers curled through the rings and pulled the doors open.

The severed head of the once loyal servant, Osbert was mounted like a trophy, within the confines of the cabinet. The mouth hung wide open, and the eyes rolled back, revealing only the whites between the drooping eyelids. The flesh had not putrefied, though this kill was obviously not 'fresh.'

Danica was taken aback. She knew this man very well. She said his name in disbelief. "Osbert..."

Osbert's eyes rolled forward and met Danica's. The mouth slowly closed as it made a gurgling sound. It answered with a hollow dead voice. "Yes?"

Danica backed away from the cabinet into the desk, scattering papers and feather quill pens to the floor. The head waited for a moment before it gurgled. Once again, its eyes rolled back, and the mouth fell wide open.

"You were to wait in that bedchamber for our return." Naamah was amused by Danica's reaction to Osbert.

The Duke stood just inside his office, arriving unnoticed by Princess Danica. He appeared to Danica in the familiar form of her old uncle, once again disguising his true form through transmutation magic. Danica eyed Payne up and down. This was the first time she had seen him in person years since before Duchess Katherine took ill. Even then, he struggled to walk without the use of one of his many walking sticks, and now he did without.

"My darling niece, welcome back to Redrock. I'm pleased to have you once again, as a guest in my home. I trust you had a comfortable journey?" The Duke's words were strangely genuine and pleasant.

Duke Payne was obviously mad, and Danica was not going to play along with this strange performance. "You ordered an ambush on the King's soldiers and had them butchered by her! You use necromancy to give un-life to the dead! You are an abomination!"

Payne smiled at his niece, ignoring all she had said. "I had the best guest room readied for your stay. The one facing your aunt Katherine's beloved gardens. I remember you used to stay in it when you were a child. A bath is being drawn to make yourself comfortable after your long journey."

Payne closed the cabinet doors, once again concealing Osbert's severed head. He slowly turned to face Danica, smiling with his hand behind his back. Naamah smiled, taking pleasure at the discomfort in the princess's eyes.

Danica composed herself and stood defiant with her fists clenched. "King Ernald will never yield to your demands. Whatever power you hold over this dukedom, will be forfeit along with your life for betraying the King. You have damned your soul to The Hells for nothing!"

Naamah still stood at attention, turning her gaze from Danica to The Duke, to observe his reaction. Payne was unmoved by Danica's dialog, appearing willingly deaf to her speech.

Payne made the 'after you' gesture with his hands toward the door, letting Danica know the conversation ended. Payne and the Princess traversed Castle Redrock, with Naamah following, to Danica's new accommodations.

It was in the middle of the night, and the castle was eerily quiet and empty of life. The stars and moon of the night sky, shined through stained glass windows along their walk. Sconces and candelabras were dark, since the servants abandoned the place and their duties were left undone. Payne was oblivious to the state of his surroundings and engaged in a very animated one-way conversation with Danica, who walked without uttering a word.

The grandiose hall leading to the bedchambers was also in the same state of neglect. Ahead at the ready by the guest room door, a figure waited in the darkness.

Duke Payne smiled as the three approached, giving a nod to his valet. "Ah, good evening, Brandon."

Brandon did not speak, but instead made a low groan as he opened the door. Danica realizing that he was another undead servant of the Duke. She could smell the underlying odor of decay on his putrefying skin.

"I will take my leave now, if I am not needed your Grace." Naamah spoke with overt pretentiousness.

The Duke dismissed his general with a nod, and Naamah exited after an exaggerated low bow. Danica watched Naamah leave and the valet closed the chamber door behind her.

The guest room was lit with oil lamps, candles in sconces, and tables about the room. This one room escaped damage and looting during the uprising. Everything was in place, from the bed linens to the embroidered tapestry that decorated one wall. On the opposite wall, was the fireplace and the balcony overlooking the gardens.

Eleanor stood next to a folding screen painted with a colorful garden scene, behind which was the tub prepared for Danica. Just like the valet, Eleanor's corpse was forced to continue acting as a servant. A white nightdress lay neatly folded on a plush divan at the ready for Danica. Next to it lay a silver tray piled with fruits and sweet cakes, shared with a single goblet and open bottle of wine.

"Please, make yourself comfortable. It may be some time before the King sends another lacky to remove me. I'm certain each time it will be an exponentially greater force. I assure you each attempt will fail, and I will add the fallen to my army." The Duke paced the floor, as he talked with all seriousness.

Danica slowly moved her hand to retrieve the knife hidden within the padded jerkin, as Payne continued talking. Eleanor, was oblivious to everything, except for the task she had been given by the Duke.

"It's no secret you are my favorite niece. I admire your talents and skills in warfare, as well as being a fine tactician. Other noble ladies enjoyed their creature comforts their station in life brought them. You chose the life of a soldier. Working your way through the ranks, until you earned your own command. Perhaps, I may be able to offer such a command of my forces, if you serve me instead." The diminutive Duke stopped pacing and rubbed his chin.

Danica sprang onto Duke Payne as he was turning to gauge her reaction to the speculated offer. She plunged the knife deep into the center of his chest, knocking him to the floor, after crashing over the overstuffed chair in front of the hearth. Danica quickly crossed the room to the doors to the balcony, to escape into the gardens.

The doors were locked and would need to be broken down, unless he had the key on his person. She turned as Eleanor approached, walking in a stiff gait, clutching at the air, ready to rend Danica to pieces.

Danica grabbed a potted fern by the door and crushed Eleanor's skull. Broken pottery, soil, and greenery lay on the floor atop the corpse. The noise would surely bring in the undead valet, who would go down as easily as this one did. She would need to find another weapon.

She looked over to the hearth, thinking the poker would suffice.

Duke Payne stood with his hands behind his back, looking at the knife protruding from his chest with disappointment in his eyes. "This fine tunic was made by the best tailor in my dukedom. A kindly gentleman down south in Sommer Harbour. Always did the best work. Now look at it."

Payne pulled out the knife and cast it on the ground, then further inspected the hole with his fingers. Danica stumbled backwards, surprised.

"Humph! At least there's no blood to stain it." Duke Payne's damaged garment was his focus for the moment.

"How in the Hells are you standing? What devilry protects you?" Danica backed away.

Payne brushed off his clothing with his hands, eyeing the body on the floor. "You have made quite a mess of things in here. You even destroyed Eleanor, who oversees the cleaning of these rooms. I can't have that."

He dropped the enchantment; his image in life faded, revealing his true form. The red points of light in the empty sockets of the skull burned angrily, staring into her soul. Danica backed into the wall, as her uncle reached out his skeletal hand.

She raised her fists, as a pugilist ready to pummel him. He grabbed her wrist before she could land a blow.

"Fulgur!" Payne spoke the command, releasing an electrical charge of blue sparks that enveloped Danica's body, causing her bones to glow briefly beneath her skin.

The smell of ozone filled the air, and the princess briefly stood shaking, before her eyes rolled back and she collapsed to the floor.

Brandon shuffled into the room, then stood mindlessly awaiting orders. Payne briefly knelt over his niece, inspecting her where she lay. Her arm was blistered, and his handprint was burned around the wrist. Her chest rose, as she began breathing.

"Brandon, put my niece to bed. Perhaps she just needs a little sleep to put her mind right. I will not have such unwarranted, destructive behavior of her. She is acting out like a spoiled child, for no good reason!" The Duke's annoyance showed, as the intensity of the points of light in his empty sockets grew brighter.

Brandon shuffled to where Danica lay on the floor. He carried Danica over his shoulder and unceremoniously dropped her on the bed in the wrong direction. Danica's arms and head hung off one side and her feet the other. Payne shook his head and sighed with disappointment at his servant's ineptness.

"I want this room back in order before my niece awakens. That includes disposing of Eleanor." Payne waved his finger at Brandon.

Brandon uttered a low groan from his dead lips, as he carried out his duties. Payne exited the guest chamber, as a pair of guards approached down the dark hallway. The pair were clad in the usual chain hauberks with surcoats displaying the dukedom's colors. Both displayed wounds from a violent death during the uprising, and like the servants, were now forced to serve even in death.

"Don't allow princess Danica to leave her chamber until I summon her." The Duke gave his order and watched as the guards slowly shuffled to their positions on either side of the door.

He shook his skull and walked down the center of the hall with hands behind his back. The few dead that he was able to raise with his magic to act as soldiers and servants, would hardly replace the living that died or abandoned him. These unthinking aberrations were only able to obey his simplest commands and were too easy to destroy. The peat bog cursed by his lord, the Arch Devil Dysvakar, created far more formidable soldiers from the dead immersed within its waters. There was work to be done to prepare defenses for more incursions into his dukedom.

The undead Duke Payne had an eternity to prepare. The lands he ruled over did not.

54
Flame Broil and Snow Cones

The morning sunrise would mark the return of activity to Redrock. Some semblance of life continued within its walls, despite everything. The deputy mayor was thrust into his new position with the 'premature departure' of the former without ceremony. His hopes were to join the others in the exodus from the city. Unfortunately, he was under scrutiny from the Duke, so leaving now wasn't an option. The new mayor headed planning and budgeting for a new city revitalization. Scaffolding was along the walls, and construction materials were about the grounds of the immense Redrock Cathedral, that was in active use.

Redrock Cathedral suffered damage during the short siege, that ended with the capture and subsequent sacrifice of Bishop Caitlin, in the dark ceremony at the marsh. Now the structure underwent renovations and repairs to serve its new lord, Dysvakar. However, Dysvakar was only one of several dukes of the Hells, who vied to increase his influence in this world.

Flynn and Izzy were in rat form, outside of the range of the lanterns that hung around the site. Izzy scuttled across the courtyard and ducked behind a pile of lumber. Standing on her hind legs, nose and whiskers twitched as she sniffed the air. Flynn slinked across the courtyard, sticking to the shadows. His red eyes scanned the area for guards, but none were posted outside of the cathedral.

The once magnificent doors, that were covered in bronze relief sculptures depicting highlights from the story of The Mother, were gone. In their place fifteen-foot-tall, gloomy, black iron doors set with spikes, transformed the once inviting place of worship into a dark hall, where Dysvakar's unholy dogma was spewed. The stained-glass windows were smashed during the siege and were now shuttered, awaiting replacement.

Randall, Juliana, Madok, and Ashdown watched from afar, in the shadow of the alleyway. Esma brought them this far, before she and her brethren returned to the sewers. She promised to keep Mosi safe during this foray, leaving one to keep watch on the cathedral. Peter and his remaining three loyal followers, used this time to make their exit from the city. Their part was done.

Flynn darted over to join Izzy at the lumber pile. Izzy had not detected any immediate threat outside of the cathedral walls. Assuming the front doors were secured, she scurried along the side of the building, looking for an opening. Flynn followed behind at a short distance, keeping watch as Izzy climbed the wall to the first window ledge.

The arched cathedral window was boarded up from top to bottom, but not so secure that it couldn't block a view of the interior. Izzy could see the front of the nave, which had taken the brunt of the damage during the attack. The pews that were not heavily burned or damaged remained and the others removed. Nothing remained that showed this was once hallowed ground. Izzy took a little more time looking for any signs of life within. Nothing, not even one candelabra was lit.

Finding the weakest spot in the wood barricade, she began chewing with her sharp rodent incisors. In minutes the hole big enough for Izzy to squeeze through. Flynn looked over to his friends watching from the alleyway, before climbing the ledge and pushing through the hole.

"They're in. Grab their gear." Madok whispered and crossed the courtyard.

The others grabbed the wererat's bundles of weapons and clothing, before joining Madok. Madok was in conversation with Flynn, who was now in his human form hanging out through the window.

"Toss those up. Those doors are not only locked, but barred from the inside. Someone or something else, must be lurking in here." Flynn waved over to Randall, smiling.

Randall's spell, he used before, would be useless against the doors being barred. Luckily Izzy's special talent would come in handy once again, he thought. Randall tossed up the first bundle with Izzy's gear to Flynn, who had his hands held out to receive. Not even close. The bundle fell back to the ground. Flynn's smile disappeared.

"I got this." Ashdown tossed up the bundles, one at a time, successfully.

Randall felt the urge to transform Ashdown into a pond hopping, amphibious creature. He would have to research that spell for a future date.

"Izzy says she will have the door open in a moment. She says the lock isn't beyond her skill." Flynn said, reassuring the others.

Izzy stood before the great iron doors with her lock picking tools rolled out on the floor before her. Flynn already removed the heavy bar and stood guard. The night sky above was turning to dawn, as the fire damaged roof allowed light to filter into the nave through the charred rafters. Birds roosting in the rafters above, watched with curiosity.

Izzy inserted another thin, twisted, metal, lock picking device into the keyhole only to have it snap. "Rats! This one is tougher than I thought."

"Keep at it, Izzy, but hurry." Flynn sensed something lurking beyond the nave in the darkness, deeper in the cathedral.

"Izzy, we are not alone." Flynn drew his rapier and took a defensive stance, as shapes advanced toward them.

"Keep them busy! I think I almost have it." Izzy blew on her fingers, as another snapping lock pick scraped her knuckles. The wound healed instantly, but it smarted nonetheless.

"Right." Flynn snapped back at the girl, before cautiously approaching the guardians.

Three hooded figures, shrouded in dark gray cloaks, floated floor toward him. They moved unobstructed, passing through the columns supporting the damaged roof and pews, as if they did not exist. Under their hoods there was only blackness, save for two glowing red points of light. The ends of their robes were empty and within only blackness.

The three made no sound, but circled Flynn, just out of the reach of his blade. Flynn's heart raced and beads of sweat rolled down his brow. Izzy looked over her shoulder at Flynn struggling to ward off the guardians. She put her full attention to the lock, realizing they were over their heads.

Flynn thrust his blade at an apparition, but it dodged with great agility. Even when he plunged it into one's form, it passed through harmlessly. With each swipe Flynn took at one he faced, another flanking him would strike at him like a serpent. Each hit by the wicked creatures felt, as searing venom was coursing through his veins. He felt his strength leaving his body, and every step felt like he wore boots of lead.

Flynn dropped his rapier before, he too, collapsed. The three apparitions continued to strike as he writhed in agony. Flynn lay motionless as the three slowly circled his body.

Izzy screamed, turning their attention to her. The translucent floating forms billowed like sheets on a clothesline, as they sized up the little girl. Izzy frantically went back to work on the lock. This time success.

Izzy's scream pierced the morning calm, echoing through the cathedral and alerted the others to the imminent danger. Madok and Ashdown each grabbed hold of the massive ring set in one of the iron doors, and as a team pulled it far enough to pass through.

Juliana stepped through first, spotting Izzy darting through the nave, as the three apparitions gave chase. Izzy was very quick, ducking and tumbling, just out of their reach and then cutting back and forth between, as each lunged at her. Their red eyes glowed brighter as they were infuriated by Izzy's superior agility. Madok and Ashdown stepped through with swords drawn, and Randall brought up the rear.

"Help!" Izzy squealed, narrowly missed by the ghostly creature.

Madok and Ashdown rushed in, without hesitation, to engage. The apparitions turned to face the fighting men, leaving Izzy to crawl to her fallen friend, Flynn. The men fought back-to-back, to prevent attacks to their flanks, as they were circled.

Their swords passed through the spirits without any effect. They knew this would be impossible to win.

Juliana retrieved her blessed holy symbol and held it in her hand as she approached. Ashdown was struck by one of the creatures on his shoulder. Its icy touch caused agonizing pain to flow through his body from that point of contact.

Juliana called out to her comrade-at-arms. "Your weapons will have no effect on those spirits. Retreat!"

The two heeded Juliana's warning and made a fighting retreat. Madok was struck as he backed away, causing him to reel. They were not going to allow them to escape.

Juliana held the silver amulet boldly, so their red gaze would fall on it. "In the name of The Mother, I command you to remove your vile presence from this place!"

Piercing shrieks of torment filled the cathedral nave, as the apparitions retreated from Juliana, as she continued walking forward. The symbol held before her; she faced each spirit in turn as each attempted to inch forward, only to be driven back again.

"What can we do against these things?" Madok shouted out desperately, feeling weakened.

Randall spoke up. "I believe that they are not invulnerable to this... Flatus illum!"

Pointing his finger at the spirit that retreated up into the rafters, Randall's incantation called forth five bolts of force. Unerringly, the missiles struck their target, causing it to react as if it had been pummeled.

The smoky apparition felt the effects, but it wasn't enough to destroy it. Enraged, it dived at Randall, ignoring Juliana.

"Oh shite!" Randall cried, paralyzed with fear.

Before it could reach Randall, Izzy's dagger struck the undead foe. The strange blade did not pass through the incorporeal spirit, but lodged in its smoky body. It shrieked and spun, before its smoky form dispersed in the air. The dagger hit the floor with a clatter, as Izzy swooped in to collect it.

"Who trespasses here?" A voice called from deep within the darkness, hidden from the morning light.

Madok challenged. "Show yourself! You are the ones that don't belong here!"

Juliana stepped forward with Madok and Ashdown, holding the silver symbol to keep the remaining apparitions at bay. "We have come to remove you from this house of The Mother, and return it to Her and Her faithful. Stand down and I promise to be merciful!"

"I think not! Et erit lux!" The voice spoke words to an incantation.

Sickening green light glowed deep within the cathedral. Its source was a rectangular great iron altar with a smooth, flat surface to receive a living sacrifice. There were grooves around its edge to capture spilled blood. These would channel blood to strategically to spill out of the mouths of the twisted grotesque faces along the front of the alter, to fill vessels used in an evil blood ritual. Dried blood showed that it had been used recently.

The antithesis to Bishop Caitlan, who once led the faithful, stood behind the altar. He had a shaved head and diabolical pointed goatee. Roused from his bedchamber, he hastily donned his iron gray vestments, and a blood red priestly stole draped over his shoulders. High contrasting gold embroidery bore inverted pentagrams on the stole.

Rising from the choir stalls on either side of the raised altar, stood dozens of figures cloaked in long iron gray robes with hoods concealing their faces. Slowly, they shuffled out of the choir stalls to form defensive lines before the alter, four deep and six across. Each held a sword in one hand and a wooden buckler on their other arm. They stood perfectly still in their formation.

Izzy helped Flynn sit up, the best she could. He was weak and could barely stand on his own, needing her for support. Ashdown and Madok glanced at each other without speaking. Juliana's eyes narrowed, studying the robed warriors and determined their true nature quickly.

Randall fumbled through his reagent bag. To summon a ball of fire to engulf the whole lot, he needed a ball of bat guano. The little jar storing it was open, creating a smelly mess in the bag. "Shite, shite, shite!" Quite literally.

Juliana addressed Ashdown and Madok in a low voice. "Those that stand between us and him, are undead of his creation. They have greater numbers, but they can easily be handled by you two. Keep them busy so I can get to him."

"What about those things flying in rafters?" Madok looked upwards.

"Randall and Izzy will handle them." Juliana said with confidence.

Randall looked up hearing his name. "What?"

Izzy held her dagger at the ready, leaving Flynn to hit the floor. "Sorry Flynn!"

The priest shouted the command to his robed defenders. "Kill them all!"

The robed force slowly moved forward, swords raised for attack and shields raised to defend. The sound of their many feet shuffling across the floor was drowned out by the sound of the low tormented groaning of this deadly 'choir.'

Ashdown and Madok charged, each taking half of the first line of guardians. The dead moved slowly, unable to fend off the fighting men's assault. Juliana's assessment of these foes was correct. These were recently deceased, forced into servitude in a dark ritual by this servant of Dysvakar. Their movement was stiff, their attacks were clumsy, but their numbers could overwhelm them if they were surrounded.

Juliana called out to Her, with her silver amulet held tightly in hand. "Mother, I ask for you to protect your servants and help us vanquish these unholy foes!

The ghostly mace materialized, bathed in blue light, only feet above the battle below. Juliana concentrated, intending to send it onward, to crack the skull of the defiler. As the weapon began its way to Juliana's intended target, it was stopped. Another ghostly mace materialized, bathed in sickly green light, blocking the advance by slamming into it.

The priest's counter to Juliana's spell emboldened him. Juliana could see him chuckling.

"Mr. Randall they're coming back!" Izzy shouted.

The spirits that retreated into the rafters, swooped down at Izzy and Randall. The morning light however, prevented them from approaching them further. The morning sky grew brighter and the interior of the cathedral, where they held their ground, was bathed in it. The apparitions did not appear harmed by the light, but they refused to pursue them into it. Instead, their attention turned to the darker interior, where the roof still shielded out the light of the sun. Their target was now Juliana.

"Randall, stop them!" Izzy pleaded.

Randall scooped out enough of the mess from his bag and was quickly rolling guano into a ball in his fingers, while sprinkling in sulfur from another vial. Hoping he had enough of these components for the spell, he shouted out a warning to his friends. "Hit the floor!"

Madok heard Randall's warning, knowing the magic he was about to use, was probably not completely under his control. He tackled Ashdown to the floor. Juliana dropped and covered her head.

"Globus ignis occidere eos!" Randall pointed at the mob of creatures and concentrated. A small glowing ember shot from his pointed finger, deep into the cathedral.

When it reached the target, it exploded into a large ball of fire, that engulfed the space before the altar, from the ceiling almost touching the floor. The apparitions were caught in the fiery blast and were erased from existence. The lowly dead guardians were blown down by the blast, and consumed by the flames.

Juliana, Madok and Ashdown escaped Randall's spell, but the rafters high above were set alight. Yellow flames licked at the wood timbers of the naked rafters and were spreading to the roof. The priest found cover behind altar to shield himself, escaping the fate of his undead minions. Peeking over the altar, he saw his foes approaching.

He hoped to barricade himself in the sacristy, but Madok and Ashdown had already made it to the top of the dais and blocked his escape.

The priest backed away to deliver a monologue and stall for time. "You are the ones that attacked his Highness, causing havoc in Redrock! You will answer to Dysvakar for-"

Madok and Ashdown cut his diatribe short with a few swings of their swords. The priest fell across the iron altar, with gaping wounds to his belly and across his back. Small bubbles of blood sputtered out of his mouth, as he exhaled his final breath.

"Juliana, the fire is spreading. We need to leave this place!" Ashdown pointed to the rafters above and the smoke that was now escaping from the missing roof section.

Juliana looked at Randall, who was already surveying the flames. "Randall, can you extinguish the fire?"

Randall was excited to share a solution. "Absolutely! I learned something from that wand I had. I was coming up with the formula for the incantation that would allow me to-"

"Do it!" Juliana was uncharacteristically short.

Randall shut up and nodded. He retrieved the prism he had used before, when reading magic inscriptions. Extending his arm, he pointed the prism toward the fire spreading through the rafters and spoke an incantation, while making an ever-widening circular motion with his hand. "Conus frigus!"

Arctic air blasted from Randall's hand and snuffed out the flames. The exposed rafters and ceiling were left in a layer of ice and frost. He admired his work, rather impressed with himself and expected the others to shower him with praise.

"Stop fooling around Randall, help Flynn to his feet!" Madok barked.

"Right." Randall took Flynn's arm and helped him follow the others.

The heavily reinforced iron door leading to crypts below Redrock Cathedral was intact after the siege. Izzy did a quick inspection ensuring there wasn't any nasty trap to spring, before picking the lock. This one opened far easier than the main doors.

Descending the ancient steps into the vaulted chamber of the undercroft, it was evident many crypts were desecrated. Statues toppled, lids to sarcophagi smashed with interred remains violated. The central shrine to The Mother was desecrated with feces and garbage.

Juliana was angered by the blasphemy, but kept a cool head. She walked the crypt searching for St. Vittoria, hoping that her resting place was unmolested. They split into two groups, with Randall and Juliana each bearing their stone to light the way. Flynn sat at the foot of the stair recuperating, while Izzy kept watch on the door.

Randall and Madok passed defaced crypts, reading aloud names chiseled into the granite. Ashdown and Juliana did the same on the opposite end of the undercroft

"What is that name again?" Randall squinted to read the tarnished brass plate affixed to a broken sarcophagus.

"It's still Vittoria. It's hard to believe a man with your intellect can struggle to remember a name, yet quick to access a dangerous situation and change the course of events to our favor. If not for you, we would not have survived everything we have gone through. Many times, over." Madok felt feeling guilty for misjudging him since they first met, during the days of his employment to Geoffrey.

Randall was genuinely touched by Madok's words. This was a bonding moment. Randall responded the best he could. "I, uh... Thanks."

The search ended before they reached the end of the undercroft, when a lone sarcophagus drew Randall's attention. The lid had been removed from it and smashed on the ground. Around it, lying on the ground, were the decomposing corpses of what must have been fighters that were part of the attack.

"I see something. I'm not sure just what." Randall called to the others.

Juliana and Ashdown hurried to join them, and together they moved in cautiously to inspect. The corpses of the three were badly decomposed, but were whole showing no sign of being killed in battle.

Juliana then read the name on the sarcophagus. "We have found her."

55
A Pressing Matter

Naamah looked across the crenelated wall of the castle, toward the smoke, rising from the cathedral in the distance. Whatever had happened, it appeared the flames had been extinguished. Naamah immediately suspected the troublemakers The Duke was obsessing over.

"Captain, inform His Highness that the Temple of Dysvakar is under attack. I am going to see who the intruders are myself." Naamah crossed her arms, while surveying the cathedral from afar.

Miles averted his eyes from Naamah, who stood naked before him. "General, I will take a company of men there to investigate, to give you time to don your armor."

Naamah grabbed Captain Miles by his chin and forced him to look upon her naked body. "You will not disobey my orders. Do as I say, or I will throw you over this wall."

"Yes, General." Miles responded by saluting Naamah when she released him.

Naamah closed her eyes tightly, bowed her head and went into deep trance-like concentration. She muttered the words repeatedly. "March to The Master's temple."

Naamah opened her eyes, regaining her faculties and looked again to the ruined cathedral in the distance. Spreading her feathery white wings, Naamah leapt atop the battlement wall, then launched herself into the morning sky. Captain Miles cursed, as she flew over Redrock toward the smoking temple. Acting as a servitor to the evil, that now ruled over the dukedom and its traitorous acts against the kingdom, weighed heavy on him.

The distance was a quick flight over the rooftops and city streets, that were filled with the morning traffic. Naamah wasn't unnoticed on the ground. It was now common knowledge in Redrock, that a winged woman commanded Duke Payne's forces. The citizens on the streets of Redrock, pointed and gawked as she soared overhead, unconstrained by clothing. Many fled in fear, leaving any burdens they carried in the streets.

Naamah flew over the ruined cathedral, circling overhead, surveying the area around it. The carpenters and the engineers just arrived for work, but didn't enter seeing the smoke rising through the roof. The iron door remained slightly ajar, but no one dared go inside.

Naamah hovered at the façade, eyeing the onlookers, before addressing them. "Did anyone enter or leave the temple?"

The frightened crowd stared at the devil, collectively shaking their heads 'no.'

Looking across the faces, she searched for anyone that appeared to hold back the truth. Satisfied, she set her feet on the ground and folded her wings behind her. Drawing her sword in one hand, she stepped inside, and pulled the door shut behind her.

✳✳✳

Below in the undercroft, Juliana stood by St. Vittoria's open sarcophagus, aiming her light on the remains within. The others approached, taking care to avoid the bodies lying on the ground.

The moldering remains were skeletal, her ceremonial armor rusted and pitted. Lying atop the body with the hilt grasped in the corpse's gloved hands, was the Blessed Sword of Saint Vittoria. The plain black leather scabbard protecting the blade, showed no sign of rot and was clean.

"Remarkable... It appears as it would have been, when it was interred with her centuries ago." Ashdown marveled that it was indeed, the real thing.

Madok had his suspicions. "Why would the cathedral be ransacked, and this left behind?"

Randall looked again at the three decaying bodies on the floor. "Could there have been a booby trap, Flynn? I don't see evidence of a magical ward that would result in this."

Flynn and Izzy joined the others and took a few moments looking over the sarcophagus, finding no evidence of a triggered trap. This was something else.

"It is the will of The Mother, not to allow the sword to fall into the possession of Her enemies. Madok, take the sword. With it, you will be able to defeat Duke Payne and send him to face punishment in the Hells." Juliana touched his hand, looking into his eyes as she spoke.

Madok smiled, then reached for the blade.

"Stop!" Ashdown grabbed Madok's arm before he could touch the sword.

Madok pulled his arm out of his grasp. "What is it?"

Paul Wolff

"The sword of Vittoria is not for you to wield, Madok. If you were to touch it, you would befall the same fate as those three. The Mother will only allow a servant she has chosen, to wield this weapon." Ashdown spoke sternly.

Madok's eyes narrowed. "You think you are the one who should carry the sword?"

"No, I wasn't chosen for this task either. Juliana is the one The Mother chose. She is the only one pure enough in heart and mind to take up this sacred weapon." Ashdown looked at Juliana.

In turn all eyes fell on Juliana, humbled by Ashdown's words.

"Juliana, I think he's right! You are the nicest person I know." Izzy smiled.

Juliana knew his words were true. She was just denying herself the truth. Events were set in motion as part of The Mother's plan.

Juliana gently moved aside the gloved hands of Saint Vittoria from the hilt of the sword. Randall stepped back, unsure what was going to happen next. She lifted the sheathed sword out, without harm being done unto her. Slowly she pulled the blade from its leather sheath. The steel, like the scabbard, showed no sign of aging and held a keen edge. A gentle warm white light was shed along the length of the blade, ending at its wire wrapped hilt.

"I have not trained with a sword." Juliana held the sword straight out, inspecting it at arm's length. It was light in her hand and strangely felt as an extension of her arm.

"The Mother will be with you, guiding your hand in this fight." Ashdown smiled.

Randall grew tired of the discussion of swords, The Mother, and divine plans. He also noted that Flynn needed complete bed rest, after the attack from the apparitions.

"We should retreat from here, before someone takes notice of our 'intrusion.'" Randall urged the others, waving them to follow.

"I agree. The city will be on alert, once our handiwork above is discovered." Madok pulled Flynn up to his feet.

"Juliana, is there anything you can do for Flynn?" Izzy took Flynn's hand, as he leaned on Madok for support.

"The wounds that Flynn sustained from those spirits will require more than a simple prayer. Those creatures were draining him of his life's energy, which may not come back to him with only rest. It may require an offering to The Mother, for the ritual to restore him." Juliana sheathed the sword and hung it from her belt, in place of her mace.

The stone lid to Saint Vittoria's sarcophagus was put back in place to protect her remains, before they ventured to the ground floor. The group made their way to the ground floor of the ruined cathedral, with Madok supporting Flynn all the way.

Morning light poured through the damaged roof, and the smell of the scorched rafters lingered in the air. Ashdown surveyed the area around the altar and the choir, before moving in further. The priest's body still lay across the altar and the burned guards were also untouched. Ashdown waved 'all clear' and continued in. Izzy joined him, followed by Juliana and Randall. Madok and Flynn took up the rear.

Izzy stopped, halfway down the nave. "Hey, that big door is shut."

Randall pondered over what magic he would need to call upon. Juliana drew the sword, wielding it with both hands. Flynn propped himself up on one knee, to keep himself off the floor, as Madok readied himself to defend. Izzy drew her dagger and darted for cover under a pew. Ashdown cautiously moved ahead, searching for signs of a threat.

The disembodied voice of Naamah, boomed in the cathedral from all directions. "Great Dysvakar, accept the sacrifice upon your altar, and send more of your children to serve me in defending your temple!"

Randall was bewildered hearing the voice of Naamah, and looked wildly about for its source. His eyes fell upon the altar and the body of the slain priest laying across it. Unnatural green flames spread across the altar, casting their sickening glow around the dais it sat upon. The flames grew larger and their glow brighter, as they consumed the body of the priest. Within seconds the body vanished, and the flames were snuffed out. All that remained on the altar was the blood spilled upon it.

Madok moved joined Ashdown, then called to the invisible devil. "Show yourself coward!"

The silence was deafening in the cathedral. Randall could feel and hear his own heart pounding in his chest. The dread was worse than anything he had experienced, since this whole tragic mess started in the cell below Geoffrey's mansion.

Ashdown pointed at the altar. "Over there!"

Three pillars of green flames sprang from the floor around the base of the altar. The flames' green glow cast light across the cathedral and grew until they licked the ceiling above. Each pillar spun as a vortex and within each an amorphous shape took form. The flames did not consume, but created, the fiends that Naamah summoned from The Hells to her aid.

Three figures stepped out of the fiery vortexes atop the dais and immediately the flames were extinguished, leaving no trace. Standing side by side, three tall muscular man-like devils eyed their foes. Their red skin was wrapped in blackened chains, covered in barbs that bit into their flesh. The chains were to torment them, as much as they were to be used as weapons against the enemy. In their hands they held the free ends of the chains, that dangled to the floor, ending in evil pendulum-like blades. The fiend's glowing blood red eyes, were the only features of their faces free from the barbed chains that wrapped around their heads. The creatures didn't utter any words. The only sound from them was the metal blades that scraped the stone floor.

They turned their heads in unison to face Randall and company. Once they locked eyes with their foes, they swung the chains in their hands, increasing the velocity of their rotation until the blades appeared as deadly blurs.

Juliana stepped before Ashdown and Madok with the sword of Vittoria before her. "These creatures are thralls of The Hells. There will be no retreat or quarter allowed by them."

Randall looked about the scene frantically. "Who summoned them here?"

Flynn forced himself to his feet in his weakened state. "I recognized her voice. It was the fiend that The Duke calls his general, Naamah."

Juliana closed her eyes and prayed aloud. "Mother, I call upon You to bless your servants, to aid us that we may remove those that occupy Your house."

A shimmering, faint, white glow enveloped Juliana, and the others then quickly faded away. Randall felt a warm sensation throughout, from his head to toes, overcoming the once overwhelming feeling of dread.

"The Mother's divine blessing is temporary! We must act quickly!" Juliana led the attack.

Randall hung back with Flynn, as Juliana charged the devils, alongside Madok and Ashdown. Each chose a single foe to engage, and the hell spawn accepted their challengers.

The three closed in on the fiends that awaited their approach. The devil's barbed chains were released from their circular rotation, and ended with the pendulum blades flying at their targets. Madok dodged a blade, aimed at his throat, and with swing of his sword deflected the second away from his chest. The chains sprung back and the devil pulled back to prepare its next attack.

Ashdown pushed forward, to fully engage his foe, before it was able to release a chain attack on him. He charged between the chains, focusing on its belly to plunge his longsword. The devil, in a feat of acrobatic skill, performed a standing backflip to the iron altar. Ashdown was caught off guard by the maneuver, giving the fiend a chance to counterattack. It released a chain and with blinding speed, catching Ashdown around his neck. The length of the chain wrapped around his throat and barbs dug into his flesh, as Ashdown gasped for breath.

The devil used both hands to pull the chain, which bound Ashdown like a dog's leash. Ashdown fell to his knees, as the blood vessels in his eyes burst and he turned purple. He grabbed the chain with both hands to play tug-o-war with the fiend, desperately trying to snap his neck.

Juliana backed away from the devil that was encroaching on her quickly. It launched its barbed chains with serpent-like strikes, but Juliana was able to evade each attack. The fiend grew angrier with each failed attempt and its blood red eyes burned with fury. The Blessed Sword of Vittoria's soft white glow intensified, until its light bathed her in a holy aura. Juliana pressed forward now, and she swung the blade with a whirlwind of slashing attacks.

The devil launched its chains at her again, but Juliana didn't allow any to land on her. The sword easily cut through the hellish links of the barbed chains, as if they were merely twine. The bladed chains flew in different directions, with their blades imbedding harmlessly into an ornate pillar behind Juliana. Disarmed of its bladed chains, the fiend went on the defensive and tumbled away from Juliana, as she slashed at it with her longsword.

Madok furiously blocked the bladed chain attacks from the devil, but was unable to land a blow to it. The creature was quick and unrelenting, and its red eyes smoldered with pleasure. The attacks came quicker, as the blades launched at Madok and sliced across his shoulder and another slicing his thigh. The cuts were not deep, but they burned and bled.

"Randall! Quit fooling around and do something helpful!" Madok barked, as he blocked another chain that lashed out at him.

"Yes! I'm already on it!" Randall had already retrieved the spell book pilfered from The Duke's tower, and dropped the haversack to the floor. Thumbing through the pages of the tome, he searched for a spell that he thought might be able to save them. He didn't have it committed to memory but reading it directly from the pages should work. He found the spell that would send one of these creatures back to The Hells.

Ashdown was in the most immediate danger, while Juliana's foe was retreating from her. Madok was holding his own, but suffered from the unrelenting barbed chain attacks, though his blade was finally finding its mark on his opponent with the help of The Mother's blessing.

Randall held the large book in both hands, and he read the incantation aloud. "**Reditus ad planum existentiae unde vocati estis numquam redire!**" The inked words on the illuminated parchment glowed, as he recited each, then vanished from the page with the surrounding illustrations. The pages were left blank, as if a quill and ink had never touched them.

Above the devil, thick purple mists swirled and blue charges of electricity crackled throughout it. The devil's attention was drawn from Ashdown to the mists above it. Before it could react, the mist enveloped the creature. The chains, that held Ashdown, fell to the ground, and then were drawn into the mist. A silhouette of the devil glowed brightly from within, then in a blinding flash, disappeared. The purple mist dissipated, leaving no trace of the fiend.

Ashdown was doubled over on the ground, gasping for his breath, as cuts left from the barbed chains oozed blood. The other devils paid no notice to the disappearance of their brother and continued facing off their foes. Randall looked to Flynn, who was still in a weakened state.

"Randall, help him. I'm good." Flynn urged.

Randall returned the tome it to his haversack on the ground.

Izzy scrambled to Flynn, from her hiding place. "I'll protect Flynn, Mr. Randall!"

Juliana with the sword of Saint Vittoria in her hands and with The Mother's blessing, had her foe pushed into a corner. The creature felt the sword bite into its flesh and its bladed chains were severed, leaving it defenseless. It had nowhere to go, other than head on with Juliana, using its brute strength.

The devil made no sound, but its red eyes showed its rage, as its large hands clenched into fists and shoulder and arm muscles flexed. The devil leapt to tackle Juliana. The protection of The Mother's blessing quickened Juliana's reaction, dodging her foe, and causing it to fall flat on the stone floor.

The devil quickly recovered from its fall and sprang up to face Juliana. Juliana was ready. She swung the sword with one hand, connecting with the devil's thick neck. The blade lodged deep into it, but not enough to sever with the first blow. It staggered backwards, holding the wound, while putrid black blood gushed forth. Juliana finished the creature with a second swing, severing its head. The body hit the floor, transforming into a bubbling black sludge, before evaporating, without a trace.

Madok and his opponent were on equal footing as a matchup. Neither was allowing the other to land a blow, dodging the other's attacks. Juliana joined Madok, to flank the last fiend.

"Ashdown, take my arm!" Randall crouched down, offering him support.

Ashdown was shaking off the pain and waved Randall away. His neck was oozing blood. The whites of his eyes were now red and watery. He retrieved his sword and looked at Randall with his pained eyes. "There is one more evil entity amongst us. We must find the one that summoned these thralls of The Hells."

Randall remembered the commanding feminine voice and Flynn's warning about Naamah. He looked about the cathedral. Across the dais, Madok and Juliana finishing off the overwhelmed final devil. Flynn was on his feet with his rapier in hand, and Izzy stood in front of him, with her enchanted blade ready to slice anyone daring cross her path. Randall looked to the choir and the nave, but both appeared as they were, with the bodies sprawled across the floor.

He turned back to the fight to see Madok finish the devil, with a thrust and twist of his sword. Like the other, it evaporated into vapor.

Randall turned his attention back to Ashdown. "Perhaps it fled? We made quick work of..."

Ashdown dropped his sword, and his body stiffened as Naamah's sword impaled him from behind and through his chest. She reappeared behind Ashdown, as she pulled her sword from his body. Before Ashdown hit the floor, she quickly swung her blade to decapitate the dying warrior. Randall froze, sprayed with Ashdown's blood, looking into Naamah's eyes as she smiled.

"No!" Izzy screamed.

Flynn grabbed Izzy, to prevent her from making a suicide attack.

Naamah towered over Randall and stared unblinking, as she slinked over to him with her sword pointed at his throat, as the sharp tip of the blade touched gently under his chin. Naamah lifted his head with her blade, forcing him to peer into the unworldly gaze of her red eyes.

"Pathetic mortal boy. I would grind you out of existence like a worm beneath my foot, but His Highness wants you alive." Naamah cooed.

Naamah pulled Randall to her and pointed her blade at Juliana. Randall's face was smashed into Naamah's breasts. A different set of circumstances at any other time, place or with a mortal woman, Randall would have happily submitted. However, the devil's skin was uncomfortably hot to the touch and had the acrid smell of brimstone.

"Let him go and face me!" Juliana commanded.

Naamah backed away, as Juliana and Madok continued moving toward her. She smiled as she stepped from the dais, making her way into the central aisle of the nave. Randall struggled to breathe, and flailed his arms uncontrollably, causing Naamah to laugh. She adjusted her hold on her prisoner after sheathing her sword, allowing Randall to face forward.

"Your request is denied, child. You will have a more pressing matter to attend to." Naamah hissed. She turned, unfolded her feathery wings, and shot into the air, through the hole in the roof.

Everyone ran to the nave, to catch a glimpse of Randall disappearing with Naamah, into the sky.

"She killed Ashdown and stole Mr. Randall." Tears welled up in Izzy's brown eyes and ran down her dirty cheeks.

Madok growled. "What do you make of this 'pressing matter' she mentioned?

Flynn was the last to join the group, with Randall's haversack thrown over his shoulder. He sensed danger approaching. "Shhh... Listen!"

The four stood quietly in the center of the nave, bathed in the light, listening.

The sounds of screams and of weapons clashing, could be heard outside the cathedral. Juliana looked at the others, as they discerned what was happening. Then all went silent.

Izzy pointed at the iron doors, as they slowly creaked open. "Look, someone is coming in."

The four readied themselves to face the new threat, without having a moment's rest from their encounter with Naamah and her minions.

"Perhaps the city guard has been sent to arrest us." Madok mused aloud.

Juliana's eyes narrowed, as the doors opened wide, revealing who was on the other side. "We would not be that lucky."

Izzy ducked behind Juliana, who stepped before the others, with the white light of the sword of Vittoria intensifying with the approach of this foe. Madok and Flynn stood on either side, sizing up the 'pressing matter.'

Beyond the doors, the scores of centuries old, mummified barbarians stared into the cathedral through their empty black eye sockets. They were covered in fresh blood from the unfortunate citizens of Redrock and any city guard that happened to be in the path of their march. Their numbers stretched out into the square, around the cathedral.

The first bog mummy shuffled over the threshold, holding a great axe in his boney hands and was followed by a one-armed, undead barbarian, wielding a spiked club. Others slowly filed into the cathedral.

"There are too many for us to take, without Randall's magic!" Madok shouted.

Juliana closed her eyes and whispered a prayer for guidance from The Mother, as the numbers of the undead horde grew.

55
The Escape Part 2

Danica sat in an oversized chair in the dining hall at one end of the massive table. Empty chairs lined either side of it all the way to the far end, where her uncle sat some twenty feet away. A breakfast of eggs and toasted bread with preserves was set before her, untouched. Danica was given a 'suitable courtly gown' to wear, by The Duke. Any other woman of nobility would have loved the fine silk flowing skirt and the intricate patterns on the embroidered bodice with delicate lace, but Danica was uncomfortable in such garb. Her thoughts were only of escape, and sending a message to the king.

Her undead uncle had no food set before him and no longer magically altered his true appearance. His regal clothing hung loosely on his skeletal frame. The fine, brimless, fur cap on his skull almost covered his eye sockets. He pushed it up with boney fingers every time it slipped. The Duke's valet, Brandon, stood swaying beside Danica. Other undead guards were posted in pairs, at each of the doors leading into the hall.

Danica was lost in thought, as her uncle droned nonstop since they were seated. In his new state he had lost touch with reality and spoke like a truly insane man. Danica paid him no attention.

Captain Miles entered the chamber, ignoring the guards and traversed the hall to where The Duke sat. Danica noted Miles was one of the few living persons seen, since she was brought to Castle Redrock the night before.

Miles crouched down to speak to The Duke, avoiding eye contact. "Your Highness, General Naamah has returned from The Cathedral of The Mo... Dysvakar with a prisoner. The young wizard, that trespassed your tower with the others. More concerning, the general ordered her troops into the city. They slaughtered any persons standing in their way. Common citizens: men, women, children, and members of my guard were indiscriminately murdered as they marched. You must do something to stop this, Your Highness!"

"Splendid! Have Naamah bring the prisoner to the throne room! I would like to address him there." The Duke rose from his chair, gleefully.

"Your highness, what of the..." Captain Miles voiced his concerns, giving up when his report was ignored.

"Brandon, escort Danica to her chambers." The Duke exited the hall with his guards, leaving Miles alone with Danica and the dead valet.

Captain Miles watched Duke Payne as he exited the hall. Brandon continued to sway in place, next to the princess, with a low groan escaping his dry dead lips.

Danica rose to address Miles. "Captain Miles, you ultimately serve King Ernald and defend the realm. This monster, my uncle, is an abomination and a threat to the entire kingdom."

"You think I don't know this? General Jaheem was put to the sword and his family were taken away for plotting against him. Your entire company was slaughtered, attempting to march on Redrock, and you are now his prisoner. I would risk my family defying him." Miles said in a somber tone.

Brandon's skeletal fingers wrapped around Danica's arm tightly. The valet's empty sunken eyes stared blindly past her, as he mindlessly attempted to lead Danica from the table. Danica resisted the valet and kept her eyes locked with Captain Miles's.

"I apologize, Princess Danica, but I must first report to General Naamah. However, if you find yourself unattended by Brandon soon, I will be making my rounds and able to speak more. I usually start from the ground floor barracks. They have been emptied of late, due to the desertions. I will linger there for a while." Captain Miles hurried out of the hall.

Brandon continued to pull at Danica's arm, using more force as she stood unmoved. The captain disappeared from her view and the sound of his footsteps grew fainter. The valet tugged and tore Danica's sleeve, leaving scratches on her arm.

Danica pulled away from Brandon and inspected the wound as he swayed gently groaning. Again, Brandon reached for Danica's arm. She stepped back out of his reach. The valet reached again, stepping toward Danica.

The princess grabbed the undead valet's outstretched arm with both hands. She swung the creature until it was unbalanced and lost its footing, and crashed to the floor. Brandon slowly lifted his head, revealing a flattened nose and broken teeth.

Danica quickly crushed his head with a brass candle holder from her breakfast table. There was an ominous heavy quiet, as she peered down the castle's cold stone halls. No sign of life or any of The Duke's undead guards. She hid Brandon's remains under the table before leaving.

Danica was familiar with her uncle's castle and quickly made her way to the empty guard's barracks. She claimed a longsword from a weapon's rack, and quickly trimmed away the excess of the long dress she was forced to wear. Unsure of Captain Miles' intentions, she knew that getting word to King Ernald may be next to impossible. She would need to fulfill her mission on her own. She awaited Captain Miles and hoped he would find her, before she was discovered missing.

Across Redrock Castle, The Duke sat atop his throne cross legged, while he tapped his chin. Auntie Olga joined him and paced about, waving her one arm about as she spewed out all manner of curses as to what should be done with Randall.

The former Lord Mayor Geoffrey sat hunched over on the floor, wrapped in a moth-eaten blanket with an iron collar around his neck. A length of heavy chain from the collar was bolted to the floor, giving him some freedom of movement. However, the chain was only long enough to be teasingly out of reach of stale scraps on the floor before him. He stared longingly in silence.

"Will you cease with your incessant noise? I should have let you walk back to the castle and driven the coach myself, so you'd still be on the road. Then I'd have some peace." The Duke pounded his fist to silence the hag.

Auntie Olga stopped pacing and sat in the chair once reserved for Osbert. "Sorry Archie. I just want to see if Naamah has the one that took my arm. I will personally deal with him!"

"His fate is not for you to decide! Dysvakar expects his debt paid, and I will need this one for the next new moon."

"It will be dangerous to hold him while he has allies in the city!" Olga waved her finger at The Duke.

Naamah pulled Randall into the throne room, by the chain attached to the iron collar on his neck. "Quiet, Olga. This one is my prisoner, and I slew another. My army will have slain the others by now."

"Naamah, please tell me why you returned here without first seeing them finished off?" The Duke drummed his phalanges on the arms of his throne.

Naamah threw Randall flat to the floor and placed her foot between his shoulders to keep his face to the ground. Naamah was tormenting him with her words, promising all manner of painful torture up to the moment of his sacrifice, ever since they reached the castle. Randall's eye was blackened and lip split from being backhanded repeatedly, when he had tried to speak to her.

Randall saw Geoffrey for the first time in months. The memory of being sealed in a barrel, didn't leave room for pity for this shell of a man. However, he may end up in that exact position, tormented by The Duke and the rest of his evil minions until his time was up.

"I wanted to bring you this little one without delay. This is the troublesome little magician you've been consumed with for some time now?" Naamah dropped the chain and stepped off Randall's back.

The Duke rose from his throne and floated across the floor within inches of Randall, who was rising to his knees. Randall felt the icy chill from Duke Payne's skeletal form, while his eyes burned through to his soul. Overcome with fear, Randall retreated, crawling backwards.

Payne grabbed the end of Randall's chain and uttered the incantation. "Fulgur!"

The electric charge transmitted through the metal chain to his collar. Randall cried out and fell silent to the floor. After a long moment, Randall's chest rose as he took a shallow breath, in a state of unconsciousness.

"Naamah, return to your troops! I don't share your optimism that your swampy barbarian horde alone, will succeed in quelling this." The Duke ordered, as he passed the chain to Auntie Olga.

Naamah turned away from the others and stormed out of the throne room, cursing under her breath.

The Duke stood with arms crossed, watching as she passed the guards and called out once more. "Where are the book and wand that were in his possession?"

Naamah continued her exit and hissed. "Ask him."

"Bah, such insolence." The Duke shook his head.

Randall was regaining consciousness, choking as he was dragged by the one-armed hag with the chain. It was locked into the same heavy iron ring set in the floor that held Geoffrey's chain.

Payne studied Randall, as an undead guard bound his wrists in front of him with iron cuffs. "You are a troublesome little fellow. No need to worry, this accommodation next to your former employer is only temporary. There won't be any mischief with you mumbling off any apprentice minor magics."

Auntie Olga produced a knife from within the folds of her ragged dress. The undead guard pulled Randall from the floor and squeezed his throat, while another stood by holding a pair of smithing pinchers.

"Wait, wait, wait! Shite!" Randall closed his mouth, but the guard forced his mouth open wide. Randall's eyes bugged out, seeing the iron pinchers opened wide to receive his tongue.

Auntie Olga smiled broadly, as the pinchers took hold of the tip of Randall's tongue. She went to make the cut, but his tongue slipped free.

"Boy, it will be over quicker if you don't fight!" Olga cackled.

The guard was making another grab with the pinchers, while Olga was overcome with fits of laughter. Randall saw the open doors leading from the throne room with no guards. This would be his only chance for an escape.

"Ut hic de mecum in infernum!" Randall spoke the incantation so quickly, he wasn't sure if it would work.

There was the bright flash of light, and instantaneously Randall was transported across the throne room to its unguarded grand entrance. He was freed from the collar that was clasped around his neck, but he still bore the manacles on his wrists.

Randall darted through the doors, throwing himself to the floor as The Duke unleashed a bolt of lightning that struck a far wall with a loud thunderclap. That was too close, as he felt his hair stand on end. He made a run for it down a side corridor, hearing The Duke's guards chase after him. The Duke's curses and the hag's laughing fit faded as he ran.

Randall was limited on magic options without his component bag. He chanced running into more guards, if Duke Archibald didn't catch up to him first. A turn down another corridor and he could smell the kitchens ahead. Even if The Duke was a walking skeleton requiring no sustenance, there were a few others in his service that did.

The sound of guards approaching from behind, encouraged him to continue onward, even though he was out of breath. A man carrying a basket stacked high with fresh baked loaves of bread exited the kitchen into the hall on his way to the garrison. In a panic, Randall darted into an open doorway before the kitchen into a dark storage room. He ducked down just out of the light from the hall. He surrounded himself with a few large canvas bags filled with tubers, hoping the guards would pass.

They ran past the room and shouted at the baker carrying his load. He couldn't make out everything that was said, but he knew he was the subject. The whole castle would be alerted to his escape. Was it better for the guards kill him now, or face the fate The Duke promised?

"Don't move. Don't even breathe." The woman's voice whispered behind him, in the darkness.

Randall froze. The hag must be in the room preparing to force herself upon him. He wanted to call out to the guards to surrender.

The woman's hand covered his mouth, and the edge of her blade went under his chin as she pulled him closer. "Shhh..."

He closed his eyes and prepared for an oily witch's tongue to lick his cheek. He didn't know what she was waiting for as they sat quietly in the darkness.

"He didn't come this way. Double back and take the north hall. He may try to make his escape outside to the bailey." The commander's voice ordered the guards away. The sound of their bootsteps disappeared.

Randall opened his eyes again as her grip relaxed. He could see the figure standing in the doorway of the armored man, but he did not enter.

"I'm going to let you go, but you must not make a sound." Danica whispered into Randall's ear, as she slowly removed her hand from his mouth and pulled away the sword from his throat.

"Princess, are you still here? The guards have left, but others may return." Captain Miles whispered into the room.

"I am, and I believe this is the young wizard they are looking for." Danica rose and kicked Randall in his hind quarters.

Randall struggled to his feet. His eyes were adjusting to the dark and he recognized the captain, who just moments ago delivered messages back and forth between Naamah and The Duke.

"What? How in The Hells? This is an impossible situation." Captain Miles hissed at Danica, as he looked out for any more approaching guards.

"He bumbled his way in here." Danica gave Randall a push with an open palm, causing him to stumble forward.

"The Duke himself will be scouring these halls for him and it won't be possible to deceive him. The only way you will escape, will be for me to create a diversion dragging his dead body to The Duke." Miles began to pull his sword.

Randall threw up his shackled hands and backed into the wall. "Wait! I'm on your side! I came here to kill The Duke!"

"I saw General Naamah flying you into the castle as a prisoner. You are in no position to assassinate him." Captain Miles took a step forward with his sword pointed at Randall.

"We recovered the Blessed Sword of Saint... uh, someone from the cathedral when we were ambushed. We had killed the priest and the guardians, before she summoned more devils from The Hells to fight for her. We defeated them, but she made a sneak attack and grabbed me. My friends are probably already halfway here, to join me and finish him." Randall pleaded, very quickly.

Miles sheathed his sword. "They are already lost. A hoard of the dead was sent to the cathedral to eliminate your companions, by General Naamah. They will kill anything in their path. She returned to the cathedral, under orders of The Duke, to ensure none survived."

"They slaughtered my entire company without taking a single casualty. They are not simply walking corpses given unlife by a necromancer. The marshlands on the edge of the dukedom were cursed, in a deal made by Duke

Payne with an archduke of The Hells. That is where these creatures rose from." Danica added.

"My talented friends will even the odds in an impossible situation. I need to find another way to aid them. If you are not going to run me through, would you mind?" Randall held up his manacled wrists to Captain Miles.

Danica kept watch, as Miles pulled his key. Captain Miles' master key worked on the locks on prisoner's bindings and most of the doors around the castle.

"It will be impossible to smuggle the princess out, with the guards on high alert scouring this part of the castle. Divert their attention elsewhere or I will go with my original plan." Miles tapped the hilt of his sword.

"Okay, okay, wherever you are going I'll head in the opposite direction." Randall agreed.

"Good luck to you. Your actions will be honored when the kingdom is rid of Duke Payne." Danica smiled and cautiously stepped into the hall.

"I believe you are clever enough to make your own escape and rejoin your friends, once I have the princess well on her way. May The Mother guide your way." Captain Miles joined Danica.

"Yes, yes, thank you." Randall said as the two hurried away.

Randall went over the few spells he could use without any special material components. Stepping into the corridor, he heard footsteps from behind. He ducked into the kitchen as he they rounded the corner.

Very few living people still served in the castle, but the kitchen was still operating. The man who left with the basket of bread was still away. A flour covered worktable with several round balls of dough were ready to flatten to make into bread. In the hearth a stew was cooking in a cauldron. The floor was littered with scraps of potato and carrot peelings. Curled in a ball on his pillow near an empty food dish, was a fat orange cat sleeping off its breakfast. The cat looked up upon Randall's entry into his domain, then curled into a ball drifting off.

Randall armed himself with a rolling pin and ducked behind the woodpile, covering his eyes with one hand. Through the door, he heard one person enter the kitchen breathing heavily. He peaked between his fingers and saw the cook dropping the empty breadbasket by the door.

"Puddin' we should have left months ago! Now there's another mad wizard on the loose here. Yes, we should have left Redrock when everyone else did." The cook lovingly spoke to his comatose cat.

Randall studied the cook's face as he picked Puddin' up, stroking the cat as he nervously paced the floor, keeping his eyes on the doorway. The well-placed blow to the cook's head from the rolling pin knocked him out cold.

Paul Wolff

Puddin' landed on his feet, hissed, and hid behind a barrel in the darkest corner of the kitchen.

Randall dragged the unconscious chef behind the wood pile and donned his stained slouch hat and smock. "Mutare forma iunior!"

In seconds the illusionary magic transformed Randall's appearance into the cook, who snored flat on the floor. The spell failed to fool the guards at the Customs House, but Randall felt more confident about this deception because this was a common cook.

"Olly!" a gruff voice called into the kitchen.

Randall hesitated, then stood up from behind the woodpile. Looking to the doorway, he saw a pair of actual living guards.

"Oh, there you are! There's a wizard boy on the loose in the castle! He was brought in by the General this morning and escaped. He's the same one that broke into The Duke's tower, that wreaked all kinds of havoc. Oh, that smells nice." The young guard stepped in, sniffing the air of the meat stew simmering in the cauldron.

The second guard grabbed the first by his arm and addressed Randall. "We don't have time for you to take an early lunch. Did he come this way, Olly?"

Randall paused for a moment before realizing he was Olly. "Nope, I didn't see any wizards come through."

The guard's eyes narrowed as he studied 'Olly.' "You okay, Olly? You don't sound like your normal self."

"Er, I have a cold. I'm quite all right, really." Randall fumbled a bit.

The guard stepped into the kitchen, now focused on Randall followed by the hungry guard focused on the stew. Randall took one step back, stopping short of tripping on the real Olly. Randall had one more spell, that he had memorized, that could change this situation.

Randall spoke the incantation and made a quick gesture with one hand toward the approaching guard. "Amicum gratissimum."

Overcome with dizziness from the enchantment Randall cast upon him, the guard stopped and put his hand to his forehead. Shaking his head and regaining his balance again, looking upon the disguised wizard. His demeanor changed from one of suspicion to regarding him as his trusted friend. The other guard was too busy tasting stew directly from the cauldron to notice.

"I'm sorry, Olly. I can't seem to remember what we came in here for." The guard scratched his head.

Puddin' quietly slinked from his hiding place, to the woodpile, where the real Olly was just out of view. The orange cat sniffed Olly's head, then licked his face causing him to slightly stir. Randall quickly formulated a plan.

"Since there is a dangerous escaped prisoner wandering the halls, would you kindly escort me to the... tower. I need to deliver ...stew." Randall could replenish spell components and escape from the rooftop as he had before. He had no idea how to get there from where he was. He just needed to get there avoiding Payne, guards, and other nasties along the way.

"Deliver stew? To the tower?" The hungry guard dropped the spoon back into the cauldron.

"Uh, yes. Amidst all that is going on there is a guest that needs to eat. A... uh princess, right?" Randall was hoping he sounded convincing.

"Princess Danica? Oh, she's in there? I guess The Duke moved her there for safe keeping with the castle on high alert. Intruder in the castle and the trouble at the cathedral right now. I'm grateful the general didn't order us to march out there. Dangerous folk over there!" The first guard was convinced.

The remaining guards appeared to have a diminished intellect, thus preventing the capability of critical thinking. Both were willing to act as his escort, while keeping an eye out for the renegade wizard. After shooing them out of his kitchen, he gave the real Olly another lump on his head for good measure. He put together a tray with stew and covered it with a cloche.

Randall made a point of having his armed escort avoid any others patrolling the halls and avoid the throne room, so to not disturb the Duke. The undead guards in the castle ignored the three as they walked past their posts.

No guard was posted at the door to The Duke's private tower entrance when the three arrived. A stroke of luck for Randall. However, there was the possibility of one on the other side of the door.

The beguiled guard rapped on the large hardwood door with his gloved fist as Randall stood with the food tray. Luckily there was no answer, as he wasn't prepared for an action to take if The Duke himself opened it.

"Have you ever been there?" The younger guard asked the other.

"Never. Only Duke Payne's bodyguards and guests of high importance enter." The guard knocked again.

"How about you, Olly?" The younger guard said with a smile.

"Uh, no. This is the first time of course. Ever." Randall felt a bit uncomfortable, but tried to keep the tray and his head level.

"You wouldn't be lying, would you?" The young guard had a broad smile across his face.

"What are you going on about?" The other guard knocked again before looking over to his inquisitive companion.

"I don't believe what Olly said about never being in the tower before. In fact, he is very familiar with it." The younger guard covered his mouth with one hand to hold in a laugh.

Paul Wolff

"Umm, this tray is getting heavy. I've got it from here. I don't want to take away any more time from your duties." Randall had a bead of sweat run down his face.

"I don't carry a key to the tower door. Only The Duke and his advisors do. If no one answers the door it is unoccupied and of course restricted." The knocking guard turned to face Randall now.

"No worries. I have a key." The young guard produced a key and made a cackling laugh.

Randall dropped the tray making a loud crash. "Shite! No!"

Auntie Olga held the key with her one hand as her disguise melted away. The other guard was also taken by surprise, stumbling back a few steps. Randall pressed his back to the wall and the illusion of Chef Olly also faded.

"You made this all too easy. I suppose we could have saved everyone a lot of trouble and just let you walk yourself here in the first place. I'll still want that little tongue of yours. Wizard tongue has many uses in potion making. After it is properly dried, once harvested, I will let you watch me craft one before you are sacrificed. It's a rare ingredient to come across these days and the least I can do is share a little knowledge." Auntie Olga cackled and turned the key in the tower door.

The enchantment on the guard was also broken, shocked by the hag's deception. He ran away at full speed.

"This will make things a little more difficult. Nothing I can't handle course." Auntie Olga nodded.

Randall looked about desperately to which direction he should make a break. Olga punched Randall with an uppercut to the chin, dropping him to the floor. Grabbing Randall by his collar, she dragged him in the entry chamber of the tower and locked the door behind them.

Randall moaned as his eyes rolled about, unable to focus. He lifted his head, as he regained his faculties and the ringing in his ears diminished. His attention was drawn to the gurgling, coming from the cabinet behind The Duke's desk.

"Don't worry about old Osbert. He gets anxious when he hasn't had a visitor in a while. Come along now. You in there, quiet!" Olga barked out, as she opened the cabinet revealing Osbert. Olga dragged Randall through the warded door by one leg, as the voice of Osbert blathered on incoherently.

57
Null and Void

"Back into the crypt!" Flynn shouted to his companions, as more of the dead filed through the doors of the cathedral.

"That will be our own tomb if we retreat down there!" Madok called back, as they backed toward the sanctuary.

Izzy hid behind Juliana as the undead horde swarmed them. Madok raised his sword in a defensive position, ready to parry any swing of a battle axe. Flynn turned to defend their rear position as the dead encircled them, blocking their egress.

The four stood back-to-back, expecting the lifeless creatures to charge them, but they were held back. Juliana's eyes were tightly closed, as she held the blessed sword in both hands upright before her. The blade shed a holy white light, centered on Juliana and extending outwards, repelling the dead outside the perimeter.

The four looked out to the undead horde that stood shoulder to shoulder, surrounding them. Everyone pressed in closer, to stay bet bathed in the protective light.

"Juliana, how long will the light protect us?" Madok asked, as he positioned himself back-to-back to her.

"As long as I boldly hold the blade and concentrate, The Mother will shroud us in her protection. However, the sword is growing heavier." Juliana felt her energy drawn from her and channeled through the sword.

Flynn looked to the boarded window he first entered, beyond the horde of dead. Esma was in hybrid rat form, crouched on the sill, unnoticed by the others holding a large leather bag. Another wererat shared the sill with her holding a torch. The dead barbarian numbers were at their thinnest on the direct path to that window. Their number before the cathedral doors would be unpassable.

"Esma!" Flynn bumped Madok with his elbow.

"I can't see! What's going on?" Izzy desperately tried jumping up to see, but it was impossible behind the rows of dead warriors.

Esma withdrew a round clay flask with an oil-soaked cloth stuffed into its neck from the bag. She held it out for her wererat companion to set alight with his torch. Once ignited, she tossed it into the crowd before them. It shattered on impact against the head of a barbarian, whose red beard scrawled down to its belly. Burning oil covered the creature and splashed its closest comrades, engulfing them in flames.

Fire was an effective weapon against Naamah's soldiers, as the flames consumed their dry flesh and set alight centuries old hides they wore. More of the clay flasks were released upon the undead soldiers, but they didn't retreat. Instead, some of their numbers split and marched towards Esma's position. From the opposite side of the cathedral, more wererats lobbed lit flasks into the crowd of dead, also drawing their numbers away.

An effective diversion was created.

Izzy transformed into hybrid rat form and scurried across the floor away from the hoard. Dodging swings from weapons and ducking between their legs, she navigated to another boarded window, where another pair of wererats broke through. She was hoisted up by the pair, then pushed out the window to safety.

"Friends, Izzy made it. We should follow her lead!" Flynn pointed to the wererats waving them over.

The numbers of the creatures had thinned with their force divided, so Juliana could lead the trio to the awaiting rescuers. The sword continued to repel the dead blocking their path, giving them an easy egress. Fire was spreading throughout the cathedral. The rafters, that had been extinguished by Randall a short time before, were once again threatened as flames climbed the wooden pillars.

A scream across the cathedral caught Madok's attention, as he was pulled up to the ledge. A wererat was pulled from another window ledge by a barbarian engulfed in flames, then tossed into the awaiting hoard. The wererat disappeared and its screams silenced, as the dead dismembered it.

Flynn was pulled up next and Juliana stood her ground, as the dead focused their attention on her. Flynn was pushed through the window, joining Madok and Izzy in the courtyard. Other members of Esma's gang were nearby in human form, keeping watch from a safer distance and keeping the route to the sewer clear.

Izzy watched the window waiting for Juliana to appear, as Esma ran toward them now in human form.

"Quickly, we can take cover below before their attention is drawn to us." Esma urged, catching her breath.

Two wererats jumped from the window back into the courtyard with the others. Noticeably without Juliana.

"Juliana?" Madok grabbed one of the rat men by the arm and looked into its red glowing eyes. The creature shook its head and pulled away.

"It was too late. We were being overrun by those things. We must leave before they follow!" Esma spoke hurriedly, urging them to join the others in the alleyway.

Izzy squeaked, and climbed the cathedral wall to the window.

"Izzy, no!" Flynn called out, as she pulled herself up on the ledge.

A mummified hand reached through the window, grabbing for her, but she tumbled back to the ground. More barbarians appeared in the broken windows, climbing over one another to escape as smoke and fire poured through.

Izzy transformed back into her dirty street urchin self and was snatched up by Madok. Kicking and twisting, she fought to free herself from under his arm. Flynn and Madok joined the other fleeing wererats to the entrance of the sewers with Izzy.

"Take her! Don't let her go!" Madok passed Izzy to Esma, as Flynn descended into the darkness.

"Madok, Juliana!" Izzy cried, as Esma handed her off to another waiting wererat.

Madok swore. "I am not abandoning her."

Esma nodded at Madok, and she climbed down into the darkness. The last rat man pulled the iron cover into place over the sewer hole. Madok ran back into the courtyard, as the undead barbarians were now escaping the burning cathedral through the windows and the front doors.

Madok swallowed, preparing himself for an unwinnable fight; a barbarian took notice of him and advanced. The last of the creatures pulling themselves through the windows, fell to the cobblestone ground engulfed in flames. They tried to advance, but the flames consumed them wholly, reducing their remains to blackened embers.

"Juliana!" Madok called out, scanning the approaching crowd of dead filing out across the courtyard against the backdrop of an inferno. There would be no wizard's magic to squelch the flames now, as it raged out of control.

The first barbarian reached Madok with a great axe, held in a tight grip in its skeletal hands. Its mummified skin on its face stretched and split, as it opened its mouth giving only a silent war cry. Madok dodged the creature's swing and spun about, thrusting his blade deep into its flank then pulling it free. It made no reaction to the gaping gash in its desiccated skin. More dead barbarians approached Madok, as he parried and dodged the swings of the axe man.

A quick change of strategy was needed. Madok circled to its rear and dropped to a knee. He slashed through the dead man's leg below the knee, as it swung its great axe. The creature lost balance and crashed to the ground. It made attempts to rise on one leg, but continued to fall, as its comrades closed in, encircling Madok. Hopelessness set in.

"Madok!" Juliana's voice carried across the courtyard.

Madok looked through the crowd and called back to her. There was a parting in the hoard of the dead, as Juliana advanced through their ranks with the Sword of Vittoria held before her, shining its holy light. Juliana appeared drained as she pressed forward, as if she were trudging through thick mud.

Madok was fending off the attacks of two undead barbarians, as the one-legged one held his leg. He wriggled free of its grasp, rolling aside as another barbarian swung an axe past his head.

Juliana pushed forward, and as the sword's holy light touched the creatures engaged with Madok they retreated. Flames engulfing the gables of the cathedral consumed the timbers, and the roof collapsed. Black smoke poured from the windows and the boards that covered them were all charred embers. The heat and acrid smell of smoke made the square a hellish landscape.

Flaming debris from the cathedral was caught by the wind and soon the fire was spreading onto the wooden roof of the Merchant's Guildhall. The city of Redrock was in danger, as the chaos ensued in its streets. The barbarian dead were indifferent to any of it. Or maybe even oblivious? They encircled Madok and Juliana, just out of the sword's protective light, even as burning debris landed amid their outer ranks.

"We will be burned alive if we remain here! Push forward through them." Madok urged.

Juliana nodded, with a bead of sweat dripping off the tip of her nose and her dirty blonde hair stuck to the sides of her face. Slowly she moved forward with the sword held before her, growing even heavier. The barbarians were just out of reach, but they followed along, keeping them surrounded as they made their retreat. Madok wiped his brow with one hand, while looking for any openings to take advantage of.

The undead barbarian's numbers parted to the south, opening a way out of the smoke and flames. Madok was quick to catch this and saw a chance for them to make their retreat through an alley. He made a quick tug on Juliana's arm, drawing her attention.

"This is it. We will need to run now!" Madok shouted and Juliana acknowledged with another weak nod of her head.

Madok ran forward through the opening, which widened, as the dead parted the way to draw him out. Behind Madok, the dead filled the gap, separating him from Juliana. Madok found himself outside the circle of the barbarian dead, yet they didn't approach him. Instead, they all faced Juliana in their center.

"Juliana!" Madok called out to her. The holy light of the sword continued to hold the enemy at bay, but Juliana was hidden in the crowd.

Juliana closed her eyes and mouthed the words of a prayer to The Mother, to deliver Madok to safety if she were to fall. The dead stood at attention around her, unwavering. They waited for her faith to falter and the protection of the sword to fail.

Madok moved toward the dead men he just escaped, preparing to fight his way back to Juliana. The outer ranks turned to face him as he approached, but did not raise their weapons against him. Their empty eye sockets stared beyond him. Madok stopped and spun to check his flank all too late.

Searing pain pierced his belly where Naamah's sword was thrust. She became visible once she made her sneak attack on Madok. Madok's longsword clattered, as it fell from his hand to the cobblestones. With a push from her foot, she pulled it from his belly. Madok pressed his hands to the wound, as he doubled over and collapsed.

Once again, the barbarian dead parted a path directly to where Madok lay and Naamah stood over him. Holding her bloodied blade in one hand, she outstretched her feathery wings, then folded them behind her. Her naked form was splashed with Madok's blood, as well as the dried blood of Captain Ashdown. Her glowing red eyes looked from her fallen foe up to Juliana. She smiled and kicked Madok over onto his back, while he still clutched his opened belly. The flow of blood spread onto the cobblestone beneath him. Naamah pushed the tip of her blade to Madok's chest.

"Cast down the sword and surrender to me and I will spare him. Refuse, and you both will perish here and now." Naamah purred her offer to Juliana.

Madok turned his head to Juliana, locking eyes with her. In his weakened state, he could only mouth the word, "Don't."

Juliana knew that the she would never be true to her word and the only advantage she had was the Sword of Vittoria, which protected her from the reach of the dead warriors. Ridding the world of this entity would be the best way to serve The Mother. Madok knew this as well and was ready to face death.

"I do not seek to save our mortal lives, only to return you to The Hells, to suffer eternal torment." Juliana proclaimed, with great resolve.

Naamah's brow furrowed with a deep crease and her feral eyes glowed bright red. She looked down at Madok, who's eyes were now dimming, though still locked on Juliana. Naamah stomped down on Madok's throat, and with a twist, she ended his life. She looked up at Juliana and hissed. "Come then!"

Juliana screamed, finding the strength to charge forward through the path left open by the dead hoard. Naamah smiled, then vanished.

Madok lay just feet before her and the barbarian dead behind her didn't move. Juliana went on the defensive, preparing for the devil to reappear and strike her from behind. Juliana listened to the sounds around her, hoping Naamah's position may be given away by the flap of her feathery wings. The remaining portion of the cathedral's roof collapsed with an explosion of flaming embers, denying Juliana the warning.

Juliana cried out, as the dagger Naamah hurled plunged into her thigh, and became visible again. Juliana dropped to one knee and the grip on the sword loosened as she fought to hold onto it. The dagger was coated with venom that was weakening her further. She looked in Madok's lifeless eyes and was overcome with hopelessness.

"You will lay down that sword and submit to me." Naamah slowly stepped forward with her blade pointing at Juliana.

Juliana looked Naamah in the eye, pulling the dagger from her thigh and tossing it away. Blood trickling down her leg, as she forced herself to stand. Naamah smiled and her red eyes flickered from pure anger to amusement.

Juliana pointed the sword at Naamah, challenging her. Juliana tried to put on a brave face and ignore the pain, but Naamah saw through her, reveling in her suffering.

"The poison will not kill you, but it will immobilize you. The crippling pain will soon consume your entire body, and you will lay at my feet begging me to end your suffering. Lay down the sword and it will not have to end that way." Naamah smiled, as she took another step forward.

Juliana felt any moment that her legs could buckle beneath her. She knew The Blessed Sword of Vittoria prevented the devil from approaching her, the same as it did the dead. This was only as long as she was able to keep the sword in hand and concentrate on its protective powers. The venom was spreading into her back now and her face drained of color. Her leg was crimson with her own blood, and grew dizzy as her body temperature rose. Her sword arm grew numb, and her grip loosened on the blade.

The sword dropped from her hand and Juliana dropped to both knees, with her eyes locked with the devil's. Naamah smiled broadly and began to cover the ground between them, raising her sword to strike. Juliana spotted the silhouette of a small figure charging out of the alleyway into the square.

"Izzy, stand down!" Juliana screamed.

Ignoring Juliana's command, she leapt onto Naamah's back, wrapping her legs around the devil's waist and an arm around the neck. Izzy's rat eyes glowed red with rage, as she plunged the dagger repeatedly into Naamah's side.

Naamah spread her wings out and violently flapped them to shake the rat girl from her back, as she spun about. She grabbed Izzy's little arm and then with a yank dislodged her from her back swinging her overhead before slamming her to ground.

Naamah touched the wounds on her side and examined her black blood as it dripped from her fingers. Izzy lay on the ground struggling to breathe, before losing consciousness. In one hand she still held the dagger and in the other a handful of Naamah's white feathers.

"Enough of this! Kill them!" Naamah commanded her army of dead warriors to finish the task.

The mummified barbarians did not move. Naamah's eyes went back to Juliana. Juliana held the sword once again in her hand and her other hand pressed on the wound. She spoke the words of healing, and the light of The Mother glowed around her hand, surging into her thigh. Blood vessels joined together and the deep wound that cut into her flesh deep into muscle, sealed up, repairing the tissues from the inside to the surface. Her leg was drenched in her own blood as was the healing hand, but the venom from Naamah's blade still coursed through her veins. She would not bleed out, but the poison was weakening her further. Juliana rose to her feet and once again pointed the weapon at Naamah.

"You will return to The Hells!" Juliana addressed the devil with the sword of Vittoria leveled at her.

Naamah's face contorted as she made an unworldly roar in rage. Her brow furrowed with deep lines, her fair skin reddened and her white wings darkened to black, as if they were charred in the fires of the underworld. The totality of Naamah's true appearance was unveiled, as her feet transformed into cloven hooves and her legs took on a bestial appearance, with her knees bending in the opposite direction.

"I will be bringing you with me, fool!" Naamah's voice now had a dark, deep threatening resonance, absent of all feminine tonality.

Naamah and Juliana faced off, eyes locked on the others, in the heat and smokey haze. Naamah's hooves clopped on the worn cobblestones, in contrast to the light click of Juliana's boots. Naamah smiled, as Juliana struggling with the venom spreading into her other leg, fell to the ground.

From out of the smoke, Izzy appeared and was joined by Esma and the other wererats. Pushing through the smoke and fire and past the barbarian undead, they caught Naamah off her guard. Only Izzy's enchanted blade was able to cut through the devil's flesh. The other wererats grappled Naamah's arms and legs, pushing her away from Juliana.

Naamah flung her attackers off one at a time with brute force, but another would take its place. Izzy's dagger was a bane to Naamah, with each stab black blood issued forth from the wound, spattering her in the tar like gore. Naamah's sword arm was free, and she still had strength to make quick work of two of her attackers, that were not quick enough to dodge the swing of her cursed blade. Esma pulled Izzy away and held her back.

Naamah's visage took on more pronounced diabolic features, as her rage grew. She raised her sword in both hands again, readying to finish off the nuisance before her. A roof of another building engulfed in flames collapsed with a loud crash, sending more embers into the square. The light of the sun was blocked by thick smoke, as only the glow of the fires illuminated the scene in a color spectrum of reds, yellows, and orange.

Naamah, shrugged off the pain of her wounds and pushed forward toward Esma, who stood defiantly with her sword in hand. Naamah's sword struck Esma's sword, breaking it in a shower of sparks. Esma fell back on Izzy and both hit the ground. Naamah raised her blade again to finish her foes.

Naamah stopped before she made the killing blow. From her belly, a bright white light grew, as the Sword of Vittoria broke through the skin. Juliana held onto the blade and pushed with her remaining strength, until the hilt stopped it from going further. Naamah's wings buffeted wildly, as she fought to fly but was kept grounded by the defiant Juliana, who held tightly to the sword.

Naamah's wings slowed as her life force escaped, and her strength waned. She dropped her sword and collapsed to her knees, as black blood bubbled from her mouth. The Mother guided Juliana's hand to perform the coup de grâce, just as Naamah had done many times before. Juliana drew the sword from Naamah's body and in one graceful swing, decapitated the devil before she fell to ground.

Juliana fell to one knee, and then the other. Izzy threw her arms around her. Juliana balanced herself with the glowing sword and squeezed Izzy with her free arm. Esma looked about the square at the bodies of her kin, reverted into human form after their deaths from Naamah's cursed blade. Others, now engaged in combat with Naamah's dead fighters in the hellish environment.

The head and body of Naamah instantly putrefied, and the skin bubbled off the skeleton into a thick black ichor. Soon even the bones and ichor evaporated away, leaving behind only the sword forged from The Hells.

The barbarian bog mummies immediately stopped all movement. The defeat of their general ended her command over them. The creatures stood in place, lowering their ancient weapons. Wererats engaged in combat stopped and cautiously backed away. The barbarian dead crumbled where they stood, into moldering piles of bone, mummified flesh, and rotted gear. The Duke's contractual obligations made by Dysvakar, were null and void.

Esma and Izzy returned to human form and helped support Juliana, after she sheathed the sword and collapsed again.

"The poison… I can't fight it anymore." Juliana strained to speak.

Esma nodded and took Juliana's arm. "We need to escape to the safety beneath the city before we become trapped in the fire. I can treat you there."

"Madok…" Izzy cried, pointing to his body as she held onto Juliana's other arm.

"We have lost many of those we loved today, but we don't have time to mourn them just yet, child. We must hurry." Esma urged Izzy along, while guiding Juliana through the square to the alleyway, to make their egress.

Wererats in hybrid and human form returned below, to the safety of the sewers as the fire raged from the center of the city spreading unchecked building to building. The black smoke could be seen for miles away to the Redrock Mountains, beyond the Ironwood Forest, or as near as Castle Redrock.

58
Showdown

R andall slowly opened his eyes and was face to face with a gargoyle. The statue-like creature knelt over, him wringing its clawed hands, looking at Randall as if he were a treat. A string of drool fell from the corner of its mouth to the ground, just missing Randalls face.

"He's not for eating idiot! Just do as you were told and watch over him!" Olga shouted at the ever-hungry beast.

The creature snorted, bared its teeth, then took a few steps back to its original position, eyes locked on the wizard.

Olga looked over the crenellated tower wall at the city below. Fires raged, mostly unchallenged, through the city into the evening. The city below was an inferno and glowed as it was being consumed. The smell of smoke was heavy in the air.

Randall's hands were not bound and he still had his tongue. The hag's blow to his head took him out for hours, and left him with a horrible headache. He was able to speak, but lacked material components to perform the magic to escape from the tower.

"Uh, ma'am. Any chance of getting a drink. I'm a bit parched from the day's events." Randall asked politely.

Auntie Olga looked over at Randall, who was laid out on the roof. "You'll get nothing. I'd prefer that moron eat your innards before you, while you still breathe. However, The Duke wants you whole."

The gargoyle licked its chops.

Randall scanned the rest of the tower top and saw the large brass brazier in the center of the floor.

"Uh, ma'am. Any chance I may be able to use a privy before he returns?" Randall asked, just because.

Olga cringed. "Soil yourself where you lay. You're not going anywhere."

Randall sat up, causing the gargoyle to respond with an angry 'grunt.' It made one hop over to him and with one finger pushed Randall's head back to the ground. The creature snorted, then backed up to its original position.

"Ma'am, would it be too much trouble if I were to sit on that bench over there? It's quite uncomfortable here." Randall asked politely.

Auntie Olga was growing more irritated with the young wizard. "Boy, your comfort should be of no concern as you will not be breathing much longer."

Randall knew his situation was dire, but if The Duke and Naamah were not around, it wasn't completely hopeless. "So, The Duke wants to have a talk with me? Will we be expecting him back soon?"

"Quite soon. In fact, he is returning." The hag pointed into the night sky, toward the small figure flying toward the tower.

Duke Payne was personally searching for Captain Miles and Princess Danica. They escaped successfully that morning on horseback with several days' provisions. The city was in total chaos and there were no guards to maintain order, as all had abandoned their posts. Without General Naamah and her company of dead barbarian warriors, another favor would need to be called in from Dysvakar.

The Duke touched down onto the tower, in his embroidered purple slippers that covered his boney feet. The sockets in his skull burned with a furious red glow.

The gargoyle cowered and retreated to its perch, a few steps at a time. Randall propped himself up on one arm and shielded his eyes from The Duke's burning gaze.

"Naamah failed me! She allowed the rest of his companions to escape and leave my city to burn to the ground!" The Duke furiously waved his arms, pacing the tower top.

"Your Royal Highness, all is ready. Shall I light the brazier and begin the ritual?" Auntie Olga asked timidly.

The Duke looked over to Randall, who was studying the rooftop layout. Nodding his skull, he reluctantly replied. "Yes, no more delays."

The coals of the brass brazier were set alight and the ritual commenced. The red coals began to glow green, sending magical green flames roaring high into the sky. Auntie Olga refrained from performing the throat singing, which offended Dysvakar's musical sensibilities.

While Payne and Olga were preoccupied, the gargoyle hopped up to its perch, fearful of who was being summoned. It quietly flew off into the smoke-filled sky, abandoning its post, resigning without giving notice.

Randall slowly rose to his feet, noticing their attention was on the brazier. The gargoyle had the right idea, and its sudden departure wasn't noticed by The

Duke. The door down into the tower was open, with a wedge of warm yellow light beckoning him.

The green fire formed a vortex that rapidly turned into a pillar of flame high into the air, bathing everything in a green glow. From that pillar of flame, the disembodied head of Dysvakar appeared. Once again, a direct line of communication was formed from The Hells into this world. Dysvakar cast his gaze first upon Olga, then to The Duke. He appeared very displeased.

"My Lord, O great Dysvakar. I wish to—" The Duke began his address to his benefactor, but was cut short.

"Silence! Payne, it has not even been one moon cycle since you last called on me. I was in an important meeting with a couple of demonic contractors. I hired them to oversee the renovations on the vacation palace I purchased from Beelzebub over a millennia ago. I should have known what to expect, signing a contract with The Lord of Lies. My goodness, I should have inspected that dump, but I bought it sight unseen, just because it overlooks a rather spectacular lake of fire. Now I'm dealing with crumbling ramparts, sagging roof, bad foundation, and it's so poorly insulated I'm heating a whole level of hell. Now, if I don't keep on top of them, they will waste another millennium, with the idiot work crew of damned souls, they recruited from the 9th level of The Hells. Fortunately, I'm paying them for the complete job and not at the normal century rate. So, what is it this time?" Dysvakar scowled.

Payne and Auntie Olga both bowed and took one knee. Olga kept her head bowed, as The Duke looked up at the green fiery visage of Dysvakar.

"My Lord, I just wish to offer the sacrifice of the young wizard ahead of the New Moon. To show my gratitude, for all you have done for me as your most loyal servant." The Duke then bowed his head.

"Well, well, well. This is a nice little treat." Dysvakar managed a smirk, even though he was quite irritated.

"Bring forth the prisoner!" Duke Payne called out to his gargoyle guardian, followed by an uncomfortably long silence.

The Duke stood and looked across the entire rooftop. No gargoyle and no Randall. He slapped the kneeling Auntie Olga in the head, to get her attention. Olga rose to her feet and looked across the rooftop as well.

The Duke motioned for Auntie Olga to track down the elusive sacrifice. The hag backed away from the brazier, with a low bow, then ran around the rooftop looking in, out, and around any place a young wizard might hide, while cursing under her breath.

Dysvakar shook his head and rolled his devilish eyes. "Payne, you are really getting my dander up! Is General Naamah there with you? I want a report from her of your affairs on that world." Dysvakar frowned with one eyebrow cocked, wrinkling his bald head.

"Um, no my Lord. The general has retired to her chambers now." The Duke would be sweating, if he still had the flesh covering his skull to do so. It could take a year before Naamah's soul would return to The Hells, where she could fill Dysvakar in in person. Payne hoped he could form a cover story in the interim.

The conversation between Payne and Dysvakar continued, as Olga finally realized Randall left the rooftop altogether and had delved into the tower from the roof entrance and barred the door. The conversation behind her was getting heated, as she knew Dysvakar could see through all deception Payne was presenting him with. She dared not interrupt to avoid Dysvakar's ire turned on her.

Randall was once again in The Duke's laboratory. He knew time was of the essence and it wouldn't be long before they found him. Scattered on tables were pieces of parchment, containing spells and of course the small jars of the material components, needed for casting spells required for them. It looked as if The Duke may have been writing down from memory, spells from the book Randall had stolen from his library. This was exactly what Randall was hoping to get back into the tower for.

Randall heard noise coming from the door up the stairs. That bar he put into place, was there to deter a nosey gargoyle, but would do nothing to prevent Duke Payne or the hag from passing. He grabbed the papers under his arm and stuffed his pockets with components, as quickly as he could empty them from the jars. Dropping balls of guano and insect husks in his pockets, was the price of doing the business of a wizard. Retrieving the right ingredient for the appropriate spell would be his main challenge. The last item was a small clear piece of quartz from a wooden bowl holding a variety of colorful crystals

He appropriated as much of Payne's property as he could grab and was determined to make a quick exit from the tower, through the ground floor of the castle. He had no idea what become of his friends since he was stolen away, and imagined they escaped Redrock together. He was on his own now and hoped his friends were safe.

Randall left the laboratory to use the express levitation portal to the ground floor. He approached the first portal and the magical glyphs that circled it glowed, waiting for him to step into it. He felt he might make it out.

Auntie Olga's long boney fingers grabbed Randall by the collar of his tunic, and with a quick tug pulled him out of the portal just as he stepped in. She tossed him against the wall, causing him to drop the papers tucked under his arm. Randall slid to the ground, dazed.

Olga cackled, as she lifted Randall up by his throat, until his feet dangled above the floor. Her grip was tight, and her sharp nails dug into his skin. Randall gasped for breath, as he tried to break her hold with both of his hands.

"I'm done playing with you, boy. We will leave all that right there for now. He awaits." Olga snarled.

The hag lowered Randall back on his feet and pushed him into the laboratory. "You think you're a clever mortal? Your soul will face eternal torment after you are removed from this world."

The pair climbed the stairs, with Randall in front, prodded forward by the hag and her sharp nails. The Duke stood before the giant green head of the devil, receiving further admonishment as they approached from behind.

"Kneel before our Lord, the Great Dysvakar!" Auntie Olga commanded Randall, as she gave him one last strong shove in the back.

Randall stumbled forward a few steps toward the floating head, then dropped to his knees shaking. Duke Payne turned to look at the young wizard, then back to Dysvakar. The devil looked down his nose on Randall without any change of expression for a short moment, then blinked a few times before turning his gaze back to The Duke.

"So, this is the one that has gotten the best of you over and over again?" The disembodied head of Dysvakar, rolled his eyes and 'tisk-tisked' Duke Payne.

Payne was offended, holding his rage in check, but the red points of light in his sockets began to burn brighter. "My Lord, it was only a setback. He's a formidable foe, thus making his soul a most suitable sacrifice."

The hag grabbed Randall's hair tightly in her hand, pulling his head back to look up at Dysvakar. Randall was bathed in the flickering green light of the flames of the devil's head. He looked down upon the wizard, whose face shown the abuse of Auntie Olga. Randall averted his eyes across to The Duke who held the same sacrificial dagger Naamah used to take the life of Bishop Caitlan.

Dysvakar looked down on the wizard, expressionless. "By what name do you go by, boy?"

"Uh, R-Randall sir." Randall was shaking uncontrollably.

"Randall? Not the name I would expect a 'powerful' wizard, that is making a fool of my thralls to go by. You should probably think about changing that to something a bit more foreboding and mysterious. Something that would command respect. Like, 'Sebastian caller of the Firestorm,' or 'Ballard Blight Bringer.' Those names would be remembered and people would shudder in fear when they heard them. The name Randall has the same impact as, let's say 'Archie.'" Dysvakar rolled his eyes when saying the last name.

Auntie Olga stifled a snicker. Duke Archie fumed.

"Sir, I would take that into consideration. However, I don't think I'll have the chance." Randall said with a squeak.

"My Lord, I offer you this soul as a token of my gratitude, in debt of my servitude to you. When the life of this mortal is extinguished and his soul delivered to you, I humbly ask that I be granted a favor again, to better serve you, O great Dysvakar!" The Duke knew he was asking too much of the arch devil, but everything was crumbling before him.

Randall heard the exchange between Payne and Dysvakar's avatar, but did not hear the actual words they spoke. He was reviewing his mistakes in life, that lead him to where he was now. His betrayal of Master Williamson, by stealing the magic tome from his private library and abandoning his studies. Coming into the employment of the Lord Mayor of Port Gwynn, and conspiring with him and his cronies to enrich themselves. Bringing the attention of Duke Archibald Payne, to himself and his only real friends, leading to their pain and suffering.

However, Randall also felt his involvement was part of a bigger picture. The Duke brought turmoil and suffering to the realm. The actions he and his friends were taking prevented The Duke's plans from reaching fruition. Were events set into play for a divine plan?

Randall's attention was brought back to the present by the booming voice of Dysvakar, shaking the tower. The Duke's request was denied.

"You are a fool to believe you could hide your failings from me! Too many unpaid debts for the loss of what I bestowed to you. The destruction of my servants Barnabas and Naamah, the defeat of the army of dead warriors, and of course my golden mirror of scrying. I was foolish to entrust you with anything. Yet again, you ask for more of me. I leave you to the devices of this world to suffer whatever doom awaits you. Never call on me again!" Dysvakar's voice caused all to cower with dread and fear.

"My Lord, I beg! Don't abandon me! I have always been your loyal servant!" The Duke, who should never express fear, acted as a frightened child being separated from his mother.

Auntie Olga released her hold on Randall's hair and backed away, much like the traitorous gargoyle, as The Duke pleaded with Dysvakar. She pulled a black stone from her purse and disappeared into the ether. From there she would watch things unfold, and escape any potential harm from fallout between the two.

Silence fell, and the full attention of the head of Dysvakar and Payne, were upon Randall.

Paul Wolff

"This boy made both your servants disappear. That is quite a good trick. Maybe he is the superior wizard." Dysvakar looked across the top of the tower, noting the absence of Auntie Olga and the gargoyle.

Randall didn't want more attention from The Duke. The head of Dysvakar was chuckling, with a diabolical laugh. Duke Payne was also looking across the tower roof, searching for Olga and his gargoyle minion.

"Enough of this!" Payne screamed in his unearthly voice. He went through the motions of casting and spoke the incantation. "Pessulum autem fulgur!"

Randall knew what was coming and threw himself flat on the floor, as the forked blue bolt crackled across, striking the crenelated wall of the tower. Pieces of masonry broke and splintered, showering the tower top with shrapnel, followed by a deafening thunderclap. Randall escaped the full force of the spell, but was covered in dust and had a black scorch mark on his breeches. The smell of the electrified ozone mixed with the smoke of the fires.

No time to waste, he withdrew a ball of bat guano from his pocket and pointed his index finger at The Duke. He returned the favor, speaking the arcane words, "Globus ignis occidere eos!"

A pea sized orange ember flew on its direct path to The Duke, exploding into a bright ball of fire that engulfed half of the rooftop. Payne was thrown off his feet to the ground. The blast area was blackened, and his robes were smoldering.

Dysvakar laughed at the drama unfolding before him, and was impressed with Randall's prowess. "Payne, it would appear you underestimated this young one's command of the arcane arts. Boy, if you would destroy my failed servant, I will reward you with even greater power. You need only swear fealty to me and it will be yours!"

Duke Payne cursed as he arose, patting his garments which were still smoking. Randall was shocked by the Devil's offer, though flattered. Dysvakar's words were clouding Randall's mind. 'Randall the Ruthless' danced around his head briefly. However, Duke Payne was not going to allow him time to daydream.

Payne shouted out. "Succendam eum culi!"

Howling winds blew, and the temperature at the top of the tower dropped, while glowing embers from the burning city floated upward into the night sky. Air rushed past Randall, drawn into The Duke's open hand. The Duke closed his hand into a fist, as if he caught a ball and made the motion of an overhand throw.

At the end of the follow through, a blast of the collected wind was released and concentrated on the young wizard's position. Randall lost his balance and was flung through the air to the crenellated wall of the tower. Randall clung to the edge of the tower wall. The gust had the strength of a hurricane wind, and he struggled to keep his grip as flying debris pelted him.

Dysvakar laughed at the spectacle playing out before him. The discord, brought forth from his influence in this world, gave him pleasure. The disruption of the faithful to the gods from The Heavens, was a win to the rulers of The Hells. There would be others to tempt to do his bidding, if The Duke defeated the young wizard.

The wall was weakened by the lightning bolt and the wind caused it to crumble and fall far below, onto the rooftop of Redrock Castle. Randall was not able to open his eyes, nor speak as his grip was slipping in the deafening winds.

Payne kept his spell concentrated on Randall as he walked toward him. Dysvakar's full attention was also on Randall and Payne. Neither noticed the small clawed hands, reaching over the opposite side of the tower.

Izzy struggled to pull herself over the crenellated wall, then dropped to the floor. She drew her curved blade and crouched down in her hybrid rat form. Nervously, she took everything in.

Another clawed hand followed, and Flynn pulled himself over the crenellated wall, dropping next to Izzy. He followed her through the tunnels of the undercity for hours, to find a safe way to reach the castle from the raging fires. Flynn kept up with his young companion, in his weakened state. No other wererats dared follow. Izzy would not let Mr. Randall suffer a cruel fate without her intervention.

Izzy slinked across the tower that was bathed in the light of the green flames of the brass brazier. Flynn attempted to grab the hem of her dress, but she was too quick. The rat girl charged The Duke, leaping to backstab him with the enchanted dagger.

The dagger plunged into The Duke's back through his regal robes, disrupting his spell. The winds ceased immediately and Izzy pulled the blade loose, then stabbed again.

The Duke spun around with the dagger lodged in his ribs. Izzy dropped and rolled, as he reached to pull the blade free. "Filthy vermin! You are finished!"

Dysvakar observed without speaking any words. Randall pulled himself back to the rooftop, before the stone he was holding broke away and tumbled to the ground far below. Izzy was darting around in attempt to get behind The Duke to get her blade, but he was too quick.

The Duke spoke the words of another spell. "Sursum et auferet!"

His feet lifted from the tower rooftop as the spell took effect. Izzy made a running jump and grabbed hold of his leg.

"Izzy! Let go!" Flynn called out.

Duke Payne tried to shake her off, but Izzy held tight. She did not weigh enough to pull him down, but she was slowing his climb. Payne reached down and touched Izzy's hand, speaking the incantation. "Fulgur!"

The blue charge of the electric sparks transferred from his hand to Izzy's and she dropped to the roof with a loud squeak. Duke Payne made the attempt to gain elevation, but now Flynn took action. He mustered what remaining strength and jumped for his legs. He held on, as they lifted off from the roof and moved toward the edge.

Izzy sprung up grabbing onto Flynn's leg, and scurried up his body, until she was clinging to Duke Payne's robes. The combined weight of the two were pulling The Duke downwards. Izzy pulled her dagger free to make another attack.

"Fulgur!" The Duke again used his magic, discharging the electrical shock of blue sparks into Flynn's arm.

Flynn's hold was broken and he dropped to the rooftop. Izzy plunged the dagger again into the The Duke's back as she held on with her legs.

"Mr. Randall!" Izzy made a desperate plea for the young wizard to come to their aid.

Randall stood up and looked at the fiery green visage of Dysvakar floating above the brazier. The Arch Devil intently waited to see Randall's next move. Duke Payne was again rising high above the tower, with Izzy clinging on with one arm. The Duke was desperately trying to reach Izzy, but the nimble wererat dodged each time.

"Randall, do something!" Flynn called to him, as he pulled himself up.

Dysvakar looked at Randall with one eye cocked, intently waiting for his reaction. Desperately, Randall dug his hand into his pockets, moving around the components he lifted from The Duke's laboratory. He withdrew the clear quartz. Randall was compelled to use another power he learned from that wand.

The Duke was ten feet above the tower roof, when he made contact with Izzy. The electric shock made Izzy lose her hold and she fell, crashing onto the tower roof. Flynn pulled her away.

Duke Payne's eyes now appeared as flames, that licked out the empty sockets. His fury was to be unleashed, as he prepared a spell to annihilate all those that were on the tower. He gestured with his arms and spoke the words to invoke the incantation. "Ignea meteoris destruere inimicos!"

The night sky that was black with soot, now had tumultuous clouds of fire red rolling in from above, looming low and heavy. The sound of low rumbling from the sky shook the ground, setting vibrations up from the foundations to the top of tower.

Duke Payne circled over head, as Flynn covered Izzy with his body and Randall fought to keep his footing. Payne pointed his finger down at the tower roof and in his unearthly voice spoke. "Perdere!"

From the sky, an explosion erupted with a blinding flash of light. A fiery meteor fell out of the red sky with a trail of smoke and debris trailing behind it. The missle crashed into the side of the tower and exploded with a ball of flame, collapsing a small section of the outer wall. Randall lost his footing, as the tower shook.

The brazier teetered and the head of Dysvakar flickered, but then came back strong. He looked up at The Duke and then to Randall, watching intently. The Duke high above, was preparing to summon forth another meteor.

"Mr. Randall!" Izzy forced her way out from under her protector, who pulled her back under his arms.

Randall stood and held the clear quartz crystal in his hand toward Payne. He spoke loudly the words of the incantion and made a figure eight motion. "Glacies murus!"

There was another loud explosion in the sky, summoning forth another fiery meteor. Randall continued to make the figure eight motion with the crystal, even as he appeared to be directly in the meteor's trajectory. The crystal glowed brightly and a silver ray shot forth toward Duke Payne.

A sphere of ice formed in the sky, targeted directly on The Duke, who became entrapped in its center. The thick ball of ice crashed onto the rooftop of the tower. Planks on the rooftop cracked, but held. The opaque ice ball rolled, until it came to rest against the crenellated tower wall.

The meteor tracing downward through the sky fizzled out harmlessly, as The Duke's spell was disrupted. The summoned red clouds disolved into the black of the night sky. The only sound now, was the inferno raging far below in the city.

"Well done, boy. Archibald Payne always proved to be quite annoying. I see you as someone with great potential." Dysvakar congratulated Randall as the victor in the duel.

"Thank you, sir. I don't understand why you would praise me for this. The Duke who served you loyally, held power and influence and greater command of magic. I'm nobody." Randall said, nervously.

"Yes, but he is a fool, and an uncharismatic one at that. In you I see potential, that I will help groom and mould, into one that can wield true power. One that would reap great rewards for helping me spread my sphere of influence in your world." The devil smirked and nodded his fiery visage with approval.

Paul Wolff

"I, I don't know. Something doesn't feel right about this." Randall felt Dysvakar's words were tempting him toward the corrupt path Duke Payne followed.

Dysvakar continued with his pitch to Randall. "We will have time to discuss this further in greater detail. All you need do is think what more you can achieve with this mortal life in my service. There is just a small investment and sacrifice you would need for a binding contract. A small price for-"

The brazier tipped over with a crash and the glowing green coals scattered on the tower roof extinguished, going cold black. The disembodied head of the Arch Devil Dysvakar flickered out. The line of communication from this world to The Hells was broken. Flynn and Izzy stood behind the brazier in their exhausted human forms.

Flynn shook his head and looked at Randall. "I didn't care much for the path that conversation was going."

Izzy looked at Randall with her arms crossed, shaking her head. "Juliana would not have liked that one bit."

Attention was drawn away from the conversation, back to the sphere of ice. A red glow grew from within its core. As it grew brighter the frozen exterior of the sphere sweated and water puddled around it. The interior glow grew and the silhouette of The Duke could be seen moving from within.

"That may have been just a temporary delay to our problems." Randall pointed at the ice sphere, which had steam escaping from fissures forming over its surface.

Before the three could make another move, Duke Payne's ice prison exploded in a ball of fire. Ice shards that would have acted as fatal shrapnel, instantaneously evaporated from the heat of the magic fire. Payne brushed off his robes, while looking defiantly upon his foes.

As the three picked themselves of the ground, The Duke prepared a spell to finish the interlopers off. He traced a sigil in the air with his hand, as he began speaking the words to the incantation.

"Don't let him finish!" Randall shouted to his companions, as he charged Duke Payne.

Izzy and Flynn followed suit, rushing him, as the sigil was being replicated on the ground before them, in a barely discernable golden glow. Randall threw himself at The Duke in an effort to disrupt another deadly spell. Payne glided aside and Randall crashed into the wall.

Izzy was next upon him with the glowing curved dagger in hand. Payne evaded the attack of the girl, continuing the spell while gliding up between the crenellations of the tower wall. The gold sigil on top of the tower was almost complete, and the glow bathed everything its golden light.

392

Flynn was the last to reach Payne. He knew if he failed his friends, that more innocents would perish. He threw everything into his running leap and connected with Duke Payne. As he collided with The Duke, he wrapped his arms around his skeletal waist and the two tumbled off of the tower wall.

Izzy screamed and climbed to the top of the wall, looking below for Flynn. "Mr. Randall! Flynn fell!"

The sigil was not complete and its golden light faded, leaving the tower dark. Randall climbed next to Izzy, looking down below. The two had fallen to the rocky cliffside, outside of the city, untouched by the raging fires. From this vantage point in the dark, Randall couldn't make out anything.

"I think I see Flynn!" Izzy pointed.

"What about The Duke?" Randall squinted his eyes.

"Maybe? I'm not sure." Izzy spoke fast and frantically.

There's no quick way for me to get down there, unless I could find a wing feather for that one spell." Randall patted the pockets.

"Mr. Randall! Mr. Randall! I have these!" Izzy pulled a handful of white wing feathers from her pouch and passed them to Randall.

Randall looked at the feathers Izzy plucked from Naamah that morning. "These will work! Hold my hand."

Izzy took Randall's hand, as he spoke the incantation of the spell. Together they stepped off the tower wall and gently floated to the bottom of the cliffside.

Randall picked up a small stone and cast a light spell upon it, to illuminate the area. Izzy already left him behind to reach Flynn, who she spotted not far away. Randall did a quick look around for any sign of Duke Payne lurking about, before following.

Izzy kneeled, sobbing at Flynn's body that lay bloodied and broken from the fall on the rocks. She held his hand to her face, with tears streaming down her cheeks. Randall felt tears welling in his eyes as well, knowing that his friend made the ultimate sacrifice for them. The fall was too far for even a lycanthrope to survive.

He held the stone up higher, shining its light across the rocks and spotted the remains of Duke Payne. He also did not escape the fall. Splintered pieces of bones were strewn about, from impacting on the rocks in the fall. Randall moved in closer and tripped over what he thought was a rock and dropping his light as he broke his fall.

Looking over his shoulder, he realized it was The Duke's skull and not a rock. The jawless cranium sat on the ground, seemingly mocking Randall. Or so he thought. Its sockets were dark now, and the battle won.

Randall sat up and took the skull in both hands, studying it for a moment. "You gave up everything for power and this 'existence?' You were a fool Duke Payne. You brought so much death and suffering for nothing. May you eternally rot in the pits of The Hells."

Pins of red light began to glow in the black sockets of the skull, and intensified as if they were flames licking out from them. Randall yelped and tossed the skull away and crawled backwards across the rocks.

The skull slowly levitated and followed after Randall, as he retreated. Bones scattered about the place scuttled across the ground into a pile.

The skull of Duke Payne glided toward its target, filled with rage and contempt for the mortal who dared defy him.

"Shite! Enough of this, I'm done living in fear of you!" Randall reached up and grabbed the floating skull from out of the air.

He could feel it trying to resist and pull from his grasp, but Randall had his fill. He smashed it against the rocks. Every time he struck it to the ground, the flames in the sockets went dark then reignighted. The other remains of The Duke were pulling together, reforming its skeletal structure.

The skull finally escaped from Randall's bloodied hands and floated toward the skeleton. It was now almost completely reformed, with its jawbone held aloft in one of its hands, waving it for the skull to reattach.

Izzy sprang out of the darkness into the glow of the blue light, leaping atop Duke Payne's skull, taking it to the ground. The enchanted dagger drawn, she plunged it into skull over and over, until it cracked apart and bits splintered away. The fire in the sockets finally dimmed to cold blackness. The skeletal remains that had risen to stand, fell apart and scattered on the ground.

Izzy cried as she walked over to Randall, who took her in his arms for a long hug each patting the other's backs.

"I didn't want to lose you too Mr. Randall." Izzy said, with her voice cracking.

"Nor I you, Izzy. Let's rest here for a moment." Randall released Izzy and fell flat across the rocky ground.

"If we must, Mr. Randall." Izzy curled up next to him, both falling to sleep immediately.

59
Epilogue

Izzy and Mosi walked hand in hand, having navigated their way touring through some of the devastated areas of Redrock. Many buildings were burned to their foundations, others showed signs of major fire damage, and a few inexplicably escaped the fires completely. It took three days for the fires to be brought under control, by Redrock's braver citizens. Most were left to run their course and burned out. This morning the sprinkling of rain helped extinguish the few remaining smoldering areas, leaving the smell of the burn heavy in the air. Esma and her people remained hidden away, beneath the city to wait out the troubles above. They chose not to involve themselves further and turned Randall and company out as soon as they safely could.

It was now a week since the battle on the tower. The pair stood at the apex of a stone bridge that crossed a rivulet, acting as the border of the Low Quarter, home to the many of the capitol city's impoverished citizens. This buffer had spared its inhabitants the loss of what property they had. The night of the fire, they were united in protecting their quarter, with every able-bodied man, woman and child taking part. Izzy pointed out to Mosi the buckets left lying along the riverbank, used by the "bucket brigades." Old dilapidated buildings and shacks serving as homes and places of business, were still standing on this side of the river. On the other were the burned remains of structures of the citizens that had fled through the city gates.

Mosi and Izzy approached Castle Redrock and its tower. Izzy told the story of the events of days prior, and the bravery of Ashdown, Madok, and Flynn. Mosi was traumatized by the captivity of the hags in that tower, only to be watched over by wererats in the dank filth of the city sewers. He only wanted to be out in the open, feeling the rain on his face and to think about his mama and baba, whom he missed dearly, not fully understanding he would never see them again.

Outside the city walls of Redrock many of the citizens that fled had set up camps, making do with what they brought with them. Fear of the unknown was what most faced. There were only rumors circulating of the events leading up to the inferno that destroyed their homes. Many believed The Duke was still in Castle Redrock, and were waiting for him to send help. There were few that saw the barbarian dead marching through the city, slaughtering all in their path. Fewer witnessed Naamah flying overhead and addressing the crowd gathered at the Cathedral, or even The Duke himself, killing the deserters in the guard tower, using dark magic forbidden in his own dukedom. Many citizens believed these to be tall tales created to start dissent against Duke Payne.

Randall and Juliana set up their temporary base camp in the guard barracks, in the bailey of the massive Castle Redrock. Juliana had prayed to The Mother and her healing powers, to neutralize the effects of Naamah's envenomed dagger and now only bared a scar from that wound. The body of Captain Ashdown was never recovered, but Madok and Flynn's remains were buried in the lush grand gardens of Duchess Katherine, that she adored in life. Juliana performed the ceremony with only Randall, Izzy, and Mosi in attendance. Simple wood markers baring their names, marked the graves hidden away off the main pathway, beneath an ancient oak tree. Juliana would visit their gravesides for her morning prayers. She would spend a moment in silent meditation by Madok's marker before leaving.

Food stores from the castle were now being rationed out and distributed to the people. Juliana organized and led this undertaking, with the help of citizen's remaining in the city. Olly was working sunup to sundown in the castle's kitchen, with the help of Puddin' and a team of freshly recruited bakers for the effort. The Great Hall was serving as an infirmary and the surviving sisters, once serving Bishop Caitlan in Redrock Cathedral, now tending the sick and injured.

Randall was shying away from the immediate duties of acting as Juliana's assistant. He even took time to visit Geoffrey, who was still babbling insanely while under the care of the sisters. Randall wished to distance himself from this damned city and get a fresh start elsewhere. Perhaps venture outside of the realm of King Ernald III, to other lands that wouldn't consider his practice of the arcane arts as 'devilry' and be persecuted by its ruler who was in league with a devil. Then he thought of Madeline, and if she was okay, and if she would have feelings for him still.

His tome and the one stolen from The Duke's library, were safe in the magic haversack, which he was once again carried on his person. He dared not leave them anywhere in this city, without them being under his watchful eye.

He was thankful again to Flynn for their safekeeping, after he was stolen away by Naamah.

He hoped to get back into the tower one last time to search it thoroughly at his leisure. There was obviously more knowledge to be gained and interesting artifacts to be discovered. Juliana forbade him to return and made him swear to her that he wouldn't. She wanted everything to be left as it was, when representatives of the King arrived to investigate. Riders were sent out with messages, and of course Randall's story of Princess Danica and Captain Miles escaping, gave hope that help may already be coming.

Randall made a stop at the kitchen and helped himself to a bowl of stew. He felt guilty about the lumps he left on Olly's head, but they were healing on their own nicely. Olly still didn't know what had hit him. Puddin' didn't mind Randall petting him and scratching his ears.

Returning to the castle bailey to join Juliana, he saw riders mounted on warhorses in full plate armor baring the standard of The Kingdom. They were heavily armed and many more were waiting outside the walls of the castle.

Juliana stood before the five soldiers and was speaking with their commanding officer. Randall set his bowl aside to join her.

"Good day kind sirs. We are very happy you have come to take over this operation! It's been a bit overwhelming and this type of work is out of my element." Randall greeted the commander with a bow.

The commander removed his helm and passed it to the man to his right. Scruff from days of riding covered his chin, and his greasy brown hair peeked out from under his arming cap. He looked Randall up and down for a long moment. "Duke Archibald Payne is to be arrested under orders of his Majesty, King Ernald III. Any who aid in resisting will be put to the sword. Stand down, boy."

Juliana looked at Randall and without a word he stepped back, with his arms behind his back and looked down at his shoes.

Juliana gave an approving nod to Randall and turned her attention back to the commander. "Sir, as I told you The Duke is dead. The destruction of the city is directly his doing as is the loss of many innocent lives. Our involvement was from a divine call of The Mother. We will gladly assist with the investigation; all I ask is you allow us to continue helping Redrock's citizens who are in need."

"Madam, this will be taken into consideration as we begin." The commander was of the faith, but he was not trusting of anyone.

Another group entered the castle baily on foot. Princess Danica and Captain Miles was with them, both in shock over the destruction that surrounded them. Danica and Miles had joined the contingency force that was sent out by King Ernald, after communication was lost with the Princess.

Danica pointed at Randall and shouted as they approached. "That one there! I want to talk to him."

Randall looked around, then pointed to himself when his eyes met the princess's. "Me?"

"Yes you! You are the one that escaped The Duke that morning in the castle?" Danica approached Randall, with one hand on the hilt of her sword and the other to her side.

"That was me. I apologize for any inconvenience." Randall nervously expressed himself, best he could.

"You were true to your word, keeping The Duke occupied, while we made our escape. For that I am grateful." Danica put her hand over her heart.

"You're... welcome?" Randall answered sheepishly.

"We saw the smoke from the direction of Redrock filling the sky days before we made it back here. I just couldn't have imagined this. What word of my uncle, The Duke?" Princess Danica asked.

"He is dead. Well, deader than he already was. We were atop that tower when the fighting broke out. My friend sacrificed himself to end this madness and save us." Randall gave the short version.

"What of that wicked devil, General Naamah?" Captain Miles stepped forward and asked.

Juliana answered, this time saddened. "It is dead, along with the force of dead warriors it commanded. The fires decimating the city originated in the battle at the cathedral. We also lost two other friends who fought bravely there, without whom we would not have made it."

"Hey, I was there for both of those!" Barefooted Izzy proclaimed, appearing out of thin air standing between Randall and Juliana, holding Mosi's hand.

Juliana put her hand on Izzy's shoulder and smiled. "Yes, this one is our protector and was key in taking down The Duke and his subordinates."

"Yes, sub-ud-i-nant-sss!" Izzy struggled with that word.

The commander dismounted and looked up at the tower and then around the bailey from where he stood. He then spoke gruffly. "That is a well, but I am under orders by the King to do a full investigation. Since Princess Danica from the original investigating force survived, due to the will of The Mother, she is still under orders to be instated as the viceroy of the former dukedom of Duke Payne. I assume you can show us the remains of Duke Payne?"

Randall spoke up first. "Well, not really. He's mostly scattered about, at the base of the tower. It was a long fall and my friend; Flynn was the priority and not a pile of bones."

"I can take you there!" Izzy raised her hand and jumped a bit.

The commander smiled. "Good, I'll send you with two men and a stretcher to recover the body."

"Oh, you'll just need a sack." Izzy corrected.

The commander got back to business and into character. "Right... Redrock is officially under the protection of King Ernald III and temporary governorship of Princess Danica. You three are to be put under our protective custody within the castle, as the full investigation proceeds. The Grand Inquisitor and his entourage will be arriving within a few days."

"I protest! What I said is true and we agreed to assist." Juliana was taken aback.

Izzy wrapped her arm around Juliana and stood beside her with Mosi. Randall clutched the haversack tighter.

"You will be confined to quarters within the castle, as we proceed with the investigation. You are not prisoners yet and will be allowed out of your room with armed escort of course." The commander announced.

The four complied with the order. As a sign of goodwill, they were not stripped of their weapons, nor Randall his books and allowed their personal belongings. However, they would not be allowed to carry weapons on their person. The four now shared a room that was once a well-appointed guest room, with a balcony overlooking Duchess Katherine's gardens. The chamber was neglected, since there were no servants to keep things perfectly fresh. A single guard was

posted outside the door.

✻✻✻

It had been two days since the arrival of Princess Danica and the King's men, and everyone was getting restless. The well-appointed room as comfortable as it was, began to feel like a prison. Dinner was already digesting in their bellies and the evening sky would be very dark after sunset, for the beginning of the new moon cycle.

Randall kicked his feet up on the desk, after removing his shoes, and poured over his book once again. Juliana sat on the floor with Mosi and was teaching him verses from her small prayer book. Izzy sat at the small table they took all their meals at.

The tray with leftover scraps of food, along with and plates and mugs were pushed to the side. Izzy had taken over the rest of the table with her small spread of belongings. The curved dagger, her lockpicking tools, sorted stacks of coins, a leftover feather from Naamah and other more mundane items, including her bone comb.

The most unusual item, was the small platinum box with gold filigree inlays. Izzy kept it stashed in the bottom of her bag, wrapped in a cloth to protect it. It was forgotten since it did nothing, other than looking pretty. She thought about selling it for more coins, in another town in the future. Now Izzy was just bored and growing more restless. She accompanied the king's men to collect The Duke's bones on the first day, but had not been outside the castle gates since.

"Mr. Randall, some more men came up from Port Sommer to help here in the castle. I overheard them talking about a problem down there with 'rat folk.' Do you suppose that could be the Captain and those sailors from the *Lady Anne*?" Izzy asked, as she ran her thumb across the teeth of the comb.

"Yeah." Randall mumbled and continued reading, without looking up. He had his light stone in hand, to shine a little extra light on the text he was reading. He also nursed a mug of the elusive Grummandy beer. The firkin of the drink sat on the desk for easy access.

"Mr. Randall, I think we should go back there and help them. When someone first gets bit and turns, they don't know how to control themselves when the moon is full for a long time. Maybe I could be their leader, if you would help me! Well, that is if his Lordship hasn't already headed there and took over." Izzy tried to tickle herself with Naamah's feather.

"Uh hum." Randall continued reading, without looking up.

"Mr. Randall, perhaps if I bit you and turned you into one of my kin, your hearing would improve and you'd listen to me." Izzy crossed her arms and scrunched up her nose.

"Yeah." Randall grunted.

"Izzy, Randall is busy with his studies. We all would rather be somewhere else right now, but we shouldn't antagonize one another." Juliana closed her prayer book and Mosi yawned.

"Mmm hmm." Randall was nose deep in the book.

Izzy walked over to Juliana, after throwing Randall a dirty look and sat on a cushion next to her and Mosi.

"We should probably turn in for bed tonight. The Grand Inquisitor is due tomorrow, according to Princess Danica. So far, they have treated us decently and allowed me to continue helping the people who are in need." Juliana stretched and put her arms around Izzy and Mosi, hugging them tightly.

Randall looked up from his book over to Juliana. "Well, I'm not looking forward to his arrival, and I don't trust any of these guys. An Inquisitor sounds like trouble. Why do you think I've been studying these books late into the night? They may decide to burn me at the stake for heresy. Not to mention what they would do to Izzy, if they discovered her true nature."

"They wouldn't dare! I won't let that happen!" Izzy stood, waving her fist.

"I don't believe you will! The power of The Mother protects us, and the truth is what we will tell them. However, remember that we are the ones that ended the reign of a monster. It is unlikely a few of the king's knights would be a match for us if they were to challenge us." Juliana was aware they could be in danger.

Randall stood up, set his book on the desk, then stretched his arms out to receive. "Goodnight, everyone."

Izzy and Mosi ran to him and hugged him around the waist. Juliana joined in and everyone held one another for a long moment. Randall's eyes grew misty, and a single tear ran down his cheek.

"Alright, alright off you go. I'm going to keep after it." Randall stretched before returning to his chair and opening to where he left off.

The others changed into night clothes and Juliana modestly changed behind a screen, before piling into the large feather bed together. The ever-cautious Izzy slept with her dagger under her pillow. Juliana kept the Sword of Vittoria within reach, just in case.

A few hours passed. Randall's light spell on the stone had winked out an hour prior. The three in the bed were sleeping soundly and Randall was asleep with the book open on his belly. Only silvery starlight, through the open doors to the balcony, dimly light in the room. The first night of this new moon was peacefully quiet. The only sound was the light breathing of the four friends and an occasional snore from Izzy.

Izzy's treasures were still spread across the small table, along with the dirty dishes as she had left them. The platinum box sitting amongst the items began to vibrate, ever so slightly at first. Vibrations grew stronger, setting up vibrations in the table, as well causing the stack of coins to fall over.

No one's sleep was disturbed, as the box's gold glyphs began to glow increasing in brightness. At its apex, the lid sprung open and the internal palladium lining was exposed. A small non-corporeal glowing orb escaped and floated above the box, as the gold light dimmed back to darkness.

The glowing orb floated away from the table, making its way slowly around the room, pausing first by the bed for a long moment, before moving toward Randall sleeping at the desk. Again, the orb paused, bobbing as it hovered near the young sleeping wizard.

The orb floated away from Randall toward the box it had escaped from. It rotated slowly at first, and increased its velocity until elongating, becoming cylindrical. It grew to the size of a man, taking on a blurred humanoid, form as the rotation continued increasing in speed. The features of a skull became clearer, and the skeleton's individual bones were more discernable with each rotation.

The spinning stopped and now His Grace, The Duke Archibald Payne, stood in the room whilst everyone slept. The empty eye sockets once again glow red with the pinpoints of light from within. His arms were crossed as if he had been laid to rest in a sarcophagus, though his skeletal body was not covered in a burial shroud. The Duke lowered his arms to his side and looked upon the others in the room.

He glided across the floor to the screen after spotting a hooded cloak. He wrapped his bones in the gray garment and pulled the hood over his head.

The others slept, as Mosi began to stir. The boy scratched his big head of unruly hair and yawned before opening his eyes.

The Duke floated across the room toward Randall, who snored softly. He looked upon him and the book that laid across his belly, held firmly in his hands. Payne shoved each of his skeletal feet into the shoes of the former owner, where they conveniently sat on the floor beside him.

Mosi sat up in the bed and saw the dark shape moving about the room. He closed his eyes and rubbed them, adjusting them to the dark believing it was Randall. He squinted and watched the figure turn to look directly at him with its glowing eyes.

Mosi's mouth opened wide to scream, but he couldn't make a noise, instead he shivered with fear.

Duke Payne put a finger to his mandible. "Shhh"

The cloaked figure floated to the table and took the platinum box in his hands. The Duke floated backwards through the open balcony doors, watching the occupants the entire way.

Mosi was breathing heavily and shaking. Izzy began to stir and reached one hand over to the boy.

"Mosi, be still you woke me up." Izzy patted his arm.

Mosi pointed at the silhouette of the cloaked Duke, standing at the edge of the balcony against backdrop the starry sky screaming. "The Duke!"

Izzy sprung up out bed and drew her dagger. Randall fell out of his chair, flat onto the floor with a thud. Juliana rolled out of the bed and drew her sword.

"Et erit lux!" Randall called upon the spell to create light once again.

The room was illuminated by the blue light on the stone, and they rushed to the balcony. The Duke was not there. They returned to the chamber as Mosi sat on the bed, up to his nose in blankets shaking.

"Perhaps he was dreaming it?" Randall presumed.

"It's been a traumatizing time for Mosi as it has been for all of us." Juliana walked over and put her hand on his head.

"No, I saw him! I wasn't dreaming it." Mosi cried.

"Hey, my pretty metal box is gone!" Izzy looked at her collection on the table.

Randall picked up his book and noticed his shoes were now missing. "Alright, who is trying to be cute."

"I saw him! The Duke stole it and left out there!" Mosi pointed at the doors again.

All four looked to the open balcony doors again, in silence. Immediately they knew Mosi's words were true. There would be no rest for anyone.

✳ ✳ ✳

The morning was a wash of colors: purples, pale blues and rosy, pink clouds painted in the sky, as the sun peeked over the horizon bringing the dawn. Duke Archibald Payne wrapped in the cloak of gray, walked on his own two feet, through the night on the cobblestones of the High Road. He carried only the platinum box in his hands, which protected his blackened soul allowing him to return to his "unlife." He did not grow fatigued, he did not require food, water nor sleep. This setback he could recover from, even if it took him a century. Time means nothing to one who is already dead. He lost all he had in life, but possessions and titles mean nothing to one who is already dead

Another cloaked figure stood waiting, off the side of the cobblestone road at the edge of the overgrown track into the vale to the marshlands. The one-armed hag said nothing. Only the sounds of insects awakening to the light of the morning, broke the silence with the flittering of their wings and chirping calls.

The Duke stepped onto the overgrown path and descended into the vale. Auntie Olga patiently waited with her head bowed, then trailed a few steps behind him, and both disappeared into the marshlands.

Time means nothing to one who is already dead.

End of Book I

About the Author

Paul Wolff's interest in fantasy was first sparked by role playing games with his friends in middle school. Around that same time, he dove into fantasy novels by the usual suspects of famous authors. During the early 1980's Hollywood was releasing many fantasy movies that he was instantly drawn to, some good, and many bad ones. These influences made an impact on his creative mind. A good helping of British comedy helped twist that impressionable mind.

Devils & Wizards is his debut novel.

Paul is also an artist whose other interests include music, bicycling, and drinking unhealthy amounts of black coffee. He, and his wife Samantha, share their home with their dog, Toots, and cat, Winky.

www.ingramcontent.com/pod-product-compliance
Lightning Source LLC
Chambersburg PA
CBHW020651110726
47901CB00001B/139